50+ Explicit& Taboo Sex Stories For Adults (4 in 1): Forbidden Fantasies Erotica- Threesomes, Gangbangs, BDSM, Rough Anal, Cuckold, Orgasmic Oral, First Time Lesbian, Tantra& More

By Rachael Richards

Filthy& Orgasmic Erotic Sex Stories: Threesomes, Sex Games, First Time Anal, BDSM, Gangbangs, MILFs, Femdom, Lesbian, Wife Swapping, Cuckold & More! (Forbidden Fantasies Series)

By Rachael Richards

Contents

The Gym Trainer's Awakening

My husband told me going to the gym would be fun. At first, I thought he was crazy.

Little did I know that I'd meet *him* of all people.

It all started out pretty innocently. I was walking in after putting my gym bag and clothes away, holding my water bottle. I looked around, seeing my husband already hitting the weights, and I couldn't help but feel a little bit intimidated.

What do you do in this kind of situation? Do you just ignore the nagging feeling and hope for the best?

That's when I heard it, the sound of a tenor voice, pulling me out of my thoughts.

"You alright there miss?" the man asked.

I whipped my head around, and I came face-to-face with a super-hot trainer that worked here. He was tall, muscular but not super beefy, and he had sandy blonde hair that swept partially over his face.

For a moment, I didn't know what to say. I was fucking floored, amazed that someone so...attractive was talking to me. And in truth, I didn't know how to form a coherent speech as I looked into his eyes.

"Y-yes. I'm looking for Paul. I have a training session with him," I said to the nice man.

His lips curled into a smile, a chuckle that made my hairs stand on end filled through me. God it sounded so hot, and I could feel my pussy grow hot with need.

"That'd be me. Must be my lucky day, working with such a cutie like you," he said with a wink.

For a moment, I had no idea of what to say. I mean...what do you do when someone approaches you like this? I quickly smiled.

"Yes, I'm very excited too!" I replied. Of course, I was excited because this would mean so much more. He guided me over to the training area, and we started to stretch. But I could see him locking eyes with me, giving me flirty little smiles, and I couldn't help but smile back.

I knew that Timmy my husband would make fun of me for this. He wasn't necessarily the jealous type. In fact...we actually talked about the possibility of a third a while back. I'd been looking for one, but none of the guys who even showed remotely any interest really caught my eye.

That is, until now.

As I stretched over I let out a small moan and he looked at me, a bit of surprise on his face.

"Feisty aren't we?" he said.

"Maybe I am," I purred.

After all, I liked guys like this. Those types who usually don't know what to say, who don't know the first thing about talking to a woman. That was one of the things I found thrilling.

We then began training, where he showed me how to do bicep curls, triceps extensions, and we even worked with the lat pulldown machine. Every time he was right behind me, and I couldn't help but get a whiff of his musky, manly scent, sighing.

"You're doing great for your first time there," he said to me.

I smiled, excited about that. The way he gave compliments made me turn into music practically.

"That's because I have a great teacher," I purred.

"Well I love knowing that I can teach you some great things," he said to me, practically whispering in my ear.

I felt a bit guilty. A part of me wanted to get Paul involved, but he did tell me if he found someone, I could approach it and start this.

I continued to go through the motions of training, but my mind was so focused on him that it was hard not to just lose it all right then and there. I worked with him, enjoying every single motion, every single little flirty touch that he provided to me.

Finally, after we finished the workout routines for the day we sat down, and he spoke.

"You're definitely showing some great potential. It's a shame that you're only here for a half hour every few days," he said.

"Maybe I'll come in more," I said to him.

He smiled.

"Well I'm working this shift every day, but I do have nights off. Perhaps we can…meet up for something else," he said to me.

The way he flirted with me was driving me mad. I knew I needed to take care of this before I went to go see Timmy.

"I'll let you know," I said with an alluring smile.

As I left the training area I went back to the locker room, grabbing my stuff and rushing into the shower. As the hot water hit my naked body I slid my hands down, between my legs, pressing two fingers in.

The idea of Paul inside me, filling me up. Having Timmy in my other hole, pushing in deep and filling me up completely…it was just too much. I was being driven insane with each thrust, and as I played with my clit, pushing the socked fingers in deep and curling around that bundle of nerves, I could feel my orgasm take me. I bit my lip to stop the small whine that came out of my mouth, coming down from that high.

This gym trainer was already driving me mad, and my pussy was still throbbing after all of that.

I wanted him, and I knew that Paul would be the target I was going for next.

That night, when Timmy and I were back at home, we started to put dinner together, but I noticed his eyes look over at me, a flirting smile on his face.

"I saw you talking to the trainer earlier. Looked like you were having a fun time," Timmy said, leaning in and kissing my neck.

"Yes. He's something. Honestly…I was thinking of inviting him over. He knows that we're together, but that didn't stop the flirting," I said.

"Of course. I know we've talked about this. And Timmy is nice. I've spotted him before on his bench. He's a young college guy, about a decade younger than us. It'd be fun," he teased in my ear.

I was going for it. I needed this. And I'd warm him up to the idea, and then get him to come with me.

I continued to go to training sessions every single week, but every time I did, I could see the eyes wandering further and further, causing my body to stand on edge, and my pussy throb. I felt horny all the time after working out. At first, I thought this was due to the endorphins and other hormones.

But no, it had to be because of Paul.

I couldn't get him out of my damn mind. It was like he sat there rent-free in that space, turning me on and making me feel the ache of need as time continued on. I couldn't take it. It was driving me utterly mad.

I had to do something about this. There was only so much masturbation and fucking could do before I knew these fantasies needed to be acted upon.

And they needed to be acted upon soon.

Finally, I got the courage to ask. It was one evening at the gym. The usual crowd was gone, and I'd just worked on some squats with Paul. His hands were so dangerously close to my butt I could feel the tension there, but I didn't tell him. after we finished with the weights, we sat there, stretching. Timmy already agreed to this, so I figured Paul would be fine with this too.

"Something the matter?" Paul finally asked me.

"Yeah, I wanted to talk to you about something," I told him.

"What's the matter?" he asked.

I looked around, wondering if anyone was around. When I saw not a soul was near, I spoke.

"I was wondering if you…wanted to come home. My husband and I talked and well…he wants to meet you too," I said.

Paul's expression changed. A smile was on his face.

"Does he now?"

"Yeah, he heard all about how you've trained me so well, and he wants to know a bit more. He wants to see what the training you've done has helped with," I told him.

I could see his eyes widening. He quickly nodded.

"R-right. Well I can do that," he said, too shocked to say much more.

"Yeah, plus we wouldn't mind having you over for dinner. You've helped me a lot with getting in shape and going to the gym. I almost didn't do this had it not been for him," I replied. I tried to pretend that this was some sort of innocent thing, but from the look on my face, I'm sure he could tell from a mile away it wasn't.

And it sure as shit wasn't in my mind.

"Yeah, just let me clock out. I'll follow you home," he said.

"Here's my address too if you fall behind," I said.

I gave him my address, and we soon parted ways. I met with Timmy in the car, sighing.

"Did it work?" he asked.

"Yeah, I think so. He's coming," I said.

He grinned, and I'm sure that he was surprised at how much I wanted this. But the fantasy of two guys like this, taking me and teasing me in all the right away, it was just…too exciting to bear. I could feel the heat driving me wild.

Before I knew it, we were back at my place, and Paul followed. We went inside, and I got dinner out, which was already slow cooking beforehand.

"This looks delicious," Timmy said.

"Sure does," Paul replied.

We ate dinner, with Timmy and Paul both talking and making small exchanges at me. Finally, I stood up, smiling towards them.

"I'll be in my room, if you two want to join that is," I purred.

It was so rare for me to be this daring and sexy like this, but I quickly rushed in, tossing off the shirt and shorts that I had, revealing the black lingerie that I had. Moments later, the door opened, and Paul, followed by Timmy appeared.

"O-oh," Paul said.

"You like what you see?" I said.

I wasn't in bad shape even before hitting the gym, and I could see from the way Paul's eyes glazed over my body that he certainly enjoyed what he was looking at. Shortly before I knew it, Paul moved closer, his hands nervously touching.

"I-is this okay?" he said.

"Yes, Timmy and I both agreed. He said if I found a good enough guy that he liked…we would do this together," I told him.

I mean, I've had threesomes with girls before. It was nice, but also…I could feel the bubble of excitement that came with this one, the thrill of having sex with the personal trainer that I had. Suddenly, he pushed me down on the bed, his hands touching my body. My husband soon joined, and I felt his hands on my ass, while Paul's moved towards my hips and eventually upwards.

"W-wow," he said.

"Yeah, I certainly didn't get any worse after marriage," I said with a purr.

"You sure as fuck didn't," he said.

Then, our lips crashed against one another, touching, teasing, the pleasure immediately driving me mad. I moved forward, but I felt a pair of hands against the front of my panties, rubbing me there. My wetness was already obvious, and I could hear the low groan of arousal in my ear from Timmy, followed by the dancing of his fingers there.

Paul's lips felt heavenly. He was a good kisser. He was younger, much more awkward than us, but I could sense that he liked it. I felt like the mature older woman who knew exactly how to make him feel good, and that's when

I felt a tongue press forward, meeting my own. Our tongues teased and moved against one another, his hands moving upwards, touching the edge of my bra, causing me to let out a small moan of excitement as things started to heat up within me.

I didn't know how much more of this I could take. Kissing was nice and all, but there was something about...the way he kissed me that made every part of me stand on edge, causing me to let out a series of moans which sounded delicious, and the excitement and need growing even more so as time went on.

I felt Paul's hands move under my bra, touching the very edge of my breasts, teasing the nipples there, causing me to let out a small hum of pleasure as we continued to do this. Everything was driving me crazy, and I couldn't help but enjoy everything that was happening. My body ached for him, needed him, and I could tell that the way he was teasing me was only getting me closer and closer to the edge.

With deft hands I felt one of them take off my bra, tossing it to the side. I let out a small gasp as I felt a pair of hands move from behind me. Timmy's hands cupped my breasts, teasing the edges of my nipples, pinching them in his hands as he breathed against my ear, licking my neck and ear.

"You like it babe?" he said to me.

"Y-yes," I finally breathed out, moving forward. I felt a hand against there, rubbing me there. The heat only bubbled more within me. I arched my back, crying out, but that was just an excuse to get Paul's lips against my own, our tongues moving and mingling together. I felt Timmy's lips move towards my neck, pressing against there, biting on the flesh, and I felt like I was in heaven as I felt all of this.

It was heavenly. It was passionate, and I knew for a fact that he was enjoying this s much as I was, and it only made me hunger for more, ache for more, and I desired so much out of him it was driving me crazy.

I knew he wanted this, as much as I did, and I knew from the way their lips kissed, touched, and teased every single part of me, I was only getting closer and closer to the edge. I could feel the heat bubbling.

It was rare for me to be so close to the edge without orgasming. I felt like I was being purposefully edged, and I knew that he enjoyed this too.

Paul pushed me down on the bed, his hands roving my body. I could see Timmy there, watching me, smiling as I saw him stroke himself. Pauls' hands traveled down my body, to the tips of my nipples. He reached out, grabbing them and teasing the tips of them. I quickly moaned, pushing my body upwards and feeling the ravaging desire of his hands, enjoying the sensation of this, and wanting more from this man as he continued to touch, tease, and take me like this.

Everything about this was enough to drive me mad, and I knew that I was getting closer to this. The lust I felt from their hands, just exploring and taking me like this, was enough to turn me on.

Paul's lips moved to the tip of my nipple, capturing it and touching it slightly. I shivered, crying out loud as I pushed my hips upwards, feeling the sudden, aching pleasure of the flesh take over me. I felt his hands reach out, teasing my other nipple, pinching and pulling on them as I bit my lip, crying out in pleasure, enjoying the way he just...made me feel amazing.

I felt Timmy move his hips a bit, shuffling his pants downwards. He stroked his cock, but I took it against my hands, rubbing the shaft and teasing the tip of it while Paul's lips continued the onslaught on my body.

"Y-yes," I finally breathed out.

I turned my head to the side, grabbing my husband's cock and pushing it into my mouth. I sucked on the tip fervently, teasing the very edge of it while I felt Paul's lips travel downwards, moving to the bottom of my lingerie, which was wet with my juices, tossing them off of my body, spreading me apart and diving right on in.

I cried out as I felt his lips touch the very top of my clit, pressing against there. The small, subtle touch against this bundle of nerves caused a heat to flood through my body that I didn't expect from this. Before long he pushed his face in deeper, touching the very edge of my pussy, rubbing it there and making me shiver with delight, enjoying the sensation of that there. For a long time, I felt his lips continue to descend and touch against my body, enjoying the crevices, touching, teasing and pleasuring every aspect of it.

He then pushed his tongue inside, the sensation of his wet muscle fucking me making my eyes widen, and my jaw become agape. I didn't know what to say, other than I just kept pressing my hips forward, fucking his tongue with my hips, feeling him spread me out and penetrate me.

Timmy moved forward, grabbing my head and pushing me down to the base of his cock. I eagerly took him all the way down, feeling him groan against my lips, and as I stayed there, enjoying the sensation of this, it was only a matter of time before I knew I was close to the edge.

He then pushed himself balls-deep against me, his cock filling my mouth completely. I could barely breathe, but that didn't matter. I let out a small scream, muffled by the dick in my mouth, as I felt my orgasm.

It was amazing, and as Paul moved back, he leaned over to me, kissing my mouth. I could taste his juices. Paul moved his hands to his pants, pulling them off and when I saw his cock there, my eyes widened in surprise.

He was bigger than Timmy. Timmy was pretty sizable himself, but the way it stood there, throbbing with need and attention, only made me lick my lips with need. I quickly moved over, feeling a pair of hands on my backside. I wiggled my butt for a moment, and Timmy groaned, smacking my ass.

"Yeah go gobble that cock down honey," he said, encouraging me to take Paul all the way.

I moved onto all fours, Timmy's cock right up against my entrance, and soon, I moved my lips to the tip. I took part of it in, and that's when I felt the cock all the way inside, filling me up. I cried out around the dick, but that didn't stop me from moving down on it.

Paul's eyes became lidded with lust, and soon he reached out, his hands lightly in my hair, holding it as I moved downwards, taking him about halfway.

"Come on Paul, you can be rougher with her. She likes it," Timmy said, encouraging him. I wanted to chuckle because he wasn't wrong. Usually, I was much more into the roughness.

Suddenly, I felt my hair get yanked down, and soon his cock filled up my mouth. Paul grabbed my head, fucking my mouth hard while Timmy fucked my other hole.

I wanted to scream and cry out, but the feeling of the cock inside both of my holes muffled it. The only sounds that I could hear were the slippery sounds of sex, my own moans, and the groans of need that came out of both of these guys. Timmy's thrusts started to go in deeper, and I could feel it hitting that one spot, but that didn't stop Paul from pulling me all the way down, until I was deep-throating his cock.

It was some fucking miracle that I didn't gag once he did that, but he pulled me all the way in, holding me there as he fucked my face hard. They continued this, until I felt Timmy pull out, groaning in pleasure.

"You've got to feel inside her. She's amazing," Timmy said.

I knew Timmy sharing me with someone was definitely not what he was used to, but I could sense from the way Paul acted, he was enjoying the little adventure. Paul quickly spread me apart, pulling me so that I was back down on my sides, and then he pulled my legs up. I was against the bed, and then, I felt him push his cock all the way in.

I suddenly cried out, surprised by how full this felt. I didn't expect him to be so...big. But here he was, all the way inside of me, and I couldn't help but let out a small series of muffled screams, enjoying the feeling of being used like this.

The element of control. It was gone, replaced by the feeling of raw pleasure. They both knew exactly where to touch me though, where to treat me right. His hands moved downwards, pressing against my clit, and that's when I tensed up, letting out a small, guttural sound as I felt him get closer. He pressed there, but then he pushed my hips slightly back, thrusting in, and when it hit that spot, I lost my ability to speak for a brief moment.

I was...shocked by how good this felt, by how he knew exactly where to touch me, where to fuck me, and everything about this. He continued his thrusts, pushing harder against me, and I felt him press that spot once more.

When I came, I let out a loud cry, one that I didn't think I'd ever made before, the feeling of my orgasm just completely taking over me, making me shiver with delight.

I was completely immobilized by pleasure, enjoying the thrill of my orgasm. But that's when I felt a pair of arms move behind me, picking me up.

I noticed Paul grab me too. He looked into my eyes, a gentle smile on his face.

"Wrap your legs around him," he insisted.

I couldn't believe this. But I listened. It was the only thing I could do, right? I quickly wrapped my legs around, only to feel both of their cocks inside of me.

Suddenly, I felt the tightness of my hole once more. I felt like I was being stretched out, and as I held onto them both for dear life, I wanted to cry out in both pain and pleasure at the feeling of this.

I was immobilized by the pleasure, enjoying the sensation of this, and completely enraptured by it all at the same time. They continued to fuck me hard, holding me there as they each took turns, pushing themselves deep into me. It was like I couldn't go a damn second without one of their cocks inside of me, pushing me to the limit, making me cry out with sheer pleasure and lust.

After a few more moments, I felt them both inside, pressing against there. That combined with Paul's lips on my nipple and Timmy's hand on my clit made me cry out, completely overwhelmed by lust, and that's when it hit me.

The thrill of the orgasm, the moment I'd been waiting for, and something I couldn't get enough of. I felt completely immobilized by this, overtaken by lust, and suddenly, I felt something else other than my orgasm happen.

I squirted.

They held me there as I finished, laying me down. I was completely overtaken by lust, feeling them both groan as they saw me there, enraptured by pleasure and completely smitten.

"Fuck," I heard Paul say.

I looked at them, both of them still hard. I scrambled upwards, taking them both and jerking their cocks, taking them against my lips every so often. I could see Timmy's eyes widening. He was probably shocked that I could go for so long.

Truth be told, I had no idea how I was still going after all of this. I felt like I was on complete autopilot at this point, aroused by this, and I knew that they were enjoying this just as much as I was.

I took Timmy against my mouth, and then, he groaned, pumping himself deep into me. His seem was in my mouth, a familiar taste, and I gobbled it down, looking at both of them with a small smirk of approval at all of this. It felt so damn good, and it was only a matter of time before he would get to this point too.

But Paul didn't stop. As he saw Timmy finish up he let out his own groan. He grabbed my chin, pulling my face so he could look me in the eyes, and then, he cried out.

Strings of cum hit my face, decorating me with his white seed. It tasted a little bit saltier than Timmy's, and I quickly gobbled it up, enjoying all of this, loving the sensation of this hot seed as it hit my face. He pulled back, and I moved my hand to my face, taking the shots of cum that didn't hit my mouth and licking it.

"You taste pretty good," I said to him.

He smiled, a small bit of redness from both embarrassment and from pleasure hitting him.

"Of course. I know I taste great," he said with a smirk.

I enjoyed it too. I stayed like this, not moving at all, and then, shortly after, I simply collapsed on the bed. I was so happy, the orgasmic bliss a permanent feeling at the present moment. I don't know what it is, but after the two of them penetrated into me, filling me up with their hot seed, I couldn't do much else besides accept the moment, and enjoy the way things were.

They each moved next to me, both of them laying down on the bed as well. We all fell asleep there for a bit, exhaustion and bliss from the sex that we had definitely a feeling we all had.

When I woke up, I saw that Paul was getting his stuff on. I looked at him, and he smiled.

"I definitely wasn't expecting this…but I enjoyed it," he said.

I beamed.

"I really did too. And I think Timmy did as well," I said.

There was a groan, and I saw the bedsheet move over. Timmy looked over at the two of us, a small smile on his face.

"Yeah, I did," he said.

"Yeah. I wouldn't mind doing this again if you two are up to it," Paul said.

I looked at Timmy. It was up to him. I certainly would, but I knew with something like this, it took both parties.

"Sure," he told us.

I smiled.

"See, it all worked out," I told them.

"Sure did," Paul said.

We all looked at one another, the enjoyment obvious. Paul gave us both a small hug goodbye. He told me that he couldn't stay longer because he had to go train someone in the morning.

That's when I realized it. I was going to be trained by Paul once again during my next class. I flushed at the realization of it.

"Well that was something," Timmy said, moving behind me and giving me a hug.

"Sure was. But I had a blast you know," I said to him.

"I'd be lying if I said I didn't have the same feelings babe," he said.

I leaned in, enjoying the feeling of the hug that he gave to me. It was refreshing, relieving, and it made me realize just how happy I was here.

"I'm really glad I got to do that with you babe. I had an amazing time," I admitted.

And it wasn't just because I got penetrated so hard I ended up squirting. But he nodded.

"I sure did too. I wouldn't mind doing that again if we ever had the chance," he told me.

I smiled.

"Same here. We'll see how this goes. I think I could use a shower and some rest before anything else," I told him.

He nodded.

"You and me both," he replied.

We both went into the shower, our lips and hands on one another as we got in there. I loved taking showers with Timmy. It was a small, intimate act that we could share together, that both of us enjoyed.

I knew he enjoyed this as much as I did. He loved sharing me, whether it be with a man, or with a woman, and I enjoyed it too. The feeling of hands on my body, each time taking control of me, it was just exciting, thrilling, and I knew that he liked it too. And honestly, from the way I was taken care of I would do it again in a heartbeat.

Of course, I wouldn't do it right away. Paul was nice, but I didn't want to get his hopes up with any of that. But it did make me a bit more excited to go to the gym, to work out hard, because I knew that I'd get to experience that thrill again. That feeling of two men inside me, making me feel good, and the feeling of pleasure that I had just discovered recently, but it was a feeling of pleasure that only made me more excited with time, and gave me the thrill that I'd been looking for when it came to bedroom adventures, and the fun that it brought to me both as a temporary high, and a long-term one too.

Rejuvenating The Love

Scarlet wished that Andy would say something to her.

Her husband, her best friend for many years, now felt like someone who she barely even knew these days. She wondered if there was a way for them to come back.

To rejuvenate the love.

Scarlet looked for something. After being together for ten years, this was something that seemed to be inevitable, but that didn't mean it didn't hurt any less. She wanted Andy to reach out, to be with her, and to tell her that he loved her.

She remembered how he used to make her feel. Those nights when it was just their bodies. The way his lips moved towards the tip of her nipples, capturing it there. It made her flush thinking about it, her hand between her legs and a moan of need escaping her mouth as she thought about those nights...nights long gone from before.

Scarlet wanted that back.

Now, they had gotten older, and Andy was working a lot. They were around one another a lot, and everything still felt comfortable...but it felt like the spark was gone for some reason.

She wanted more. She wanted this. She wanted to feel that love once again in the bedroom, the passion and need igniting under her, making her shiver with delight at the sight of it.

She wanted more.

Their anniversary was coming up. 11 years. It felt like it hadn't been that long, but also...she knew that they'd been through a lot. From new houses to moving to even the struggles that couples went through...she remembered it. But she didn't want things to end on a poor note.

Instead she wanted things to be normal once again, where they could both just accept one another and whatever it was that they were about to go into.

She wanted to rejuvenate the love.

That's when she got an idea. Scarlet came home early from a day at the office, checking for different vacation spots, when she found out there was some sort of vacation getaway with a twist: every couple would have their own place, and they'd be given some...incentives in order to try the games out. Supposedly, those who have done this ended up having better, more progressive relationships with their partners afterwards.

Scarlet looked at it. It was on a beach too, and they'd be given a cabana, and that's where the games were located. She wondered what would happen if they did this.

She thought about asking Andy, but she didn't know for sure whether or not it would work with Andy. After all, he was always working so damn much that it made her wonder if hue would even care at all.

Only way to find out would be to ask him.

Scarlet sat down at the dinner table, looking at Andy as he finished texting a message to someone on his phone.

"Hey babe," Scarlet started.

Andy looked at her with a curious glance.

"What's up babe?"

"I wanted to ask you if you wanted to go somewhere for our anniversary. We've been together for a while, and I didn't know if you spent any time looking for places yet or not," she stated.

He looked at her and nodded.

"Yeah, I wanted to ask you about that. I'm down for whatever you have planned babe. I haven't really done a ton of looking around, but whatever you want to decide is fine with me," he replied.

She nodded, realizing that it was ultimately up to her.

"Well, why not here?" she said.

She showed him the location, his eyes widening.

"Really? This is something else! It's beautiful too," he said.

"Yeah I was thinking we could...have some fun together there," she said.

Scarlet made sure to pack a bunch of lingerie for it, and she wanted to learn more about what kinds of "Games" this place had. He looked hesitant, but then nodded.

"I'd love this. I've heard this is a wonderful location, good for many things," he said to her.

Scarlet nodded.

"Yeah, I am really happy about it," she said.

He agreed, so they made sure to have that weekend doff. Apparently, it was a three-day adventure for them to explore one another, and Scarlet did her research. Many of the women who came back were oftentimes much happier than they were beforehand. Scarlet didn't find much else, but this was definitely something promising, and may fix the awkwardness of her current relationship with him.

On the day of the event, both Scarlet and Andy flew out. When they got to the location, the plane docked itself right along the shoreline. They got off, and suddenly, a woman who wore a bikini came over, smiling.

"Hey there! Welcome! You're here for the weekend?" she said.

"Yeah. I heard we have a cabana for this?" Scarlet asked.

"Oh yes! Follow me," she said.

They quickly followed the woman to a small little cabana. It was right on the beach, and very far from the others. It was like they were in their own little world.

"Have a look inside. Showers are down the pathway there. They are separate, but we also have couples ones too. Have a good time. If you need food, just walk down that path. We have a large selection of various dinner options," she said.

"Yeah, that's fine," Scarlet said.

They walked to the entrance of the cabana, realizing that they were all alone. The bed that was there certainly looked nice to lay on, but Scarlet's eyes looked over at a small series of cards and a box of them neatly stacked up. There was also a bottle of lube on the nightstand too.

"Looks like they came prepared," Andy said.

"Yeah," she said.

She wanted to look at it, but the growl of her stomach said otherwise. Andy chuckled.

"Why don't we get some dinner here?" he said.

"Yeah, let's do that," Scarlet said.

Andy's phone was off, along with hers. That was one of the rules of this place: if you have your phone on, you must turn it off. It probably is to add to the anonymity of the island, and also to offer a more intimate place for them. They sat down atm dinner, which was overlooking the ocean. The sun began to set, and Andy sighed with contentment.

"You know, we haven't done this in a long time," he said.

"Yeah. A part of me was worried about that," Scarlet said.

He reached out, taking her hand and holding it.

"Don't be. I'm sorry…work just got a bit overwhelming. But I realized that the one person who matters the most to me is you babe. You're someone who…I really do love and care about. And I hope this weekend dis magical for both of us," he said.

Scarlet nodded, gripping and holding his hands there.

"Yeah, I hope so too," she told him.

They stayed like this for a long time, just holding one another and lightly brushing against each other's hands. She could see the need in his eyes, the lust that he had, and I was excited to see what he had planned for tonight.

Scarlet went back with him after they had dinner, a couple of cocktails later. She looked at Andy, who had a grin on his face. His taut, muscular body that he kept up, his beautiful blue eyes that she fell in love with all of those years ago…it all made her shiver with delight, and the need only grew more so as they got to the entrance of their cabana. The lights came on in there, creating a dim, ambient atmosphere that made her smile.

"Looks beautiful," she said.

"Like you babe," he said to her.

He pulled Scarlet around, and she gasped. Their lips crashed together, both of them enjoying the feeling of one another. She held his waist, staying like this there, and as they explored the feeling of their lips against one another, she couldn't help but shiver with delight.

"I need you," she said to him.

"I do too. But wouldn't…a couple of little games be a bit more fun first?" he said.

She looked at the cards that were on the bed there. That's right…that was the little quirk of this place. You had to play the sex games that they had. She walked over, looking at the box, and the instructions.

The instructions are simple:

You must draw a card, and whatever's on there, you need to act it out with your partner. Learn to explore what you like about your partner's body.

You will definitely enjoy the result of this.

Scarlet read it. So they'd have to draw cards. She wondered what they'd be about. She looked at it, and then at Andy.

"I guess I'll draw first," he said.

She looked at him, nodding.

"Y-yeah," she said.

He picked up the card, drawing the first one and humming.

"I see."

"What is it?"

"Well, it says here that I should use the blindfold and cuffs and cuff you to the bed. If I don't do that…I have to of course tell you a secret," he said.

A secret? Like what?

"Do you…want to?" Scarlet asked.

He paused, shrugging.

"I kind of want to try the blindfold and handcuffs. It says to just do that," he said.

Scarlet nodded.

"Yeah, I also have something else that I want to show you too," she said.

She moved forward, taking off her shirt and shorts, revealing a set of black lingerie. His eyes widened.

"W-wow," he said.

"Yeah, I figured I'd wear something nice for the moment," she said.

Scarlet looked high and low for different lingerie that would appeal to Andy. She knew how much he loved black lingerie, and she could see it in his eyes. He was completely enraptured.

His hands immediately moved to Scarlet's waist, touching, teasing, feeling up every part of her body. She let out a small gasp, moving her hips up and down slightly, enjoying the sensation of this. She craved more of this touch, her body aching for his hands to move against her, under her lingerie, and then move there.

"All right, I'm going to put the cuffs on," he said.

She looked at him, and then nodded.

"O-okay," she said.

He secured them on, and while they weren't super tight wrist straps, she could sense that it did offer less mobility. He then took the blindfold, putting it around her.

"There we go," he said.

"A-alight," she said.

She liked this. The fact that her sense of sight was devoid, and she was at the mercy of Andy was something kind of fun.

"I guess I'll have to pick the next card," he said.

"Yeah, you will," Scarlet said.

But he didn't just yet. Instead, his hands moved against her neck, moving towards against her collarbone, between her breasts. He moved under her shirt, pressing his fingers to the tips of her nipples.

Scarlet's moans immediately echoed within the cabana, her body moving forward, and she soon let out a series of small gasps. Surprised by the touch. But it wasn't just that. The sheer force of his touches was enough to make her cry out, and everything felt like her body was a spark about to ignite. The little touches were driving her insane, making her realize that the need for him was much larger than she thought.

"That's right. You like this...don't you," he said to her.

"Y-yes," she said.

He teased her body, and Scarlet could feel both his fingers against her nipples. She moaned, moving about, but wasn't able to do much due to the restraints. The feeling of helplessness that came from this, it was...arousing.

She could hear the small grunts from Andy's lips too as he explored her body, his gentle touches making her feel on edge, close to the limit.

"Alright. The next card says to edge your partner, but don't let them cum. If you can do that, then they get to choose what's next," he said.

Fuck, he was going to edge her. Scarlet shivered.

"A-alright," she said.

He moved between her legs, his hands moving towards the entrance of her pussy. He circled his finger around, causing her to let out a moan, suddenly feeling the heat that was all over her body pool into but one location.

Scarlet enjoyed the touches, but she knew he was taking it slow. She bit her lip, pressing her hips up as his fingers danced against her clit, teasing her passionately.

"Fuck," she said.

"You like that babe?"

"Yes," she said. It was a familiar feeling that she missed. She wanted Andy to take her to climax. She missed these touches, but then, as soon as he got her close, he pulled his hands away, causing her to let out a gasp of frustration.

"I'm just following the rules. But I think it's your turn," he said.

"Right," she replied.

He undid the cuffs and pulled off the blindfold. But she kind of liked it. She picked the next card, looking at it.

"Oh," she said.

"What is it?" he asked.

"It says that I'm supposed to be spanked...with whatever one of the instruments I want to try. I can be handcuffed or blindfolded. Otherwise...I have to say a truth," she said to him.

This seemed like some weird truth or dare shit, but she wasn't going to lie, she enjoyed the sensation of this a whole lot.

"I see. Want to...try it?" he said.

"Yes," she said.

Andy spanked her before in the past, but there was something different about this time. She wondered what would happen next.

This time around, there was a riding crop, a paddle, and a flogger. In truth, she wanted to try all of these.

"Ready?" he said.

"Yeah," she replied.

But Scarlet changed things up. While it did say that she didn't need to, she put the blindfold back on. She wanted to know what it felt like.

"You sure?" he asked.

"Yes," she replied.

He grabbed the paddle, moving slightly, then pressing it against her backside. As she did that, she let out a small cry of both pleasure and pain, surprised by the force of the motion.

She cried out, feeling the sting of both the paddle and the way the edge of it contacted with her ass. She let out a small gasp of surprise, pushing her hips forward as he did it once more.

"What's that? You like that?" he purred in her eat, hitting her once again with it. She let out a garbled sound, pleasure and anticipation driving her to the point of madness.

"Yes, more!" she cried out.

She knew she could trust Andy. After all, they've been together for so long that it only made sense. Every single touch, every single sting, it made her shiver with delight, causing her to cry out, loving every moment of it as it occurred. She could feel the anticipation and the tension grow even more so, making her want this, and making her desire even more from every single move.

He then hit her with something else, something that was a lot harder, but only hit a part of her backside. She howled with pleasure, enjoying the feeling of this. There was something about letting Andy take control. Even though their relationship was on the rocks, she knew that she could trust him, since of course, he knew exactly what it was that he was doing, and how to make her feel good.

Every single touch, every single motion, all of this was making her get closer and closer to the edge, causing her to let out a series of shiver and moans, her heart and mind aching for this.

Everything was getting to her, all of this was making her want more and more, everything taking her to the point.

Then, there was the flogger. Each touch caused her body to feel like it was sizzling, the moans that escaped her mouth music to his ears. He let out a small groan of desire as he heard this, every single touch and press making

her cry out. It was amazing, completely arousing, and she knew that he was enjoying this as much as she was. It was a feeling of lust, of pleasure, of need that only made her want more.

Everything was making her body stand on edge, the feelings that he gave to her, and the moans that escaped her mouth.

It was driving her closer and closer to the edge, and as she felt the stings, she knew that there was nothing else that would make her feel better than for him to continue. Each touch, each feeling of pain and pleasure, it only made her hungry for more.

But then, Andy stopped.

"Your ass is red all over," he said.

"Good. That's how I wanted it," Scarlet said.

He looked at the cars, pulling one of them out.

"The next game is to have sex in a place that you've always wanted. Well...I've wanted to do it on the beach," he said.

Scarlet turned to him, taking off the blindfold and nodded.

"Yeah but first...I want to do something to you," She said.

She felt like she got her spark back. After all this time, it was all flooding towards her, and she loved it. She took the contents of the cards, pulling it towards her. She shuffled through them, until she pulled one.

"So we can have sex on the beach but beforehand I need to...drizzle chocolate syrup on your dick and lick it off," she said.

She did feel the urge for a little snack. Andy flushed, but she quickly grabbed the contents, pushing him towards the edge. She drizzled the contents on his dick, watching him groan in arousal.

She flicked her tongue against the tip of his member, watching his eyes widen with surprise. She then took the first half of his cock into her mouth, and soon, she pushed her lips up and down against him, enjoying the sensation of his cock down her throat, and the groans that she so missed from this. She pushed her head the rest of the way down, getting to the base of his cock.

She bobbed her head up and down, watching his eyes grow wide as Scarlet worked her magic. It was a series of delicious sounds that she'd been waiting for. Andy and she did this plenty of times, but there was something arousing about tasting not only the chocolate of this, but also the mixture of his precum with that too.

She pulled her face further downwards, taking it all the way in, watching his eyes widen and his body start to jerk forward, each and every thrust hitting the back of her throat, causing her to let out a series of gasps and moans, enjoying the feeling of this. It was all becoming more and more arousing, but she knew that there was only one other thing she wanted.

She pulled back, looking at him with a smile.

"Want to go out there?" she said.

"Yeah but first let me grab a couple of things," Andy replied.

She was surprised by this, but then, he walked towards the nightstand, grabbing the lube, and some of the cards that were there.

Were they going to play out there?

The darkness of night hid their bodies, and all they could see were the waves, and of course the moonlight reflecting off their bodies.

"This looks good," Andy said.

They went to the sand, but before sitting down, Andy grabbed one of the cards.

"I figured this would be a good time to draw another," he said.

At this point, Scarlet didn't even know what the game was anymore, but she nodded.

"Yeah, I'd love that," she said.

He took the card, pulling it out and smiling.

"Perfect. Get on all fours," he said.

Scarlet did as she was told, getting there. She then felt a hand on her ass, grabbing it and rubbing it, causing her to let out a small moan. She knew that it was tender, but the touch of it, even just the little massages, were more than enough.

She then felt something against there pushing in deeper and deeper, causing her to let out a small gasp of surprise as he filled her up.

"Ahh!" she cried out, feeling him in there.

"You good?" he asked.

"Y-yeah," she said, feeling it very tight, but also feeling amazing.

"There you go. Very good," he said. He began to lightly move his hips up and down, in and out of her, and the squelching sensation of their bodies, and the sound of the waves were the only two things that were heard. The moans they had together as he thrust into her, holding onto her hips as she cried out caused Scarlet to feel like she was being taken to a higher level, another plane, and a whole different feeling of pleasure.

After a few more thrusts, she could feel his hands down below her, touching her there, rubbing her clit, and it was all that she could do not to completely lose control right then and there. After a brief second, he pulled back, causing her to let out a sigh of need.

"I think it's time to draw another card," he said.

"W-what do you mean?" she asked.

He grabbed a card, giving it to her. She pulled it out, looking at him.

"Something you've always wanted to try," she said.

"Well, what are you thinking?" he said.

She flushed, looking at him with embarrassment.

"This might sound weird but...I want you to put it in my butt," she said.

21

He looked at her with slight shock and surprise.

"really now?"

"Yeah. I would like that," she said.

"Well I'll be dammed. Sure," he said.

He grabbed the lube, bringing it out so that he can prepare her. She shivered as she felt the first finger against her pucker. For a second, she held her breath. She knew that it would feel weird, but she also knew that some of her friends enjoyed this. She felt the first finger inside, the tightness of it making her cry out.

"Fuck," she said.

"Do you want me to continue?" her asked her.

"Yes," she said, almost too quickly.

He then inserted another finger into her, causing her to let out a small gasp of surprise. The feeling of this was almost too much to bear, and she knew that he enjoyed it too. For a long time, she could feel him all the way inside, and every single finger stretched her out. It was a different feeling, but it was one that she didn't necessarily dislike.

"You...ready?" he asked.

"Yes," she said, suddenly surprised by the forceful sounds that came out of her. Was she really this aroused? It shocked her, but at the same time, she knew deep down this was what she needed.

He then spread her legs apart, pressing two fingers inside, teasing her. She cried out, surprised by the feeling, but then he pulled away.

"I think you should...choose the position too," he said.

She flushed.

"Get in the sand. I want to be on top," she said.

It was more like she wanted them to be in one another's arms, but he did as he was told. She grabbed the lube, putting it on his cock, rubbing it in, and then, moments later...she slid the tip of it into her.

It was tight. Much harder than she expected, but she knew that this was indeed what she wanted. She let out a small cry as she pressed herself deeper and deeper, enjoying the sensation of this. She then was all the way in, and when she did so, she looked down at Andy.

He was in bliss as she moved her hips up and down, and she couldn't help but enjoy the feeling of this. She started moving her body slightly, thrusting up and down a bit more and a bit harder, looking into his eyes.

"You good there?" she asked.

"A-amazing," he said.

She felt good too. The way his cock angled into her felt good. But then, shortly afterwards, she felt a pair of hands on her hips, thrusting in deep.

She let out a choked sound, the moans escaping her louder than before. She was worried for a brief moment that she was too loud for this place, but at the same time, it didn't feel like anyone was complaining either. She was

silenced by his lips, and then, something moved in between her legs. It was two fingers penetrating her, and one thumb circling her clit.

As soon as she felt this, she let out a small gasp of surprise and pleasure, feeling her hips move up and down. The feeling of being penetrated in two holes while their lips moved and mingled together was enough to make her feel like she was being driven to the point of insanity, but she also knew that he enjoyed this too.

For a long time, the sounds of their moans and groans of pleasure were the only things that were uttered while they fucked on the beach, both of them lost in the pleasure of one another, and she couldn't help but feel as if she was getting closer and closer to the point of no return, the edge that she'd been waiting for.

Finally, he pressed in deep, the two fingers digging into that one spot, his hands forcefully against her clit, and his tongue inside. She screamed from within, feeling like everything was going blank.

This was one of the most powerful orgasms that she ever had, and she knew that he enjoyed this as much as she did too. He finished, groaning as he filled up her butt with his seed, pulling out to cover her butt.

When he finished, they laid there naked on the beach. The night was still young, and thankfully nobody seemed to be out here to tell them to go put clothes on. Not that either of them wanted to.

They were so enthralled with one another that the pleasure of this was enough to make Scarlet not regret a damn thing. She looked at him, smiling.

"You good?" he said.

"Better than just good," she admitted.

It was rare to be this aroused by the sheer mention of him, but he looked at her, smiling warmly.

"Good. I'm excited for more of this. Remember, it's only night 1 babe," he said to her.

"Yeah, it is," she told him.

It was the first night. That meant that they still had two more nights. He then looked at her with a smoldering glance.

"I wouldn't mind having more fun with you over the next two days. If you know what I mean of course," he purred.

She smiled, taking his hand and holding it.

"I'd love that. But are you ready for what's to come?" she asked him.

"Depends. What do you have in store for me?" he said.

She leaned in, giving him a soft kiss.

"That's for me to know, and for you to find out babe," she said.

Scarlet couldn't help but wonder what was in those games. After all, this seemed like the perfect way for them to connect. It showed them things that they liked that they weren't expecting, and of course, helped them learn a little bit about the other person.

And it pulled Andy out of the funk that he had. He got up, taking her hand, and they made their way over to the showers, both of them getting into one of the couple showers, cleaning while making out with one another. They tried to not have sex, but that was soon thwarted by Andy pushing her against the wall, slipping his cock into her, making her cry out slightly, but she tried to bite her lip as he thrust into her.

It was the perfect vacation though, one of them that they could share with one another, that allowed them to explore one another's bodies in ways that neither of them expected. For both of them, it was the start of something new, something amazing, and for both of them, it was driving them both closer and closer to the edge, and towards one another.

For Scarlet, she noticed that Andy was happier too. When they got back to the cabana that night, she noticed that he seemed a whole lot more open, and less hiding about things.

"I noticed you have a bit of a change of heart," she said.

"Yeah well, I'm sorry for being so distant Scarlet. I do love you, and this has been one hell of an anniversary weekend so far," he admitted.

He was right. She didn't expect this kind of anniversary present, but she was happy about this, and it made her smile.

"I'm happy about it too. Definitely one hell of a time. And I guess we can see where this takes us down the road," she said.

He took her hands, holding it there.

"Yeah, we can see where this goes too," he said.

For the first time in a long time, Scarlet truly did feel happy. Andy was the rock that she relief on for so long, and someone that she definitely was happy to be around. She knew that even though there was tension before, it was now gone.

They were able to rejuvenate the love, and be with one another, and Scarlet knew that their relationship was destined to work, she was sure of it.

The vacation rejuvenated their love and then some, and she knew that things could only get better from here for the two of them.

Trying Something New

Something new.

That's what I thought when I walked into this club. It was a strip club, but I was alone. I mean, I've always found women and men attractive, but I've never...been to a place like this before as a woman alone.

I could feel my heart race, my body start to feel on edge as I got to the doorway, seeing the guy there. He looked me up and down, smiling.

"You looking for a job here? You have the looks," he said.

"No I'm here to go into the club. I have the cover fee," I said, awkwardly shoving the cash in his hands

He looked at me, surprised by my words, but then nodded.

"I see. Come in then," he said.

I nodded, paying the club fee and moving inside. This place was different. I knew that the girls here would give you more if you paid the right price. Or if they thought that you were something worthwhile.

I looked, seeing the different people that were here. There was something almost exciting about this, and I didn't know why, but the prospect of...someone coming to me, to hit me up and talk to me felt a bit...liberating and fun.

I sat down, watching the girls move their bodies, gyrating. I could feel my heart race, my whole body start to grow hot with need, and that's when I saw it.

Her.

She was the most beautiful woman in the club. With long red hair, blue eyes, and a body with delicious curves, I couldn't help but lick my lips, seeing her there. I wanted this, and I knew as she moved her body on the pole, sliding up and down and giving little teasing winks, this was the one that I wanted.

I got a drink, sitting down at the bar and sighing. Why was I already so enthralled by her? I that she was someone that I craved, needed, and wanted more than anything else. She gave me a small smile before I gave her some cash.

"I'll be over later," she purred.

Those words they...they made me feel a warm, fuzzy feeling that excited me. I scrambled back to my seat, sitting down and waiting for her. The excitement, the need, the tension, all of this was driving me crazy, and as I watched her finish up, there was something familiar about this.

Why did she give off that energy. No way, could it be....

It was.

It had to be Lydia. It was a girl from my college classes, a redhead who was meek and timid. But I didn't realize it was her because normally she wore glasses and oversized hoodies, and would pull her hair back into a messy bun. But here she was, moving her body like it was a machine, working her magic, and I was enthralled.

To say I had a crush on Lydia was an understatement. She was a girl that I did want to get to know better. But I always...feared talking to her. She was so different from me, and so incredibly smart.

We did work on a project together once, but for the most part she stayed silent while I did a chunk of the work. She also ended up giving it to me.

She was mysterious and alluring, and honestly, I wanted to learn more about her, but I didn't know much. I mean, jhow do you bring this up to someone when you barely know them. I definitely felt a bit scared by this, and unsure of what to do.

But as I sat there watching her body move and meander, I could feel my heart race, and my lips lick.

When she was done, she left the stage and I sat there in the club. I got another drink, hoping the liquid courage would help me...experience something. Anything.

I waited and waited, but I didn't see where she was. Did she realize it was her classmate, a girl who seemly seemed out of her league, and then fucked right off?

Maybe. Maybe she was trying to figure out why I was here.

I could see that, but also...I knew that there was something that held me there, practically begging me to talk to her.

About thirty minutes had passed, and I assumed that she was gone. But then, I felt a presence heavy, something that seemed so damn familiar that I knew who t was without whipping my head around.

"Guess who," the voice said as she breathed in my ear.

I let out a small gasp, realizing that it was Lydia. I turned, seeing her there.

"I was wondering what you were doing here Alice," she said.

"Oh I was just...visiting," I said.

That was the truth. I knew that coming to the club like this would awaken something within me. This newfound sexual exploration definitely made me curious, and I didn't know why, but it made me feel an excitement that I didn't know how to achieve.

"I see. Want to come back with me?" she purred.

The back area was where the private dances were. I did have money for that.

"Sure," I said.

She gave me a smile, and I couldn't help but feel my eyes glaze over her body, looking at her curves which were hidden under a pale blue bra and panties. She wore stilettos, which made her tower over me, giving me that thrill of being with a tall woman.

I wasn't going to lie, I'd thought of her before. When I was in bed, my panties down and my hand stroking my clit, I thought about her, but I didn't think of her as this stunning redhead beauty. I thought of her as the nerdy girl that was hiding her true potential.

Maybe that wasn't necessarily wrong. She was showing her true self here, and I was completely mesmerized by this too.

"You good?" she asked me, whipping me out of my thoughts.

"Y-yeah. Sorry, just thinking about things," I told her.

I wasn't going to lie, I was excited for this. I knew that she would make things fun and exciting, that's for sure.

She grabbed my hand, and I could feel the sparks start to fly from there, and soon, she brought me to the back. But instead do the private areas that were usually used for dances, she brought me back further.

"This should be good enough," she said.

"But wait, I have to pay more for this, right?" I said.

I didn't want to have to pay a bunch of money for something like this. I thought about the dance, and then maybe giving a little bit of extra. Maybe some petting and maybe a little bit of kissing or something.

But she put her hand to her lips, smiling.

"Don't worry, I'll keep this a secret," she said to me.

I couldn't believe this. She was willing to risk it all for me?

"But what about this place? Don't the other girls need it?" I asked her. I was worried that there may be something wrong and the head of the club may come on in, and we'd be in trouble.

But she scoffed.

"Trust me, the boss doesn't care. He knows that I'll make money, and I definitely don't think he'll mind me entertaining customers. You can give me some cash to help with this, but if you want, I can also cover for this," she said.

I was completely enthralled. I was amazed by this.

"O-okay," I said.

She looked me over, surprise on her face.

"Is this your first time with a woman?" she asked.

I flushed, but then nodded.

"Y-yeah," I said to her.

"Wow, I'm honored. I'm sure you're wondering why I'm so...different from the usual self that you see here," she said.

"Yeah I do wonder that," I told her.

"Well, I made a few decisions a while back, got into stripping and well...I love it out here Alice. I've been dancing for a bit to pay for school, and I know that it's where I want to be," she said.

"That...makes sense," I told her.

"It does. I know that it's not easy for you to understand Alice but I'm happy," she said to me.

"I'm glad that you're happy Alice. I just...I came here originally because I heard the girls do a bit more if you gave them money. Then I saw you and I was floored and then I realized...it was you," I told her.

She laughed.

"Yeah, I get that Alice. I would ask for you to keep it a secret, because the last thing I want is the guys knowing that I'm doing this. I get asked out a whole lot by some of the guys there, and I'd love it if they just never learned about this. You're nice Alice but some of those guys..."

"Yeah, they're something," I told her.

I remembered one of them tried to ask me out. I humbly declined, but that didn't mean that I wasn't a bit worried about her too. I quickly sighed.

"Anyways...what now?" I asked her. I didn't know how you're supposed to...start something like this.

"Ever had a dance?" she asked.

"N-no," I said, flushing crimson. I thought about it, but I never had a chance to experience one.

"Well have a seat. I've got something to show you," she said.

I did as I was told, sitting down on the chair. It was pleasantly comfy, and I looked forward, seeing her there. She then climbed on the chair, smiling.

"How about I turn on a little bit of music for this?" she offered.

I nodded, and I watched her slide off the chair, heading over to the radio that was there and the stereo system. She pressed a few buttons, and some techno song with EDM beats echoed through the room. I watched her gyrate her hips, giving me this sultry little smile.

She climbed on the chair, hovering over me, her breasts mere inches from my face. I licked my lips, looking at her with surprise. I couldn't help but feel the rush of excitement and pleasure that came from this. She then moved all the way down, her crotch moving against my own.

I bit my lip, trying to stifle the moan that threatened to escape my lips. I wanted her, I craved her, and I ached for her.

She then moved her body up and down, her breasts pressing against my own, then in between my face, and then, her face was mere inches from mine. I shivered, watching her with rapt attention, amazed by the way that she looked.

"Fuck," I moaned to myself.

"You like?" she purred.

"Yeah. I do," I told her.

"Good. Because I like you as well," she said to me, her voice laced with pleasure, excitement, and lust. The aching need that came off her voice definitely made me shiver with delight.

For a moment, she moved her body against me, and I could feel my hands reaching out. She rubbed her hips against my own, and I let out a small cry of pleasure.

"That's right...you like this don't you?" she said in my ear, rubbing her hands against my sides. I started to shiver as I felt her hands there, touching my hips, moving down towards the crevice of my thighs.

She moved my legs, spreading me apart, and then she leaned forward, rubbing against me. I cried out, moving my body upwards, and she smiled.

"What's the matter? You enjoying this Alice?" she purred.

I nodded letting out a small gasp of surprise as I felt her move her body, touching, teasing, moving every single way that I could.

"Y-yes," I moaned, suddenly moving forward, pressing my body there.

She then leaned towards my neck, rubbing her face there, and it was all I could do not to lose control right then and there. The passion, the need, everything it just…drove me insane. I shivered, crying out loud and moaning in response to her actions.

"Fuck," I said, feeling my whole body become aroused with pleasure, enjoying the sensation of this this too. I wanted her, I needed her, and I wanted to just…experience everything with this woman.

She then moved her face near mine, immediately causing me to let out a small gasp of surprise. Her lips were so dangerously close to mine, that there was something that just…excited me about all of this.

Then, I felt her lips meet mine, kissing me suddenly my body reacted, kissing her back and moaning slightly. Our lips met one another, and I noticed her press closer to me, making me shiver with delight as I felt her body lean in closer. She then kissed me passionately, and for a moment, I was lost to her lips.

I've kissed and fucked guys before, but when I kissed Lydia…it felt different. Her lips were soft, a plush texture that made me shiver, crying out with delight, and I loved the feeling of this, knowing for sure that this is something that I needed. Our lips lightly moved and touched one another, and then, I felt something touch against me, a slight press of her tongue, and as it mingled against my own, I felt the heat rise through my body. I wanted her, I needed her, and I knew that she was enjoying this as much, if not more than I did.

When I fantasized about this, I always thought that I'd be the one to take the lead. But instead io was at the mercy of her touches, her teases, and I loved everything about this.

She moved her lips slightly away, giving me a playful smirk.

"Go to the bed," she said.

I wondered how many people used this. But then, as if on cue, she spoke.

"don't worry, this hasn't been used in a long time. It's a very VIP experience, and usually the boss doesn't care if people use it as long as the clean it afterwards. So don't worry about that," she said.

I sighed with relief. I didn't want to make things worse for either of us.

I followed her over to the bed, laying down. She got on top of me, grinding her hips against me, and I let out a groan of passion and need. She quickly pulled me close, our lips crashing and teasing once again.

Her kiss was like a subtle dance, our tongues moving and mingling against one another. I noticed her hands became a bit grabbier, touching my sides, moving upwards towards my breasts, teasing the tips of them through my bra. I shivered, moaning out loud. The passion and need was only growing hotter, and it made me excited for what was to come.

She then moved her lips downwards, teasing the edges of this, making me shiver with delight. Her kisses touched the sides of my neck, pressure building within me. She didn't leave any marks, but it felt like with every kiss she left a little touch of her behind, which was something that I wanted more and more, and something I so desperately needed.

She then got to the collarbone, lightly licking the edge of this, moving herself upwards and touching the very edge of this, pressing against my neck. I cried out, excitement and need flowing through my body, the aching tension only growing as time went on.

She then moved her tongue down towards the hollow of my neck, and I felt that small pink muscle press against there, causing me to let out a small gasp of pleasure.

Her hands snaked under my shirt, touching my breasts from the outside. I shivered, feeling the pleasure, need, and desire only grow even more so as time began to pass. I moved forward, groaning out loud and with a need that I couldn't stop or contain.

"You like that?" she purred in my ears.

"Yes," I said, feeling my body react.

She smiled, moving towards the hem of my shirt, pulling it off, over my body. She then moved her hands upwards, grabbing my breasts and playing with the exposed nipples that she saw through the bra.

From the moment she touched them, I felt like I was on edge, completely smitten and satisfied. I was losing my mind, feeling all of my self-control just disappear right then and there. I wanted her, and I knew that she was only going to make me crave more, just from the touch of her body alone.

I noticed her hands began to move towards the back of my bra, pulling at the clasps like she'd done this many times before. I started to moan, feeling her hands touch the very edges of my breasts, teasing the flesh of the orbs. I shivered, knowing this was only going to drive me to the edge. Her touches were soft because her hands were soft. Even though she worked the pole, the softness of her hands was something I couldn't get enough of, and that's when I felt the tips of her two fingers press against the edge of my breasts.

"Ahh," I cried out.

It was different from a man's touch. While the guys in the past were a bit...rougher, she treated me like I was a delicate piece, making sure that I was okay. She continued to press the tip of her fingers to my nipple, playing with them and watching me moan and groan with pleasure, enjoying the sensation of this.

I wanted this more than anything. I could feel the need only growing more and more as she continued to tease me, playing with my nipples. She moved her body so that her tongue was right over one of them. When I felt her breath, I suddenly shivered, moaning out loud and with a look of pure desire on my face. She continued to play with them, taking one of them into her mouth, while her other hand pinched, touched and teased them. I felt them harden against me, and the sudden wave of need, pleasure, and so much more driving me closer and closer to the point of madness, my body aching for this too.

She looked at me, a smile on her face as she watched me writhe in pleasure underneath her. The way her soft hands played with me, showing me just how good it was, I couldn't help but lose my mind and crave more of this from her.

But then, she moved away, moving her hands to the back of her bra. I moved forward, pulling the clasp off, my hands moving towards her own breasts. I felt the soft orbs, much bigger than mine, in my hands. as I massaged them, I felt her let out a gasp of pleasure.

"Fuck that's good," she said.

"You alright?" I asked her.

"Yeah I'm just...I'm watching you and it's wonderful. You're so cute," she said.

I flushed, feeling her body against mine. My hands moved towards the tip of her nipples, brushing against there. I watched her shiver with delight, crying out as I continued to tease her body.

But I wanted more. I desired her, and I knew that she wanted the same thing. She then moved her body downwards, pressing her lips against my stomach, brushing there. She moved further and further downwards until she got in between my legs, pressing her lips against my thigs, enjoying the sensation of this. She pressed her lips against my thighs, pressing upwards as she continued to look me in the eyes. Then, when she got to the very edge of my pussy, she kissed the panties that were there, teasing me slightly.

"Ahh," I said out loud, pressing my hips upwards.

Her hands felt like silk, dancing between my legs, brushing against my panties. I looked into her eyes, enjoying the feeling of this, and for a long time, I simply sat there, enjoying the sensation of this. She continued to press there, enjoying the sounds that I made, making me lose control. My mind raced, my heart skipped a beat, and as her hands explored me, I sat on the bed, humming in pleurae as she continued this.

She slipped her hands to the sides of my pants, pulling them down along with my panties. The cold air hit me, causing me to shudder almost on instinct. She looked me in the eyes, but not before moving her hands forward, pressing towards the tip of my pussy, playing with my clit as she continued to look at me.

"You like that? She said sweetly in my ear.

"Y-yes," I said, my mouth struggling to form words. There was something just so....exciting about all of this. I knew that she enjoyed this tease as much as I did.

A hand moved against my clit, rubbing the nub there. I shivered, moaning in pleasure as I moved my hips slightly, pressing them upwards and enjoying the touch and the sensation. She gave me a small smirk, rubbing the tip of it, moving towards my ear.

"You like that?" she said.

"I-I do," I told her, choking out the sounds that I made. She smiled, pressing against there, pushing in deeper and deeper until she got towards my entrance. The first finger moved against my entrance, pushing into me.

I cried out, arching my hips as she slowly pumped in and out, leaning on top of me. She captured her lips against mine, pressing a finger into there, her thumb grazing against my clit, touching, teasing, making me slowly but surely lose control with every touch and press. It was driving me insane, making me shiver with delight, and I knew that this onslaught against me wasn't going to stop until she was satisfied.

She then moved the second finger against me, pressing there and then slowly into my entrance. I shivered, moaning out loud and enjoying the sensation of this. I knew that she was liking this too, and with every single touch, every single motion, I knew that she was driving me insane. She knew exactly what made me tick, and with every subtle graze against my sweet spot, I could feel the urge to orgasm loom over me.

I moved my hands forward, pawing at the front of her panties. She looked down at me, seeing the look of pure desire, the need for her, and the desire for everything start to take over. She smiled, pulling at the sides, letting the garment fall off.

I explored her, using my fingers at first and then pressing one of them into her like she did me. The sounds she made were different. They were still moans, but they sounded like whimpers, and I couldn't help but love the way she seemed to be losing control with every action, and the desire for well...everything that came from her.

For each touch that she had, I could see it in her eyes. The look of pure lust. That's when I moved another hand upwards, cupping her breasts as I looked into her eyes.

The ravishing need. The temptation, which was there, it was only going to make me want her more and more. I captured her lips, feeling Lydia gasp in surprise, but then slowly moan out, enjoying the sensation of control, of pleasure, and of everything else that came along the way. Our lips were mingling together, both of us gasping and crying out one another's names as we continued this. I didn't know how much more of this I could take, but it was only a matter of time before I could sense her body getting closer and closer, and it was then when, after a few more thrusts, I could feel her pressing upwards, causing me to let out a small gasp.

I was at my limit. She plunged her fingers there, her thumb moving against my clit, our tongues dancing a passionate dance with one another. The sound that I made was loud, but it was muffled by her lips, and I felt my eyes widen in both surprise, and of need over time. I could feel the high of this driving me insane, and I knew that she enjoyed this as much as I did.

After a few more moments, she thrust her fingers in deep and I cried out, feeling the pure, unadulterated lust that came out of my mouth. I shivered, crying out loud and thrusting my hips towards her, savoring the feeling of my orgasm.

I then did the same thing to her, but I pulled my fingers away, replacing it with my lips. My tongue teased her clit, than pressed deep into her entrance, causing her to let out a series of small moans and sounds that only made me ache for her more and more. After a few mere moments, she let out another soft, subtle cry, and she came hard, and as I felt the juice drip from her mouth, I looked at her, seeing the satisfaction that came from her as I did this.

I couldn't believe how good this was, how it was just so...so damn perfect. I knew she enjoyed this as much as I did, and everything alone was making me feel like I was about to hit my limit. She pulled back, looking me dead in the eyes, a smile ghosting her face.

"You good?" she said to me.

I didn't know how I felt. I felt like I had hit my limit and then some. But I nodded.

"Yeah just...too amazed to speak," I told her.

She smiled.

"Well good. I like seeing you like this," she teased.

I liked feeling like this. I looked at her, knowing full well that I could trust her. Even though she was...so different from what I expected, I embraced this.

The girl pulled away, looking into my eyes, a smile on her face.

"Good. I wouldn't...mind doing this once again if that's what you're into," she said to me.

I mean, Lydia was amazing. I didn't expect her to just...make me feel a certain way, but here she was. She had s smile on her face as she did it, and I couldn't help but feel a warmth in my heart.

"You, I'd like that, I told her.

"Good. Because I like it too," she replied.

I knew that she liked this as much as I did. The tension that was there before was definitely only growing even more so. I looked at her for a moment, and then, she spoke.

"I do need to get back to the club floor. Gotta make some money," she said.

"Yeah. I was only expecting a dance. Not all of that," I told her.

I felt a flush of embarrassment wash over my face as she looked at me. She then smirked.

"Well, I would love to continue this. Maybe we can…meet up for coffee at some point, she offered.

Coffee. That definitely was a prospect. I nodded.

"Yeah. I'd like that," I told her.

She beamed.

"Great. Then consider it a date honey," she said.

"Yeah, definitely," I replied.

She gave me a kiss, smiling warmly before leaving the room. However, before she got out of the area she turned around, looking at me.

"By the way, make sure to close the door on the way out. I don't want anyone funny around here," she said.

"Yeah, that's fine," I said.

With that, she was gone. I sat there, the post-orgasmic bliss hitting me hard. I didn't know what to tell anyone, other than I had the best experience with a woman.

She changed the way that I felt, made me excited about the future that I had. I tried to date guys before but there just wasn't a click. But with Lydia, I knew that we clicked.

She was different. She was the quiet, timid nerd that I'd see come Monday in class. She probably would ask a question or two while I told her the answer, giving her all of the important information. But I knew that underneath it all was a woman who seemed to be the right one for me, the one that I'd been waiting for. She was someone who changed me for the better, and made me excited.

And that of course made me feel a heat of excitement. I wanted her, and I knew that she wanted me as well.

As I was about to leave the club, I heard a small sound. I whipped my head around, expecting it to be the club owner about to cuss me out, but to my relief, it was Lydia.

"Hey so…I just realized I never gave you ,my number. Here's my card. Text me some time," she said.

I took the card, beaming.

"Yeah, I sure will," I replied.

I noticed her smile, seeing her rush on off, leaving me alone once again. I looked, understanding that this was the beginning of a whole new life for me.

As I left the club, I turned around and looked back, realizing that Lydia would be there, waiting for me next time. I smiled, feeling a satisfaction at the fact that she would be here. I knew that if I ever wanted to come back to the club, she'd be there waiting for me.

But there was so much more than that. I knew that on Monday we'd meet up, and I'd give her the same flirty smile. I knew that, even though we were separate for now, I could still taste her on my tongue, and I couldn't wait for the next time we crossed paths, and the fun we could share together.

It was my first time with a woman, but it was an experience that I'd never forget, no matter what happened next.

Take Over Control

Life's been busy as hell lately. Everything just felt like it was passing on by. Between time, my own efforts, well...everything really. It just felt so overwhelming that I wanted to scream.

I needed something. Anything. To help me get in my place.

That's when I met up with him. my dom Terry.

Terry was a different kind of guy. He seemed like a meek and timid man, but he knew how to completely control me, turn me into a puddle of goo, making me shiver with delight and crave more.

I learned about Terry from one of the fetish clubs that I used to frequent with when I went out with my ex-roommate. We aren't on bad terms, they just got a girlfriend and now they're doing their own thing, living with them and stuff. But they introduced me to this fetish club, and I started to go on my own.

That's when I met him.

His name there was Stone. That's because he had the personality of a rock when you first met him, but as you got closer to him and he opened up, the way he opened would be markedly different.

At first, Stone and I were a bit awkward around one another. But then, one night I moved over towards one of the play areas, going to the area they restrained you at. He restrained me and I felt the crop just barely graze against my behind. But as I felt it, I let out a small moan of surprise. It felt...nice to say the least. I liked the way it tickled against my backside, making me shiver and cry out with delight as he continued to tease me. But that's when I felt it.

The flick of the wrist, and the small cry that I let out. But then he went over, putting a gag in my mouth, moving towards my lips.

"Now, you know better than to make noises like that. I want to watch you squirm," he said.

He gagged me. He knew that if I needed out there was a sign, but then he did it again, and I cried out. This feeling of control. This need that made me ache for more. It turned this businesswoman into a wed puddle of need, crying out with every single touch like she was the mess of the whore that she was before.

And that's what I wanted.

I wanted a man who knew exactly how to shut me the fuck up so I could enjoy the feeling of not being in control.

The spanking session continued, this time with harder hits from the flogger. But I grinned and bore it, holding onto the edges, moaning as I felt the hot leather hit against my backside.

I felt so naked, even though I still had my panties and bra on, and yet...there was something liberating about being taken over like this.

When we finished he untied me, getting the restraints and gag out of my mouth, bringing me over to help ice my butt. It stung, but there was something riveting about this.

"You okay?" he finally asked.

I turned to him and nodded.

"Very okay," I said.

I was then approached by him to see if I wanted to possibly…take this a bit further. To possibly start a long-term thing. I decided sure, and then he showed me the contract.

At first I thought those kinds of contracts were of course, something that a person would have in the movies. But I read it, realizing it was all there and true, and I quickly signed it, agreeing to all of this. I'd be his, bound to his word, and there was something exciting about this. Perhaps it was the freedom of possibly making sure that I finally got to experience the lust and power that I've lived for.

Maybe it was that inherent desire, that need within me, something that caused me to sign this immediately without any worries.

And that's what we agreed to. It was kind of like we were dating, but not really. I didn't see myself dating anyone right now with work, and we agreed to start this slow and steady.

The first thing we did together was spend time of course at the dungeon together. There he helped me unlock new fetishes and feelings. The idea of being a sub was so enticing to me.

It was because I always was in control. Being the CEO of a company that I made and ran was exhausting, and sometimes, just being told what to do was riveting. And the physical pleasure that came out of this only made me more and more excited.

But I craved more, and after different play sessions, I would ask for more.

Until one day, I asked for it.

"I want you to fully take control of me," I said to him.

Stone looked at me with surprise.

"Are you sure about this Minerva?" he asked me.

That was the codename that we made up for one another. I never wanted to use my real name here, and always made sure to look different from what the photos and the like plastered on the internet had.

"Yes. I want this," I said.

I craved the idea of being tied up, of just…being used like this. It may seem cruel to some people, but the idea of letting go, and allowing someone to do this to me was a novel feeling, and one that I so desperately wanted.

So he agreed to this. We agreed that we'd do this at his place, since he had a dungeon. I'd been there before, and Stone was a professional dom. When I got there, I rang the doorbell, my body excited, my pussy wet with desire.

The door mysteriously opened as I stepped inside. For a moment, I thought this was some sort of prank, when suddenly, I felt an item against my lips, holding it there.

It was a scarf, a gag that was tied around my mouth. I let out a series of small cries, but they were stopped by the item. Then, I heard his mouth lower, right up against my ear.

"Aww you're here. You're ripe for the picking. Master's been waiting my little kitten," he said.

I let out a muffled sound. Just hearing this man's tenor voice made me want to just melt completely. He picked me up, carrying me, bringing me up the stairs. I shivered, enjoying the closeness of our bodies. He then brought

me to another room. I knew of course that he had the dungeon, but that was in another part of the house completely.

I muffled out a "Where are we going" but then I felt the slapping of my bottom, causing me to let out a small groan of pleasure.

"You'll find out what we get there kitten. I have something special for you tonight," he purred in my ear.

I knew what he meant by this. There was that thrill of course of being taken like this. When we got to the room he opened it up.

It was like the dungeon, but it had a bed with restraints and a whole bunch of rope.

"Tonight I'm going to tie you up, tease you completely, and make you squirm. And you know exactly how to get out of this if you need to," he said.

That's right. He wanted me to snap my fingers and cross my toes. One or the other would be enough for him to stop the scene completely.

It may not seem like enough for some people, but I knew that he'd take care of me, and that I could trust him, which was more than enough for me. He then moved me towards the bed, restraining my arms and legs, my eyes wide and the sounds of moans coming out of my mouth.

He quickly discarded my clothes, leaving on the little sheer lingerie which showed my hard nipples and the obvious wetness of my pussy. He moved his hand towards there, rubbing me down there, making me cry out slightly.

"Look at you, so desperate for master already. But you came here, so I'm going to make sure you get everything that you've desired, and what you want," he said.

That's right. This wasn't just for him. This was for me. This was something that I explicitly asked for, and I knew that it was something that he enjoyed doing. He loved teasing me like this, making me cry out, the small sounds of pleasure coming out of my mouth as he continued to tease me completely, making me shiver and cry out with pure, unadulterated delight as he did this.

I wanted him to take over control like this. He soon moved his hands forward, grabbing them roughly, but not enough for it to hurt, putting it in the bindings.

"You'll be tight, but not too tight. We can start with this kitten," he said.

I nodded, my eyes curious at everything that he had planned. He finished restraining me as he looked me up and down.

"You look so cute there, all desperate and needy for master. I can't wait to tie you up in a hogtie, making you moan and scream my name," he purred there.

His hands moved downwards, the smallest, most sensual touches making me shiver with delight. He got of course right over my nipples, which were already hard. He tugged on them, causing me to let out a small cry, shivering with delight.

"Look at you! All desperate and needy like this. I love it," he said to me.

I shivered, enjoying the sounds that escaped my mouth as he did this, loving the feeling of his hands and lips against me. He lightly trailed his kisses downwards, until of course, he got between the crevice of my breasts,

touching me there. The little touches were enough to make me cry out, but nothing could really be heard because of the gag.

"You know, I want to just *rip* this off of you…but first I have something a little more fun to do," he said.

I looked at him, curiosity killing me as he walked on over, reaching for his drawers, grabbing the clamps.

There were two tat were across from one another, and one that was a bit further away.

I squirmed about, the realization of what this was immediately driving me forward.

He grabbed the clamps, putting them on each of my nipples, placing them there. The pinch caused a gasp to escape my mouth. But then he spread my legs, pushing the other clamp against my clit, holding it there.

I felt the dull ache and pain that came out of this, causing me to shiver and cry out, the gag muffling all of the sounds. After he finished putting them on, he smiled.

"There you go. You look ravishing my dear," he said.

The way those words came off of his mouth made me cry out, suddenly feeling completely aroused and used by this man already. He slowly reached for something. Was it a remote? But then he pressed the button and the surges of energy hit me, causing me to let out a small cry of pleasure, the ache and need growing within me.

I squirmed about, watching him smile as he started to dial this up further, watching me shiver and cry out with delight as he did this.

"Look at you. So used and enjoying this," he said.

I let out another muffled sound as he continued this, enjoying the way he just completely took over me, causing me to feel the pleasure and the surge of need grow within me. Everything was making me cry out with delight, losing all semblance of control as he continued to tease me. This had different vibrations that caused me to let out a series of small cries, enjoying every single moment as I continued to lose all semblance of control, my hands beginning to form fists as I cried out.

Then, as soon as I felt that the pressure and pleasure was becoming too much, he turned it off, looking at me. He moved his hands between my legs, pressing against the obvious wetness there, lightly rubbing and teasing this slightly.

"Look at you. Such a mess." He said with a smile. I cried out, squirming about, but then, he took the clamps off. I watched him walk over and grab something else.

It was a bit of ice. I looked at him as he started to smile, taking the cubes and holding them in his hands.

"Wow. So desperate. I can see the look in your eyes. The anticipation. The need," he said to me.

That was there. I wanted him so badly. I needed him inside me. He's fucked me while tied up before, but the intimacy of this was driving me insane. It was different this time.

This time, it wasn't just two people indulging in fetishes.

I really was his kitten, and he was my master.

He then took the ice cubes, ripping off the lingerie, tossing the ruined garment over to the side. He grabbed the cubes, putting them right above my nipples. I let out a small hum, squirming about.

"What's the matter? Are you anticipating the feeling of cold, the sensation of this as it hits you?" he asked me.

I looked at him, eyes wide and ready, and that's when I felt it.

The first drop. It hit my right nipple, causing me to immediately react. I felt everything clench up, the pleasure of this almost intoxicating me completely. He smiled, watching me squirm and lose all semblance of control as he did this.

"Aww! Such a mess," he purred into my ear.

I was a goddamn mess. I couldn't have it any other way though, completely and utterly lost to the pleasure of the flesh, the touch that this man bestowed upon me, and the aching need for so much more as time continued on.

He moved the ice cubes right over my nipple, just barely grazing against this. That's when my eyes widened, and I let out a garbled cry, pushing my hands and feet upwards, wanting more of the touch there.

"Getting hot and bothered over ice. How cute," he said to me.

I was a mess. I wanted him to just use that all over me, making me shiver and cry out in pleasure from everything that came out of this. I wanted him to continue this onslaught against my body, making me shiver and cry out in complete need and lust.

That's all I desired from this man, and he was making me feel things that I didn't even expect to feel, a level of pleasure and desire that hit me on a different plane.

I felt the ice lay against the tips of my nipples. He smiled as he rubbed them and my body just instantly reacted. I threw my head back, moaning the little sounds that I could, as muffled as they were, shivering with delight as he rubbed them slowly, against every single part of it. My nipples were now rock-hard and cold as shit.

There was a thrilling feeling about all of this. Maybe it was the fact that he knew exactly how to tease and pleasure me, to the point where I was enjoying this far more than I cared to admit, but I loved every single touch, craved the feeling of this as time went on, and I needed it more than ever.

I wanted him, and I knew that after a bit there was only so much that he could do.

When he pulled the cubes away, he tossed them to the side, looking at my flailing, desperate body as he smiled.

"Look at you. I haven't even tied you up and fucked you yet. Maybe I should. Or maybe I should just tease that body of yours more..."

He moved his hands against there, skating over my flesh. The little touches were enough to make me lose control, the excitement of this driving me insane.

For a long time, he just skirted his hands around, nails digging into every part of my flesh. When they skirted the soft parts of my flesh, I let out a guttural sound, enjoying the sudden sensitivity that came out of this too.

Every touch was driving me to the point of madness. Every single motion was enough to make me ache for more, desire more, and need even more too.

It was only then when after a little while he moved his hands away, going over to the little wraps. He undid them so that I could be freed, but that freedom only lasted a short while, before he blinded my eyes once more.

"I want you to feel everything tonight kitten?" he said to me.

I shivered, moaning and crying out with every single touch. It was driving me crazy, the insanity only making me want more and more out of him. before I knew it, he soon had his hands right over the very edges of my body, slowly moving this over in the direction of wherever he was putting me.

It was then when I was over at the edge of some place. He grabbed my hands, pulling them up and tying them up somewhere. I felt the rope there, suddenly realizing that I was at the mercy of his touches. He took the rope there and then also put it against the edges of my feet, suspending me there.

I shivered, feeling the burn of the rope hit me. But this was what is signed up for. I wanted this, and he damn well knew this too. When I was suspended in the air, hue grabbed something. He then brought it over, letting it skirt against the very tip of my back,

I realized what it was.

A flogger.

I shivered with delight, feeling the item just barely touch my back. And then, before I knew it, I heard the crack of it, and the scream that came out of my mouth.

It was a bit harder than I expected, probably because of the lack of sight. He then stopped, grazing it there, asking me something.

"Are you alright kitten? You know you can just say the word and I will stop," he said.

He then lightly moved there, but I shook my head. I didn't want to stop, and he damn well knew this. He knew I enjoyed the feeling of this more than I'd ever care to admit, and that I was lost in the feeling of pleasure that came out of this.

He let out a grunt of excitement as he moved his hands then slowly over my arms, down to my backside, and then between my legs. He pressed two fingers in, causing me to let out a small gasp.

"I want to hear those cute moans of yours," he purred in my ear, lightly nibbling on the shell of my ear.

I shivered, aching for him, but then he moved his hands to the back of the gag, undoing it, and when it was gone I let out a small gasp of excitement.

"Now kitten, back to what we were doing," he purred.

That's exactly what I wanted. He slowly moved his hands towards my backside again, this time shoving three fingers into me. I cried out, completely aroused by the pleasure of this. He then grabbed the flogger once more, reading it, this time near my right side on my back.

When it hit, I let out a sudden moan, feeling the pleasure along with the mild pain just flow through my body. It was driving me crazy, and everything just felt so...so right. I ached for this. It was the best thing I'd have ever experienced, and there was something about being taken like this that only made me want to enjoy this again and again.

He hit me with the flogger three more times, each time making me whimper and cry out with pleasure, enjoying the sensation of this, loving every single moment of this too. It was amazing, and I knew that he enjoyed this as much as I did. Every single touch, every single motion, it was all just...so damn good.

I loved the feeling. The pain turned into pleasure every time he did this. I was aching for more, and I knew that he was enjoying this as much as I was.

Everything was making me feel like all of my sensitivity was turned up to 11. And that's okay, because I knew he enjoyed this too.

He continued to use the flogger, reaching over and teasing every part of me, hitting every which way. I shivered, crying out every single time, enjoying the feeling of this man's touches, losing all sense of control as he continued to touch every part of me.

He then stopped, putting the flogger down. I was a little disappointed, but then I felt something against my feet.

It was a tickler. He tickled between my toes, making me giggle, slowly laughing more and more. It was weird because it was both arousing, but also incredibly sensitive too. I started to feel him continue this, enjoying the sensation of it, watching him as he smiled at me.

"You like that? You enjoy being tickled? Turned on by it?" he said.

I couldn't say anything, the only sounds coming out of me was laughter as he moved from my feet up towards my sides, letting the tickler explore those sensitive parts of me that I normally wouldn't let anyone dare to touch and find out about.

There was something thrilling about letting go and letting him take complete control of me. He then moved the tickler away, moving towards my feet to get them down.

I was soon on the ground again, and my arms were freed. He gave me a moment to let the feeling come back, but the dull ache of my arms felt so damn good. He then pushed me down onto the bed, grabbing my arms and legs, and with a skill and finesse that I didn't even expect, he tied me up in a hogtie.

I was shocked at how limited I was. But there was something almost riveting about this. The liberating feeling of being tied up like this, enjoying the feeling of losing control. He then moved himself so that he was in between my legs, pressing his fingers into me.

He shoved two into there, causing me to let out a small moan. But then, I felt him pull back, grabbing something from there.

"I have something a little extra for you tonight," he said.

He moved my cheeks apart and then padded my other hole. I suddenly tensed up, feeling a bit unsure about all of this, but then, he moved to my ear.

"If you want out, remember there's always the magic words or actions. You want this kitten?" he asked.

I was a little bit nervous, but that's what I liked about Stone. He took me to different levels. There was something liberating about your limits being tested to no end, enjoying the pleasure that came from this too.

"Y-yes," I told him, pushing my hips there.

He giggled, but then moved between my legs, pushing the toy into my pucker. I suddenly felt the object within there, cand I felt it fill me up a little bit. It's a bit bigger than I expected, but it wasn't that bad.

But then, I felt my legs move upwards slightly, and then there was something else between my legs. Something big and hot, and when I realized it was his cock, I let out a small cry.

He slid in with ease, probably because I'd already came a couple of times. But this felt so good, my senses immediately heightened. I felt his cock sink in, filling me up completely. But that of course was nothing compared to the feeling of his body moving over me, holding my legs upwards, fucking me with a full abandonment of thought and logic.

And I loved it.

Every single pump, every single thrust, every single touch was making me feel a sense of excitement that I hadn't tapped into yet. It was then when, after a few more thrusts, he moved in, pressing his lips to my ear.

"Are you good?" he asked me.

I cried out, thrusting my hips upwards, suddenly lost in the feeling of pleasure that came from this. He then turned on the device, the vibrating sensation of the butt plug in my ass causing me to let out a series of low, guttural sounds and screams.

Everything about this was amazing, the perfect moment that I'd been waiting for as he continued to fill me up, thrusting into me.

After a few more thrusts though, he hit against my g-spot, and it was then when I felt my entire body tense up, the need of my orgasm hitting me completely, and it was then when I suddenly lost all semblance of control, losing it all and feeling my orgasm hit me completely.

I screamed out, cumming hard as he groaned, pressing into me, breeding me with his seed. I then felt him pull out, leaving me there with the cum dripping out of me, and a satisfied smile on my face.

Just like that, the entire scene change. He immediately got me out of the bindings. I rubbed my hands a little bit, the string of it reminding me of the fun that I got to have. he then pulled the blindfold off, and I squinted my eyes, realizing I was back to reality from the pleasure that I felt.

It was heady, but I felt really good. He grabbed my body, holding it in his arms, stroking my head as he looked at me.

"Are you good?" he asked me.

I nodded.

"Yeah just...wow. I didn't expect this," I told him.

"Well I wanted to give you something amazing. You told me how stressed you were recently, so I figured this was the least that I could do," he purred.

I smiled happily. Having someone like this who cared about me just felt so nice. It's a rarity for me. I felt more appreciated by stone than I did anyone else really.

He brought me over to the bathtub after drawing some water, gently laying on me and rubbing some ointment on the bruises that began to form. A couple of them drew blood, but that's okay. The fun of the moment was worth all of the pain that I just endured.

"You good?" he asked me.

I nodded.

"Amazing," I admitted.

"Good. I was worried I'd been too much for you back there," he said.

"No you're fine. Trust me," I told him.

I was glad that I got to experience this. He then looked into my eyes, seeing the obvious lust that was there, and the happiness too.

"What's the matter?" he inquired.

"I don't know. It just…feels really good you know. It feels so right to experience this with you," I said to him.

He nodded.

"I feel that. The feeling's mutual there," he said.

There was a bit of a long silence, and there was something that I wanted from him. I looked at him, and then for a moment, neither of us knew what to say.

There was a feeling of trust when I was near him. but there was also that feeling of something more.

I knew that no matter what, I could be with him.

After he finished cleaning me up, he got me some hot chocolate and some chocolates, something that I loved after we had these sessions. I sat there, munching on it, but I could see the look that he had, and there was something he wanted to say, but feared saying it.

"Something the matter?" I asked him.

"No it's just…I wanted to ask you something. About us," he said.

"What do you mean?" I inquired.

He turned to me, looking me in the eyes. There was a bit of desperation there on his face, but also there was that desire to ask me something, whatever it was.

"It's about us," he said.

"You mean like…this relationship?" I asked.

"Sort of. I kind of…want something more. I know it's ultimately up to you. We can keep the contract but…I like the intimacy of this. There's something about you that's different from the others that I've dommed before. I feel this connection with you. we don't need to take it fast or anything just….something for you to consider," he said to me.

I paused, thinking about this. I knew what he meant. It was not something I'd thought of before, if he wanted the truth of it.

"Are you sure?"

"Yes. I'm sure," he said.

I looked at him, pausing. Trying to figure out how to approach this.

"Yeah. Let's just…take it slow you know? I don't want this to be too fast," I admitted.

"Heavens no. I don't want that either. I think us taking a bit more time, getting to know each other and seeing where this goes is a good thing for each of us," he replied.

I smiled, thankful that he understood my thought process.

"Thank you so much for getting it," I said.

And then, for the first time in forever, he leaned in, capturing my lips.

"It's Ryan by the way. My real name," he said after he pulled away.

I smiled, my body warm. I didn't think Terry was his real name, just the dom name.

"Vanessa," I replied.

It was a deepness that I hadn't experienced with others before, but there was something about this which just felt so damn right. I knew I wasn't making a bad decision here, and this wouldn't bite me in the ass, even if other people may find it strange.

Her Son's Best Friend

"Hey mom," my son Gavin said.

"Oh, hey there honey," I said to him.

He smiled, but not before running up to his room, closing the door and staying on his computer. That's pretty much how everything's been for the last three years. Except now he's 1, coming home from college and ignoring his mom.

I sighed. Sometimes I wished he would realize the annoying things he does, but it's not like I can sit there and scold his ass either. He's a young boy, he probably doesn't realize just how much of an antisocial asshole he is at time.

Still though, you'd think as an adult things would get better.

"Hey Gavin, dinner's ready," I told him.

"Yeah mom, coming," he said.

He walked over, sitting down across from me. As we ate though, I looked at him.

"So have you figured out what you plan to do this summer break this year?" I asked.

Normally, Gavin would take a job as a lifeguard, but I had no idea what his plans were for this one.

"Actually, me and Cody are working for this guy. Cody's dad's friend. He wants us to move things. And also…Vicky wanted me to come say hi," he said.

"Oh yeah Vicky! How is she?" I asked him.

"Well she's alright. And also Cody's doing well too," he said.

I remembered Cody. He was a bit of a punk ass kid back in the day, but maybe he's managed to turn over a new leaf.

"They're invited over if you want them to stop by," I offered.

"Yeah Cody said he would. Vicky…I don't know," he said.

I kinda chuckled to myself. My son definitely had a little crush on Vicky, but it wasn't going to be like…weird that I mentioned it or anything.

He was terrible at hiding it for starters.

But when I saw him look at me, seeing the flush on his face, I could tell he was a bit embarrassed.

"Actually mom, they're also going out to the lake too. There's a party that night. I may spend time there," he said.

"That's fine dear. As long as you have something planned. I'll of course be running my business during the summer," I told him.

"Right. Sounds good mom," he said.

I ran an online retailer business, and it was definitely a bit of an experience. But I also liked it, and I knew that it'd make me the money that I needed not provide for both myself, and for my son.

Over the next couple of weeks, I started to see Vicky here more often. But I wondered where Cody was. Finally, Gavin rushed inside, looking at me with surprise.

"Hey so uh...Cody and Vicky are coming over," he said.

"Oh really? Great!" I said. I mean, I liked them both. It'd been about three years since I've seen both, since Cody weas a year older than my son and was already in college before "Gavin got in, and Vicky was the daughter of some rich family, but maybe they chilled out now that she was an adult.

Either way, I was excited to have them over.

That night, I got the place set up for four people. I had a four-person dining set, and when the doorbell rang, I grabbed it. First, it was Vicky, who said hello.

She matured into a fine young woman. I've known her family for a while, and even though Gavin wouldn't admit it, I knew he had a huge crush on her.

But then, the door opened, and Cody showed up, 20 years old and looking amazing.

He matured into one hell of a man. He had short blonde hair, blue eyes, and was tall. The hint of muscle that I saw immediately caught my attention, and I tried to hold back licking my lips.

Wow, Cody grew up, and he was definitely a piece of eye candy these days.

"Hey Ms. Baxter," he said.

"Hey there Cody! My it's been a long time! Come on in," she said.

He gave me a hug just like Vicky did, and those large arms practically smothered me. I wanted to feel this again. But I quickly brought them to the dinner table, all of them sitting around.

Of course Cody and Gavin talked about video games for a bit, but I could see that Cody was a bit nervous.

"Everything alright?" I asked.

"Yeah mom, don't worry," he said, totally brushing me off.

"Hey man, she was just asking. Everything okay—"

"Don't worry about it Cody. Seriously," Gavin said.

Whatever Gavin was trying to hide was both kind of hilarious, but also slightly frustrating.

Vicky touched his shoulder and then he stopped.

"Sorry mom. Hey, is it okay if I take a break. I think I'm done," he said.

"Sure dear," she said.

Vicky finished her food, looking at me.

"Thank you for the food Ms. Baxter. It's really good to see you again," she said.

"Same here. How's college?" I asked.

"really good. I've been talking to Gavin whenever I can and—"

She blushed, and I couldn't help but hide a laugh. My son was really bad at hiding the fact that he had a girlfriend, or at least had a crush on her.

"Anyways, yeah I've just been getting my degree. Parents want me to go into business, and I want the same thing, so I'm working on that degree," she said.

"Great. That sounds like fun," I told her.

She beamed.

"Sure as hell is. Anyways, I need to go. Gavin's upstairs, right?" she said.

"Yeah, he is," I replied.

I watched the two of them head upstairs, and then there was Cody, who scoffed.

"It's always like this," he said.

"The two of them?"

"Yeah...I've been left out all this month. I didn't know that he was talking to her all the time, and I didn't know that they were basically dating. But yeah, sorry for that Ms. Baxter. They invited me over because I told them that I missed seeing you, but now I feel like it's a waste of time," he said.

"Not at all. You've grown into a fine young man. And I'm sorry that Gavin's like this. He's not always the type to do this. Maybe it's because it's Vicky," I explained.

I didn't care who my son dated as long as they had protected sex and she wasn't some sort of drug addicted mess. And I knew Vicky's family. They were the type who were strict with her, but not to the point where she'd rebel.

In truth, I didn't mind the two of them getting together but I could sense that for him, this was hell.

"Yeah, I'm surprised you didn't hear about it sooner. They've been kind of seeing one another. They haven't told me, but I guess that's par for the course. Because well...I expected things to go different. That's all," he said.

"Hey, don't worry. And you're welcome to come over at any time. I'm sure my son and Vicky will be busy," I told him.

Cody laughed.

"They will be. But thanks Ms. B. by the way...are you doing anything next Friday?'

"No, want to come over?"

"Well I was thinking that. There's this party and well...I don't think I'll be going. As much as I love Gavin, seeing Vicky and him necking all night wasn't my idea of a fun time," he said.

I laughed.

"I get that. Yeah you're more than welcome over dear. I'll just be here," I said.

"Thanks."

"Y-yes," he said to me.

I nodded.

"By the way, you taste better than my ex," I purred in his ear.

He flushed crimson, but quickly got his pants back on.

"I'll see you next Friday," he said.

"Alright, have fun," I told him.

He rushed on out of there, ignoring the little laugh that I had. I watched him scurry out to his car. They really did take separate cars.

I felt bad for him, but even though his best friend now treated him like a third wheel, I of course could step in and make things a little bit better as well.

I sighed, realizing it was the first time in a long while I felt that level of arousal. Not since…well when I last had sex with my ex. Before of course we got a divorce. It was breakup sex, and it was fun. But there was something about this which was far more thrilling than boring ass breakup sex with a mediocre dude.

This was a thrill. It was fun, and it made me excited for what was to come.

Over the next couple of days, I noticed that Gavin was spending a whole lot more time at Vicky's house. When he did come home, he spoke to me a little bit, but was distant.

"Hey Gavin?" I asked.

"Yeah mom?" he asked.

"You're…using protection and everything right? With Vicky?" I asked.

"W-why are you asking mom?"

"Come on Gavin, you're a terrible liar. I know that you and Vicky are…together and all," I told him.

He flushed, but then nodded.

"Yeah, what about it?" he muttered.

"Nothing's wrong dear. Just be safe. And I guess that's why Cody is mad too, isn't it?" I asked.

He nodded.

"Yeah, Cody's pissed about it. But it's not like I can help it! She's just…she likes me mom," he said to me.

I understood that. I certainly could see it in his eyes.

"Well, whatever you do is up to you dear. At the end of the day it's your life, your sexual health, just be smart. All I'm asking for," I told him.

"right. Thanks mom," he said.

"See, that's not so bad," I said.

Then, Friday came. I waited, wondering if he would actually show up. Gavin left early, saying he needed to help with "Setups" with Vicky, but I imagine it was something else. About an hour had passed, and I wondered if he'd show up. He hadn't as of yet, which made me worried.

I thought I came on too strong, but then the doorbell rang. I rushed on over, getting it.

"Oh there you are Cody," I said.

"Hey Ms. Baxter. Sorry about that. I had to deal with Gavin and Vicky before heading over here," he said.

"Is everything okay?" I asked.

He paused, looking away.

"I'll tell you inside."

I let him in, watching him head to the couch, plopping down and sighing.

"I don't understand. We used to be such close friends! And now I feel like he doesn't give a rat's ass about me," he moaned.

"You mean...Gavin?" I asked.

"Yeah, I just feel like all he cares about these days is Vicky. I hate it. I wished I could have that but...I don't know I can't. and I can't stand it," he said.

"I know. It's hard. But sometimes...if it's meant to be, it's meant to be. I know Gavin doesn't dislike you dear. He's just bad with time management and the feelings of others," I said.

He did this when he turned 18 a year ago too. Rushing off, ignoring me. Even during his teenage years he wasn't this bad. Cody sighed.

"That should've been me with Vicky. I told Gavin that I liked her, but he just swept in, and then took her away. Ugh," he said.

"I know it's hard. But I'm here for you," I said, reaching out and touching his thigh. He paused, looking at me.

"So we don't need to talk about this with anyone right? I mean, you're my friend's mom. If people find out—"

"Nobody needs to know dear. Not even Gavin. I can be the mom that consoles you through this," I said with a smile.

"Really?"

I nodded.

"Course," I said.

He smiled, and looked at me.

"Thanks," he said.

Before I could say much more, his lips were quickly on mine. There was that feeling or urgency that came from younger men. I did prefer younger men to men my age, and Cody had grown up to be quite a cutie.

We locked lips, both of us moaning as I felt my lips press in harder against him, and I could sense the urgency in his lips too. The kiss that we shred was different. There was a clear desire for more there, but there was also that explorative nature to it that came with the kiss as well.

As we kissed, I felt his hands move slightly towards my backside, touching gingerly. It was cute, seeing a young man like him so inexperienced. I thought he'd have a girlfriend or two in college, but I guess that wasn't the case for a guy like him.

Oh well, I knew how to make a cutie like him feel good.

I pressed my tongue to his lips, and he quickly opened up, moaning in surprise as I mingled my lips with his own. We let our tongues move and dance with one another, groaning and moaning being the only sounds that we made as we made out on the couch.

I'd never tell Gavin about this, and I'm sure he'd keep it a secret too. After all, I knew his secret about Vicky and all. For a long time, we just experienced the thrill and feeling of one another's lips, until of course, I pulled back, sighing.

"Damn," he said.

"I could say the same yourself," I told him, rubbing my crotch against his. The obvious tent in his pants was growing more prominent, and of course, I could see the look of pure desire in his eyes, and way he licked his lips.

"Want to continue?" I asked.

"Do I? of course," he said excitedly.

He moved, his hands exploring my body. He touched my sides, moving forward towards my breasts, touching them there, playing with the orbs through the fabric. I let out a small grunt of satisfaction, but then I quickly pulled it over my head, tossing the garment over to the side.

His eyes widened like giant saucers, looking at me with shock and surprise.

"Wow," he said.

"You like?" I said to him.

He nodded.

"Yeah. They're…big," he said.

"I can let you feel them too," I told him with a smile.

He reached out, touching the orbs with his hands, playing with them from outside the bra. But then I sighed, moving my hands to the back of my bra, undoing the clasp, pulling it off.

The look on his face when he saw them was one that I wanted to remember forever. The way his eyes just widened at the size of my chest was amusing. I did have large boobs, but they weren't as perky as they used to be. However, he didn't care, grabbing the large orbs and touching them with his hands. His fingers moved against the tip of them, causing me to let out a small humming sound of pleasure.

"Fuck that's nice," I said to him.

He played and explored, suing his hands both gingerly, and with little touches and pinches, causing me to let out a small gasp of surprise, moving my hips slightly as he continued to explore me like this.

51

It was only a matter of time before I could feel my whole body just start to lose control, and the way he touched me felt different from others. He seemed almost innocent with the touches, and it made me feel excited about this too.

Before I knew it, his lips were on one of my nipples, sucking on it fervently. His other hand moved towards the other nipple, pinching it slightly, and I let out a small gasp, enjoying the sensation of this as he continued to touch, tease and pleasure my body.

I ached for him, I wanted him, and I knew that he was enjoying this as much as I was. He continued to play and tease with my breasts and nipples, enjoying the sounds that came out of my lips, and the feeling of this.

"You good?' he asked me.

"Yeah," I told him with excitement.

The little touches and teases wee enough to drive me crazy, but then I felt his hands move downwards, rubbing between my legs.

"Oh so that's what you want," I purred.

I moved off of him, getting on his left, spreading my legs and teasing my pussy for him to see.

"Y-yes," he said.

He was already all over me before I could say anything else. He then moved his hands there, rubbing my clit, touching there with the smallest of touches, I could feel my whole body on fire, the pleasure growing, and the need increasing.

"Fuck," I breathed out, feeling his hands there. He reached towards the sides of my panties, sliding them off, revealing my shaven, pink pussy.

My pussy throbbed with delight, and I watched as he extended his tongue, reaching out and lapping at the tip of my clit. As he did that, I shivered, shuddering in pleasure as I felt him gobble me up, completely overtaking me and making me feel amazing. I shivered with delight, feeling the moan escape my body, and the pleasure rise above. I wanted him to continue this, and then, before I knew it, he moved his face forward, pushing his tongue out, and then pressing it into me.

I screamed out, surprised by how good he was at this. He was so experienced, even though he supposedly never did this before. Maybe he did have some experience but just wasn't letting on.

Either way, I was enjoying this, wanting him to continue his onslaught on my body, and the pleasure that reverberated through my bones.

I felt him push his tongue against a certain spot, and I suddenly cried out, struggling to hold back the wave of pleasure that completely overtook me for but a brief moment. But then, he pulled back, smiling at me.

"I-I want to fuck you MS. Baxter," he said.

"Then go on ahead dear," I purred in his ear.

He looked at me, slightly nervous, but then I reached out, cupping his pants.

"Why don't I get you a little ready beforehand," I said.

"O-okay," he said.

I pulled down his basketball shorts, seeing his cock there. I quickly took half of the shaft in my hands, moving my lips there. I licked the sides of the shafts, and then the underside, and he let out a small cry of desire and need. I looked at him, smiling.

"There we go," I purred, taking him all the way down. His cock was big, and it did require me having to relax my gag, but I son felt him moan, fucking my throat slightly. But we took it slow. I didn't want him to blow his load like that.

But then I pulled away with a plop, spreading my legs and pussy apart.

"Go ahead," I said.

He looked starstruck, but he quickly spread my legs, holding them there as he pushed into my entrance, letting it sink in.

The feeling of this was definitely more surprising than I expected. I looked at him, seeing the look of pure bliss on his face as he plunged into me.

I held my legs up, letting him rest himself all the way in. He let out a gasp as I got deep inside, feeling him in there and pulsating.

"Holy shit. It's so warm. And so tight," he said.

"That's how it should be. You feel great," I said.

He began to thrust in and out, and I felt my eyes practically roll to the back of my head, the pleasure that I felt driving me crazy.

He was big, but that's the way that I liked it. It's what I enjoyed, and even thought this was all novel to him, he seemed to know exactly how to use his cock.

He thrust in and out, moaning slightly as he looked at me, the sounds delicious and music to my ears. I held him there, thrusting my own pussy against there, watching his eyes widen and the moans that he uttered echo through the room. The sounds of our bodies, and the moans that we shared were the only things that we could hear.

But then he grabbed me, holding me against the edge of the couch, plunging all the way in. I suddenly cried out, feeling the pleasure of the moment drive me insane. I could see him holding me there, his hands touching my body. I felt a pair of hands against my breasts, holding them and teasing the nipples. I shuddered, crying out loud, completely lost in the pleasure that this young man gave to me.

He continued the thrusts, but then he pulled out, looking me in the eyes.

"Could I fuck you...doggy style?" he asked.

My face curled into a smile.

"Course."

I got on all fours, feeling his cock enter into me, plunging deep inside. I let out a moan, the pleasure igniting through my body as he thrust in deep, filling me up completely with his seed. The excitement, the pleasure, the feeling of this, it was all just...wonderful.

I was lost in the pleasure of the moment, the pleasure of the flesh, and I knew that he felt the exact same way, enjoying the sensation of this too, loving the feeling as much as I did.

He held my hips, thrusting in deep, but then I felt his hand plunge down, grabbing my ass and holding it.

"Damn Ms. B, you have a nice ass too," he said.

"T-thanks," I said, feeling him hit that one spot, causing me to let out a choked sound.

But then he stopped, pulling back. I looked at him with concern.

"Something the matter?" I asked.

"Yes. I'd like...to fuck you against the wall," he said.

I looked at him with surprise at the request.

"Sure," I said.

I moved back there, but then, to my surprise he pulled me into his arms, his cock plunging into me, holding all of my weight as he thrust inside.

I moaned, shocked by the feeling of this. Not even my ex could do this. I wrapped my arms around him. The pleasure igniting my body, and it was then when, after a few more moments he let out a small grunt, holding me there as he thrust in deep, causing me to let out a small scream of pleasure. I didn't know how much more of this I could take.

He reached down, rubbing my clit as he thrust against that one spot, and it was then when he plunged in deep, groaning.

The cum warmed me up inside, and I moaned as I felt it rush in. He pushed against that one spot that I had, causing me to feel the force of my orgasm as well.

It hit me like a ton of bricks. I shivered, crying out loud, the moment driving me slowly but surely to the point of madness. I thrust my hips up, feeling it all just come tumbling down, and then as soon as the high of the orgasm hit, I suddenly felt the low as well, the feeling of the drop, and when he put me down, I could feel the cum leaking out of me.

I was spent, and when I looked at him, he let out a groan too.

"Damn," he said to me.

"You got that right," I panted, shocked I could even get a word or two out of my mouth.

"Well that was fun," he told me.

"Sure was," I finally managed to breathe out.

He helped me up, and I did move. But then, he grabbed me, holding my body against his own. I let out a small hum of contentment, enjoying the feeling of this as well.

"I enjoyed the hell out of that," he said.

"I did too," I replied.

"I would love to...to do that again," he said to me.

I nodded.

"Yeah, I would love to," I replied.

But first I needed a shower. I went up to my room, taking a shower to wash off. I also took some plan B just in case. It'd been so long since I sued that, and yet...I kind of liked that. I did have an implant sure, but better to be safe than sorry.

Especially with how big the load was.

When I finished, I walked outside, seeing that he cleaned everything up and was chilling out there. I sat down on the couch next to him, sighing.

"So what did you think? You liked your first time with a mom?" I said.

"Yeah. I didn't expect that Ms. B. That was just...amazing really," he said.

I beamed.

"I aim to please," I replied.

We sat there, enjoying the feeling of one another for a long time. But then, he sighed.

"So do we tell Gavin about this? Because I sure as fuck wasn't," he said.

"I'm sure not. He's also busy with Vicky anyways. Let him have his fun, and you can of course, have your fun with me," I told him with a smile.

He grinned.

"You're right. I do get to have my fun. I'm sure he's probably doing his own thing too," he said.

"Yeah," I said.

He then leaned against me, sighing.

"Thank you though. I feel a lot better. And not just because I nutted, but because I feel a lot better about everything. I was really worried about this," he said.

"You're good. Trust me, I know how Gavin is. He's always the type to make you feel like you're bad for this. But I know that he's probably just acting out because he's younger. And he doesn't want people to know about his girlfriend," I said.

"Yeah, probably at first I was a bit jealous. But then after well...what we just did, I don't feel nearly as jealous anymore. My first time got to be with you," he said.

I chuckled.

"And we can do this again too, if you want?" I offered.

I wanted to, but again, this was up to him. I didn't want to overstep my boundaries or anything.

He paused, hesitating for a second, but then nodding.

"Yeah, I'd like that actually," he said.

"Then that settles it. Whenever you want to come over, you're welcome over," I told him.

"Thanks Ms. B," he said to me.

I smiled, feeling good about all of this. After a bit we relaxed and cuddled on the couch. Vicky and Gavin didn't come home that night, but that's fine. I had Cody in my arms.

It was his first time with his best friend's mom, but it certainly wouldn't be the last time that we got to have fun like this, at least not on my watch.

We said goodbye early in the morning, and Gavin came home shortly after that. He didn't know about what I did, but he also didn't need to know. It would be my little secret, and one that I planned to keep with me for a long time.

I wouldn't stop thinking about Cody, and I knew that, for at least the duration of the summer, I'd get to have my fun with a cute college guy for a while. Whatever happened after that was up to fate, but I sure as hell wasn't going to complain about the fun I was having either

Taken By the Businessmen

"Come on Katie is that ready yet?" my boss Wes asked.

"Sir, I'm trying to get this as quickly as I can get it completed," I said to him.

I fumbled with the orders that were there, looking through them. My eyes felt like they were permanently glued to the screen as I read through the contents of this.

I was the second-in-command for one of the country's biggest retail chain suppliers.

I was supposed to be happy about this, but the truth was, I was stressed. I did so much for these guys, and the one thing I got from them was a bunch of grief and bullshit.

But now, I wanted to impress them. That's because they were offering a huge salary bonus, and I needed that. I'd been working at this company for so damn long that I felt like I needed this, even though of course, there was that part of me that was worried I'd fuck this one up.

"Come on Katie, I need that report yesterday," Wes snapped.

"I'm getting this done as quickly as I can! Sheesh," I muttered to myself. I wished that Wes was a bit nicer, but it was either I accept this bullshit, or I'd get fired.

And this was the best job I've had since graduating. I couldn't fuck this bullshit up.

After I finished with that report I finished off with the rest of the crap that needed to be done, looking over at the calendar.

It was tomorrow.

I had a huge meeting with a few of the board members, a group of guys that would determine the next steps of action for the company. They were the bigwigs, and I wanted to impress them. And of course Wes would be there with me.

There would be six people in total including me, and I was nervous as shit. I knew that I had to impress these men, no matter what it took. Even if I had to kiss some ass, I'd get the job done.

And of course, what I didn't realize was that I'd actually have to do that, and so much more as time passed.

I worked tirelessly into the night, the excitement pouring through my body as I looked around at everything that was going on. I wanted to make this work, and I wanted to be the best person for the job. Maybe it was in my nature to suck up to the bosses, but I'd been here for far too damn long not to just let this get away.

The next day, I heard the sound of a knock at my desk. I sprang forward, looking at Wes.

"Hey there sleepyhead," he said.

"Oh, hey there Wes," I said to him.

Wes was a pretty attractive boss, I'll give him that. Golden blonde hair, big green eyes, and a muscular frame. I could see my eyes threatening to waver every time I was near him. He looked at me with a bit of concern on his face, nodding.

"Everything alright Katie? You're never the type to slack off like this," he asked.

"I'm just getting everything ready for this tonight. That's all," I said to him.

That wasn't even a lie either. But he frowned.

"Yeah don't fuck this up. I'm putting you in charge of this because I know that I can trust you Katie. And I'm worried that this slacking will be a continuous thing," he said.

"No it won't be. Trust me on this," I muttered.

I didn't want to slack off. But it was all so damn overwhelming. I don't remember the last time I hadn't felt stressed.

Maybe when I was in college? No back then it was stupid stress. This was actually what my career was based on, and I damn well knew better than to fuck this one up.

Wes nodded.

"Well let's get this show on the road then. We're meeting up in the Arbor meeting room at nine on the dot. That's after everyone's days are done. I don't want you messing this up," he said.

The words that he uttered made me nervous. I had no clue what would happen to me now. I quickly nodded.

"Got it. Will do sir," I said.

I furiously got all of the shit together, looking for everything. I crossed all my Ts and dotted the Is. And yet, I felt like there was something I was going to fuck up on.

It had to be my damn imagination. I couldn't fuck this one up.

Could I?

I didn't want to put that bad juju here, but I started to wonder if I'd inherently fuck this one up completely.

But nine came quickly. I got all the way up to the meeting room. It was a fancy room that was on the other side of the company. This was where all of the big meetings would happen, some which would determine the ultimate fate of the company. I'd only been up here a handful of times and usually as the person who would take notes and then bring it down for Wes the next morning along with his favorite coffee.

But tonight, I was the star of the show.

I would be the one to present the budget report. Wes was definitely counting on me, and I could feel the nerves getting to me.

Finally, when it was time, I walked to the door, and Wes was there.

"Alright, you know what you have to do," he said to me.

"Got it," I told him.

The door opened, and there I was, right there in front of a group of board members. But what surprised me, was that all of these men were much younger than I thought they'd be.

58

They were all in their twenties and thirties. I always thought the people who ran that shit were usually old fogies. But they weren't.

"Wow ummm hi there," I said to them.

"Hello," one of the guys said.

"Hi so uh….I'm here to give the budget report, and then tell you all what the plan is. I hope that you're impressed with what we have to offer," I said.

The plan of course was to show the budget, and then the next expansion plans. The board would of course fund the budget and the plans, and we'd grow as a company. They helped out not just us, but also other companies too with this.

I showed them all the stats, got it all together, even had the plans in place. But something was telling me that I didn't do it all. When I finished the report, I could feel the dread that sat there as I looked out at them.

"Alright, and there it is. I guess the next steps of course, would be to figure out a good middle ground and—"

"Nope," one of the voices said.

I turned, and it was the guy from before. He had brown hair, brown eyes, and had an impish grin on his face.

"What do you mean?" I asked, my voice shaky.

"You showed us all of that, but I don't think we'll be putting our money into your company. I appreciate all of the work Katie, but the guys have decided to pool our resources into Trevin corp," he replied.

That's when I saw it. The look of pure, unadulterated annoyance that was clearly on Wes's face.

"You can't be serious!"

"On the contrary we made the decision the other night. We just wanted to see what you had to offer for us Wes. And while it looks great…I'm not feeling it," another guy said. This one had long brown hair, a pointed nose, and a very defined chin. He looked a lot more dignified than everyone else who was here.

"Come on Quinn. You know this is our big break," Wes said.

"I'm talking to her," Quinn snapped.

"Yeah, we can't just accept this. We made our decision," Glenn one of the guys said.

I looked over at the happy guy, who I remembered to be Tony, who smiled.

"Sorry Katie, the rules are rules," he said.

"But they're meant to be broken, right?" I heard Wes say.

"Depends. Not sure why you'd want to break these rules. They're right there," he replied.

They all laughed, and then I looked at the guy on the very end. Brady. He simply sat there, nodding.

"I'm terribly sorry Katie, but we're not going to take this. We'll be pulling our resources elsewhere," he said to me.

I looked at all of them, shock settling into my body. I couldn't…believe they'd let me go down like this.

I couldn't let the boss down. I just couldn't! I quickly took deep breath, smiling as I moved my hands to my shirt.

"You guys are willing to listen if you have another...incentive, right?" I said.

I had no idea if this would work. This seemed like one of those stupid ideas that I'd have, and I'd bank on it. But they all looked at me with surprise.

"What are you doing?" Wes said.

I turned to him, giving him a wink of excitement.

"Getting us out of this mess," I told him.

He looked at me with complete confusion as I undid the buttons on my shirt, a smile ghosting over my face.

"Tell you what guys. I know that you've been...interested in a while. Perhaps we can make a deal. How about that?" I asked them.

They looked at me with shock on their faces. But then, Brady of all people spoke.

"Humor it," he said.

"But sir," Glenn added.

"You and I both know that she's offering something...we all would like. I'm willing to put this little mess behind us if you...offer your body to us," he said, letting out a low chuckle that reverberated through the room.

I saw Quinn's eyes glaze over my body, causing a shiver to envelope over me. I didn't know why, but seeing his eyes there, whisking over my body, was driving me crazy, and I felt my pussy wetten.

"Are you...sure about this Katie?" Wes said. I knew Wes had his own feelings. He was an attractive boss, but I knew that the best way to get out of this shit would be to do this.

"Do you think I'm fucking around? I'm not," I said.

I wasn't going to lie either. The guys on the board were attractive. And I mean, I could see the look of pure desire that was on their faces as I looked at me, undoing every single little button on my blouse, pushing it aside. My large breasts were housed in a pink bra, making their eyes all widen in surprise.

"Wow," I heard one of the guys say. I think it was Tony or Glenn.

"Very nice," I heard Quinn mutter.

"Not bad at all," Brady said, a smile on his face.

Brady was the first to step forward, pushing me down on the desk. His body was much larger than the rest of the guys, his dark skin a contrast to my pale ones. I could see Wes there, too shocked to say much else. But I simply smiled.

There was a thrill in being taken like this. I didn't know why, but I liked this a lot.

I felt Brady's hands ghost up my thighs, between my legs for a second, and then slowly creeping up towards the tip of my bra, and then to my chin. He looked me in the eyes, smiling.

"I'm going to have some fun with you tonight," he said.

But then, before I knew it, my lips were pulled into a passionate kiss. I was lip locking with one of the heads of the entire company, and I didn't think I was alone with this. All of the guys slowly came over, each of them touching my body. I had no idea whose hand was whose as they continued to slowly move against my body, touching every part of me, feeling up my curves.

I let out a small gasp as soon as I felt more and more hands touch me, causing me to let out a low groan of excitement as they did this.

There was something almost thrilling about the way they touched me. The little touches, the caresses, the feeling of Quinn's lips against my neck. I shivered, moaning out loud.

Before I knew it, my clothes were off. I wasn't sure if it was Tony or Brady that took them off, but I laid there, my breasts out on display for them to see. Glenn moved there in front of me, lightly pressing his hands against them, his thumbs teasing the very tip of my nipples.

"Look at you….very nice," he purred in my ear.

I let out a small gasp, surprised by how nice this felt, enjoying the sensation of his hands against my body, feeling my curves and touching them slightly. There was something just nice about all of this, and I couldn't get enough of it.

Then there was Tony, whose hands started to move against my thighs, touching the large meaty muscles that were there. He held them, squeezed them, and then groaned as I let out a small cry, tensing up as I arched my back.

I took a moment to look over at Wes, who was sitting there, struggling to hide the obvious erection in his pants. I knew this could potentially get me fired, but at the same time, I didn't really care.

I wanted to show these guys what I was really like, and with a smile on my face, and a purr emitting from my breath, I quickly began to move my hips.

That's when I felt it, two fingers inside, pumping me. I let out a big gasp, surprise on my face as I moved my hips forward, looking over at them with a smile. It was Glenn who played with me there, shoving two fingers into my pussy, touching, teasing, moving his fingers against my insides, causing me to let out a small gasp of shock and pleasure, enjoying the way that this felt. He continued to move his hands there, pumping me in and out, enjoying the delicious sounds that came out of my mouth as he did this.

"Look at her. So desperate and needy for something already. You could've thought that she was going to ask for this sooner," Quinn said with a smile.

"Ahh," I cried out, feeling the fingers press upwards, curling into me and making me shudder with delight, enjoying the sensation of this, loving every feeling that this gave me, and the pleasure that came from my lips as I started to feel the teasing, tender sensations of them even more.

Every single touch sent a rapturous feeling through me. That feeling of need, of lust, of want for something…more in a sense. I wanted them, and I knew that with every single motion, there was no way that they could keep their hands off of me.

Quinn pushed their hands away, looking at me with a smile on his face.

"Look at this little princess, already turned on and looking like she needs a good fuck. I thought that this was a planned thing between you and Wes. Until of course, I saw the look on his face just now," he said with a chuckle.

61

I saw Wes there, struggling to keep it together, enjoying the way that I looked.

"Well, it doesn't have to be planned. I know you guys are enjoying this as much as I am," I said.

"Maybe we are. Maybe we like seeing you become the desperate slut that we know you are," he said, shoving another finger into me, pressing in deep. I cried out, but not before I felt Brady's large hand against my pucker, making me shiver with delight.

I looked at him, seeing the smile on his face. I wanted to see them, to feel them, and I wanted them.

Glenn was the first to let out a sigh, undoing his pants pulling out his erection. He stroked it, and my eyes widened with surprise.

He was much bigger than I thought. The awkward nerdy guy who liked to poke fun at me was well...packing. He then moved forward, and I took the cock in my hands, teasing and massaging it.

"Wow, already getting to us I see. I can see that you can't wait much longer," Tony said.

I looked at him, giving him a small wink before he moved towards me, pulling his pants down, and then another sizable cock came out. I looked at it, my eyes wide with shock and amazement as he pushed his cock into my hands. I took it there, moving my hands against it, feeling his long shaft and the big cock that both Glenn and Tony had. I knew that there wasn't much time before they'd fill up all my holes, taking me over.

Next was Quinn, who let out a low groan, undoing his pants, shoving his cock into my mouth. I looked at him, feeling the cock fill up my mouth, making me gag slightly as it moved right up against my inside, pressing against the edge of my throat, causing me to let out a small gasp of surprise.

He started thrusting slowly, moving his hands slightly against my face, thrusting in deep. I teased his cock while I felt the other two cocks inside of me. But there was that hunger, that need for more, and when I felt three fingers inside my pussy, rubbing me, teasing me, making me shiver with complete and utter need, I knew that there wasn't much else I could do. I wanted them, and I knew that they wanted me too.

Finally, Brady groaned, caving as he undid his pants, pulling out his cock and stroking it as he looked me in the eyes.

"God you drive a hard bargain there Katie," he said.

He then spread me apart, my wet pussy throbbing with delight. He soon pushed himself all the way in, his cock filling me up.

He was huge. I did expect him to be big, but he was bigger than anything else I'd ever experienced before. He started thrusting into me, holding my legs apart as he fucked me on the desk. I let out small little gasps and grunts but they were muffled by Quinn's member, which was only making me shiver with delight, and I wanted more. He pushed my hips up and a bit further, giving more of a range of motion as he continued to press in deeper and deeper.

I cried out, but the cries were muffled. But then, after a few more thrusts I felt his hand against my clit, touching, teasing, playing with me. I shivered, moaning in pleasure as I was used by this man, and as the other guys continued to let out small grunts and moans, making me shiver and ache for more.

Finally, Brady let out a small groan, pulling himself out, cumming on my stomach. I suddenly noticed one of the cocks in my hands tense up, followed by the spurt of cum, covering my breasts with the seed there.

I was already partially covered in cum, but I wanted more. Brady sighed, pulling back and looking at me.

"Have at it boys. She's giving us a nice little bargain," he said to me.

I loved hearing those words. The desperation on their faces, the moans of their own voices, and the feeling that this gave me.

It was a liberating feeling, and what I needed as well.

He soon moved back, and that's when I felt both Tony and Glenn move away from me. But when I looked at Glenn, who had just come, he was already hard as a rock.

"W-what are you guys doing?" I asked.

"We're going to make you feel good. Fill up all your holes," Glenn said.

"Yeah, going to use you like the bitch you are," Tony said.

Hearing them talk to me like this was exciting, liberating, and so damn fun. I loved that I was used like this, completely overtaken and enjoying the sensation of this. Suddenly, I was pushed onto the desk, right where Tony was. His cock slid into me like it was nothing, and I shivered, moaning out loud and with a delight that knew no bounds. He pushed himself up and down, causing me to let out a series of garbled sounds, but that was soon muted by of course Quinn's cock, which was still in my mouth.

"There we go," Glenn said, watching my hips move up and down against him. He grabbed something out of his pocket...was it lube or oil? He coated his hands with it, spreading me apart, shoving the first finger into me.

The foreign sensation felt good to say the least. It wasn't the worst thing that I'd experienced, but definitely was a little different from what I thought. He then moved another finger into me, filling me up with both of them, thrusting them in turn with Tony's motions.

"God you have such a tight little ass," he said.

Those comments made me grunt in response, a sound of approval probably in their minds. Soon, before I knew it, a third finger was put in, and at first I was a bit hesitant. I had to hold back from crying out in pain, simply because of how tight it was. But he touched me, teasing me there, watching me let out a series of moans and grunts, excitement flooding through my body. He continued the onslaught against my body, moving his hands about, and then, he pulled back a little bit, looking me in the eyes.

"You good?" he asked.

I nodded, pushing my hips back, wanting his cock inside of me.

I'd never been DP-d like that before, and I felt excited about it. But he continued to tease me, pressing his cock inside my pussy instead, joining Tony's there.

The tightness of both the cocks inside of there made me shiver with delight, enjoying the sensation of all of this. Everything just felt so perfect, so damn nice, and so amazing.

I continued to feel them both inside of me, pounding me completely, making me shiver with delight, enjoying every single thrust, every single push, and all that was making me lose all semblance of control.

For a long time, I felt them both thrust inside of me, and then of course, I felt Quinn's cock jammed down my throat. A pair of hands moved towards my breasts, touching and playing with them. For a second I thought it was Tony but then I realized it was Glenn, who touched and teased me there.

"Fuck," I managed to mumble out.

But then, moments later I felt something thrust in deep, and then, the feeling of orgasm hit me.

I cried out, feeling my whole body tense up, cry out, and then the feeling of release. They both pulled out, covering my body with their seed. Glenn covered my butt with it, and Tony covered my stomach.

I thought I was done when they moved out of the way, but then Quinn pinned me down on the table, holding me there as he teased me.

"Look at you, so useful for us. If I knew that it would be this easy, I would've given this offer a while ago. What about it Wes? Wouldn't you like to give her a little something too?" Quinn said.

I looked at Wes, who had his cock out, stroking it. I looked at him with complete, unadulterated need. I started to look at him, seeing the lust in his eyes as he took a look at me, enjoying the way that my body seemed to react to him like this.

I suddenly felt something enter into me, causing me to gasp out, touching the edge of the desk. It was Quinn, and he was buried in my ass. He fucked me forcefully, giving Wes a look, and soon, Wes walked over to me, looking at me with pure, unadulterated lust.

"Give it to me Wes, you know that you want to," I said.

I knew that he was hesitant. I liked seeing him nervous like this. He soon groaned, saying fuck it and taking off his pants, pushing his cock into my mouth, filling me up with it.

I shivered, feeling my whole body tense up as I felt his cock enter deep into there, fucking me forcefully, causing me to enjoy everything that came out of this.

He continued to push deep into me, but then I felt Quinn's cock press in too, spitroasting me from both sides. He groaned as he slid into me, filling me up, and I began to take Wes all the way down to the base of my mouth, feeling his cock there tensing, teasing, making me cry out and shiver with delight as he continued to fuck it forcefully. Every single motion, every single touch, it was all just overwhelming, my orgasm getting closer and closer, the need driving me insane.

It was a hunger, and I wanted both of them.

A pair of hands moved towards my butt cheeks, clutching them, holding them there as he thrust in deep, causing me to let out a small moan of surprise and excitement as he continued to groan, pushing into me, enjoying the sensation of my butt as it met with his cock.

"God you're so tight. This is so good," Quinn said.

Thrusts and moans were the only things that were heard in the office , and then, after a few more moments, I felt quin plunge in deep, groaning as I felt something warm and hot fill up my ass.

By that point, Wes let out a small grimace, making me shiver with delight, and then, I felt the explosion of cum as it hit my lips, filling my mouth up.

Moments later, the guys all pulled away, causing me to fall onto the table, exhausted but satisfied by everything that just transpired.

"You good?" I heard one of them say. I think it was Quinn.

"Yeah," I told him.

I tried to get myself cleaned off, but then, I noticed all of them were all put together. Minus Wes of course. They looked at me, my whole body covered and dirty, and then, I heard one of them chuckle.

"You drive a hard bargain there. You know, I think we can make amends and maybe hear out what you have to offer. In terms of the new growth of the company of course," Brady said.

"Yeah, we can let your budget go through. I think you've…given us enough incentive," Quinn added.

I mentally was definitely happy with this. They all waved goodbye, and then, they were all gone.

Except for Wes of course.

Neither of us said a word there. He couldn't believe what just happened. I'm surprised this worked out the way that it did too.

"Wow," he said.

"You weren't expecting this, were you?" I said with a chuckle.

"No. and that probably was incredibly reckless…but it worked. So thanks Katie. For doing that," he said.

I beamed, excited about this.

"I told you that I'd make sure that this was all done to your standards, and that you'd get what you wanted. It just…took a little bit of a different direction," I said.

"Yeah. And thanks," he said.

"For what I did?"

"Yeah. It was reckless…but also really hot. I wasn't going to jump in until he said something. Ut I'm kind of glad that I did," he said.

I nodded.

"It is what it is. I had a good time though," I told him.

There was an obvious nervousness that went along with it. I looked at him, and then, he sighed.

"Do you think that maybe…you can of course do this again? Or maybe just the two of us together and—"

"Are you asking me out?" I spat out.

He flushed, but then nodded.

"Yeah. I guess I am," he said.

I laughed, surprised by the forwardness of this.

"Well sure. I'd like that," I said to him.

"Thank fuck. I'm glad that this was working out as nicely as I expected. I weas a bit worried there," he said.

"You had nothing to worry about. Seriously," I told him.

"I know. It's just…refreshing to hear it from you. But it was pretty hot seeing you like that. And I guess that's definitely a good thing for us," he said.

"It sure is," I replied.

We looked at one another, the tension obvious there. But then, we kissed, a passionate liplock between both of us.

He then pulled away, looking me up and down.

"I can help sneak you over to the shower, but we should be careful. Don't want other people to know about what happened there," he said.

"You're right," I told him.

He smiled, taking my hand and sneaking me over to the bathroom so that I could get cleaned up. It's wild, Wes was a lot better and nicer towards me than I thought he'd be. I appreciated it though, excited for whatever the future may bring for us. I didn't expect to do what I did, and I definitely got lucky with them letting me off the hook when it comes to my decisions.

But I was happy. I truly, utterly, really was happy, and I definitely don't regret a single thing that I did so far, even though others may feel otherwise.

The New Girl at the Office

"A new assistant?" I said to my coworker.

"Yeah, Lynn had to quit. She ended up having a kid. She told me she would've been back if possible, but given recent events and how much of the attention she has to give to the child…she's unable to continue to perform her duties," he said.

"That's some bullshit. Lynn was amazing at her job. I can't believe this," I said to myself.

I was the CEO of one of the top fashion magazines in the world. We had a huge schedule and some publications which needed to go out. I couldn't possibly have this happen, could I?

But I looked at him, seeing the somber face that he had.

"I'm really sorry about this Rory. But this is what we have to do. We brought on a new assistant., her name is Candice, and she's just as qualified as Lynn was, perhaps even more," he told me.

I couldn't believe that HR did this without my approval! What kinds of motherfuckers did they think they were? I hated this, and it made me realize just how irritating it fucking was.

"I'm so annoyed," I said to him.

"I'm sorry Rory, but this is what we ended up doing. I know that you like to have a say in this, but we needed to fill the position fast and—"

"Just…leave me alone," I said, anger flooding through my body.

He put his hands up in a "Don't shoot the messenger" sort of manner before scurrying off. I watched him leave this place, closing the door behind him, and I sighed.

I couldn't believe that this was happening. I just couldn't believe it. I was pissed beyond all measure, and I knew that this could get bad for us. I wanted things to get better, and I wanted things to be alright. But I didn't know for sure.

I definitely wasn't sure about having a new girl here at the office. They'd either be good, or terrible for the job.

If they were bad, I could always fire them. But I didn't think that the HR department would step in and give me a shitty assistant.

At least, that's what I thought.

I quickly went down to her office. Apparently Thomas and the others already set her up. When I got to the door, I realized it was open, which surprised me. Lynn always had her door closed.

I knocked on the door, waiting a moment, and then, she came to the door.

"Hello there," she said.

For a second, I thought that time had stopped. I was stunned, completely floored by the cutie that was here. Big blue eyes, long brown hair that she tied back, a curvy, cute frame that looked utterly divine. It was all just…amazing really.

I bit my lip, trying to figure out how to tell her that she looked absolutely delightful and I wanted to just take her and do many nasty things to her. But I kept to myself.

"Hi, I'm Rory. I'm your boss," I said.

"Oh hi there! I didn't get a chance to meet you. They said that there was a ton of work, so I took it upon myself to make sure I got it started," she said.

This woman knew how to do her job? Without me having to chase it up? Maybe there was hope for her.

"Wow. You're a first," I said to her.

"pardon?" she asked.

"It's not usual for me to not chase newbies up. You're definitely pulling your weight already," I told her.

She beamed, that radiant smile making me feel things. Things I shouldn't be feeling right away for a woman like this.

"Thank you. I'm so glad that I can help you," she said.

"Great. I guess get started. I'll call you whenever I need you," I told her with a small grin.

She nodded, heading back inside to continue her work. But my mind was swimming, thinking about this attractive woman.

Lynn was nice, but she was nowhere near as pretty as Candice here. She was loyal too, but there was something different about her compared to Candice. I couldn't put my finger on it though.

Maybe it was the fact that Candice didn't seem to be the type to take shit from anyone, while also being incredibly helpful and attractive as hell.

I needed to stop thinking about this. It would only make me more aroused if I did so. I hummed, trying to think of something else different to focus on. But my mind kept going back to he, to Candice and everything.

Over the next couple of weeks, Candice fit right in, making me realize that I probably made the correct choice in letting HR take care of hiring her. She was incredibly loyal, really helpful with getting emails and the like out, and she definitely knew her way around the fashion industry.

But I told her I wanted her to work closer to me. It wasn't just because she was so damn good at her job, but it was also the fact that she was also very easy to talk to as well, and also I like having her around as well.

"You're cool with having my office next to yours, right?" she said.

"Of course. I like having my assistants close by. Lynn was just different. She was very independent," I told her.

In truth, I couldn't stop thinking about her. Maybe it wasn't the smartest decision to have her working near me, but she simply smiled.

"Good, I'm excited to work nearby," she said.

I smiled back, happy to provide this. I knew that she was keen on working for me, no matter what happens next.

Over the next couple of weeks, she worked hard with me, helping me get the editorials out, putting the magazines together, and contacting different publishers to help with this. And it was no wonder why they hired her so quickly.

She was so damn easy to talk to, and so easy to work with that I'd never experienced anything like this. Even Lynn had her heads she but with others with.

It was nice to have such a reliable woman working for me. But it was more than just that.

There was that...desire for more. That need that grew within me, and that aching desire which only started to grow more and more prominent as time went on.

I caught myself staring at her body, which was perfectly pressed up in those tight suits of hers. The way that her body just...looked so amazingly tight in all of this made me lick my lips, causing me to let out a small gasp of need and want, the desire only growing even more so.

"Is something the matter?" Candice asked.

"Oh nothing. You just look great today," I said to her.

Of course that was me holding back that inexplicable desire to just push her against the wall and kiss her. But I knew better than that.

However, the schedule was getting more filled due to interviews and the like. Most of the time, I'd admire Candice and her hard work from afar.

One day though, about a week before one of the biggest publishing events of the year, I finally got the courage to do it.

I looked over at Candice, who was finishing up the last of her emails. She bit her lip, and I immediately felt the heightened arousal push through me.

"Say Candice?" I asked.

She whipped her head around, looking at me.

"Oh, hi there Rory," she stated.

I didn't know how much of this I could take. That inherent desire, that need for her, that lust for her, it was driving me utterly mad. But then, I took a deep breath.

"Say, I wanted to ask if you'd like to go to the publisher's party together. Since you're my assistant and all," I said.

It was a gathering to talk with other publishers, but this was very different. This felt...like a date. She immediately nodded.

"Course. I'd love to go with you," she said.

I felt like I won the lottery as I heard those words. I beamed, getting myself ready for the event.

When the time came, I made sure to dress sexy, but within reason. The black dress that I wore hugged my frame, making my butt look bigger and my curves more obvious. I put my blonde hair back in a bun, looking over at Candice as she finished getting ready.

"You ready to go?" I asked.

"Yeah. Sorry about that," she said, slipping out of the office. She wore a purple dress that made her breasts very prominent, hugging the garment and threatening to split out. I couldn't stop staring, my body suddenly salivating at the sight of this.

"You look...wow," I said to her.

"Thank you Rory. I'm glad to be coming with you. It's an honor," she said.

"No, the honor is all mine," I purred.

The truth was, I wanted her, and I knew that she felt the same way about me too.

We drove over to the venue, where we were immediately greeted by reporters. We ignored them though, heading on inside. That's when we were both greeted again by a few of the other publishers, who talked our ear off for a bit.

I wanted to be excited of this, but in truth I was so damn tired of talking to people about the most trivial shit. I looked over at Candice, who seemed exhausted too.

"You alright?" she asked me.

"Yeah, I just think I need some fresh air. Care to join me?" I purred.

She looked at me, nodding.

I knew this place like the back of my own hand. There was a quiet series of rooms upstairs, which may be nice.

But I knew an even better place.

I moved out the side door with Candice following suit. We walked together through the gardens, until I hung a right.

"Where are we going?"

"To a more private location," I said.

I knew about this place because I tried to hide from a really creepy dude a few parties back. He stalked me, and I couldn't find a way to avoid him, until I found this. I laid low here, making calls and doing business, until he fucked off.

But now I was using this to my advantage.

We went through the bushes to a small clearing, with a bench there.

"What's this?" Candice said.

'oh, it's a secret place. I've used this before when I needed to get away from weirdos," I told her.

"Oh yeah, you probably get a lot of those. Because you're pretty and everything," she said.

I flushed at the compliment, surprised by her words.

"Pretty you say?" I teased.

"You know what I mean. Like...really nice," she said.

I chuckled.

"Well I appreciate what you say to me. I'm definitely happy about this," I replied.

I sat down on the bench. Candice sat next to me, our thighs touching. I then sighed.

"This is nice. I've never come here with someone, and you're the first to do so. I like it," I said.

"I like it too Rory," she said.,

There was an awkward silence, and then, moments later, she spoke.

"Say Rory?"

"What is it?" I ventured to ask. Surely she couldn't be confessing something...could she? But then I saw the embarrassment on her face, the flush that made me smile with delight.

"I'm sorry for being so nervous. It's just...there's something I've wanted to ask you for a bit," she said.

"Hit me with it," I told her.

"Okay….have you ever had a crush on someone but know that it's not the right thing to do? Like they're off-limits and all?" she said.

I knew that feeling and then some. I chuckled at her words.

"I know that feeling all too well," I purred.

"Okay so it's not weird for me to talk about this then. Because there's this person that...I really like them. And I'm worried about what this may imply and stuff. And I don't want to get in trouble or anything," she said.

"Why would you get in trouble? It's just a crush," I said.

"Because of their position. If people found out...this could be bad. I'm just nervous. Maybe I'm reading way too much into this," she muttered.

"Perhaps you are Candice. But I think that...if you like them, you should tell them your feelings," I offered.

It was the least she could do. After all, it's obvious from the look on her eyes that this was eating her up inside.

"I'm just worried I'm coming on too fast you know?"

"I don't think you'll be coming on that fast dear," I said.

She paused, looking at me and then nodding.

"Okay. well I guess I can tell this person that I have a crush on them. I just hope they feel the same way back," she said.

I was torn. I wanted what's best for Candice, but if that person wasn't me...I don't know what I'd do.

"Who is the person?" I asked. I knew this could open the door for some awkward shit, but then, she sighed.

"You really want to know?"

"Of course," I replied.

It wasn't just because there was that aching part of me that made me want to just find out if she felt the same way about me as I about her, but there was that desire to know whether or not I was overthinking this or not.

She took a deep breath, steeling herself for whatever was going to happen next. Finally, she spoke.

"Okay…so since you really want to know. It's you Rory. I…I have a crush on you, and I feel bad about it," she said.

I laughed, feeling a bit bad that I just blurted that out, but it's the only response that I did have.

"That's all huh?"

"Wait, you're not mad?" she asked with an incredulous look on her face.

"Course not. I'm going to be honest, I'd be lying if I didn't feel the same way," I told her with a purr.

She looked at me, amazed by the words that came out of my mouth. She then nodded.

"Wow. You do feel the same way then," she said.

"That I do dear. I like you a lot. but I know how it is. You like them, but you don't want this to get in the way of everything," I told her.

"You're right. I'm just scared Rory. I have no idea what'll happen and all. I know that it's not something normal. It's a bit taboo, but I can't stop thinking about you and everything and—"

That's when I did it. I moved towards her lips, pressing my own against hers, silencing her there. We stayed in this garden, kissing passionately.

I knew this was a taboo thing. Fi anyone in the office, or even any other publications, found out about this shit, we'd be in deep trouble. But I wasn't going to worry about that until things got to that point. For now, I just kissed her, our lips mingling and touching one another's, enjoying the feeling of one another as we continued to make out.

Things felt perfect as we kissed one another. We enjoyed the subtle, teasing feeling of one another's lips as we continued to move against one another. It was a passionate dance between the two of us, enjoying the feeling of one another, loving everything about this.

The motions of our lips, the feeling of our bodies moving again stone another, the aching tension and need that came from this, it was driving me to the point of madness.

I wanted her, and I could sense that she wanted me as well.

The garden was the perfect place for the two of us to express our feelings without others knowing. Our lips moved, touched, and teased against one another, enjoying the feeling of our bodies together, the excitement, the need, the desire, all of this was only growing even larger and larger as we continued to press and touch there together, the aching need driving us both crazy.

I then moved my tongue against hers, lightly massaging and playing with hers tongue. She let me continue this, and for a long time, the only sounds that were heard were of course the sounds of our tongues, the sloppy sounds of our lips, and the pleasure we experienced.

It drove me mad. And I knew that she wanted this too.

When I pulled away, she paused, looking at me with a flushed face.

"Wow. You're the first girl I've kissed before," she said.

I chuckled, pulling chin up, giving her a look of pure, unadulterated desire as we continued to lock eyes.

"Don't worry, I certainly will make this first kiss special," I told her.

I couldn't believe I was taking her first time. Usually I didn't attract the first timers, but there was something thrilling about being able to touch, tease, and play with her while making her feel really good.

I began to move my lips toward her neck, gently pressing kisses there. It took everything in my power not to leave marks there, simply because I knew that someone would ask if she came back with that. But I gave her gentle kisses, enjoying the little sounds of pleasure that came out of this as I began to move my lips downwards. I pressed my hands to the back of dress, and when I got to the apex between her breasts, I pulled the back of the dress apart, her breasts spilling out.

"Ahh," she cried out, surprise on her face as I looked at her. There was clear shock and awe there as I moved closer, touching the very tip of her nipple with my lips, enjoying the sensation and sounds that came out of her mouth.

"Fuck," she said to me.

I smiled to myself as I continued to lick and suck on her nipple, teasing her there. I suckled on the flesh, letting the nub tease and move against my teeth and tongue. My other hand moved towards her other nipple, pressing against the tip there with my palms, before taking it between my fingers, pinching the little nub until it hardened under my touch.

The sounds that she made were delicious. It was the sound of struggle to stay quiet combined of course, with the pure lust that came from her lips. It was to die for, a divine sound that only made me desire her more and more.

I continued to tease and play with her nipples, pressing against each part of her body, listening to the little moans that she had, the sounds of complete and utter need that escaped her body.

But I wanted more. Seeing her there, looking flushed and desiring me was only making me hunger for her more. I wanted to taste every part of her.

I played with her nipples for a second, teasing her once again but this time, I moved my lips downwards, pressing against the very edge of her pussy with my hands, moving her dress upwards and spreading her thick thighs apart, touching the soft flesh. She let out a small cry, but then, as I was about to get between her legs, she moved her hands to my breasts, pushing down my dress, taking both of the nipples into her hands, pressing there.

"Fuck," I breathed out, moaning as I pushed my hips upwards. I wanted to show her a good time, but her fingers danced against my body, making me lick my lips with delight, thrusting my body upwards as she continued to tease me like this. I didn't know how much more of this I could take, feeling her fingers pinching slightly over my nipples, rolling them in her hands, and then, she leaned down, taking one in her mouth, licking and teasing it slowly while she rolled the other nipple there.

I let out a sound of complete need, feeling my heart race and breathe out as I felt her continue to touch and tease my body. I just wanted more.

I didn't ,know how to feel about anything else, besides the lust that came off my body as she continued to take me like this. I didn't know what else to say, other than to moan.

But then, I stopped, pressing against the heat between her legs, rubbing against there. She let out a small yelp, which she silenced over time.

"Shh. You better be quiet. You don't want anyone to hear us, right?" I purred in her ear.

"S-sorry," she said, struggling to hold back her sounds.

I loved teasing her like this. I let my fingers climb up her delicious body, until I got in between her legs. I rubbed her for a second, watching her hips move upwards, and the moan that escaped her silenced with her fingers. She bit her lip, but I could see the flushed face there, the eyes of complete desire, want, and need that only grew even more obvious as time began to continue forward.

I pulled her panties down, licking my lips as I saw her there. Her fluffy, fat pussy was dripping wet for me, and I spread her apart, touching her sides, teasing her slightly. I pinched her clit, touching the nub there, playing with it as I watched her throw her head back in pleasure, thrusting her hips up.

Seeing her lose control like this was a look of pure desire that only grew more and more obvious as time went on. I continued to play with her, tease her like this, and I knew that she was slowly losing all semblance of control that started to make me wonder just what in the world she'd be doing next.

I then moved my finger inside, watching her tense up, the small yelp that came out of her mouth really cute, but then I started to press against there pushing in and out, looking at her glistening juices as I did this.

"F-fuck this feels amazing," she said.

I smiled, happy to hear those words from her as I continued to press my fingers in and out, up and down, feeling her pussy tighten around my digits. I added in a second one, watching her eyes widen as I continued to tease her. I then moved towards her clit, touching and capturing it there, and the sounds that came out of her were delicious, and only made me hunger for more.

"Look at you. Losing control like this," I teased.

She didn't say anything else, but just moaned as I continued pumping her, using my lips, tongue, everything that I could to make her feel good.

She had the cutest little moans, and when I pushed my fingers up there, touching her sweet spot, her eyes shot open and she began to fuck my fingers as I continued to press them into her.

I moved them faster, flicking my tongue against her clit, trying to bring her over the edge. Moments later, she tensed up, thrusting upwards, holding her breath as I saw the face of pure lust come by as she orgasmed.

She couldn't hold it back, so I moved forward, capturing her lips with my own. We made out as she rode her orgasm, and when she finally pulled away, I saw the look of surprise on her face, the shock that she did something like this on her face.

"Wow," she said.

"You good?" I asked her.

"Amazing. I'm just...wow. Sorry, trying to figure out what to say. Still coming down from it all," she told me.

"You're good," I told her. A smile was on my face as I looked into her eyes.

There was a clear need for more. I wanted to ask what she wanted, but then she moved downwards, getting in between my legs. She pressed her hands to my dress, pulling it upwards, looking at me with a curious glance.

"You okay?" I asked.

"Yes. I want...I want to taste you," she purred.

I smiled, seeing the look of curiosity on her face.

"Be my guest then," I offered.

I wasn't going to deny her this. It's very clear that she wanted this as much as I did. Even though it was her first time, there was a clear need for something, anything, the need for more that only grew as time went on.

She then spread my legs, causing me to let out a small gasp of surprise. She extended her finger, touching against there.

What she didn't know, was that I was sensitive. I'm talking stupid sensitive, and I had no way of controlling any of this. I looked at her, seeing the smile on her face as she began to rub me there, causing me to let out a small gasp of surprise as she moved her fingers gingerly.

"You good?" she asked me.

"Amazing," I breathed out, unable to think straight. I thought I was going to die and head to heaven as she continued rubbing me.

She then moved her hands to my thong, undoing it and then pushing it downwards. I shivered, feeling the cold air hitting me as I gasped, feeling my body tense up. She pushed a finger there, rubbing against there, and I started to move my hips forward, pushing my body against hers. I started to look at her, seeing the look of pure lust on her face as she continued to push her fingers there, rubbing my clit, and then, moments later she pushed her fingers in, causing me to let out a small gasp of surprise.

She knew what she was doing, and that surprised me. Usually with the first-timers, there was always that awkwardness that came with this. But not her. She was like an expert, and I wasn't going to stop. I began to thrust upwards, watching her smile as she continued to press in deep, making me shiver with delight as I continued to feel her push her fingers into there.

She then extended her tongue, flicking it over my clit, pressing her fingers deeper and deeper, fucking me harder, and I knew that there was only a bit of time before I'd lose it right then and there.

When she pushed her fingers upwards, hitting that one spot once more, her tongue right against the nub of my clit, I suddenly felt as if I saw stars. I shivered, crying out slightly as I thrust upwards, feeling the pleasure of my orgasm begin to take over me as I thrust my body forwards, enjoying the height and pleasure of my orgasm.

For a long time, after she hit that spot, I let out a small cry, holding back the sounds that I wanted to make. I was not only sensitive as shit, but I was also pretty fucking loud too. But after a brief moment, she finished up, pulling out her fingers, licking them. I groaned as I looked at her, seeing the way that she was looking at me, a smile on her face.

"You taste great boss," she said.

"Thanks," I said, my face flush with delight as I heard those words.

"By the way...I really enjoyed this," she said.

"I did...too," I told her.

There was that awkward tension there. We got our dresses back on, looking around. The reality of the moment came back to us. The realization that we were still at a fancy party, and I just got her off and she got me off. I didn't know what you're supposed to do from here. Do you just...talk about this like it's nothing? Do you ask them out? I mean, I'd never done this with a person I worked with before.

"I'm sorry for overstepping my boundaries and—"

"What are you talking about Rory?" Candice asked.

I looked at her, completely surprised by the feeling that this gave me. Did she...like it?

"You liked it?"

"Of course I did. In fact...I loved it," I heard her say.

My eyes widened with surprise, shock settling in.

"Wow. I'm surprised, I told her.

"Yeah, I'm normally not the type to make moves like this, but this was...different. In a great way. And I did find you attractive Rory," she said.

That's a relief. I thought she was going to tell me that she did this out of pity or something.

"I'm glad," I finally said.

"Which brings me to the next thing. What now?" she asked.

What do you do now?

"Do you want to...see where this goes?" I asked.

She nodded.

"I wouldn't mind it Rory. We don't have to tell anyone about this. We can keep it our little secret if you know what I mean," she told me with a wink.

I looked at her, surprised by the words she said.

"Yeah, I'd love that," I told her.

She grinned, giving me a kiss. I could taste myself on her.

"We should probably head back. But keep it on the down low what happened out there," I said.

"Course," she replied.

We held hands for a moment, looking into one another's eyes. There was that inexplicable desire for ore, that need that was clearly there, but I also knew that we'd have to keep this secret.

But it would be our little secret, one that only we knew about, one that we could share together, and one that I'd take with me to my grave. It was something that I was proud of, that's for sure but I also knew that this was something that would be the start of an amazing relationship.

It was the beginning of a new life, and I was ready for it.

Swapping Fun

"Oh it's been so good to see you!" my friend Mindy said. I rushed over, giving her a long hug.

Mindy and I have been best friends for a long time.

"So Giselle, you two been taking care of yourselves?" Mindy asked.

I saw her eyes immediately turn to my husband Rob. I could see the smile on her face, and in a strange way, I kind of liked it. I knew about Mindy's little crush on Rob, but she also kind of knew that I had a thing for her husband Thomas.

"Yeah, we definitely," have," I said. I looked at her husband Thomas, who was a muscular guy, a little different from Rob, but also a sweet man.

"That's great. I certainly am glad that both of you are taking care of yourselves," she said.

We continued to talk the talk a little bit, but I saw Thomas give me a small, flirty smile and I gave him one back.

In truth, I thought Thomas was insanely attractive, and I'd be lying if I said I wasn't the least bit jealous of my best friend for nabbing a guy like that. But also, at the same time, I knew that jealousy wasn't necessarily the smartest thing to have, so I kept it to myself. But there was always that part of me that wanted to tell her that she was so lucky, and let her know about the small crush that I had on Thomas.

We sat down, all of us having drinks and dinner together. Mindy and I really did enjoy the company of one another, and both Rob and Thomas did enjoy this too. We talked for a long time, the drinks being drank and the laughs and smiles we had warming up the room.

I didn't know how many drinks I'd had at this point. Maybe it was three or four? I'm a bit of a lightweight, so a little goes a long way for me, but during all of this, Mindy looked at me with a devilish grin.

"What's up?" I asked her.

"Oh nothing. Say uh Giselle, you ever thought about maybe we could...switch things up for a bit?" she said to me.

Switching things up? What the hell did she mean by that?

"What are you talking about?" I asked her.

"Well, I do think Rob is a cute guy, and well...you have a crush on Thomas, don't you?" she said with a devilish smile.

I flushed. Was it that obvious that I had a crush on him? she then smiled.

"You're bad at lying you know," she said to me.

"And what if I do?" I asked.

"Well, this is a bit of a shot in the dark, but I was thinking maybe after all of this, we could...switch things up a little bit. I know that it'd be fun and different! Plus it wouldn't mean anything different between us. You're my

best friend Gis, and I know that you have a huge crush on him. I don't blame you, my husband is hot as fuck," she said with a laugh.

Did she really not take offense to that? I was trying to figure out if this was a product of her being drunk or not.

"So like…a four-way?" I asked her.

"Yeah silly! You'd get to try things out with Thomas, and I get rob? I can assure you that this is something that would be super fun for us, and I'm sure you'd love it," she said with a smile on her face.

I didn't know what to think. I looked over at Thomas, who seemed to be in support of this.

"Don't worry, we've discussed this before. She'll be fine. Mindy just needs to drink a little bit to admit her feelings on this kind of shit," he said to me.

That made sense, and I knew for a fact that this was something that was definitely not something we were against, but I felt nervous.

"Well…what do you think Rob?" I asked him.

Rob paused, his eyes focused on Mindy. I knew that he thought she was hot. He mentioned it a few times, and I'd be lying if I didn't think the same thing. I had a little crush on Mindy, but I doubted it would ever amount to anything.

But now here we were, all of us drinking and having a bit of fun. None of us were too drunk to consent, and I definitely felt the excitement flow through my body.

"I wouldn't mind it," he said, keeping a poker face, but I knew for a fact that he was just as excited as I was.

"You sure?" I inquired.

"I didn't say no, right?" he said to me.

He was right. He didn't say no. It's so weird to have a husband in full support of this, but I was fortunate to have that.

"You guys sure about this?" I asked them.

"Positive," I heard Mindy say.

"Yeah, we talked about this already together," he said.

That was a relief. I didn't feel as bad for wanting this then. I turned to rob, who nodded.

"Alright, we're in," I said with a smile, taking one last drink, feeling the liquid courage hit me.

This was one of our few adventures we had tighter. Since we were all pretty busy, meeting up was a struggle for us. But we decided on the Lancaster Casino because there was a hotel attached to it. But little did I know that this would be the beginning of something new for us.

A band began to play, and I looked over at Mindy, who stood up with Thomas.

'Tell you what, why don't we…dance a little?" she said to me.

I looked at her and nodded.

"Yeah, I'd like that," I told her.

I took Thomas's hand, and we went out to the dance floor. He was a bit bigger, a lot thicker, and the way his hand fit in mine made mine feel fucking diminutive compared to his.

We began to dance, and in truth, I adored the feeling of it already. Our bodies were plastered next to one another, and it took a moment to drink in the sight of Thomas.

He had dark hair, a little bit of gristle on his cheeks, a large, muscular frame, and a smile with perfectly-white teeth. His chiseled jaw and large thighs which strained against his pants made me shiver with delight. But what excited me the most was his voice, not just the fact he knew how to dance with me.

"I'm surprised you agreed to this," he said.

"Well, it was more like both of us agreed," I told him.

"I see. Rob is a good man. He's probably just as nervous as I am," he said.

"Yeah, we're all nervous," I told him.

But he pulled me in, resting my body against his. The heat and friction between us, the desire for more, all of this was driving me wild. We held onto one another, both of us taking one another there and feeling the passion between our bodies. It excited me to no end, and he enjoyed it too.

For a long time, we stayed like this, dancing, touching, and teasing one another. But finally, I pressed against him, letting out a small groan.

I looked over at rob, seeing the head of blonde hair with the fiery redhead that was Mindy. They were both super attractive, and there was something about this which turned me on more than anything.

"Thinking about them?"

"Yeah. It's so weird how this worked. I guess that's what friends are for," I told him.

"Yeah, I wanted to try the wife swapping thing, but I didn't know who to do it with. When Mindy suggested you...I definitely was into that," he said.

"I like the idea of it too. Just took me by surprise," I told him.

We continued to dance until it was making us both hot and bothered. He then took my hand, leading me upstairs. When we got to the room, he unlocked the door, pulling me inside, and then, his lips were on my own.

His kisses were far different from Rob's. They were amazing, completely turning me on, and as he kissed me, I drank it up, feeling the excitement and pleasure that washed through my body. I ached for him, I needed him, and as he continued to touch, tease and pleasure me, I felt my body grow hot, the fiery need within me growing even more so.

He then grabbed me and pushed me down on the bed, touching my curves, feeling my curvy, sensual body as I looked into his eyes.

He was so nice to feel against me, the touches large and expansive, but there was something that I loved about it.

We made out on the bed, grinding our hips against one another, when suddenly the door opened again, and I looked up.

There was Mindy, pulling my husband inside, kissing him passionately. The sight of them making out was hot as fuck, but then my attention was brought back to Thomas, who gave me a long, passionate kiss.

I didn't pay attention to much else, just enjoying the feeling of Thomas's hands against me, exploring every part of my body. His hands moved towards my breasts, nestling against there making me cry out suddenly as I felt the finger graze and touch against the nipple.

For a long time, I couldn't help but love everything about this. It drove me mad, and there was definitely that feeling of lust and desire, making me shiver with delight and enjoying everything about this. For a long time, he simply stayed there, touching, teasing, and then playing with me.

Then, I felt his lips trail downwards. I shivered, tensing up, and I noticed Rob teasing Mindy too. But I was turned on by the sounds that she made.

I wanted her to make those same sounds for me. The thoughts of that aroused me, making me want her, need her, and ache for her.

But then a pair of hands moved towards the back of my dress, grabbing the backings and pulling it downwards. I gasped as I felt my dress slowly come undone, flushing as mi realized how naked I was in front of him. but that didn't matter. There was something about being naked for this man that excited me, that aroused me, and made me want to embrace it.

His hands moved towards my nipples, playing and pleasuring them, and I cried out, feeling my whole body ache for him. but then, his fingers moved to my other nipple, and I felt his fingers pad the tip of it. He touched it very slightly, but then rolled it against his fingers, and as he did that, I shivered and cried out, holding onto him there as I tensed up, aching for this, watching his smile grow as I started to feel him take control of me, making me shiver with delight, enjoying the sound of this too as time began to continue forward.

His lips captured one of my nipples, taking it in his mouth, touching, teasing, pleasuring my body with his large hands. I felt the subtle touch of his stubble against me, making me shiver and cry out, the pleasure overwhelming me as he did this.

I looked over slightly, seeing Rob doing the same thing to Mindy, and I couldn't help but find it completely arousing. I should be jealous, but I'm not. Instead, I found it hotter than anything.

He then moved down my body, getting in between my legs, and when Thomas hiked my skirt up, he looked me in the eyes, a look of pure lust in his eyes. He then dove into my pussy, pulling my panties apart and pushing his face in. He touched the tip of my clit, causing me to let out a series of small gasps and moans, surprised by the nature of this. I thrust my hips upwards, feeling my body smother him with my pussy.

Everything was making me hot and bothered, and I enjoyed everything about this. For a long time, he continued to touch, to tease, and to move his lips against my body, enjoying the sounds that I made.

He knew how to touch and tease me.. There was something about this which made me aroused and needy. I turned to my right, seeing Mindy do the same, the sounds that she made turning me on.

I didn't know how much of this I could take though. I quickly felt my hips move forward, my body start to tense up, and that's when it hit me.

The force of my orgasm took over my body, and as I rode his face, I felt that hunger for him. That need for his large, fat cock to just completely destroy me.

And that's what he wanted to.

He pulled away, but not before I got to his pants, pulling them down along with his underwear. I took his cock in my hands, playing with it, watching his eyes begin to widen as I continued to do this.

"You like that?" I breathed out.

"Y-yes," he said, groaning as he pushed his hips forward.

I smiled, the sensual feeling of this making me feel more and more aroused with time. For a moment, I watched him tense up, but then I kissed the tip of his cock, taking it into my mouth.

The sounds he made were music to my eats as I continued to suck him off, taking him deeper and deeper into my mouth, enjoying the delicious utterances that came out of him. I continued this, hearing the little cries in his mouth become more and more audible.

I looked to my right, seeing Mindy do this again, and I smiled. There was something so hot about seeing my best friend suck off my husband like this, and in truth, I wanted to do so much more to her while my husband fucked her.

But there was no time for that. I needed his cock inside of me now. I moved back, flipping over so that I was on my stomach with my legs up, my ass there for him too.

"Fill me up," I said, the desperation and need laced in my voice obvious.

He grunted, surprised by how desperate and needy I was, and shortly after he pushed himself into me, filling me up.

He was a lot bigger than I expected. I knew that he would be big, but holy shit. I was not expecting this. I quickly moaned, holding onto him as he pounded me, holding me there as he did this. I shivered, crying out loud as he continued to thrust in deep, holding onto the sheets.

Then, I saw Mindy move over, her face right up against mine, a grin on her face.

"Doesn't he feel great?" she said.

"Yeah," I said, barely able to form words. In truth, I was trying to hold back from making out with Mindy as I continued to feel him pound me, smacking my ass and making me shiver with delight, enjoying the feeling of this as well.

For a second, I wanted to tell her how I felt, how I wanted her to make out with me, how I wanted her to stuff my face in between her legs, but then, she leaned min, capturing my lips with her own.

I widened my eyes in surprise, shocked that she wanted this too. But there was a small moan that exhaled from her, and I silenced it with my own mouth. She continued to kiss though, our tongues touching and teasing one another, my pussy being pounded in the process.

She then pulled away, a trail of spit connecting us, but then she gave me a devilish grin.

"I've wanted to do that for a while Giselle," she said.

"M-me too," I said.

"Damn, I didn't know you wanted me so badly. I would've suggested this sooner," she said.

I kind of wished that she did suggest this sooner, but I didn't have much more to say, our bodies moving closer as we made out with one another.

I felt Thomas pick me up, holding me min his lap, his cock still buried inside of me as I continued to mov up and down, feeling his fat member penetrate me completely. But then, Mindy moved towards me, making out with me, her hands on my breasts as Rob held her the same way that Thomas did.

We bounced on their laps, making out, our hands exploring one another. I touched her breasts, which were far smaller than mine, and she cried out, tensing up and moving towards me, pressing against my pussy.

I felt her crotch against mine, the rubbing of that combined with the cock inside of me making my head spinney.

After a few more thrusts, I heard Mindy tense up, throwing her head back and crying out as she orgasmed, the little trail of her juices coming out and against my husband's cock.

I wanted to lick it up, to taste her juices, but then, she moved back, smiling as she stared into my eyes.

"Want a taste?" she offered to me.

I couldn't say no. I moved my head downwards, touching the tip of her pussy, feeling her clit there against my mouth. I hummed against it, feeling her tense up and cry out, rubbing her face against my own. I shivered, feeling her drench me in her sweet pussy juices as she did this.

Thomas wasn't going to stop either. He continued his thrusts, this time pulling me back into doggy-style, holding me there as I explored her folds.

I heard Mindy moan for a bit, aroused by the little sounds that she made, but then moments later, I heard the sound of muffled words and moans. I looked up, and Rob stuffed her with his cock. Her mouth was full, but that didn't stop her from riding my face.

And I loved it. She tasted so damn good, and everything about her was a joy to have around. I continued to explore her pussy, enjoying the feeling of her folds, loving the way that she sounded against my mouth. After a few moments though, she pressed against there and I dug my tongue in, exploring her deeper.

She cried out, suddenly moving against my face, fucking it, but also sucking off Thomas. After a few more thrusts she screamed out, and then, something came out of her.

She squirted in my face. Most people would be shocked by that or turned off, but I quickly licked it up. I wanted to taste her, and she sure as shit gave it to me.

Thomas then pulled out, groaning as he let out a sigh, cumming against Mindy's mouth with little strings. She was soon covered in his seed, smiling excitedly.

"Fuck that was good," she said.

"Sure was," I replied.

I wanted more, and Thomas seemed to understand that. He then pulled me into his arms again, letting me stay on top, but then, he moved his hand between my cheeks, rubbing my pucker there.

I moaned. What most men didn't know was that I loved anal, and Thomas enjoyed pounding me. Both he and Mindy were out of commission, but I did tease my hips around, looking over at him with a teasing smile.

"Want to put it in my ass?" I asked him.

"Yes," he breathed out.

He soon began to move himself against me, holding me there, and it was moments later that he started to plunge the finger inside of me, pushing two of them into there and making me moan as I continued to rub on his cock. I felt his cock hit me in all of the right places, and then, moments later he pulled out, slowly shoving it into me.

My eyes widened in surprise, and soon, I felt him plunge deep into me, holding me there as he thrust up and down, making me cry out, a sting of pain and a whole wave of pleasure overtaking me.

He thrust in, pushing in faster and deeper, filling up my ass. Mindy finally recovered, moving towards me, smiling as she spread my legs apart, pushing her face in between there, teasing me.

I suddenly shivered. I didn't expect Mindy to return the favor, but she pulled back, giving me ta teasing smile.

"You thought I wouldn't return this? Come on Gis," she said to me.

I moaned, hearing her teasing voice as she continued to push herself against me, her tongue coming out and licking every part of my folds. For a long time, I simply just embraced the moment, enjoying her there as she continued to tease and caress my folds, enjoying the sensation of this. For a long time, she explored me, but then she got to my clit, rubbing it with her tongue, and then sucking on it.

That, combined with the feeling of the cock in my ass hitting that spot, only made me want to just lose all semblance of control. I tensed up, moaning out loud and in pleasure, feeling the sudden force of my orgasm hit me like this. I then screamed out, thrusting against her, and then, the force of my orgasm hit me all at once.,

I came hard, feeling her right there, licking up all of my juices like it was the last thing she'd ever get to have. She then pulled back, looking at me with a smile on her face as she rolled her tongue against there licking up the contents and then smiling.

"Fuck that was good," she told me.

"T-thanks," I told her.

She looked at me, reaching in, giving me a long, passionate kiss. As she did that, I felt Thomas thrust in deep, plunging into my ass and then moaning as he came right inside.

I felt the cum move deep into there, filling up my entire ass. When he was done, Mindy pulled her lips away, and suddenly, I felt the sudden heaviness of my post-coital bliss hit me.

That was amazing. But now I was exhausted. I laid down there, feeling the realization of what I did start to hit me.

But of course Mindy didn't stop there. She then got in between my legs, pushing her tongue deep inside, burying inside of there. She rubbed the nub of my clit, and it was then when, after a few more moments I tensed up, thrusting upwards, shivering with delight as I began to cum hard, feeling my juices smeared all over her goddamn face.

I then stopped, looking over at her, a smile plastered on her face.

"You like that?" she asked me.

"I sure as shit do," I told her. I flushed as I uttered those words, feeling like I may've overstepped a few boundaries, but then, Thomas was the first to excuse himself.

"I'll go take a shower first," he said.

He went inside, turning on the water and taking a shower., I looked over at Mindy, who smiled.

"I think Thomas is surprised by the crush that I had on you," she admitted to me.

"What do you mean?" I asked.

"Well...he kind of knew about it, but he wasn't expecting that, " she said.

I flushed. I hope I didn't upset him or anything. But then Mindy leaned in, giving me another kiss. I quickly moved towards there, making out with her for a long time as well. I knew that Rob liked to watch it, and when I looked over, I saw him jerking it off to the two of us.

"Want to help him out?" I said, pulling back and looking at that.

"Sure," she said.

We both got to his dick, and soon, I took my lips and encased them against the top half of his cock. I moved up and down, enjoying the little gasps and sounds that he uttered. I looked over at Mindy, who was near the base, sucking on his balls and holding onto them with her lips.

He groaned, tensing up, and then moments later he came hard, filling my mouth up with his seed. I swallowed all of it, but then Mindy pulled me away, making out and sharing the cum with me. Rob let out a low groan, of arousal at the sight.

"If I knew this was what you had planned for me, I would've agreed to this a whole lot sooner," he said.

I didn't think this would work out as swimmingly as it did, if you wanted the truth of it, but when I looked at Mindy, she gave me a teasing smile.

"I didn't think this would work out half as well, but here we are, enjoying the feelings of one another, and I can't get enough of either of you two. And I know that Thomas enjoyed you as well," she said.

Thomas came out, a towel wrapped around his waist. Rob was the next one, and then Mindy and I went into the shower together. We took the shower together, making out and enjoying one another. In truth, this "Wife swap" thing ended up bringing us both closer together.

While we were in the shower though, Mindy smiled.

"So how long have you had a crush on me?" she asked.

I blushed, but then sighed.

"For about a year now. I didn't want to make it weird, but I realized I was bisexual because of you," I said.

"That's sweet. I've always thought you were quite the cutie Giselle. I wanted to tell you, but I wasn't sure if you'd be upset with me or not," she said.

"Nah, I appreciate it," I told her.

"Anyways, we should probably get out of here. Don't want to keep the guys waiting," I said.

We walked out, seeing the guys on each side. We got in between them, smiling at one another. I sighed in happiness and contentment at Rob's hands as they held me there.

"This is nice," I said to Mindy.

"Yeah, this was a good thing for both of us," she told me.

"It sure was," I said.

"I enjoyed it too. Definitely worth the effort," Thomas said.

"Yeah, I'd most certainly love to do it again," Rob said with a wink.

I laughed, knowing exactly what he meant by that. He wanted us to slobber on his cock again.

"Yeah, maybe the next time we can all meet up like this...we can do it again," I said to them.

We all agreed to this, the swapping a big success. We did go back to our own respective hotel rooms after a bit, but I noticed that Rob was red as a tomato.

"I'm not going to lie...I thought you and Mindy together was super hot," he said.

"Yeah, it was. I loved it," I said.

"I knew this would be good for both of us. Mindy is a cutie, but I'm glad it could help you with your sexuality too," he said.

It did help me. I did have an inkling that I was bi for a long time, but I never really explored it.

"Well, I finally got to explore my sexuality with my best friend. If that's not something to be proud of, I don't know what is," I told him.

"Yeah, I'm glad that you could do this," he told me.

I beamed, but not before moving in, giving him a passionate kiss on the lips. It felt nice to do this, because this was certainly what we both enjoyed. We made out, making love once again that night on the bed together. With Rob, he seemed to get it, and I enjoyed that my husband partook in this with me as well.

The next morning, we all met up for breakfast, exhausted from the night's activities, but still meeting up to have enjoyable conversation with one another. But then, I saw Mindy give me a little wink, and I smiled back.

"Well, I say this was a success. I'm glad we got to catch up and then some," she purred.

"We sure did," I replied.

She then gave me one last kiss, smiling before leaving.

"I'll text you when I get home. How's that chica?" she asked me.

"That'd be great," I told her excitedly.

She beamed, heading out with Thomas, who gave me a little smile too.

I looked over at Rob, who was processing all of this.

"Well that went better than I thought," I told him.

"Sure did. And I think it helped us all grow closer together. I thought it was hot as shit seeing you and Mindy make out like that," he said.

I flushed, but nodded.

"Yeah, me too," I replied.

We took one another's hands, both of us knowing that the swap was more than just us getting to share our husbands and wives, but it was also the discovery of our sexuality. I enjoyed it for that.

I did think that Thomas was incredibly hot, and I was a bit jealous Mindy got to tap that every night. But I was also pining for her as well. Now that we got to do this, I didn't regret a damn thing.

When we got to the car, I got a text from Mindy saying that she had a bunch of fun, and that she'd love to do this again and again. I told her we could set up a date that worked with all of our schedules, so that we could swap and have a good time.

It was the beginning of a new, fun, and innovative experience, and I knew that this swapping would continue to be a fun experience for everyone, no matter where we went next.

The Gardener's Arousal

I walked outside, waving hello to Carlos, the gardener that we had. He waved back at me, giving me that smile that just...made me feel warm and fuzzy inside. It was no lie that I had feelings for Carlos.

But the truth was, I wouldn't dare act on them.

Carlos was a gardener that we hired to take care of the property. We could afford it, with my husband being a successful businessman and I being an interior decorator.

It paid well, and it gave us a nice home. And of course, we had a decent life...but I always felt like something was missing.

It didn't help that whenever Carlos looked at me, giving me the once-over and looking me up and down, I couldn't help but smile.

"How much do you have to do today?" I asked him.

"Not a ton miss. I'm actually going to be done relatively soon," he said with a smile.

"Great job! Keep yup the good work," I told him.

He gave me a small smirk, and I winked at him.

I wasn't going to lie, I did find him very attractive. There was something about Carlos which made me excited, a thrilling sensation.

Was it because he was young and attractive, about a decade younger than my husband and I at least? he was a young college guy who worked for me for a few extra bucks, but I also could feel the attraction between us grow and grow even more so as time went on.

For a long time, we both simply made small talk. I'd be lying if I said I didn't have a crush, but I'm not sure what my husband would think about that. However, I realized I spent way too much time chatting and flirting with Carlos, so I waved at him and then ran off.

"Oh, have a good day Mrs. Simpson," he said to me.

"I will," I told him with a grin.

He looked me over, smiling as he gave me a small, flirting look. I took a moment to figure out what to say, my mind suddenly entrapped by the idea of fucking this man. But then, I dropped it, realizing that it was just a fleeting feeling.

There's no way that my husband would be okay with this...right?

But that night, when we sat around in bed, he turned to me, smiling.

"Say babe....I was wondering....it's a bit embarrassing, but have you ever had a fetish that you wanted to discuss, but feared embarrassment?" he asked.

I paused, unsure of what to say.

"What do you mean?"

"I'm sorry, it's probably wrong, something bad to assume, but I just…"

"Tell me babe," I said to my husband.

He flushed crimson, and then spoke.

"I've seen the way you look at Carlos," he said to me.

My face grew pale.

"What do you mean?"

"I know that you find him attractive and well…I don't know. I'd like to see you and him. Together," he said to me.

My eyes widened with shock. I couldn't believe this. I mean, I did find him attractive, but I didn't think my own husband would agree to this.

"You're serious?" I asked him.

"Yeah. I'm a little embarrassed but I've been watching more…cuckolding things and I'd like to try it. I wouldn't mind seeing it," he said to me.

I paused, surprised by those words. I thought he was joking, but given the way he looked me dead in the eyes as he said that, hue certainly wasn't joking, that much was certain.

"Wow. This is a little different from what I expected," I said.

"Sorry, I know that it's embarrassing. I've never…told someone this, so I'm a little nervous. But maybe you get it," he said.

In a way, I felt like I hit the jackpot. He wanted me to fuck him! I thought he was just messing with me, but I don't think he was.

"You're serious though…right?" I said to him.

He flushed, nodding.

"Y-yes," he said.

"Good. Because I wouldn't mind that either," I said to him.

He looked me in the eyes, nodding.

"Yeah. I guess you can talk to Carlos and set it up. I don't know, I just see that he looks at you like that…and I kind of want to see what he can do," he said.

I never thought my husband would be the one in support of this. I thought I'd have to weasel my way into telling him about this fetish. But it makes it a whole lot easier.

Which makes me wonder…how far does he want this to go?

The next day, I woke up, seeing that Carlos was already downstairs, cutting the bushes and waving at me. That young man always made my heart race, the excitement obvious when I looked into his eyes.

"Hey there Carlos," I said.

"Hello there Mrs. Simpson," he said.

"Call me Layla," I purred.

"Oh...okay then, " he said.

His face was red as a tomato. He seemed so young, so damn innocent, and in a way, I couldn't help but feel the excitement grow as I thought of the idea of feeling his dick inside me, while my husband watched. There was something thrilling about this, and the fact that he was so open and willing to do this was just...nice in a way.

"Anyways, I wanted to ask you what the heck you were planning on doing next Friday," I said to him.

That's what my husband and I agreed upon. That way he could be home at a reasonable time, and I'd get to have my fun.

"So far nothing. Why though?" he asked.

"I was wondering if you wanted to possibly...stay over a bit longer. I have something very important I need to talk to you about," I purred.

He turned red, and I felt that thrilling sensation of making this young man squirm. I don't know why, there was something just so fun about this.

"Yeah. That should be fine," he said.

"perfect. I'll be seeing you then cutie," I told him.

He flushed, but then nodded. I could sense that this was something he wasn't expecting. In truth, I wasn't expecting my husband to go along with it either.

But there was something fun about this. The feeling of this man's cock inside me was a thought that I had quite a bit, and I'd be lying if I said I didn't masturbate to that idea once, letting the toy sit inside of me, a big dildo that made me imagine it was his fat cock, plunging deep into me.

I shuddered just thinking about it now. I needed to get my mind off it. I'd think about it later when I had some time off.

Over the next couple of days my thoughts were occupied with Carlos and the impending plan. My husband told me he did want to watch. Maybe he got off to this kind of thing. But Friday soon came around, and shortly afterwards, I noticed Carlos was sticking around as he finished with the last of the trimming.

His body was caked in a line of sweat, and I could see it moving down his rippling abs, drenching him. His warm, sweaty body against mine as he pounded my pussy made me shiver with delight. As I got ready, throwing on the lingerie and the robe that was there, I heard the knock on the door.

It was my husband. He looked me over, whistling.

"Looking good there love," he said to me.

"Thanks. I think he'll like it," I said, feeling the thrill of those words. I had a feeling Carlos would adore it, but I'd wait of course until then.

When the time came, he marched right on upstairs, and there was a knock at the door.

"Umm...Layla?' he said.

"Oh come on in," I purred.

He opened the door, flushing crimson as he saw the dim light, looking me up and down. I could see him licking his lips as he stood there.

"Wow. You look...good," he said.

"Thank you dear. In fact, I have something special for you," I said to him with a purr.

I pulled the robe apart, watching his eyes widen in surprise as he looked at me

"W-what do you mean?" he asked me.

"I have something delightful for you," I said.

I tore the robe off, tossing it to the side by my husband, revealing a black lingerie set that highlighted my curves. Despite my age I was still rocking it, and he soon licked his lips, looking me up and down.

"Wow," he said to me.

"You like what you see?" I told him.

He nodded.

"Y-yeah," he purred.

"Well, why don't you take a moment to...explore? I know you look at me a lot while you're gardening, and this is the chance that you've been waiting for," I said to him.

He couldn't believe it, and I could see it in his eyes. He soon moved his body so that he was getting closer and closer to me, moving downwards, and then shortly thereafter he let his hands lightly touch.

"W-what about your husband though?" he inquired.

"Don't worry, he's right there. He wants to watch and see what you can do," I told him with a purr.

Watching his eyes widen at the sheer shock of it all was entertaining to say the least. I saw his eyes widen with surprise, but then shortly after, he nodded.

"This is okay then, right?" he asked.

"Very okay dear," I said, pulling his chin upwards. Then, I gave him a long, passionate kiss.

It caught him off guard, but shortly afterwards, he kissed me passionately. I looked over, seeing my husband already palming his pants.

Did he like this as much as I did?

I couldn't help but wonder, but then, moments later I felt something move towards my lips. It was his tongue, and then moments later I let him in, kissing him with a lustful passion that I didn't know what to believe.

Before I knew it, his hands were soon against the edge of my breast touching it, looking at them slightly. He looked at me, surprised by this.

"You have wonderful breasts ma'am," he said.

"Oh stop with the formalities dear," I said to him, lightly chiding the young man. He probably wasn't used to it, but that didn't mean that I liked it either.

However, he quickly shut up, moving his lips down my neck, lightly exploring his hands against my body, touching my breasts and thumbing his fingers against my nipples. I shivered, moaning out loud and enjoying the sensation of all of this. It was riveting, amazing, and there was something just so damn exciting about this that only made me ache for more from him.

He then moved his lips downward, awkwardly fumbling with the bra. I tried to help him, but then, shortly afterwards, he soon groaned, pulling it off my body. The bra fell to the side of my body, and he tossed it there, his hands moving towards my breasts. He cupped them, causing me to let out a small gasp of surprise and pleasure as he started touching me. There was that thrill that came from this, and I couldn't help but moan in response to his actions.

"You good?" he asked me.

"Yeah," I breathe out.

He lightly touched my breasts, taking it nice and slow, playing with my nipples between his fingers. I looked over at my husband, who was starting to slowly undo his pants pulling his cock out, stroking it to the sight of me being teased and pleasured by our gardener.

It was something that I never expected him to be into, but there was something thrilling about this.

Soon, I felt his lips move down, suckling on one of my breasts. He played with it, lightly touching my nipples and tugging on them, causing me to let out a small gasp of pleasure, arching my back and moaning in response to his actions.

He groaned, rubbing his cock against me. I felt him between my legs, and I knew one thing was for sure.

He was big.

And my pussy was already tingling just thinking about it. I wanted this man inside of me, to take me, to make me feel good. I looked over at my husband, who was jerking it slightly to the sight, a low groan escaping his lips.

I wanted to continue this. I started to rub myself against his member, feeling his large shaft right up against my own body. I ached for it, enjoyed this, and for a long time, I simply just enjoyed the feeling of this too.

For a long time, we simply just continued to tease, his hands, lips, and entire body on my own. I ached for this, I wanted even more, and I knew that this was only making me shiver with delight, enjoying everything about this.

Moment later, I felt him move downwards, touching my thighs and massaging the inner parts of them. I groaned, arching my back slightly and enjoying all of this. His hands were exploring my body, enjoying the touches, the sensation, the pleasure that escaped my lips as he did this.

For a long time, he simply explored, enjoying the little sounds that came out of me. But not before of course, moving his hands towards the edge of my panties, rubbing me there and teasing me.

The little teasing alone was enough to make me shiver, and making me ache for him more and more.

I could feel myself losing control slightly, enjoying the tension, the pleasure, the need that came over my body. He soon pressed his hand towards my clit, pressing against there and playing with it, making me cry out, pressing towards it and arching my back.

This was something that I'd been waiting for.

For a moment, I could feel my vision go a bit blank, and my body aching for this. I was hungry for his cock, hungry for him, and I knew that he wanted me just as much as I wanted him.

He soon pressed his hands against the very edge of my panties, sliding them downwards to reveal my naked, hot pussy. I was wet with desire, and his hands soon moved there, rubbing the nub of my clit, causing me to throw my head back, moaning out loud with pleasure as he did this. I didn't expect the gardener to make me feel this way.

But he was skilled. He was young, but he knew how to make me feel good.

"H-how are you so good?" I said.

He'd never seen my body before, but he knew just where to touch me.

"I just do. I'm quite...experienced," he said.

He pressed a finger inside, making me shiver with delight, moaning in response to his actions. He slithered the finger into me, thrusting against my body, and I soon threw my head back, moaning out loud at the pleasure that I felt as he did this. Every single touch was enough to turn me on, making me ache for him, and when he pushed two fingers inside, pressing them upwards, I let out a garbled cry, enjoying the sensation of this.

I was getting close already. But I didn't want to cum yet. But then, I felt his head between my legs, removing his fingers, and then lapping at my folds, exploring me like I was the last thing he'd get to taste on earth.

And I couldn't believe how good this felt. I threw my back upwards, pushing my hips forward, the sounds coming out of my mouth both music to my ears, and music to my husband's ears.

He was still jerking it to us, stroking his cock, and it was taking everything in me to tell him that he could join. Or maybe that's what he was getting at. That he wanted me to invite him.

Well maybe I'd do that in a few moments. I felt a finger press upwards, touching that sweet spot within me, and when it pressed there, I shivered, crying out loud, throwing my arms up, holding onto his head as he continued to slobber and tease all over me. Everything was just...wow.

I wanted more, and I ached for more. He continued this for what felt like forever, and then, moments later he pulled away, just before I was about to cum.

I groaned, feeling my pussy throbbing, the need for a cock inside to breed me only growing more and more so. He then moved to his pants, but I slapped his hands away, smiling.

"I've got it," I insisted.

He looked at me with slight surprise, but then nodded. He soon pushed his hands away and I undid his pants, sliding them down and brining his cock out to play.

I touched it, feeling it pulsate in my hands. He groaned, and I realized that he was a bit bigger than my husband. Which surprised me, but it wasn't like I was necessarily complaining either. For a second, I stroked it, listening to him groan in response to my motions, enjoying the sensation of this, but then, I touched the top of it with a couple of kisses. I also flicked my tongue over the tip of this, and he let out a small, garbled cry as I looked into his eyes.

The need. The passion, the desire. All of this was there as I started to take him partially into my mouth. With each suck, I could hear the sounds of need emitting from his mouth, and I could see the look of pure lust in his eyes.

He wanted this, and I sure as shit did too.

I got a bit braver, pushing my face downwards, feeling him tense up against me, holding my head there as he started to thrust upwards. He continued to gently rock there, and I let out a small gasp of surprise, enjoying the feeling of this as he continued to push my head further downwards, making me gobble up his cock. I let out a small gasp as he pushed my face halfway down. I took a chunk of his cock in my mouth, feeling it tighten against my throat, but I loved it. Being stuffed like this made me shiver with delight, and I ached for more.

He continued to fuck my throat, looking me in the eyes as he held me there. I took him further and further down, my husband stroking it to me sucking this man's dick. I continued to move my lips up and down, feeling it penetrate the back of my mouth, and it was then when, after a few more thrusts he pulled away, my spit still on this.

He looked me in the eyes before pushing me down on the bed, grabbing my legs, and then, without any further sounds or words, pushing into me.

I cried out, feeling his cock completely fill me up. He was bigger than my husband, and I wasn't used to that. I suddenly felt him pull my hips up, angling his cock, and when it penetrated me deep, I suddenly felt the room begin to spin, and my moans were the only thing I could register.

He continued to hold me there, thrusting his cock in deep, making me cry out with each and every single thrust. Every single touch was more than enough for me, and as he continued this, he looked me dead in the eyes, smiling.

"You good? You like that?"

"Yes, fill me with your cock," I cried out, losing all semblance of control as I felt his fat cock plunge into me.

He pushed his cock in deep, holding me there, rubbing against the tip of my clit, holding me there as I let out a series of small, garbled expressions, making me feel like I was speaking in tongues as he continued this.

After a few more thrusts, I started to feel my whole body tense up. He placed his finger against the nub of my clit, pushing in deep, and that's when I screamed out, feeling my whole body tense up, crying out as I came, and he let out a small groan as he pushed himself into me.

When he finished, he pulled out, a trail of cum there. He looked me in the eyes, smiling.

"That was amazing Layla," he said.

"Sure was. Did you like it honey?" I said to him.

He let out a groan, struggling to keep it together.

"If you want…you can finish inside me too. But only if you clean up his cum first," I said, laughing slightly.

He looked at me, surprise on his face, but then, he walked on over. I placed my foot on his back, pushing him downwards, forcing him to lap up the cum that was there. Not only did I cuck my husband, but I'd also make him feel like a little bitch.

I knew he was a bit subby, but I wanted him to work for it.

"That's right gobble it all up," I said, digging the heel of my foot into his back. I left them on for a good reason, and the sound of complete amazement and arousal was definitely not what I was expecting, that's for sure.

He finished, and finally I let him come up for air, looking at me. I cupped his chin, rubbing my foot against his cock, lightly putting pressure on it. He groaned, arching himself towards me.

"What's the matter? You like it when I step on your fucking balls?" I said.

"Y-yes," he said.

"Now you can finish inside me...but only if you let me spank you while Carlos fucks me," I said to him.

This was an idea that I had.

"Really now?" Carlos said.

"You can go again, right?" I asked him.

Carlos was already standing at attention. I didn't need to ask the man twice. He nodded, moving forward, spreading my cheeks, pushing me inside there.

I let out a gasp, but then grabbed the paddle that I had, placing it over my husband's ass.

"That's right, you like watching me get fucked because you're a little bitch, aren't you?" I said, hitting him with the pad.

He cried out, pushing his hips forward. I loved making him squirm like this. I paddled him again, watching his eyes widen, his body tense up, and a small cry of arousal escape his mouth.

"Just look at you. Coming apart like this. How cute," I said, spanking him once again.

He let out another hiss pushing his hips upwards. I found a thrill in this as he continued to become putty in my hands, and as I watched him lose control like this, I felt a sense of excitement. But then I felt also the feeling of arousal as Carlos grabbed my body, holding me there as he fucked me.

I paddled him again and again, teasing his balls with it, lightly paddling those, but then hitting his ass again. After a few more hits, he let out a small cry, and I saw a little dribble of cum come out.

"Look at you...getting off to me paddling you while I got fucked by Carlos. How pathetic," I said.

I hit him once more and he screamed out, but then Carlos put me down. I flipped my husband over, sliding onto his cock.

"Feel this? Carlos's cock was inside me just now. And now yours is. Look at you, getting hard because I fucked another man. Damn, you must really be a masochist," I said.

"Y-yes I am babe," he said.

I felt the thrill of teasing him, the excitement and fun that came out of this. I started to move my hips up and down, enjoying this. Carlos came over pushing his cock in my face, and I soon took it in my mouth, feeling it get shoved halfway down my throat.,

I stayed quiet, enjoying the feeling of the cocks in both my holes. I continued moving, feeling the thrill of this all hit me like a ton of bricks.

Carlos didn't last long though. He pushed in deep, crying out, and then he filled my mouth with his next load, filling me up completely with his seed.

I gobbled it up, enjoying the taste of this, looking at him as he laid down, completely exhausted.

"See that babe? He even came in my mouth too," I said.

I then moved my mouth over his, letting the cum dribble down into his mouth. He let out a groan, thrusting forward, and then I angled my hips a little bit. Moments later he let out a low groan, filling me up completely with his seed, groaning in pleasure at the sensation of this.

For a long time, I simply stayed there, feeling the pleasure of my orgasm moments later. I then flopped down on the bed next to him, completely exhausted, but pretty happy with the results of this. He looked at me, smiling excitedly.

"Wow," he said.

"Wow is right," I replied, unable to figure out what else you're supposed to say in moments like this. I looked over, seeing Carlos there, putting on his shirt and his pants.

"Nice job back there," I said.

"Thank you...Layla," he said.

"Good job, you remembered my name. none of those formalities bullshit," I teased.

"Yeah," he said to me.

"Anyways, you can run along. I think we need a little bit of time to ourself," I told him.

I wasn't expecting to make my husband squirm like that. And of course, his ass was probably sore too. He nodded, rushing off and closing the door.

When he was gone, we looked over at one another, the tension obvious, the nervousness prominent, but then I spoke.

"Are you good babe?" I asked him.

"Yeah, I loved it. Just a little different from what I thought would happen," he said.

"Well, what matters is that you enjoyed it dear," I teased.

"And enjoyed I did," he replied.

"Good. I could definitely get a repeat of this," I told him.

I thought about it. The fact that my husband enjoyed Carlos like this, and even let me dominate him as well throughout all of this was fun. We took a shower together, and afterwards I massaged a little bit of oil and cream into his cheeks. I did hit him a bit harder than I thought I did.

After we finished, we laid down in bed together, both of us looking at one another and smiling warmly towards one another.

"Carlos was something else," I said to him.

"Yeah he was a bit...bigger than I thought he'd be," he said with a flush.

"What's the matter? Little jealous?" I asked him.

"Not at all. I liked watching you two together. It was pretty hot. I honestly...I wouldn't mind doing it again," he admitted.

That's what surprised me. I didn't think he'd be the type that was into that. But I simply nodded.

"Well, that makes the two of us," I told him.

"Sure does," he replied.

There was an awkward tension there, one that was very obvious, and I cleared my throat, feeling slightly nervous about this.

"Anyways, I guess we can ask him again down the road if he would like to do this again. I think he enjoyed it," I told him.

"Yeah, I wouldn't mind that," he said to me.

There was a thrill to this. It wasn't just the fact that I got to cuck my husband and try things out with the gardener, it was like we were able to fulfill the other person's fantasies, no matter what the heck they were.

"Anyway, I'm fucking tired. I had a great time, but I'm definitely ready to get some sleep," he said.

"Yeah, I'm a bit tired myself. Maybe we can rest and then go from there. The night is still young, you know," I told him.

But I also was a bit exhausted. I didn't expect that to go so well, for all of that to happen. And I was happy with the results. It seemed like my husband was too.

It felt weird to have a fantasy like that get fulfilled, and neither of us were hurt by it. I was worried about that, but it seemed that the opposite happened. It brought us together, rather than tore us apart.

For me, I was just happy to make my husband a happy man. And that's what made me excited in truth too. I liked seeing him like this, and he seemed to enjoy this too.

The two of us did understand one another, even though we were a bit different as well.

The next day, I woke up, and I got ready for my day. We still had our busy lives, even after all that had happened. But when I walked outside, I saw Carlos there. He gave me a smile, and I winked at him.

"How are you?" I asked him.

"Great. Still feeling it after yesterday," he said.

"I get that. Well, maybe down the line we could do this again. The three of us," I purred to him.

His eyes widened with complete and utter surprise.

"Really?' he said to me.

"Really. I'd love to do this again with you," I said.

He was starstruck by the idea of this, and I felt a thrill that I hadn't experienced before. But I gave him a kiss on the cheek, and I headed back inside.

I finally got to experience this, and I knew that it was the start of something more, something bigger, and of course something incredibly fun for everyone.

Taboo Erotic Sex Stories Collection: Explicit Erotica For Adults- Orgasmic Oral, Gangbangs, Threesomes, Sex Games, Femdom, MILFs, Spanking, BDSM & More (Forbidden Fantasies Series)

Contents

The Bar Milfs Wild Night

"Come on, one more drink," I said with a smile as I took the glass to my lips, sipping on the dregs of this. I let out a sigh of contentment at the fact that the liquor was hitting nice and deep.

"Come on Tiffany, aren't you like….getting to your limit?" Patricia asked.

I looked at her, laughing hard as I felt my eyes start to grow a bit dilated at this.

"What do you mean? I don't have a limit," I said to her.

She shrugged.

"Come on Tiffany, you know what happened the last time you were drinking way too much. Remember when you threw up everything?" she said.

I remembered that. It was a night of dumbass choices, and I definitely regretted it, however.,…she did have a point.

"Maybe you do have a point," I said, feeling the alcohol hit my head, but not to the point where I was blackout drunk. I just wanted to feel something you know.

It was the first night out since my divorce from Chad. I was so glad to finally be out of that shit.

Chad was the biggest fucking dickhead. He was an asshole, and he only cared about himself. I hated it, especially when I caught him sleeping with the coworker that he had. He claimed they were just friends.

Right. Just friends.

I filed for divorce immediately after. That was the straw that broke the camel's back, but now….I didn't know what to do.

"What the fuck," I said, slamming the drink down with a thud. I got up, stumbling for a second. Patricia got me, and I smiled at her.

"You need to be careful there," she said.

"I'm doing the best that I can," I told her.

It's weird because for me, alcohol either turns me into a fucking horndog, or made me into a total mess.

And tonight, I was horny as fuck.

My son was at his friend's house, so I had the night to myself. Well not just that, but of course I needed something a bit different.

I looked over at Patricia, who was already on her way to the way to the dance floor at the bar. I joined her moments after I got myself together, seeing that she was in the corner with a couple of guys.

College kids. Perfect.

I smiled, pushing my hair back and sauntering over to the two guys. They looked at us with surprise, unable to say anything.

"Yes?" one of the guys asked.

"Hey there. We saw you two looking pretty cute. Thought we'd come say hi," Patricia said.

"Yes. I was thinking the same thing. Can't believe they let cute guys like you tow out like this," I purred to them.

They blushed, and the one who seemed a little timider, a blonde guy with obvious muscles, blue eyes that looked downwards, and shapely, muscular legs, spoke.

"Yeah my buddy Gavin and I were just handing out here. I'm Mark by the way," he said.

"Tiffany. So cutie, what you guys doing tonight?" I asked them.

"Damn, already jumping into there," Patricia said, lightly elbowing me.

I smirked, enjoying the responses these two guys had. The awkwardness of the conversation was obvious, but I didn't care. I just enjoyed the fact that this was happening, and the way that they looked at me with nervousness.

"We were just going to come here and see if we could find anyone. Celebrating finishing our junior year of college," I heard Mark say.

"Amazing. I'm excited for you two," I replied.

Mark had dark hair, looked Italian, and had dark hazel eyes. He was cute, but Gavin the blonde was a lot more my type. He was a bit awkward, and there was something utterly cute about this.

I couldn't get enough of it.

I licked my lips, enjoying the way he simply looked at me, my curvy body enticing him.

"What's the matter?" I asked him.

"N-nothing just...you look good," the blonde said.

I flushed. I liked it when men gave me compliments. It was thrilling, and there was something about the way that they sounded that made me feel really excited, almost thrilled really, and it made me want to learn more about this too.

"Anyways, want to head somewhere else? Or dance a bit?" Patricia asked.

"I wouldn't mind dancing with a woman as pretty as you," Mark said.

She took his hand, moving over to the corner, and soon their bodies were against one another, gyrating, shaking around, and I couldn't help but want that too.

I looked over at Gavin, who was shuffling around, nervous as all hell at the way I looked at him. I pulled him closer, our bodies moving against one another.

Gavin was both confident, but also nervous as hell. He looked at me, blushing crimson as I smiled at him. He was tall, and his muscular arms felt nice.

"So you come here a lot?" I asked him as I moved my body around.

"Yeah, but usually alone. I'm always out here...looking for new people," he said to me.

"Well, I'm a new person, and I can certainly show you a great time," I purred.

"I'd...I'd like that," he said.

I moved closer, feeling the erection in his pants start to come to life. That's when it surprised me.

He was big. Much bigger than I expected him to be. I licked my lips, looking over at Patricia as we both had the plan in place.

The goal was to get two guys to come over to the room that we had, and enjoy a wild night together. It was something we'd been working to plan, but haven't really managed to find someone.

Until now what is.

I looked over at Gavin, who seemed to be getting uncomfortable. I leaned in closer, my lips near his ear.

"Want to go back to my place so we can have some fun?" I asked him. I imagined that's what he wanted to do.

He looked at me, his eyes wide with shock, but then nodded.

"Y-yeah. I'd like that," he said.

"Well then let's go. I have a room at the hotel next to the bar," I told him.

There was a really nice hotel nearby. When I took his hand, I could see the awkwardness that was there. But then, we walked on over to the room, stepping inside and going to the elevator. Patricia followed me, with Mark's hand in hers.

"Oh, he's coming too?" Gavin said.

"Yeah, I thought this may be a fun little experience for both of us. We can...enjoy ourselves together," I purred.

He groaned against me, and I enjoyed the way I teased this man. There was something fun about teasing him that was different from other guys. We got inside, and I soon moved to the bed, grabbing him and pulling him so that he was right over me.

He looked at me, awkwardly hovering his body over mine. I smirked.

"Is this your first time?" I asked.

I'd laugh if I ended up picking a virgin, but he shook his head.

"No just...first time with a woman as pretty as you. I lost it to this really ugly chick," he said.

"Aww that's a shame. Well I can make you forget," I said in his ear.

I pulled his face towards mine, looking him in the eyes. He was definitely a cutie, and it made me feel nice and young doing this. Before I could say anything else, our lips were on our own.

There was something hot about hearing Patricia next to me, making out with Mark. Mark seemed to be the type who was a little bit more open with his actions, and he wasn't as nervous. But I did admit, kissing Gavin was something amazing, and thrilling as well.

We started Marking out, enjoying the feeling of this, loving the feeling of one another as we continued to let our lips collide, our tongues move and dance. He was pretty good at kissing as well. I wondered if I'd get to experience Mark as well.

The way his lips felt so subtle turned me on. I then saw Gavin pull away, looking at me with a flush.

"You're good," he said.

"It's because I have over a decade of experience over you sweetie. And you will get to enjoy all of that tonight," I said.

I was happy to have this experience. I mean, I was married for almost 2 decades before I caught the rat bastard cheating. I'm glad that I was good enough to make this young man flush, enjoying the way that I teased him.

For a long time, we just made out, our bodies moving closer. I arched my hips slightly, enjoying the way that he moaned in response, moving his hips near mine. I shuddered, shivering with a need that only grew more so as we continued to make out passionately. Gavin was definitely a looker, and he knew exactly how to kiss easily.

This younger man was already tearing me apart, turning me on in ways that I didn't think were even possible. I shivered, arching my back as he continued to pepper kisses there, our tongue moving together. I wanted him, and I definitely could tell that he wanted this too. But there was a nervousness there.

"Something the matter?" I finally asked as he pulled away.

"No. it's just...sorry I'm a little nervous. You're the first woman I've done it with that's been...really hot," he said to me.

I flushed, appreciating how he called me that. It was nice.

"I do appreciate it. I'm glad that you enjoy it," I told him.

"Boy do I," he said.

Our lips crashed together once again, loving the way that we felt against one another. It was definitely the thrill of the moment, the excitement of the future, the nature of this which made us both excited and turned on.

His lips moved downwards, touching my neck slightly. I shivered, looking over to see that Mark's hands were already at her clothes, tearing them off of her.

I don't know why, but there was something hot about seeing that. But then, I felt a little nibble against my neck, pulling me back to the feeling at hand.

Gavin was a little bit awkward with the way his hands touched. I shivered with delight, enjoying the way his hands barely grazed against my breasts. I could feel his hands touching in curiosity, exploring me.

"You can touch all you want," I told him.

"O-okay," he said.

He reached up, grabbing my breasts and teasing them there. I shivered, moaning in pleasure as I enjoyed this. His hands became exploratory, and I loved how they danced against my nipples.

I made quick work of my shirt, pulling it off. I pressed his face between my chest, touching his face there against the breasts.

"They're so...warm," he said, muffling them there.

"They are. And I'm sure you'll enjoy them," I said.

My breasts got a lot bigger after having my son, but I wasn't against that. I know that my husband liked them before he decided to be a cheating asshole, and I could see from the look on his face, the excitement in his eyes, and the obvious hardness in his pants, he enjoyed this too.

He moved his hands downwards, touching the nipple and playing with it there, teasing it against his hand. I let out a small gasp, enjoying the feeling of his hand there. This guy, despite being inexperienced as fuck, was a lot of fun to fuck around with, and I enjoyed it a whole lot. He soon moved his hands towards the tip of my nipples, touching them there through the fabric, making me shiver and cry out with delight, moving my hips upwards.

His hands moved to the back of my bra, touching the clasp there. I looked at him, seeing the struggle in his eyes, but then I laughed.

"Let me help you out," I told him.

I pulled off the bra, tossing the garment over to the side. I looked at him, smiling with a coy grin as he looked at me, his eyes wide with surprise.

"Wow," he said.

"You can touch them," I told him.

He quickly moved closer, refusing to say no to that offer. He took the tip of the nipple into his mouth, sucking on the flesh there. I let out a small moan, excitement growing within me as he pushed it between his lips, enjoying the sounds that I made. I shivered with delight, enjoying the way he continued to tease and play with it. His lips were soft, exploratory, and I noticed another set of fingers move upwards, teasing the nipple there. I cried out as he did this, thrusting m y hips upwards, enjoying the feeling of this.

He continued to play and tease around with them, and I let out a small moan, excited about this. His hands and lips worked their magic, and I enjoyed the sensation of this as well.

I continued to move my hips upwards, enjoying the little pinches that he did with his fingers. Mark was already between Patricia's legs, expertly eating her out. She let out a series of cries, and there was something about this that I found hot, that I enjoyed, and that I wanted to hear more out of.

But then, he pulled on both of the nipples, tugging on them, making me shiver with delight, enjoying the feeling of this. I shivered, loving how easily I was losing all semblance of control, all because of this man, and his expert hands.

Even though he wasn't that experienced, I'd be lying if I said I didn't enjoy it. But then, he slithered his fingers downwards, against my body, pushing his hands towards my pants. He touched my thighs, feeling the large muscles there, and I chuckled.

"You like?" I teased.

"Yes. Very much so," he purred.

"Good. Because I like this too," I said to him.

He then moved his hands to the jeans, pulling them slightly. He tried to tug them off, but there was no dice. My butt was a little too big for that one. I pushed my hips up, meeting his cock and letting out a small groan as he pushed it off of him, looking at me, seeing the look of pure need which was there on my face.

"Fuck," he said, taking a moment to drink me up. I knew I was needy. I hadn't been fucked hard in a moment, and I knew that his monstrous dick would do the job.

"Like it?" I said.

"Yes," he replied with a gulp.

I moved my hands downwards, spreading apart, but then, he moved his hands gingerly against my thighs, trailing little touches upwards till he got to the apex of my legs. He inhaled for a second, letting out a sigh of contentment before he pulled off my panties, revealing my shaven, wet pussy.

He looked at it, surprised by this.

"It's so fluffy," he said.

"Like it?" I asked him.

"Yes," he replied.

He moved his hands down between there, exploring me slightly. He then pressed against my clit, making me shiver and cry out with delight, pushing my hips upwards as I felt his hands explore and touch every single part of me. His hands moved towards the tip of my clit, pressing there, watching my eyes widen with surprise at the soft, sensual touches there. He rubbed me there, enjoying the sounds of my desire, the pleasure that came from this, and the aching need.

He was good. He then moved a finger inside, exploring my entrance, looking at me with a look of curiosity and desire.

"Fuck," I said out loud.

"You…good?" he asked me.

"Yeah. Amazing," I told him.

He continued the exploratory touches, pumping his fingers in and out, watching with rapt desire as I continued to move my hips slightly, thrusting upwards and enjoying this. I watched his eyes grow heavy with lust, and then, he spread me apart, pushing his tongue inside, digging into me.

I cried out, surprised by just how needy this man was, and the touches that he provided to me. Everything just felt so…amazing really. It was a thrill that I couldn't get enough of, something that I just felt that I needed more than anything else. I continued to press my hips upwards, pushing my hands to his face, smothering him with my pussy.

I heard the muffled gasps and sounds, but his tongue continued to work its magic, invading inside of me, moving upwards to tease my clit, and it got me so close that I thought I'd lose control for a moment. But then I stopped myself, looking over at him with a devilish grin.

"You good?" I asked him with a smile.

"Yeah," he replied.

"Anyways, I guess you enjoyed that," I told him.

"You didn't…cum did you?" he asked.

"God no. going to take more than that," I teased.

He flushed, but then nodded. However, I reached out, touching the obvious outline in his pants.

"Let's have a look at this, shall we?" I asked.

I slid his pants down, revealing his cock. He was big, much bigger than I imagined, and he was already leaking out precum. He was girthy too, and I licked my lips, excited for the taste of this, and so much more. I moved my lips to the tip, kissing and tasting the precum that was there, seeing his eyes grow heavy with need.

"You good?" I asked him.

"Yeah," he replied.

I smiled, seeing him struggle to hold onto this, all semblance of control taking him to a whole new place. I then moved my lips to the tip, sucking on this, watching him groan in pleasure, pushing his hips upwards, moaning in excitement and surprise.

He then started to press my had there as I took him further and further in. He grabbed my hair, holding it as he began to fuck my face. I felt the tears begin to fill in my eyes, but I held steady, taking his cock in deeper and deeper, mustering every ounce of strength not to pull back.

I got to the base before I could feel the urge to gag. I then pulled back, licking the underside of his cock. He pushed me back down again, thrusting his hips upwards, and I shivered, enjoying the delightful sensation of this. There was something fun about being used just like this, and I could tell from the way he continued to do this that he was enjoying this just as much as I was.

But then, as soon as it happened, he pulled back, smiling at me with excitement.

"You good?" he said.

"Yes. Now just fuck me," I said.

I moved down, spreading my legs apart, watching in anticipation as he groaned. He then pushed his legs towards me, spreading me apart, and then, he slid himself deep into me.

To my surprise, he fit pretty well in there, almost too well. I suddenly let out a small cry, surprised by how good this was as he continued to thrust in deep, and I let out a series of cries, enjoying the pleasure that came from this.

Every single touch, every single caress, it was all driving me to the point of madness. His cock filled me right the fuck up, pushing out, then pushing in, enjoying the tightness of my pussy.

"Yes, just like that," I said. He continued to press deep, hitting so hard that I didn't know how much more of this I could take.

That's when I got an idea.

I heard the sound of groaning and crying from someone. I looked over, seeing Patricia there, getting pounded into the bed by Mark. He was pretty big too, but of course, Gavin was bigger.

"Get me from behind," I said.

"Are you...sure?" he asked.

"Yes, I love it," I told him.

I moved myself on all fours, shaking my butt. He then groaned, grabbing my cheeks and pushing himself into me. The sheer force of his thrust as he filled me up made my eyes start to widen, and I felt the urge to salivate right

then and there. He continued to thrust in deep, pushing me to my limits as I let out a small cry, holding onto the sheets. Patricia looked at me, smiling.

"This is one hell of a way to celebrate you getting divorced," she said.

"Sure as shit is," I told her.

I then moved in, pressing my lips to hers, and as we both got pounded by these two, we made out, our tongues moving and touching against one another. There was something super thrilling about this, and I couldn't get enough of this. But then, we pulled back, as I felt him hit that one spot, the location that always made me whimper, becoming a puddle of goo right then and there.

"Holy shit," I cried out, feeling my back arch. He grabbed my hair, pounding me harder and harder. A hand was on my ass, and another hand touched my pucker, teasing it.

I groaned, feeling that need, that urge for two dicks inside of me. Before I knew it, Patricia let out a cry, passing out.

"Fuck," she said to herself.

"You okay?" I asked her.

"Finish them off," she told me.

I knew what they meant. I looked over at Mark, moving off.

"Want to go behind?" I said.

"Sure," he said.

I got myself on top of Gavin, holding onto him as I shifted my weight down, feeling his cock all the way inside of me as I let out a small, garbled scream as he penetrated me deep. I couldn't get enough of this, and I knew that he was enjoying this as much as I was.

But then, I felt something against my other entrance. At first, it was a finger, and that combined with the cock in my other hole, was already driving me crazy. He pushed himself all the way in, and I cried out, feeling him penetrate me completely with it. But then, Marks' cock replaced the fingers which were teasing me for a bit, and I suddenly let out a small, subtle cry.

"Yes," I shivered, moaning out loud as I felt it get deeper and deeper inside of me. There was a tightness, something which was common when I got that entrance pounded. But then, he was all the way inside of me. I shivered, enjoying the tightness and the fullness which came from this.

I started moving slightly, enjoying the feeling of this. But then I felt Gavin hold onto me, keeping me between them as they both began to thrust their cocks deep into me. I started to shiver with delight, enjoying me as I pushed against them, feeling their cocks penetrate my body deeply.

They thrust in harder, causing me to tense up. I enjoyed this, religion in the feeling of everything as I felt them both continue the onslaught on my holes, holding me there as they thrust in deep.

I was so close. I felt like I was about to reach my limit. Then, I felt Gavin pull me forward, looking me in the eyes.

Then, our lips met. We kissed, and he angled my hips slightly, pressing right up against the g-spot. That, combined with the location of where Marks's thrusts were hitting made me get so close that I could taste it. And I felt a

small hand move downwards, teasing my clit as I tensed up, shivering as I cried out loud, thrusting my hips upwards as I came hard.

By that point, when my tight pussy and ass clenched onto them, that was more than enough for them. Mark was the first, groaning as he shot his load into my ass.

But then, Gavin pulled out, grabbing his cock, and then shoved it right in my face. Spurts of cum decorated my face, and I stuck out my tongue, drinking the rest of it as it fell from his member.

I looked at him, giving him a small, wry smile as I saw him sit back, moaning out loud.

"Holy. Shit," he said.

"You good there?" I asked him.

"Yeah. Utterly amazing really. I just don't know what else to say. Other than...wow," he said.

I chuckled, leaning in, giving him a small kiss on the lips. I then pulled back, nodding.

"Don't you worry. We'll have more fun times like this down the road," I said to him.

There was an excitement that made me feel good about all of this. I loved the fact that he was enjoying this as much as I was. He then pulled back, sighing.

"Well shit," he said.

"Yeah, that's right. And I guess you knocked out Patricia. I knew that she wasn't the type to last long in bed, but damn," I said.

Patricia gave me the middle finger.

"I heard that."

"Sure you did," I retorted.

We all laughed, feeling the excitement and thrill of the moment begin to die down. I didn't know what else to say next, but then, I saw that Mark was looking around nervously.

"What's the matter?" I asked him.

"Well it's just....I didn't expect to have this happen tonight. Thought we'd pick up some younger girl," he said.

"What, is my old ass not enough for you?" I teased.

"Not at all! It's just...surprising," he said to me.

"Well, I enjoy this. And I'm glad that I can make you guys pretty happy too," I told them.

They all nodded, agreeing to my words. But then, Gavin spoke.

"Yeah, I'm definitely happy with the way things are going. Thanks for making things fun," he said to me.

"You're most welcome. I love having fun," I told him.

"Me too," Gavin replied.

"Anyways, you guys want to spend the night or..."

Mark and Gavin both shook their heads.

"Actually, we do need to be back at the dorms tonight," Gavin said.

"Yeah, we can't stay out too late or also the DA will get mad at us again," Mark replied.

So they were the type that snuck out after hours. What a bunch of naughty boys. My lips curled into that of a smile as I pushed my brown hair back, my green eyes scanning over the two of them. They were both a snack and then some, but I also was a bit surprised by the results of this too.

"That's totally fine. You two be safe though, you hear?" I asked them.

"Yeah, we will be. Thank you...Tiffany," Gavin said.

"Yeah, it was fun," Mark replied.

I watched as they got out of the doorway, closing it. I walked over to lock it. When I turned around, Patricia had come back to reality. I guess that dick really did do her some good.

"Everything alright?" I asked her.

"Yeah. Just was surprised at how fucking good that dick was," she said.

"Me too. Oh and by the way, you looked really hot there. I don't know, I wanted to kiss you because of it," I admitted, flushing red.

I don't know why, but there was something enticing about saying those words., she simply beamed, and I wondered if this was something she was all for or not.

"Really now?" she said.

"Yeah, I'm really glad that...we could enjoy that together," I told her.

"Well I'm glad that we could too," she replied.

I leaned in, giving her a hug, and we kissed again. It was a strange platonic friendship. I didn't want anything romantic with Patricia at all, but being with her, kissing her, all of this just felt...so damn good you know?

"Anyways, I think it's getting late. We should probably get some sleep. Unless...you want to go back down and do the same thing once again," she said.

I was surprised by Patricia. Sure that dick was good, but it'd be fun to try things out with another guy. To enjoy the thrill of more sex, the dick, and to have this again and again.

"Sure, I wouldn't mind that. Let me go take a shower. I kind of have cum all over my face you know," I said.

She laughed.

"Yeah he really got you," she said.

I went to the bathroom to freshen up, but it was nice to finally have the freedom that I'd been waiting for. My husband never let me have some time like this with the girls, even if there wasn't sex involved. But now, I got to experience this again and again, and I loved everything about it. It certainly was the beginning of a new life for me.

Maybe the singles life wasn't all that bad, you know?

I came on back, smiling warmly to Patricia, who was in a whole new outfit. I got my own outfit too. The night was young, and there were still some super-hot guys around. I had a feeling that Mark and Gavin were already gone, so we can go out once more.

"You ready?" Patricia asked.

"Give me just a moment," I said.

I stood in the mirror, putting on makeup and smiling as I looked in the mirror. I felt hot, hotter than I'd been in the last few marriages that I had, and a whole lot hotter than I thought.

It was time to go down again, to have some fun, get into more mischief, and of course, to explore the fun that would come out of this, and not just that, the adventures that we'd been waiting for, and the thrill of the next cutie that would come my way, just begging to give me his cock.

The Maid's Special Skill

I needed a job, and this was the first one that I'd managed to nab.

It was working for a mysterious gentleman. A guy named Gregory Kifman, some big-time dude who lived in a big mansion.

I was employed to work as his maid, and at first, we didn't have any contact with one another. Hell, I literally had an interview over the phone. It was so weird. I'd never experienced anything like this before.

I figured I'd end up losing the job or something to some other girl who probably sounded like a sex worker. But no….I got the job.

I was told to meet up on Monday, and so I did. When I got there, the place was practically empty, save for one red car. Did he have any other special hands.

"Is this the right place?" I asked myself. It had to be. This was what I found on Maps, and it was the right address. When I got to the door, I realized there was an intercom. I pressed it.

"Yes," the voice said curtly.

"Hi there. I'm Amanda. I'm here for the new job," I explained.

I hoped that this would work, that I wouldn't get into deep trouble because of this. But then, he spoke.

"I see that you're here," he told me.

"Yeah. Sorry about that," I told him.

"Very well. Give me a few moments," he said to me.

I looked around, trying to keep my wits about me. He probably was just some grumpy old man who probably acted like he was better than everyone else because he was an old man who had money.

But then, the door opened, and one of the most attractive men that I'd ever seen was in front of me. He had dark jet-black hair, dark blue eyes that looked unreal, and he was both small, but also had a defining build to him.

I suddenly licked my lips on instinct, but then pulled myself back to reality. The last thing I wanted was to come off like a total dumbass.

"Oh, there you are. The new maid I hired, correct?" he said.

"Yes. Amanda," I replied.

He extended his hand and I took it, almost letting out a small moan as I felt his larger hand in mine. I shivered, enjoying the feeling of this, but I knew for a fact that it was only a matter of time before I'd just up and lose it right then and there. But then, he simply laughed.

"No need to be so formal. Come with me," he implored.

I followed him, the gears in my head spinning as I tried to figure out what the hell to do next. He motioned for me to sit at the table, and there was a maid dress and a whole piece of paper.

"There you go. That's all you need," he said.

"But aren't you going to go over the job and shit?" I asked.

I'd never experienced a guy like him. He shrugged.

"What else is there to go over. I can assure you, everything's there," he said to me.

I didn't know if he was just fucking with me, or not. Maybe he was, maybe I was overthinking all of this. But I read over the papers, and at that point, he was gone.

I didn't know why, but he both annoyed me, and it turned me on how cold he was. Maybe I had a thing for someone like that. I quickly pored over the notes of this, nodding.

"I see," I said to myself.

It was a pretty simple job. Just to clean the common rooms, and to not drop anything. I read that one plate in this place was worth more than my apartment's rent for the month! I hated that there were so many factors here, and so many extra things added, but also...this was the best job that I'd gotten.

I wanted to get to know Gregory. He was a bit quiet, and a little cold. But he was gone, vanished without a trace. It frustrated me that he did that, that's for sure. I wanted to get to know him, to find out more about him, but he was gone, and I guess I was destined to suffer at this point.

But I did what I needed to do. I decided at this point to get started with the tasks. I went to the bathroom to put the maid uniform on, and I realized that it was...kind of short, and it showed off my supple breasts. I pulled my red hair back, and I blushed a little at how I looked.

I thought I was pretty.

I quickly got myself together, heading back out. But as soon as I did, I bumped right into Gregory, who looked at me with a smile, sizing me up and down. His eyes did glaze down at the obvious chest I had in this, and I couldn't help but flush, but also felt turned on by how he looked at me.

"Very nice. Glad that it fits you," he said to me.

"Yes of course," I told him.

He looked me in the eyes, a look of purely heated desire there. I wasn't going to lie, I did think he was attractive, and he could do so many things to me and I'd live for every moment of it. There was something that just...pushed me to my limit, making me shiver and ache with both need and delight, the pleasure and lust growing within me.

"Yes, anyway, I'll let you get started with your work. I have a lot going on," he said to me, giving me one last look before heading on out of there.

My head was spinning. I couldn't help but feel the excitement and need grow within me.

I could see his eyes roving over my body, studying me with a look of pure need, want, and desire. I ached for this. And I felt my pussy wetten with delight at the sight of him.

Maybe it really was what I wanted.

But the duty called. I had to make sure that I took care of the surroundings, cleaning them as quickly as I could. I started in the main areas, working my way through the kitchen.

All the meanwhile I kept seeing his eyes glaze over my body, practically mentally undressing me as I looked into his eyes. There was something just so damn hot about this, and it made me shiver with delight, ache for him, and want him as he continued to study me, seeing the look of need as he was there.

Over the next couple of days, I did just this. I came in, I worked, I saw him mentally undressing me, which I smiled at, and then I'd leave. However, a couple of times I moved to the bathroom, pulling my skirt upwards, sticking two fingers into me, shoving them in. I let out a series of small little sounds, cries of need and want, aching for him as I continued to move my hands in and out, shivering with need as I continued to feel the urge and desire grow.

There was something just so fun about all of this, that I couldn't help but want this, need this, and desire everything that came from this.

I continued to engage in these tasks, moving around, trying my best not to be seen by him. but one time, I was in the bathroom, pushing my hand against my breasts, teasing my nipples through the confines of this shirt, when suddenly, I heard a knock at the door.

"Amanda?" Gregory asked.

I let out a small gasp, which I bit back before I quickly got my bearings together, getting fixed up before heading back over to the doorway. When I opened it, he was there, a frown on his face.

"What's the matter?" he asked.

"Oh nothing. Sorry I was taking so long. I was…attending to something," I said.

"I see. Well, I hope the cleaning gets done relatively quickly. If you need help with anything, please don't hesitate to ask," he said.

I looked at him, wondering if he meant something else there when it came to helping. I tried to hold back from licking my lips, the idea of his hands on my body, helping me as I helped him becoming a common image in my mind.

"Right. I'll definitely let you know then," I told him.

He smiled at me, and I could tell there was definitely something else going on there. I shivered, wondering if he would say anything more.

I went over to the kitchen to clean a couple of things. But what I didn't notice, was the wet floor that was there. As soon as I moved, I fell forward, slipping and hitting the side of the cabinet. Sure it fucking hurt, but there was something which worried me more.

The glass that was there.

It wobbled around, as if trying to test me, when suddenly there was a clang, and suddenly the glass fell down, shattering on the ground.

I paused, trying to figure out what the hell to do next. I was torn. I had no clue what to do here, or even what to say. Suddenly, I heard the pattering of footsteps, and I saw Gregory come in, a panicked look on his face.

"What the hell did you do?" he said, his face contorted into that of displeasure.

Shit, I was totally going to get fired. This wasn't good.

"I'm sorry, the floor was wet and—"

"And? You do know how much those glasses cost, right? You can't just run in here, slip on this, and expect me to just let this shit slide Amanda," he said.

I felt scared. Was I getting fired next? Would he just say screw it and kick mem out? This was the easiest job that I've had, and now, I may end up losing it because of a fuckup that made me feel abashed.

"I told you I'm sorry," I told him.

He pursed his lips, looking at me with disdain in his eyes.

"Well, this is a problem. I can't be having a maid who does this," he said to me.

I didn't know what to do. It was like life was fucking with me, making me want to just hide away, die and forget about it all.

In fact, it felt like I was making the biggest goddamn mistake of my life.

But I had to persist, right? I had to make this work. Suddenly, I tried to weigh my options.

I could beg for him to just let me go. To let my pathetic ass slide. But I didn't think that was going to work here.

There was another option. I knew he wouldn't take any shit from anyone, so maybe there was a chance for this to work.

I moved forward, pressing my chest upwards, a sorrowful look on my face.

"I could pay...another way," I offered.

He looked at me, at first his face a little bit confused. But then, he spoke.

"And how do you suppose you'll do that? What could you possibly offer to me?" he said.

I didn't want to have to do this, but it was the only thing that I could do. It was the only thing that would work in this case.

I started to move closer, my hand right up against the tip of his cock. I touched it through the outline of his pants, and he showed no emotion sans biting his lip.

"What are you doing?" he snapped.

"Helping you out. Wouldn't you like that?" I purred.

He tensed, but then nodded.

"Maybe I would," he said.

"Well, tell you what, I can let you have your fun with me, and we can call this a little misunderstanding," I told him.

He looked into my eyes, pursing his lips and tensing up, unsure of what to do, or what to say anymore. Finally, he spoke.

"Very well," he said, but there was clearly the sound of desire in his voice, as I continued to touch him there.

It was very obvious that he was turned on, and he definitely hadn't had this much in a long time. But then, I wondered what else he'd do.

As I was about to take his cock out of his pants, he pulled me upwards, looking at him.

"Not here. I need to punish you first," he said.

I looked at him, feeling a bit nervous about this. I wondered what he'd do. But then, he pulled me up, practically dragging me to a room upstairs. It was probably his bedroom.

I hadn't been up in his bedroom as of yet, but when I got up there, I saw the beautiful sight. It was a nice space, and I was a little jealous of how nice it was. He then pushed me down on the bed, hoisting my skirt up, and rubbing his hand against my ass.

"You've got a cute little ass back here," he said to me.

I shivered, moaning with delight as he barely touched my pussy. He was such a tease, letting his hands rest there, and then move back to my backside. I felt his hand near my pucker too, and I tensed up.

I'd never been fucked there. What did he have planned for more.

Suddenly, before I could say anything more, he then pulled my panties down, revealing my bare ass.

"Damn," he said, grabbing it hard, holding it there. I let out a small grunt of surprise and pleasure, enjoying the way that this man touched me. There was something thrilling about the way his hands moved against there, rubbing my ass, touching it, teasing it, and enjoying it as well.

He continued to paw it, and then, he slapped it.

The slapping sensation was definitely amazing, and there was a thrill that came from this. I enjoyed it, that's for sure, and I knew that he liked it too. He started to smack me again and again, enjoying the way that I responded, and soon, I started tensing up, moaning in pleasure as he continued to smack me again and again, enjoying the feeling of all of this.

Everything was just so nice. It was perfect, a heavenly sensation that only made me ache for more. He continued to hit me harder and harder, enjoying the feeling of this, and I couldn't help but love everything about this too.

It was nice, that's for sure, and it was like he knew exactly how to touch me, how to make me feel good, and how to turn me on.

He then hit me harder, touching that one spot. As he smacked me, I shivered, crying out loud and tensing up.

"Look at you. Such a goddamn mess," he said to me, hitting me once again.

I cried out, arching my back, enjoying the feeling of this. His hands were tough, hardened, and there was something just so damn thrilling about him continually touching me, making me into the mess that I was.

With every single spanking, I felt my ass grow redder, and it felt a little bit tender. It definitely was getting me aroused, making me shiver with delight, enjoying the sensation of this.

But then, he stopped. I looked over, but he pushed my head down hard.

"I never said that we were done," he said.

I let out a small moan as he said those words. The power, the control, it was all making me shiver, the thirst that I had being quenched by the feeling of his body, and the tension that he created. Before I knew it, he soon grabbed something else, and when he hit me, a sting of pleasure hit my body, making me writhe with delight.

"Fuck," I cried out, shivering as he continued to hit me with the flogger. Every single touch was turning me on, driving me crazy, making me wish for more of this. I craved his touch. I needed it, and I could sense from the way that he did this to me that it was only making me ache for more. I definitely enjoyed this as well.

He continued the flogging, each lashing hitting my core. He got right by my pussy, and the vibration that I felt from the spanking touched every fiber of my being, making me ache for him, making me want more, and I needed this more and more.

I didn't know how much more of this I could take.

After a few more hits, he then stepped away. I didn't know what he had planned for me next. He then rubbed my ass, hitting it while I had my guard down, creating a garbled sound that came out of my mouth.

"You little shit. Over here breaking my stuff like this. Maybe I should make you pay with your body," he said to me.

In a way, the sound of that turned me on. I mean, if he kept me around for that, I'd stay forever. The way his hands continued to touch me, moving between my legs, teasing my clit, rubbing there, made me let out a garbled sensation, causing me to ache and moan in pleasure and need.

"Fuck," I shivered, crying out loud as things started to get even hotter for me. I was turned on, and I knew for a fact that he enjoyed this too.

After a few more moments, I suddenly felt like he was turning me on, and driving me crazy. He then pulled back, licking his fingers, but then he pulled me upwards, so that I was right by his cock.

"Take care of this," he grunted.

The sound of his voice reverberated through the core of my body. I quickly moved to his pants, undoing them, sliding them downwards, grabbing his cock as I touched it. He let out a small groan as I pushed it against my mouth, opening it as I started sucking on his cock.

I took the tip of it at first, watching his eyes grow wide as I sucked on the tip of it, hearing the small gasps as I continued to move my lips there, teasing the very tip of this. The sounds that he made were delightful.

Even though he was the one in control, I very much felt great about making him utter these sounds, delightful little utterances that were a turn-on to hear. I wanted to hear these again and again as I continued to move my lips around, sucking on the very tip of his cock, enjoying the sounds that came out of his mouth.

With every single touch, every single press, I was losing all semblance of control. It was driving me crazy, making me feel turned on, enjoying the feeling of all of this as he continued to groan.

The sounds that he made, the approval that was uttered, was something I couldn't get enough of. I loved hearing this, and every single time he groaned, moving his hips forward, I could tell that he liked this more and more.

I slowly pressed my tongue a little bit further down, moving towards the very tip of his cock, getting to the base and holding onto it there. He let out a small, garbled sound as I started to suck on the very base of his cock, hearing the utterances of approval that came from this.

The secret that I did have, was that I was great at sucking cock. I knew just what he wanted, the sounds that he uttered, the enjoying feelings that came out of this, it was all just...so damn perfect you know?

I continued to suck on him, getting to the very base of this, moving upwards, and he held my head there, forcing me to take it all the way down.

"There you go. Take all of this," he instructed.

"I'd do as I was told, pushing my head downwards, taking his load in my mouth if it did happen. I grabbed his cock, jerking it while I used my tongue, teasing every fiber of this, watching his eyes widen, and his cock start to jerk forward.

"Fuck," he said.

He pressed my head down, practically forcing me to take him to the very core. I did as I was told, sucking on him, holding him there as he continued to fuck my throat. I at this point was numb to everything, enjoying the feeling of all of this, and it was then when, after a few more moments, he suddenly kept my head down, but then pulled it back, shooting his load into my mouth, and partially onto my face.

His cum tasted way better than I expected, and I swallowed all of this, looking at him.

"You good?" I asked him.

"Yes. Great actually," he said.

But then, his hands moved to the back of my butt. I let out a gasp as he teased my pucker, encircling the edge, moving against the ring of muscles.

"But, I'm not done yet. You haven't fully paid it back. How about...I touch this part too," he purred.

My ass. He wanted my ass. In a strange way, I kind of liked it, and there was a thrill of being touched like this. I loved it, and soon, I felt my body slowly come apart, the need for him growing.

He reached over to his desk, grabbing what seemed to be lube out. He coated his fingers with it, smiling in excitement as he started to press the first digit into me. I suddenly cried out, feeling the ache of need grow within me. He then pushed his fingers into me, pressing two of them inside, and I cried out, tensing up as I felt this.

It was...different from what I thought. I definitely enjoyed this as much as he did, and with the way his fingers danced around, fingering my ass, pushing it to relax, it turned me on.

But I wanted something bigger in there. I wanted his fingers all the way inside me. He then added another finger, pushing deep within, and as he continued to fuck me, I felt the sudden discomfort turn into that of pleasure.

This was amazing. It was a turnon that only made me ache for more.

After a few more thrusts, he then pulled back, groaning once again. I figured he was hard. He then pushed the tip of himself inside, filling me up completely, making me shiver and ache with desire as he continued to push all the way in.

He was bigger than I expected. Sure I did just suck his cock, but that was different from well...having it all the way in there. I suddenly cried out, pushing forward, enjoying the sensation of this as he continued to press himself into me, turned on by the feeling of me against him. This was thrilling, a different type of feeling compared to what I was used to.

When he was all the way inside, he stopped, smacking my ass as I cried out, feeling the tightness become almost suffocating as he moved his hands to my hips, holding them there.

Then he thrust. When he did so, it touched a part of me that I thought I'd never get to feel. I cried out, suddenly aching for more, the encroaching need for him growing more and more. He continued to thrust in and out of me, each touch of this turning me on, and there was something exciting, thrilling, and needing about all of this. With every single thrust too, he smacked my ass, so I could feel him continuously tease me.

A hand moved in between my legs, entering into my pussy and rubbing my clit as he continued to press in and out, touching, teasing, fucking me harder and harder. There was a feeling of excitement and desire, a need that only grew more and more as time passed on. I didn't know what else to say, other than I was turned on, I was needy, horny, and I ached for him.

After a few more thrusts, he then pressed in, pushing his fingers upwards into me, touching my clit in the process. When he did that, I threw my back forward, tensing up, moaning out loud and in pleasure as he came inside of me.

The thrill of my orgasm hit me like a ton of bricks. It was so good, and the white that I saw in my eyes lasted a good moment or so. For a long time, I definitely didn't know what else I could do, or even what to say either. That's when he pulled back, looking at me with a smile on his face.

"There we go. Nice and punished," he said.

Sure, it may be a punishment to him, but I actually enjoyed this a whole lot more than I cared to let on. I mean, I wouldn't mind doing this again. But I didn't want to have it on punishing terms either.

"Yeah, I'm definitely learning my lesson," I told him.

"Good. As you should be. I don't want any more shit broken again. But…I did have a bit of fun with you. I'm surprised you took that so easily," he said.

In truth, I did have a fantasy about being taken and fucked in the ass like this. But I wouldn't dare tell him.

"Well I'm definitely quite happy with the results of this," I told him.

"Sure," he replied.

We looked at one another, his face still stern.

"But, I'm not letting you off the hook," he said.

"What do you mean?" I asked.

Was he really going to penalize me more for this.

"I never want to see you do this again. But, if you do accidentally do this, consider this to be the punishment. Perhaps a little bit harder," he said.

The sound of those last couple of words excited me. I mean, I wasn't trying to say that I wanted to be punished, but maybe I was as well.

"Yeah, I wouldn't mind that kind of punishment," I told him.

"I'm sure you wouldn't. and I can give you and even greater punishment too, if you're up for it," he said.

I'm sure this implied something else, and not necessarily actual punishments, so I nodded.

"Indeed. I'd like that," I said.

He gave me a smile, and then he walked on out. I laid there, satisfied by the treatment that this man gave to me, but I also wondered what else may happen next.

What did he have in store for me? Perhaps there was a lot that he wasn't just going to tell me. I quickly left the room, heading into the bathroom once more. Despite having an orgasm, I was turned on once again, pulling my dress up, teasing myself, thinking about the fact that his cum was still in my ass.

The idea of this thrilled me, turned me on, and made me excited for what would happen next. I don't know why, but there was something exciting and fun about all of this. I continued to push my fingers in and out, wondering how he'd feel inside my other holes, and I let out a small sigh, enjoying this.

I quickly relieved myself, but then, as I got out, I saw him there.

"By the way, I have one last punishment to give to you," he said.

Did he hear me? I don't even know, but I stopped, tensing up.

"What do you mean?" I inquired.

"This," he simply said.

He leaned in, capturing my lips with his own. We kissed passionately for a moment there before pulling away, smiling in contentment.

"I'm going to have a lot of fun with you throughout the next few months. Or however long you want to stay," he said.

"I am too," I replied.

Gregory gave me a small smirk, one that screamed he was enjoying this just as much as I was, and then, he quickly left the area, leaving me there. As I sat there trying to figure out what else to do, or even what to say, I took a moment to figure out just what was next.

I mean, I wouldn't mind more of whatever this is, but I also wondered what he'd do now. I wanted to ask, but also…I wanted to keep up the fun, the games, and the way he continued to turn me on like this.

I didn't know what he would have in store for me next but it did mean that I'd head on over to the bathroom, relieving myself every so often.

I left that night completely smitten, but also curious about what the next plans were. What did he have in store for me? What did he want now? I don't even know, but I could tell it was the beginning of something else.

There was a thrill that came with showing him my special skill. The one that I had that I sued my mouth with, the one that I could show off to others, including him. but I wanted to share it with him again. His cock was nice and thick, big and wonderful, and I already missed the taste of it on my mouth.

Maybe I'd get a chance to do this again sooner than later. I wasn't sure though, mostly because I didn't know what was next. But I did love this job, and I wasn't going to get rid of it if I could.

Teacher's Pet

"Alright, you have till the third to get this completed. Got it," I said to the class.

I taught biology at the local college, a fun little class for most of the students. But I didn't make it easy. That's the thrill of having a job like this. I could teach them while also making it challenging and fun.

And challenging I did. I made sure that the class wasn't too easy for most of the students either. As I gave them the assignment, my eyes locked with Marcus.

Marcus was a bit of an underachiever. He would do the work sure, but he always seemed to be behind. Was it on purpose? I didn't even know anymore, but there was also that feeling that he was doing this for some reason, to stand out, and it bothered me that he acted this way.

As the students left, Marcus and I locked eyes. I walked on over to his desk, holding my clipboard in my hands.

"Marcus," I said with a deadpanned tone.

"Hey there Hannah," he said.

"It's Miss Davidson," I said to him.

"Sorry," he said, flushing crimson.

"It's fine. Well, I found out that your grades are suffering once again. What's been going on? This isn't like you," I told him.

He pursed his lips, pausing and trying to think of an excuse. He didn't really have one, and it made me frustrated that this was even happening at this point.

"It's just….I'm sorry Miss Davidson, I'm just struggling," he told me.

"Well, why do you keep struggling? Do you…need some extra tutoring?" I asked.

The truth was, I wouldn't mind giving Marcus a little bit of extra tutoring. He was a young man, with long, sexy dark hair, big brown eyes, and looked adorable. I wasn't going to lie, I did find him cute, in a…corruptible sort of way.

He paused, flushing in response.

"It's nothing. I'm just…a bit embarrassed," he said.

"It's okay to be embarrassed," I told him.

"Well it's more like…I keep getting distracted. But maybe a little bit of tutoring could help me too," he said.

Distracted? By what though? I looked at him, unsure of what he meant by that, but the least that I could do was try to help him out.

"Sure, I think I can help you out," I told him.

"Alright," he said with a smile on his face.

And that's how the tutoring sessions began. Marcus was a smart student, but he always seemed to struggle in our sessions. Was there something else there? I didn't know for sure. I was struggling myself to understand what else to say here, other than of course, that I wanted to be the best teacher that I was to him.

We worked together over the next couple of weeks, trying to strive for the best that we could. But Marcus just...he just kept screwing around. It was getting on my nerves.

"Alright Marcus, what the hell is going on?" I asked him after one of the tutoring sessions. I felt like the little bastard was doing this shit on purpose, but I'm not even sure anymore.

"I don't know! I just...I can't seem to get it. I feel like a fucking moron," he said.

"You should know better than this Marcus. You can't seem to get this right though, so what the hell gives?" I asked him.

He paused, flushing as he looked at me with a nervous look. There was obviously something else there. He wanted to say something, but he didn't.

So what the hell was it.

"Come on, spit it out," I snapped at him.

He looked at me, nervous as all hell, and then finally, he spoke.

"It's you," he said to me.

"What about me? I'm your professor, and I'm trying to help you get to the top of the class," I told him.

He flushed, looking me in the eyes as he mentioned this.

"I'm sorry, it's a little bit embarrassing," he admitted.

"Well, you can either spit this out and we go about our evening, or you make this awkward for both of us. Or maybe...a little bit of motivation is what you're getting at?" I teased.

"No it's just! You're really pretty," he said to me.

Gosh this guy was fun. He was nineteen, fresh and young, and I mean...I wasn't the youngest woman out there, but I did have a bit of age, and some experience.

"Well Mark, perhaps we can make a little deal," I stated to him.

He looked at me with surprise on his face.

"What do you mean?" he asked me.

This was fun to do. I wondered if he would let me tease him.

"Tell you what, why don't you...help me out with a few things. I'm going to need you as a special helper for the next few classes, and I can make you my pet. If you satisfy me enough, I guess I can of course let you get away with a passing grade in this class," I told him with a devilish smile.

He looked at me, gulping in surprise, anticipation and the like.

"Wait, you mean like....like sexually?" he said.

"That's what you want, right? I mean, I can see your cock hardening there," I said to him. I raised my hell, lightly digging it into there. He let out a small cry, not of pain, but of arousal.

"What's that? You like my foot on your pathetic dick?" I said.

"Y-yes," he said.

He was submissive. This would be a whole lot of fun.

"Alright, we can keep this our little secret. On one condition: you better not dare tell anyone else," I told him.

If he did that, we'd both be fucked.

"Or else I'll fail, right?"

"That, and so much more. I can make your life hell, if you let out a peep. If you do this for me...we can have a little bit of fun," I offered.

I knew that there was a risk here, but there was something fun about taking this young man under my wing, making him my pet, and using him for a variety of things. After a bit of a pause, he took a deep breath, flushing.

"Yeah...I'd like that," he said to me.

"Good. I see that we're on the same page then. How sweet," I told him.

I liked that he was already agreeing to this. It made the next few things that I did a whole lot of fun.

That's when this little adventure began. I set up a small little contract. I was a dominatrix on the side, and I never let clients go off without those. But there was also the fact that I didn't want this little shit to let out a peep or anything either. After he signed it, that's when the real fun began, and when we both began to have the most fun relationship ever.

When he got in early that period, I smiled.

"Alright, get under the desk," I said.

"W-what do you mean?" he said.

"I'm going to use you as my pet. You're to...satisfy me while I conduct these exams. Don't worry, I'll give it to you later, and you can pass, but you're to take care of me. If you don't make me cum, you will be punished," I said to him.

He flushed, but then nodded. He went underneath the desk, and I got the handcuffs, cuffing him underneath the desk so that he didn't escape, and no other students saw. I sat down there, looking down at him as he looked at me with those big eyes.

Fuck he was cute. I loved teasing this man like this. He then moved his hands to my thighs, which caused me to jerk in surprise at his actions.

It was fun to tease him like this. With the nervousness that he had, the way his eyes continuously glazed over me, that little look of need that he had...this was more fun for me than I cared to admit.

I wanted him to be a good little pet for me.

He looked at me with expectant eyes as I sat down, motioning for the students to grab the papers. I then smiled.

"You have fifty minutes," I said to them coldly, looking around at all of them as they stared at me in the eyes.

They started to take the exam, and I felt the hands move a little bit higher. Shortly after, he gripped my milky, soft thighs, spreading them apart. He licked them, causing me to grip the desk a little bit, shivering with delight.

Such a good pet.

I looked over at the other students, who seemed to be furiously getting started with the papers. I grabbed a book, trying to get my mind off of this, when suddenly, I felt a tongue near my entrance.

I tensed up, struggling to keep it together. I moved my hands downwards, pulling my skirt upwards. I made sure not to wear panties this go. Suddenly, I felt the tongue move against my clit, licking it slightly as I shivered, trying to hold back a moan of pleasure.

"You okay there?" one of the students asked.

I shopped ,my head around, looking at one of the women who was in the class. She had short brown hair, big blue eyes, and a bit of an awkward gait.

"Yes, sorry. Do you have a question?" I asked her.

Suddenly, I felt his tongue move closer towards my entrance, teasing me there. I had to hold back. I wasn't going to sit there and just let him have this. The girl who was there furrowed her brows.

"Well, I was wondering with this one...what if there are two answers for this?" she said.

Fuck, it was a struggle just to form words at this point. I looked at her, a hesitant glance on my face.

"Then just....try to find the one that best fits the scenario," I explained to her, cupping my lips as I tried to hold back the obvious moan that almost escaped my mouth.

"Are you sure that you're okay?" she asked.

"Yes, I'm fine," I choked out.

This little bastard was already inside, using his tongue to tease and pleasure me. He was very skillful, moving it in and out, fucking me with that appendage. I was already feeling my composure slowly come apart, but I wasn't going to sit there and let the little bastard get the best of me.

"Anyways, just choose the ones that best fit, and from there, you can continue," I told her.

She nodded, and the other students continued this. By this point, I was so close. I pushed my thighs around his face, moving my hips a little bit, trying to make sure that not a soul saw the way my body moved. Until finally, after a few more moments, I tensed up, biting my lip, feeling the pleasure of my orgasm suddenly take me.

I let out a long sigh, and a couple of the students looked up at me, trying to figure out what was going on. But I gave them a small smile, enjoying the way that they seemed so confused. It was so lewd, it was definitely not what we were expecting to have today, but I couldn't get enough of this man, and there was clearly some fun to be had.

But I didn't know whether or not I could let this continue. My mind raced, my heart skipping a beat every now and then. He continued to service me, the sensitivity of my clit suddenly the focus of his lips. He sucked and teased there, and before I knew it, I pushed my hips up, my juices flowing out, drenching his face in my release.

I continued this for the rest of the class, looking around, wondering if a damn soul knew anything about this. For a long time, it was just silence, and then, when it was all over, I finally sighed, trying my best to keep my wits about me.

After a little bit, I stood up, pushing my skirt down as I did this.

"Okay class….test is over," I said to them.

They all turned in their test, getting dangerously close to where Marcus was. He stayed quiet, even though I moved my foot up, my heel right up against his cock. He let out a small whimper, and I pushed it into his face, forcing the him to gag on the hell.

"Quiet," I whispered at him. I didn't want anyone to know about this. The class all finished up, and then, when the final person was gone, I went to the door, locking it, taking a deep breath. I went over, taking the handcuffs off of Marcus, pulling him forward.

"There you go. Good boy," I said to him.

"T-thank you teacher," he said, the way his eyes looked at me was both of that of lust, and of course of mild anxiety.

I looked down at his cock, seeing how it throbbed there. I scoffed.

"You're hard already. How pathetic," I said.

I pushed my heel up, resting it on his balls. I put a bit of pressure on there, causing the man to wince slightly.

"What's the matter? You like me squishing your pathetic cock with my heels? You want me to hit them? To use all of my force in this heel to hit them?" I said to him.

He whimpered, moaning.

"Yes, please mistress," he said.

The way he became so quiet and easy to work with was fun. I then lightly kicked them, causing him to let out both a moan, and a cry of slight pain.

"Wow, you're really just taking this so damn easily. Look at you," I pointed out, rubbing his balls and watching his eyes fall to the back of his head.

This was quite fun.

I continued to tease him, but then, I moved back, spreading my legs apart.

"Lick them," I told him.

He whimpered, looking at me as he moved down to my feet. He licked and teased them, cleaning my heels after they'd been shoved in his mouth, and after I rested them on his cock.

It was fun watching him slowly come apart like this. There was a thrill of course, in letting him lose all semblance of control like this. Enjoying the pleasure and need that grew within me as I watched him let out the cutest little series of moans and cries.

I continued this, watching with delight as he continued to finish the cleaning. When he was done, I pulled back, sighing in contentment.

"Look at you. Such a mess. Well, there is one thing that I'd like to give to you as a sort of…punishment. But maybe you'll enjoy it. Perhaps I'll reward you when we're done here," I said to him.

"W-what is it?" he asked.

I fumbled in my drawers, remembering that this was here. I grabbed three things: a bottle of lube, a toy, and the strapon that I kept in here the last couple of days. I was waiting for the right moment to use this on him, and right now, with the way he looked, how turned on and needy he was, there was something exciting about doing this to him now more than ever.

"You're going to use that on me?" he asked.

"Damn right I am. But I won't do it right away., I think I'll prepare you just a little bit before I give you my cock," I told him.

Seeing him there, all innocent and looking at me with a look of pure, unadulterated desire, it was quiet fun.

I started to pull down his pants, tossing them off the moment I got them off his body. He whimpered, and I touched his butt, rubbing it there.

"You have a nice ass. Very fuckable," I told him.

I gave it a smack, and he let out a gasp, tensing up and sighing as he continued to thrust forward. The little bastard was into this.

I smirked, enjoying this, and then, shortly afterwards, I lubed up the toy. It was pretty sizable, but of course, not so much that he wouldn't be able to take it.

I looked at his hole. It was so innocent-looking and fun to tease. I inserted the first part of the toy in there, watching him tense up, groaning in pleasure, enjoying the feeling that I gave to him. I shoved the toy a bit further into him, watching him tense up, and I enjoyed the delicious sounds of pleasure that he gave to me. I slowly pushed the rest of it into him, watching his hole take this slightly.

Even though he probably wouldn't admit it, the bastard definitely took this better than he'd ever care to admit. I pushed it fully in, watching it slowly disappear into him before waiting a moment, slowly pumping this in and out, watching with delight as he let out a small cry of pleasure, arching his hips forward?.

"Look at you, you're doing so good," I told him. He really was, much better than I thought. I didn't want to hurt him of course, but I also wanted to give him the pleasure that he desired. It was fun, that's for sure, and there was something exciting about doing this to him, making him lose all semblance of control, enjoying the pleasure of everything that was going on.

Before I knew it, I could see him taking it so easily that I knew he was ready. I pulled the toy out, hearing the groan of pleasure that echoed from his lips, and then, I slowly put the strapon onto my body, watching his eyes grow wide with delight. I pushed my hands to his hips, holding them there as I steadied myself, pressing into there.

This was fun. I stayed on the desk, letting the edge of the strapon get into him. at first, he was nervous, holding tightly and letting out a small series of groans. But then, before I knew it, io slowly pushed in deeper and deeper, watching his eyes widen and his cock start to thrust up there.

"Look at you! You're doing so damn well," I told him.

"T-thank you," he cried out.

I smiled, pushing him fully so that I was inside of him. when I was finally all the way in, I stayed like this for a bit, hearing him shiver with delight, and let out a series of moans.

"Look at you, getting fucked by your teacher like the little bitch that you are," I said to him, smacking his ass.

"Yes, please fuck this bitch," he cried out.

It was a thrill. It was fun. It was amazing watching him slowly come apart as I began to move in and out of him. at first, I took this slowly because I didn't want to hurt him in any sense. But then, I started to press in deeper and deeper, watching him tense up, the moans of excitement and need growing within him.

"Look at you. Such a fucking tease," I told him.

"Ahh," he cried out, tensing up slightly, enjoying the feeling of this. I loved seeing him all turned on and a mess, and it was then when, after a few more thrusts, I took it to the next level, pressing in deeper and deeper, enjoying the way that he lost all semblance of control here. There was a thrill to be had in this case, the fun that he would get to enjoy, and the pleasure that I could give to him.

I reached down, jerking his cock as I continued to pound his ass, and he let out a small cry. I knew he was getting close, and it was then when, after a few more thrusts, I started to hear him tense up. I grabbed his hips, plunging into him, and within moments, he shivered, crying out loud in pleasure, holding onto the desk as he came all over it.

I pulled out, sitting down and looking at him.

"Look at you. Now go clean that up," I said.

He looked at the desk and then at me, moving forward and then cleaning up the remains of his seed there. He licked it up, looking at me with a flushed face, and I smiled, watching him there, seeing the needy look in his eyes, and the rapt delight that he had.

This was so much fun, and I loved having the little pet there.

But when I saw him again, his cock was hard as a rock still. My eyes widened in shock.

"Damn, you're still hard?" I asked him.

"Y-yes," he said.

Oh this was going to be fun. I moved in between his legs, undoing a couple of buttons on my shirt, pulling my breasts out.

"Well, we can fix that. I haven't finished yet," I told him.

I wanted to go again. I placed my large, soft breasts against his shaft, moving them up and down. I spat on them to lubricate, moving them slightly, and then, as I did that, he cried out.

"Fuck," he said to me, holding onto me as I did this. I smiled, moving against him. This was fun, and I loved seeing him like this, but I knew that I needed something more, something greater.

I then moved back slightly, smiling at him as I straddled his hips, looking into his eyes as he stared at me.

"What are you—"

"Don't worry, you're going to enjoy this," I said.

I pushed him onto the desk, giving him a smile as I slowly sank into him. I watched his eyes begin to widen as I pushed all the way down, sinking there and feeling him. He held onto me, shivering with delight as he cried out, my body suddenly tensing up as I looked at him. There was an excitement that was there. It was utterly

intoxicating, making me want more and more. The anticipation of this was to die for, a delightful activity that would only make me ache for more, and make me want him too.

When I got all the way down, we looked at one another, a smile on my face as I slowly started to move up and down. He held onto me, his eyes wide with shock and pleasure.

"Holy...shit," he said to me.

"What's the matter? You enjoying this?" I said to him with a smirk, moving my hips and up and down.

He immediately groaned, holding onto me for dear life as I shook my body around, jerking my hips slightly, watching his eyes widen in surprise at the teasing that I did. This was getting kind of fun, that's for sure. With everything going on, I knew that he was enjoying this, and it gave me great delight to see him slowly losing his composure there.

For a long time, I moved my hips, feeling his cock hit me in all of the right spots. I looked down, seeing him there, completely turned on and enjoying everything that came out of this. I wasn't going to lie, he felt amazing too.

His hands moved up towards my breasts, touching them slightly, and I couldn't help but moan in response to all of this. I suddenly began to tense up as he began to press himself upwards. I angled my hips, and after a few more moments, I slowly started to feel my entire body give way, moving forward as I cried out, enjoying the sensation of this. I then came hard, feeling it all just completely decimate me, making me suddenly lose all control, the enjoyment of this driving me insane.

After a brief second, I watched him pull back, looking at me. The cum dripped out of me, and I felt like I was losing my mind. I struggled to catch my breath for a bit, but there was definitely a feeling of enticement as we looked at one another.

"You good?" I asked him.

"Yeah," he said.

I quickly got myself together, looking around. I checked outside the classroom to make sure that nobody ended up seeing us. I hoped to god that nobody did. But who knows, I sometimes didn't get lucky with this shit, that's for sure.

For a moment, neither of us said anything, both of us not sure of what to say next about any of this. I mean, I enjoyed the hell out of it, but I knew that it was definitely a taboo thing. We didn't want others to know about it.

"Wow," he said, getting his pants and shirt back on.

"Yeah, wow is right," I admitted.

I can't believe I did all of that. But I could tell that he didn't seem to mind a damn part of it. I looked over at Marcus, who was flushing crimson.

"Something the matter?" I asked him.

"Well it's just...wow," he said.

"Cat got your tongue?" I teased.

"Maybe it does. Or maybe...I just liked that a whole fuckload," he told me.

I chuckled, seeing the happiness on his face, the grin that he had.

"Well, I know that you did want me to show you what I've got, and I aim to please," I told him.

"You're right. And you do," he said.

I laughed, seeing the look of pure desire on his face. But there was that curiosity on what was next, on what he wanted next, and for a moment, we didn't say a word.

"So. I guess we should talk about what this means for both of us," I told him.

"Yeah. What does it mean?" he asked me.

"It depends. What do you want from this Marcus?" I asked him.

"I just want good grades. I don't care about much else," he said.

"So....if you want, we can continue this. I'll give you good grades if you continue to be my pet...." I offered to him. I knew that this was a bit of a different situation than what we both thought about, but I could tell that he was enjoying this.

"Are you...sure about that?" he asked.

"Course. I liked it, and I know that you did too," I replied with a smile.

And liked it was a bit of an understatement. He came twice, and there was obviously that need for more that came from this.

"Okay. well I like it. And maybe you can...teach me a few things too," he said.

"You mean like how to please a woman?" I said with a wink.

"Yeah. I'm a bit awkward, and well...I do like girls I'm just shit at talking to them. But I get along with you super well. It's strange," he said.

"Well, sometimes it's like that Marcus. But if you want....we can continue this if that's what you're into," I offered to him. I knew that this would be a risky game, and that one of us could get in big trouble at any point if it's found out.

But at the same time, I loved it. I loved the fact that he was enjoying this as much as I was, and that there was an obvious need for more that came from this too.

"Yeah, I'd like to play this...this risky game," he said.

"Good. I'd like that too," I replied.

We both nodded in agreement, a bit of a small thing that both of us knew that we wanted. There was clearly a lust that was there, a desire for more, a pleasure that we both could enjoy, and I knew that he'd like this too.

We both agreed to start seeing one another for sessions like this once a week, and perhaps more if we ended up deciding to take things like this. I had no clue what in the world would transpire next, or even how things would go. I just felt a bit of a lustful excitement that came out of this.

He was fun to tease and please, and I would be lying if I said I didn't enjoy this either. It's not every day I got to have fun with a young man like this. After we both sat down and agreed to it, we ended up leaving, and I checked the clients that I had later on that night.

There wasn't much, but it was quite fun to see that I could go from dominating one man to another man. I just liked doing this, making men feel good, and making them squirm under me.

Marcus and I agreed to continue this for as long as we wanted to. He texted me saying that he had a good time, but his butt hurt. I laughed, realizing that I did go a little bit harder on him than I meant to. I told him to go ice it, since that probably would be the best way to handle it. After the phone clicked off, I sat there, thinking about what may happen next.

What was the future of this? What would happen with my teaching career? I started to grade the papers, looking for Marcus's name. I left him a B, since he did a good job and did pass, but there was always room for improvement. I made up a fake little exam and his name. even though this was wrong, I didn't really care in a way. I was having my fun, and it's clear that he enjoyed this too.

Marcus was definitely the teacher's pet, and he was a pet that I would keep around for as long as I could, and to tease and play around with till he couldn't take any more of it.

Best friend's Secret

"Yay you made it," Charles said as I stepped in. I pulled off the hoodie that I had, revealing the black t-shirt that I wore.

"I told you I'd come," I told him.

"I know Roxy. I just really missed you," Charles said.

Charles and I had been best friends since I was very young, hell since he was very young. We were practically inseparable as kids, and so many people ended up telling us that we needed to be together. Although that didn't happen, there was always that bit of tension between the two of us, that innate desire for well...something more. And I'd be lying if I didn't think about that every so often.

But Charles was also my best friend, and he weas a renowned businessman. He apparently had a girlfriend too, but I haven't seen her.

"Where's Debbie at?" I asked him.

Charles face froze. He looked around, and then at me. Obviously, there was something wrong.

"It's nothing. Sorry," he said.

"Come on man, you can't just act like that and expect me not to ask," I admitted to him.

I was worried. Debit and him seemed like such a power couple, that it made me almost a bit jealous. He was doing so well, but obviously, something was amiss.

He patted the seat, rushing over and grabbing a couple of glasses of wine, uncorking them and then bringing them over, filling up the glasses.

"I'm sorry Roxy. It's complicated with Debbie," he said.

"Did you two break up?" I asked him.

"Yeah. Sorry, I wanted to tell you in person. Yeah, we're not together anymore. For kind of a really dumb reason," he said to me.

What could possibly be so stupid that they'd break up? I always thought that Charles was the type of guy who never had petty breakups. I was almost a little bit jealous of him. but then, he sighed, taking a sip from his wine.

"Want to know what happened?" he asked.

"Yeah, hit me with it."

He paused, trying to figure out what else to say, and then he sighed.

"It's stupid. But we ended up fighting over kinks. We got upset with one another, and then...Debbie just left," he explained.

"Shit dude, I'm sorry. Wait…kinks? Like things you like to do in the bedroom? That's kind of a dumb thing to fight over. I always thought you were kind of vanilla too," I admitted to him.

Charles was cute, but I did think he had the vanilla tone to him. but he shook his head.

"You've got it wrong Roxy. I actually have wanted to explore kink with someone. I brought it up to Debbie, and instead of being supportive, she well…shamed me for what I liked. We had a heated argument, and I ended up telling her that if she can't accept me for who I am, then we can't do this. And then she just…left. Like that," he explained to me.

My heart sank as I heard that. I mean, it seems so petty to break up over that. It's weird though, since he was my best friend and all, that he didn't tell me about this.

Maybe it was because he was embarrassed by it.

It was kind of cute watching him awkwardly try to talk about whatever it was that he was beating around the bush about. Until finally, I spoke.

"Well what are you thinking about int terms of kink?" I asked him.

I'm not going to lie, I've thought about it too. I just haven't found someone that I trust enough to engage in that with. Maybe…this is a sign somehow.

He paused, looking at me and taking a deep breath.

"BDSM mostly. And well…I want to try impact play too," he said.

"Impact play you say?" I said to him.

Charles was my best friend, and he was pretty cute. He was tall, muscular, had a cute head of brown hair, hazel eyes, and a little bit of stubble on his chin. I'd be lying if I said I didn't have a crush on him.

"Yeah I just…want to try this with someone, and of course….let them experience it. But I know that it's a lot to ask for, and I thought that she'd be okay with it. But I guess he just wanted to keep everything vanilla for the most part," he said.

I felt bad that it happened to Charles. I mean, I could see the nervousness in asking, that's for sure. That's when I took a deep breath.

"I'm willing to try if you are," I told him.

He looked at me, confusion on his face.

"Wait, you mean—"

"Yeah. BDSM. I want to try it. Because well…maybe we both can learn something. I always have. and we can stay friends afterwards. I figured this may be something that may work better because we're so close," I told him.

We still were close friends. Maybe he didn't tell me about Debbie because he was worried about what I'd say. But then, he took a deep breath.

"Are you…sure about that? I don't want to make you uncomfortable," he said.

"Nah, you won't do any of that. You're pretty chill, and I know that deep down, you mean well," I told him.

He looked at me, flushing crimson.

"Yeah. Say, there is something I've wanted to tell you for a long time Roxy. You're my best friend, and someone that I know I can trust on and…I really do appreciate that," he said.

I blushed.

"Yeah. Same here. We've been best friends through thick and thin together. It's only natural," I said.

My heart skipped a beat. Charles was so cool, so chill, and we got along great. But now that we were together like this…I started to feel something more. Something deeper. And that's when I felt it.

He moved closer, his lips right over the edge of my own. He then pressed them there, sharing a kiss with me. For a second, I was a little bit nervous, but then, I relaxed, realizing that he weas a pretty damn good kisser. We stayed like this for a bit, until he pulled away, and then, he spoke.

"Sorry. Maybe that was too forward," he said.

"No you're good. If you were moving too fast, I would've told you," I said.

And I meant it. Charles was pretty cool about that sort of thing.

"So you're willing to…to try it?" he asked.

I was thinking about that. I mean, it would be just as friends, and obviously, the two of us were pretty damn close, so if there was something bad about this, we'd be able to stop it in its tracks.

"Yeah, but I think we do need a safe word," I told him.

"How about "Watermelon'," he said.

That would work. It wasn't my favorite fruit, nor did I hate it.

"Yeah, that works," I said.

"Yeah, if you say that, we stop. And I promise that I will," he told me.

"I know that you will. But thanks," I told him.

"Yeah I uh…bought a few things, and I wanted to try them, but I was a little nervous. When I brought it up to her, she completely shamed me for this, and she told me never to bring this up again," he said.

"Damn, I didn't expect Debbie to be such a bitch," I told him.

"Yeah, I was wrong about her too. But, there's not much we can do," he said.

There was a little bit of disappointment in his voice, but I didn't care. I did feel that connection, that growing desire, that need of course, for something more.

We went over to the bedroom, which looked barren now that Debbie was gone.

"Damn she moved everything out too," I said.

"Yeah, it fucking sucks," he said.

"Well, I guess I can take off my clothes then," I said jokingly.

I pulled off my shirt and pants, revealing the black bra and panties that I wore. I shook my jet-black hair, looking at him with green eyes and a smile that showed contentment and trust.

132

"Don't worry, I'm not going to act the same as her," I told him. it was weird to insist something like this, but he smiled warmly.

"Thank you. I do appreciate that," he said.

"Not a problem. You know that I'm here for you dude," I told him.

I was there for him, even though I knew that it was awkward for the two of us. He then moved over, grabbing the cuffs and blindfold.

"This was the first thing that I wanted to try," he said.

"Okay," I said.

He moved to my face, putting the blindfold over my eyes. This was the legit stuff.

"What don't you like?" he asked me.

"Anything too painful that draws blood really. I wouldn't mind trying things though," I said to him.

"Alright," he said.

I felt the excitement from this as he then put cuffs on my hands. we decided not on a gag for the first go, mostly because we were a bit nervous about all of this. Then, when he was done, he cuffed me to the bed, making me gasp.

"You good?" he asked.

"Yeah. Really good," I said.

I'd be lying if I said I didn't think that this was hot as hell. I liked the idea of being tied up, of losing all control, of feeling the excitement from this. His hands moved towards me, touching my sides, trailing them downwards towards my hips. I moved them upwards, letting out a small breath of surprise as I felt them there.

"You have an amazing body Roxy," he said.

"Thanks," I whimpered, feeling his hands over my thighs. He then moved his lips to my neck, lightly peppering kisses there. The touch felt a lot stronger than I expected, and soon, I moved my hips upwards, tensing up, enjoying the feeling of his soft, sensual kisses against my body, teasing, making me relish in pleasure, and enjoying it.

I shivered as I felt the touches slowly descend down my body, caressing every single part of me. I could feel my toes curling as his tongue and lips teased me.

"There you go. Good girl," he said.

"Ahh," I said, feeling the tension, the need, and the desire grow.

His hands hovered right over my breasts, giving them small, sensual touches. There was a heated desire within me, and then, his hands moved towards the back of my bra, undoing the clasp and moving the garment off of my body. It was a strapless bra, so easy to take off. But then, I felt the little touches descend downwards, touching right up against the edge of my nipples, little kisses and licks there.

Maybe it was because of the blindfold, but it felt like all touches were increased by manifold. There was something thrilling about this, something that I enjoyed, and something that I wanted. He continued to tease, pleasuring my body, enjoying the sounds that I ended up bestowing to him. He looked me in the eyes, smiling.

"There you go. You like this, don't you?" he said.

"Y-yes," I breathed out. He turned me into something that I thought I'd never become. A woman desperate for the touch.

His hands continued to touch my body, moving right up against my nipples, his fingers brushing against there, pinching the tips of it, making me shiver and cry out with pleasure and lust. He continued the touches, watching me tense up, moaning in pleasure as he did this. Every single touch, every single motion, it was all driving me slowly but surely to the point of madness, making me feel turned on, excited by this, enjoying the feeling of it all, wanting more from this man as he continued to touch, teasing every corner of my body.

I wanted him to pull on them, to make me feel both pain and pleasure. That's when he stopped.

Can I try something else? Clamps?" he asked me.

I flushed, realizing what he meant by that. I quickly nodded.

"Yeah," I told him.

"Alright," he told me. He soon moved his body over to somewhere, and then, I felt something tug on my nipples, holding them there. The pinching made me shiver, crying out loud in pleasure and desire. It hurt a little bit, but I also loved this, and I ached for more from him. He continued to tease them slightly, until I felt something else clamp down on me.

It was for my clit. He held the clamp there, securing it, and I shivered, moaning slightly in surprise at the action that he did. He let out a chuckle as he tugged on them slowly.

I cried out, feeling both pain and pleasure from this. It did hurt sure, but there was something about this which made me feel aroused, which made me excited, and in a strange way, I wanted more. There was that hunger there, that need within, that desire that made me get turned on and enjoyed every single aspect of this. There was that excitement which only made me ache for more.

After a bit, he then tugged on them harder, and I let out a garbled sound, enjoying the sensation of this. For a long time, I felt like I was at the mercy of this man, enjoying everything about this, and I knew that he liked it too. He continued this for a little bit, teasing me, watching me become a puddle of goo and pleasure in front of him. it was then when he pulled them off, and then, he moved to get something. I heard the sound of something being lit, and that's when I wanted to squirm.

Candles. He knew I was into wax play and temperature play.

"You're sure you're okay with wax play?" he said.

"Yes master," I breathed out, turned on by the words that came out of my mouth.

He chuckled.

"Damn, already calling me master. How cute," he said.

I let out a small cry as he continued to move towards me, and I could sense the wax dripping there precariously. I braced myself for this, enjoying the sensation of it all. He then dripped it down, causing me to tense up and moan in pleasure. I could feel the desire roving through my body, making me shiver with delight, enjoying the feeling of this. He then dripped it over the edge of my breast, causing me to shiver with delight.

It was a little bit warm, but not as bad as I expected it to be. I knew the candles burned a little bit lower in temperature. Probably because they didn't want you to burn the skin. He then dripped it there too, the dots forming something along my chest. There was something so arousing about being left out of control like this, feeling him just drip this down there, turning me on, causing me to tense up and shiver in pleasure.

"Fuck," I said, feeling it right over the edge of my nipple. It didn't go there directly, but there was that feeling of pleasure and desire that caused me to lose control at this point, making me tense up, causing an aching feeling in my body as I started to feel him drop it there again and again.

It was such a turnon. There was so much that made me feel very nervous, but this just...it just felt so damn good. It was amazing to feel, and I definitely liked the feeling of this too.

He continued to drop this down, piece by piece, until the wax was gone. I could feel it hardening slightly, but it wasn't an uncomfortable sensation.

"I made a cute design. Hopefully it stays," he said to me.

"Yeah," I replied.

There was a long pause, and then, I turned to him.

"If you want to try...impact play, you're free to," I told him.

"You're sure?"

"Yes. I want this. And if it becomes too much, I'll let you know," I said.

I had the safe word, but I didn't want to resort to that. I wanted to know what it would be like to be at the mercy of this man, unable to move out of the handcuffs, and unable of course, to see anything.

He flipped me around onto my back, pulling my hips upwards so my bottom was up in the air. He rubbed the edges of this, touching them slightly.

"Look at you, already arching and ready," he said to me.

"Yes," I breathed, turned on by the feeling of this.

He smirked, touching the edges of my ass. I let out a small cry of pleasure as I felt his hands right then and there.

"Look at you, all ready and willing," he said.

"I-I am," I said.

He then moved his hands away, and I sat there waiting for him. There was a long pause, and I wondered if he left for a moment. But then he came back, and when I felt the slap of his hand against my backside, I let out a small, choked sound of pleasure as I felt him hit me hard there. I suddenly tensed up, enjoying the feeling of this as he pushed his hand there, smacking me hard.

"There you are. Good girl. Look at you, enjoying all of this. You're so turned on, so needy. There's just something so damn hot about that," he said to me.

"Ahh! Yes," I said out loud, feeling him touch that spot again, smacking it hard. I shivered with delight, enjoying the feeling of this, loving the way that he just took me and used me like this.

He continued to spank me, and he did so very hard. It surprised me at how hard he was with this, but I didn't care. I liked the feeling of this too, and there was a thrill that came around with this, that need, that desire, and that lust for more as he did this.

He continued to spank me hard, and after a few more moments, he stopped moving himself away. I squirmed, shivering with delight as I wondered what he had planned next for me. I didn't know what he would really bring to the table with the impact play, but then I felt something a bit blunter, but covering a wider area touch the tips of my thighs and ass.

"This is a paddle. I want to see you turn red," he said.

"Yes…I want that too," I said.

He then raised it, smacking my ass hard with it. The indentations of this felt so damn different, and I let out a small cry of surprise as I felt this. He then smacked me again and again, each touch making me scream out a garbled cry of pleasure, my eyes tearing up at the pleasure and pain of the moment. He then smacked me again and again, hitting all parts of my ass with the paddle, making me cry out with pleasure and delight as he continued to touch me, tease me, making me lose all semblance of control as he continued this.

He then moved back, and I shivered with delight. Then, before I knew it, he had something else against my ass. It was a riding crop this time.

This one was small, but it would hit harder than the other paddle. I could feel him massaging every part of me, making me shiver and feel turned on. I felt the crop touch the very top of my pussy, rubbing my clit. I leaned into the touch, breathing out and moaning. He paddled that lightly, but that touch alone was enough to make me feel stimulation, to make me enjoy this and adore everything about this.

"Fuck," I cried out, feeling him press against there, hitting against there harder and harder, loving the feeling of this, enjoying the touch and teasing of it all.

He then moved back to my ass, massaging the area, but then, he moved away. I let out a small cry of need, feeling my hips move slightly, and that's when I felt it.

The crop made direct contact with my ass, making me shiver with delight, crying out in pleasure, feeling the aching moan and scream from this. They then hit me again and again, little Marks being made on my body, causing me to suddenly tense up, moaning out loud and in pleasure. I could feel them smiling at me without even seeing it. He enjoyed seeing me become a mess like this, and I loved being his mess.

I felt happy that I could give him this kind of control,, and there was a feeling of satisfaction as he smacked me again and again, harder and harder. He was careful around the other parts of my body, but I could feel the bruises and welts begin to form, and I loved it.

"Fuck!" I cried out, feeling him hit me hard. This was amazing, and my pussy was soaking wet at the sensations that I felt. I never knew how good this was.

But then, as quickly as it happened, he stopped, grabbing the final time. I thought it was a flogger. As I felt it hit my back, I shivered, crying out loud, enjoying the feeling of this. He continued to hit me, smacking me again and again, making me shiver, tense up, crying out loud and enjoying everything about this. He then smacked me all over, hitting every part of me, and I loved it. It was so good, the combination of both pain and pleasure turning me on.

When I felt it against my backside, lightly grazing my clit, I let out a small cry, tensing up, and that's when it hit me.

I didn't know that you could orgasm from this, but here we were, and I sat there, completely turned on, a total mess, and then, he pulled back, smiling at my body as I laid there.

"You good?" he said to me.

"Yes master but…"

He then let out a small grunt, and I felt the heat in my body rise. I know that this was supposed to be just the two of us experimenting, but I wanted something more. There was that desire for this, even though I wasn't sure what he thought about this.

"What is it?" he asked me.

"Well…I know this might be asking much but…I want you. Inside me master," I told him. I didn't know that I could say this. Perhaps it was the desire for him that had been sitting there for a long time.

"You sure?"

"Yes," I breathed out, the sound of need and desire in my voice making me feel like I would lose it if I didn't have him in there soon.

"Alright," he finally said after a brief moment. He then moved towards the drawer. I assume to get a condom, which was fine. He then spread me apart, slipping himself into there, and to my surprise…he was much bigger than I expected.

We never had this kind of relationship until now, but when I felt his cock all the way inside of me, filling me up, I suddenly felt turned on, enjoying the feeling of all of this. I felt like…everything was slowly starting to grow blank. I loved the feeling of pleasure that he provided to me, but then, when he got even deeper, I suddenly lost it.

He pushed all the way in, filling me up, making me shiver with delight, suddenly shocked by the feeling of all of this. He then pressed in, then moving out, and he soon moved in and out of me, causing me to slowly but surely lose all semblance of control, enjoying the sensation of everything that was to come. He continued to thrust in hard, feeling me tense up underneath him, and I could feel his hands against my ass.

"Look at you, so turned on for me. You feel amazing too," he said.

"Yes," I said, feeling the rush in my body.

I knew I was close again, and judging from the thrusts and how fast he was going, he was quite close too. And I loved that about him. There was that aching desire, that need for him, and that growing urge for more from this man. It was then when, after a few more thrusts, he reached down between my legs, whispering in my ear.

"I'm about to cum," he said.

"Then cum for me master. Cum in me!" I cried out.

He pushed in, letting out a small groan as he pressed deep, holding me there as he spilled his seed, the warm liquid within me. I shivered, feeling the heat that was there as I stayed there, looking forward. It was all blank still, and I felt a whole wave of pleasure too as it overtook me, causing me to enjoy everything about this.

For a long time, he simply held onto me, and we stayed like this, but then, he pulled back, grabbing the blindfold off of me, and helping me with the handcuffs. When it was all off, I sat there, looking around, my eyes slowly adjusting to the light once again.

"Damn," I told him.

"You okay?" he asked me.

"Yeah. Amazing actually," I told him.

This was definitely the best that I've felt in a long time, and I wasn't going to lie about that one.

"You sure? I didn't want to hurt you or anything, did I?" he asked me.

"No I'm fine," I told him.

He looked at me with a smile on his face.

"Good. I didn't want to hurt you on accident," he said.

"Nah, you have to do more than that to hurt me," I said with a chuckle.

"Well, I don't want to hurt you on accident. But that was a lot of fun," he said.

"Yeah," I replied.

I got up, wincing slightly. I looked down, seeing the welts and bruises forming on my butt.

"We should probably get some cream on those," he said.

"Yeah," I replied.

He brought some antibiotic cream, rubbing it in. it stung slightly, but also I enjoyed the feeling of his hands there. He continued to touch me, rubbing it in fully.

"There we go," he said.

I pulled back, looking into his eyes with surprise.

"Thank you. But...did you enjoy doing it? I know that this was to explore your kink, but I wanted to make sure this was what you wanted too," I said to him.

He nodded.

"I really did. I had a wonderful time," he told me.

I smiled, feeling relieved by that.

"Same here. Honestly...if you want to do it again, I'd be all great with that," I told him. The truth was, I enjoyed him, and the feelings that I had for him were real.

"Are you...sure about that? I don't want to hurt you," he said to me.

"Nah, you're not hurting me. In fact, I enjoyed this," I told him.

He sighed, happiness on his face.

"Okay good. I was a bit worried, but I can see it in your eyes. You're an amazing woman Roxy, and well,, maybe I did have a crush on you," he told me.

"Yeah, I did too. Maybe we can see where this will end up," I told him.

"Maybe we can," he replied.

We looked at one another, seeing the sparkle in one another's eyes. It was weird, what I thought would just be a normal meeting between friends turned into something...much much more. When we kissed, I felt a shiver in my body, the sparkle that I saw in his eyes. There was that feeling of excitement and desire that only made me ache for him more and more. With every single look, every single touch, I felt like my whole body was ignited, a desire that only grew even more so as time went on.

"Yeah, I wouldn't mind that. Of course, as long as you're cool with this," he said to me.

"I'd love it," I told him.

We looked into one another's eyes, giving a kiss once again. It was long, passionate, and something that I thoroughly enjoyed. As we stayed there, making out with one another, it felt like we were both impassioned there. It was the moment I'd been waiting for.

We spent the rest of the night kissing, talking to one another about what we liked and didn't like, and everything in between. There was that feeling of desire, that excitement which only made me ache for more, and that need too. We stayed like this for a long time, and then, later on that night we stayed over.

"I didn't expect things to work out like this," Charles admitted. I didn't think that this would work either, but here we are.

"Well, sometimes the unexpected happens," I told him.

"You're damn right, and you're an unexpected surprise that I can't get enough," he admitted to me.

I smiled, feeling the excitement and growth between us start to become more obvious. There was that feeling that made me smile, that excitement that made me feel good. We stayed together, both of us enjoying one another, and the feeling of the future strong for both of us.

Charles told me his secret, and I'd be lying if I didn't feel the same way. He was really good wat what he did though, and there was definitely a heated desire for more as well. A part of me wondered what may happen next, or even what we may get into, but I guess that's another play session to look forward to, and something that we could enjoy down the road, together as we explored one another's bodies, and the secrets that we had.

Pleasing the Donors

This was it.

I clutched the papers, realizing that I'd be meeting with some of the biggest donors to my campaign. I knew that it could reflect great or terribly on me, I just wanted to hope for the best. I had the plan all set out in place.

If the donors agreed to this, it would put my product on the map. I had the plan, just needed the financial assistance, and coming to this exposition with everything in place excited me.

I showed a couple of them earlier when they walked by the booth. But this would be a roundtable of all five of the biggest investors in kitchen and baking products. And I hoped that I'd stand out.

This was my dream. To be supported by one of these guys, and to make it work. That's what made me excited about this. I could change my whole goddamn life around just by making a couple of small changes, and I hoped that they'd understand, and feel the same way. I took a deep breath, making sure I had everything in place.

"Okay Mindy, you can do this," I said to myself.

I wanted to make this work. I wanted nothing more than for this to just go swimmingly.? I then opened the door, looking at the round table.

Five of the biggest investors all in one place. What I didn't realize was they were all young and attractive. The one at the center was the top-ranking CEO of one of the biggest appliance manufacturers, a guy named AJ. To his right was a man named Adam, who was a bit intimidating, but he gave me a small smile as I walked on in. next to him was Landon, who was one of the newer investors, but had a sizable income from his own investments in a variety of different companies.

To the right of AJ sat George, who was one of the older ones, but still he was barely over 40, and he looked like he was still in his 20s. his silvery-gray hair looked nice, and I couldn't help but feel my lips salivate at the sight of him.

Then finally, there was Craig. Craig was a bit controversial with long, black hair with blue streaks in it, a couple of piercings, and he tended to wear something different from the normal attire of business suits that these five usually had. They all looked at me as I gave them all a weak smile, feeling my heart skip a beat.

Don't fuck this one up Mindy.

"Hey there. I'm here to show off my product. I think it was craig and Adam who saw it on the showroom floor, but I wanted to show everyone," I explained to them.

"Yes, I'd love to see it," AJ said with a smile.

"Yes, me too," George said with a nod.

Landon also nodded. Adam and Craig both sat there, looking at me with a curious glance as I tried to get myself together.

To say I was nervous was a goddamn understatement. I didn't want to fuck this one up. Not now. Not after all that I've worked towards. But I took a deep breath, steeling myself as I got together for what would happen next.

:Alright so first of all this is the bake chop. It's a way to chop up cakes and other slices into pieces while it is baking. That way, it saves the time of cutting it up. It's a precise instrument, and it can do up to 16 servings! You just need to tell it what to do and all," I said, feeling my lips grow dry at the way they looked at me.

None of them showed any obvious emotions yet, which made me nervous. I had no fucking clue what would happen. I mean, they were all attractive men, and me, just some brown-haired mousey inventor, felt like I was out of my league with everyone there. But I had to keep my shit together. R that was the only thing that I knew how to do effectively, and easily.

But I didn't know what else would happen to me next. I wanted things to be different, to go well, but I had no clue what would happen next to me.

"So show me," George said.

"Yeah I'd love to see a demonstration," AJ said.

"Right uh…here's a cake. Let's put it in," I said.

I got the cake out, feeling all of their eyes on me. I put it in the machine, and then placed it in the oven. A few minutes later I pressed the button, and then, it cut up the cakes. I pulled it out, giving it to them.

"As you can see, the product does work. This also ties into the smart spatula I have. it will help determine the temperature of some of the items that you have in order to give the most perfect result. That way you're not overcooking any of your foods and know when to turn it," I explained to them.

"very interesting," Adam said, nodding in response.

"Yes, quite the inventions you've got there Mindy," AJ said.

"Thanks, I try," I replied with a smile.

I showed off both of these, and they all looked at me with interest in their eyes.

This may be it. This may be the moment I'd been looking for.

"So yeah, that's my product. As you can see, it's the product of a lot of hours and work, and I'm trying my best to make sure it's right for everyone and all," I said.

"I see. Impressive. I think we've made our decision though," I heard AJ say to me.

I paused, surprised that they made such a decision right away. I thought they'd listen to other people, and then determine whether they would put their funding into one or another.

"What do you mean? I thought you guys had a lot of people to go through," I asked them.

"Well while we liked it, we didn't think this was suffice to win us over. We're sorry, but we can't accept this," AJ said.

George, Adam, Landon, and Craig all didn't say a damn thing. I looked at them with shock in my eyes, and abject fear at what may happen now.

Could this really be the end? I didn't want it to be. I wanted things to work itself out, but I felt like I just blew the one chance I had for things to go swimmingly.

So I sat there, trying to figure out what to tell them. But I had nothing. There was nothing left for me to say.

I was at a loss.

"Are you sure you won't listen?" I asked.

"You heard AJ. I'm sorry hun, but we don't see a financial opportunity in this one," he said with a bit of an annoyed tone, like he didn't want me here period.

I felt ashamed, unsure of what to say to them, and in truth, I wanted to just cry.

But I kept my face a bit stoic. That's the only thing that you could do in times like this.

I needed to think of something, anything that could work for me. and that's when I thought about it.

It was a stretch, but they were all guys. So maybe I could possibly use this to my advantage.

I started loosening my shirt, pulling the tie and the top button that I had off, exposing the ample cleavage that I had. That was one of the plus points that I had. I had nice cleavage, and good boobs, and I think that...there was a chance that this could work to my advantage.

At least that's what I wanted to hope.

I started to move my hips slightly, a smile on my face as I looked at them.

"Well perhaps we could...make an arrangement," I said.

I noticed AJ's eyes look downwards at me.

"You're serious," he said.

"Damn well I am," I said.

He looked me over, trying to figure out what he wanted to do. Would he fall for this, hook line and sinker? Or was I biting off more than I could chew.

Finally, he sighed.

"Well, let's take a vote. If the guys want to do this, then I suppose we can arrange something. If not, you'll leave and never come back," he snapped.

He was serious. I looked at him, nodding.

"Alright. Take your vote," I told them.

They started to raise their hands, each of them except for George agreeing to this. I didn't expect it to be this easy, but here I was, watching the fate of my business start to fall forward in the hands of all of these men.

"You guys are serious...right?" I asked him.

"We're making an exception for you. Don't think we'll agree to just anything," he said to me.

I knew they wouldn't just agree to anything. They were obviously going to need me to pay the fuck up, and I hated that I was putting my fate in this.

But also...I knew that this would be the beginning of the future for me, and if I could get their agreement on this...then everything would work out.

And I wanted things to work itself out.

I then moved myself so that I was on the desk, pulling the buttons of my shirt downwards.

"Then you can have me. in exchange, you fund all of the research and the products that I have," I said.

AJ looked me over, nodding.

"Very well. You heard her guys. This one is putting all of her fate in all of us," he said with a smile.

AJ looked at me, and I could sense that he had some big ass plans for me. was this really the smartest decision? I didn't even know anymore or even what I should say. I started to watch him move his hands downwards, grabbing the buttons on my shirt, pulling them off with a forceful hand.

[I heard the rip of one of them, and I mentally hoped that it was one of the less obvious buttons, but the shirt was practically thrown off my body. A pair of hands moved towards my breasts, touching them there.

I looked up, seeing that it was Landon. He looked at my breasts, and then at me.

"I'm sorry but...I haven't gotten off in a long time and you look too good to resist," he said.

I smiled.

"Well I'm offering this. You remember our little deal," I told them.

They guys all started to let their hands wander against my body. A couple moved towards my breasts, a couple moved towards my pussy, cupping the heat there, and another moved towards my ass, grabbing it. I didn't expect this much attention.

The one who seemed to be the least into this was George, but a part of me wondered if he was just playing the part. Maybe he liked this a lot, and he didn't want to deal with any of this shit.

But then I felt AJ move himself so that he was right over my body, my hands splayed out. He looked into my eyes, a look of pure, raw need on his face.

"There we are," he told me.

"Yeah," I said.

He moved his hands towards my breasts, touching the very tips of thumb, cupping the edges of my breasts. He teased them from outside of the contents of my bra, the large mounds shaking slightly like jello. I flushed, moaning slightly at the way that this felt, at the pleasure that I was feeling.

I then felt another pair of hands move towards the back of my bra. It had to be George. He undid it with finesse, letting the garment tumble down, revealing my large, aching mounds. I flushed, looking at him as he grabbed the orbs, touching them there.

"Look at you," he said, smiling at me. He teased the tips of my nipples while lightly licking my neck. I let out a small moan, feeling my body react almost immediately to the sensation of this. That isn't to say that I was going to make a fuss. His hands were a bit rougher, and I winced slightly as I looked over at the other guys.

I then noticed AJ move towards the tip of my other nipple, pressing there with his fingers, rubbing it slowly, surely, and enough to make me shiver and cry out, enjoying the sensation of this. I knew that he was enjoying the sounds I made, and my body grew hot from the touch of his hands alone.

It felt good, and I could feel my entire body melting to the pleasure of the flesh, the excitement and need that this brought to me.

There was that need for more, that craving for more, and that desire to just...lose all semblance of control and give it all up.

I began to feel his lips suck on one of my nipples. Then, I felt Landon move to the other one, lightly peppering kisses there, touching the very edge of it with his lips before letting his tongue snake out, touching, teasing, playing with that there. I felt the heat rise through my body, starting to flood on through, causing a feeling of desire to envelope through every fiber of my being, making me enjoy the feeling of this too.

They continued to tease me, while I felt a hand down there, cupping the heat of my body. I shivered, moaning out loud as I felt that area get rubbed and rubbed once again. I felt everything just slowly melt, the pleasure and excitement of the moment driving me slowly to the precipice of madness. I wanted more, I craved more, and I knew that, no matter what happened next, they'd all make me feel good.

I believe it was Adam's hand that was against there, teasing me while the other hands were all over, teasing every part of my body. Craig moved towards my neck, licking and nibbling on the flesh there, causing me to let out a small breathing sigh of relief, the pleasure of the moment, the excitement of what was going on, all of this making me feel desire that I wasn't expecting to enjoy and feel either.

I loved this, and I knew that they all wouldn't get enough. Adam continued to rub me, touching the outside while his tongue moved towards the tip of my clit, rubbing against there making me shiver with delight and man out loud, and with a roaming pleasure that I only could fathom that would exist.

They continued this for a long time, until I felt AJ pull back, looking at all of them, and then at me, a devilish smile on his face.

"Enough with this foreplay bullshit. I need to fuck you," he said.

The way he said those words made me shiver with delight. I wanted him to fuck me too. There was a riveting feeling that started to flow through me as I heard those words. He soon moved his hands downwards, undoing the skirt that I had, practically forcing it off of my body. I felt a bit on edge as his hands got slowly closer and closer to the edge of my pussy. I could feel the heat there, making me suddenly tense up, enjoying the sensation of this, and the need that grew with me.

I could feel his hands against my entrance, two fingers inside, and I suddenly felt my whole body tense up, the ache, the need the excitement and desire making me shiver with delight, start to drool and feel my hips buck.

His fingers slowly made their way inside, slightly teasing the very edges of this, making me shiver and moan, the need for more growing in me. His fingers were soft surprisingly, and when I felt them move upwards in that "Come hither" motion, I suddenly felt like I was losing all semblance of control, the need and desire only becoming more and more obvious with time.

His touches were enough to drive me crazy, and they were already making me shiver and melt as I could feel him touching every perfect place. I knew he enjoyed this as much as I did, and I soon noticed his hands move a bit upwards, also touching the tip of my clit too, rubbing there.

Even though this man was a hardy businessman he knew how to please a woman. just the touch of this alone was enough to make me feel all parts of myself start to stutter, and my whole body crave the touch of this man even more.

While he did that though, I felt something against the tip of my mouth. I looked over, and it was craig's cock. It was big, throbbing, and it looked ready for me. I opened my mouth willingly, feeling his cock slide down my throat.

"Shit your mouth feels good," he said.

I felt two cocks fall into each of my hands. upon further inspection it was Landon and Adam, who seemed adamant for something, whatever it might be. My body reacted with excitement to the idea of being able to service all of these cocks. Even though this was not what I normally did, I enjoyed being taken like this, enjoying the pleasures of the moment, and the excitement of the feelings that I felt as time started to go on.

I felt them all tease me, take me, pleasure me. I didn't have any way to really do much besides service all of these cocks. AJ continued to pump, before he spread me apart. He let out a small little grunt of excitement.

"God you look so good. I think it's time for the main event," he said.

I let out a small groan, feeling the heavy excitement of everything hit me like this. I noticed he was undoing his pants, pulling them off along with the belt to reveal the obvious erection in his pants. I looked at his cock for a brief moment before craig pushed his cock further down my throat, and I soon let out a small grunt of excitement.

I wanted this, and I knew that he wanted them too.

He quickly pushed himself in, and I let out a small scream as he filled me up. He was a lot bigger than I imagined, and I knew that I couldn't really say much with the cocks in my mouth and hands, but before I knew it, I felt him start to thrust a little bit faster.

A cock moved underneath my armpit, and I looked over, seeing that it was George who had it there. I didn't expect this, but the sliding sensation made him groan, and while I did focus on it for a bit, suddenly, I started to lose control, the excitement the pleasure and the feeling of it all was driving me crazy.

I knew that I couldn't get enough of this. They were all making me feel amazing, and there was clearly an excitement and need that came from all of this, which made me feel that desire for more.

AJ pulled my legs, spreading me apart, thrusting into me faster and harder. I loved the way it felt. He seemed to know exactly where to pleasure me. his thrusts were hitting all of the right areas, and I felt that hunger, that need, that desire for so much more start to hit me. he soon pushed all the way in, letting out a grunt.

That's when I felt it. His white seed enter into me, filling me up. He pulled out, the trail of cum start to escape my pussy.

"There we go. That was pretty good. Well boys, you can have the rest," he said.

That was surprising. I didn't expect AJ to just nut and go. But then I felt a pair of hands start to moved me, spinning me around so that I was on my hands and knees. Craig still had his cock in my mouth, and I wasn't going to give that up anytime soon, but then he pressed it in deeper, groaning.

"Holy fuck," he said, looking into my eyes. I felt the cock fall all the way down my throat, his balls right up against the edge of my lips. But I took it all readily, enjoying the pleasure the feelings that came out of this, and everything in between.

As he did this, I looked over at Landon, who was a bit nervous about this.

"There we go," Craig said. He looked up at Landon and then down at me.

"You know you can fuck her you know," he said.

Landon quickly nodded, moving so that his cock was right at my entrance. He slid himself all the way in, filling me up completely, and suddenly, I let out a low, guttural scream. I loved the way that this felt, the pleasure that came out of this, the excitement of the moment, it was all just...so perfect and I couldn't get enough of this. He

continued to thrust in deep, enjoying the little whimpers and sounds that came out of this. Landon grabbed my hips, thrusting in deeper and deeper, making me cry out slightly.

"Look at her, she's taking all of this like a champ," Landon said.

"Yeah. She's great at sucking cock too," I heard Craig say.

I let out a series of small grunts, and then I looked up, seeing George there, his cock out, jerking it tot sight of my naked body as it got pleasured by both of them.

"God you're so hot. I'm sure that AJ was making the right decision with you," he said with a grunt.

I shivered, realizing that AJ was the one in charge of this. But I liked it, and I knew that they did too.

Landon pressed himself in, arching his hips and pressing upwards. I started to let out a small cry, enjoying the feeling of this, and I soon began to hold onto the desk, letting out cries as Craig fucked my mouth raw.

After a couple of moments, he tensed up, and I felt a little bit of his cum spray into my mouth. But then he pulled outwards, jerking off and letting the cum spit into my face.

I let out a small cough, but then I cried out as Landon held me, thrusting upwards hard, cumming deep inside of me. it felt amazing, and with the little hand against my clit, rubbing it, I lost all control.

I cried out, enjoying the feeling of this, my own orgasm overtaking me. it was all so damn perfect, so amazing, and I knew that there was only so much I could do at this point.

He finished up, pulling away, and I soon sighed. I enjoyed the feeling, but there was that sensation, that desire for more. And as I looked over at Adam and George, who were the last two, I felt an excitement and need grow within me.

"please. More," I told them.

I soon felt Adam flip me over, spreading me apart. I expected him to push himself into my pussy, but a finger moved downwards, teasing the edge of my pucker making me shiver with delight, and I cried out, enjoying the feeling of this.

"Holy…shit," I told him.

"You like that?" he asked.

"Yes. It's amazing," I told him.

He let out a chuckle as he started to tease the tip of my pucker, pressing two fingers inside that hole. I let out a chocked sound, enjoying the feeling of this. He added a few more fingers, till he had four inside of me, and I felt like I was losing control.

I needed him. I wanted him, and I knew that he was enjoying this as much as I was. He quickly pulled me into his arms, and I soon slid down, feeling his thighs against my backside. I felt his cock breach my ass. Even though it was a bit of a discomforted sensation and I was a little weirded out at first, as he got all the way to the very base, I suddenly let out a small cry, enjoying the feeling of this, and his cock filled me up completely.

He soon moved all the way in, making me cry out slightly. He soon let me move, feeling my hips as I bobbed up and down, moaning slightly.

But there was still George, who was jerking it to the sight. I thought he'd stay like that, but then, he grabbed my legs, spreading them apart as he slid inside of me.

I let out a cry, moaning in pleasure as I felt them both move in and out of me. Sometimes it would be at the same time, and that feeling of fullness was enough to drive me mad. Other times they'd alternate but I didn't care. Either way , I enjoyed the feelings that they provided to me, the pleasure that I got, and the way that their bodies just made me lose all semblance of control.

It was making me lose my mind, and I couldn't help but feel like I was so close to the edge.

George reached down, rubbing me, and then I felt that there was something hitting that one spot, that one part of me, and then, moments later, I tensed up, feeling like I was losing all semblance of control. I came hard, feeling my body tense up, enjoying the feeling of this.

Shortly afterwards, Adam pushed in, grunting as he filled me up completely.

Then there was George.

He pushed me onto the desk. I thought he'd just fuck me there, but instead he started to jerk off all over my body, making me shiver. When he came, dribbles of cum started to decorate my body, encasing my breasts, stomach, and other areas in white.

I felt like I was totally used by all of these guys, but I didn't care. This was exactly what I'd been waiting for. When they finished, I stayed there, taking a moment to bask in my orgasm.

I didn't mind this in the least, even though I'd been used by all of these men. There was something thrilling about this, something that made me ache for more, and something that I enjoyed.

"There we go," AJ said.

"Looks like she did well," Adam said.

"Yeah, that was really nice," Landon added.

"Indeed. We found a pretty good one," I heard Craig say.

"Yeah, even for how much of a desperate slut she was, she definitely was promising," I heard George finally add.

I didn't know whether or not this was the right thing to do, or if I had just completely fucked over myself and everything in between.

"So what did you guys think?" I finally said.

"Well, you certainly brought a lot to the table, and as some of the top supporters of many companies…I suppose we can give a little bit of support to you," AJ said with a wink.

I beamed. All of that work, and the hard work I did beforehand, paid off.

"Thank you. I promise that I won't let you down," I said.

"Course you won't. you certainly delivered on your promise too," AJ added.

"Yeah, I didn't expect you to go through with all of that. But here we are. I suppose we can let you have this one," Adam said. He was hesitant, but I think that was also just him playing hard to get.

"Yeah, we're pretty impressed with all that you did. Perhaps you do have some potential to add to the table," Craig added.

All of them seemed pretty happy, and there was clearly an exciting feeling that ghosted through my body. I started to smile.

"Great. I'm excited to continue this working relationship with you. Let me get cleaned up, and then I can do the paperwork," I said.

"Sure, take your time," AJ said.

I quickly made my way to the bathroom beforehand, and I cleaned up everything that was there. I was disgusted by the way I felt, but at the same time, I didn't regret what I did. Most people wouldn't dare do this, but honestly...I'm different from the rest.

In fact, this was definitely something that I enjoyed and I'd do it again.

I got myself together, and I prepared for coming back to see what they'd do next. When I got there, I stepped inside, the paperwork already nestled on the table, waiting for me to wrap up.

As I wrote down my name, I started to realize that this was the beginning of one hell of a relationship. It wasn't every day that I did this kind of shit, and honestly, most normal people wouldn't do this.

But I wasn't normal. I was someone who would stop at nothing to get what I wanted to get the recognition that was in place, and I knew for a fact that they were enjoying all of this too. I finished with the last of the paperwork, and AJ extended his hand.

"Well Mindy, you do drive a hard bargain, if I do say so myself," he said to me.

"Yeah, I sure as shit do," I told him.

"I take it that you find our little arrangement...fine then?" he asked.

"Yeah, for the most part I'm cool with it," I said.

In truth, I didn't know what this would mean for me, or even what would happen now, but I was just glad that I got to have something like this, and I was ready to see what would happen next.

When I left, I knew that it would be our little secret. The corporate donations would help my inventions get off the ground. While it wasn't considered the right thing to do in some cases, at the same time, I didn't care.

The future was brighter and I was way happier.

The Forbidden Patient

"Dr. Nadine, we need you in room 205," the voice on the intercom said.

"Alright," I muttered to myself.

Working at the regional psychiatric hospital as one of the top-leading psychiatrists was definitely not what I thought it'd be. In fact, it was much harder than I expected.

I was one of the top-ranking doctors that was in the area. In fact, I made sure that everyone was taken care of, and I made sure all medications and the like were intact. But I was also a normal doctor, who was in charge of medications for a variety of patients.

While most of the people I did see were typical psychiatric cases, in a few instances, there were those who were a little bit different.

And the patient in room 205 was different.

When I stepped inside, I immediately was met with what seemed to be the most attractive man I've ever seen. And also one of the most untouchable men as well.

William Merkins. The famous model. The guy with the body of Adonis, and a pearly-white smile that would make women swoon.

And he of course was the man I'd be seeing today. I just never expected him of all people here.

"William," I said to myself.

"You know me too? the other doctors kept asking for an autograph," he said to me.

"I see," I told him.

"Well, I'm here so I guess the secret is out," he said to me.

"What do you mean?"

"That I'm a fucking lunatic. My ex she...she called the cops on me. She thought that I was going to off myself or some stupid shit. They came, and then they brought me here. Said it'd be good for me. well I also was about to relapse. You know I've been to rehab, right?" he said.

I sure as fuck did, but because the latest tabloids would report on this shit.

"I do. But that's not why you're here, is it?" I asked him.

"No...I'm here because I want to live a normal fucking life. I'm so sick of feeling this way," he said to me.

"What do you mean?" I asked him.

He looked at me, sighing.

"It's complicated. I kind of came here because I needed a solution. And well...I didn't know where to look. I tried to ask others, but they kind of all blew me the fuck off. So I got a bit desperate. I should've been better about my

ex's feelings, but it also was a struggle. Have you ever had people just not listen to you? Like at all? And you want to scream for help but not a goddamn soul hears you?" he asked me.

I could get what he was getting at. I mean, I was a doctor after all.

"Yeah, I get that. You want to be heard. Is there anything personal you'd like to discuss?" I asked him.

He looked at me, flushing.

"Well mostly just about life. I came here for answers. And I heard you're one of the best around. I was worried you'd prescribe me meds and then go on your way and then—"

"No way," I snapped.

I looked at him, and then he nodded.

"Thanks, that's relieving. Well, I guess it's a crisis. I don't know whether I want to keep the modeling schtick up," he said.

"Well, anything in particular make you change your decision?" I asked him.

He started to nod.

"Yeah, lots of things. Just the modeling world is exhausting, and I don't know how much more of this shit I can take. I just need some advice, and I know that you've got the advice I'm looking for. And I'd...I'd like to talk about that. If that's okay," he said.

I nodded.

"Anything I can do to help. If you'd like, we can do therapy sessions and such too," I said.

I was a trained counselor, and that alone made him nod.

"Yeah, I'd appreciate that," he said to me.

We began to talk about this and that, and while I was doing my job, I couldn't help but flush a little bit when I saw his large, expansive body, the pecs he had, the washboard abs he possessed. It all made me want to lick my lips. I felt like I was slowly losing it, but I needed to keep it together.

For the patient's sake.

As we talked though, I could see the heat in his eyes, the look of desire. And I wondered if it was just me who was feeling this, or perhaps it was something more. Something deeper.

This went on for a little while. For the first week of counseling, we ended up talking about everything and anything. I discovered that he was having a goddamn crisis. It surprised me that he would be like this, but I guess that's the way life fizzled out at times, and honestly, I didn't blame him for feeling this way.

Shit was hard, and it was the least I could do to help the guy out.

I noticed that William was also not staring directly into my eyes when we talked, as if there was something bigger there. I wondered about that, but I didn't want to ask him about it. I felt that was wrong, like I was making a huge mistake if I did bother him about this.

Still...there was something about this which felt off.

I did notice his mood changed though during out sessions. At first, he was a bit stubborn, adamantly against talking about the pain from his past. But I'd reach out, touching his hand, looking him in the eyes.

"Trust me. I know it's scary now, but we'll make it. Together, " I told him.

"I know. Thank you for that doctor," he said.

And that's when things began to change. There was a connection there, something much bigger than a mere patient-doctor relationship. And I realized I was making a mistake too.

Then, it happened. One night during therapy.

"So tell me...has this caused you to develop any sorts of tendencies?" I asked him, writing down in my notes about his previous grappling with abusive women.

William sat there, listening to my words, and then...he nodded.

"Yeah, but it's an embarrassing revelation," he said.

"This is a doctor-patient confidentiality. Remember you can tell me anything," I told him.

Even though he was a famous celebrity, I could sense he was nervous about all that he had to say. I don't really blame him though. I mean, opening up about this is a struggle.

But then, he sighed.

"It's embarrassing," he added.

"Well if you don't talk about it now, you'll never heal you know," I said.

"You're right but...it doesn't make this any easier for me," he said.

"I'm not going to judge you, you know. We can keep this between us. Obviously I won't tell anyone about what's said during therapy and such," I explained.

I'd get in deep shit if I did that. After all, this is confidential, and it's supposed to be.

He took a moment to process what to say, taking a deep breath as he spoke.

"Fine. I guess I can tell you. But you promise to keep this a secret, right?" he asked me.

"Yeah, course. It's a secret," I said to him.

He looked around, and then back at me, sighing.

"Truth is...the abuse made me realize that I like a controlling woman. I want a woman to dominate me, but not hurt me. it wouldn't be abusive per se, but it's hard for me to take charge. I love it when women do," he said.

I flushed. I always liked taking charge over men. But I never told anyone about it. I wrote down the notes, pushing my hands through my red hair, looking at him.

"I'm sorry that you've struggled with a lot. but I get that. You want someone powerful," I told him.

"Yeah Nadine. And the thing is...I have always craved for a woman to just dominate me. To make me their bitch, and I know it's degenerate, but I can't stop thinking about it," he said.

"I see. As someone who is a bit more dominant-leaning, I get that. It's something you desire," I told him.

He then blushed, looking around, and then at me.

"That's I guess...why I wanted to ask you this. I know it's wrong, and I know that if I tell you, I'll probably be in deep shit. But I can't stop thinking about it. Ever since we started meeting for these kinds of sessions, I've felt the urge to tell you, but I have no idea what you'll think of it," he said.

"Whatever do you mean?" I asked.

He then blushed, looking away, and then turning to me.

"Could you...dominate me Nadine? It wouldn't just be for you, but it'd be for me too. I want to feel a woman overtake me, make me feel like I'm powerless. It's something I've desired more than I thought I ever wanted something, and I know that it's wrong, it's embarrassing, but I can't get my mind off of this," he said.

I couldn't believe I was hearing what he wanted. He wanted me to break this contract, to do...that.

And yet, I wanted to.

There was an urge there, something which continued to haunt me as he offered this.

"You're serious," I said.

"Yeah. I want you to do this. I promise that...we'll make it a secretive thing. I just want to be dominated by someone strong and powerful. Please. I feel this would help me immensely," he said to me.

I looked him in the eyes, and then I nodded.

"You promise confidentiality, correct?"

"Right. If anyone found out about this...you wouldn't be in trouble. I would be," he said.

"I could get my license taken away William," I told him.

"I know but....I also want to explore this. Just the two of us. It doesn't have to be a long-term thing. It can be just the two of us learning about one another. That's all," he said.

I pondered this. It was super risky, and the rational side of myself knew this. But that other side, the one that was curious about what may happen next, who wanted to explore this further, immediately smiled.

"Well, I guess we can settle this. Tell you what, get on the little lounge there and we can get started," I said.

He looked at me with a look of relief, and slight worry, but I simply smiled. I knew this would be new for both of us, but the truth was, I wanted to explore this too. I knew that it was wrong, that I'd get in serious trouble if a soul found this one out.

But I didn't care. I was horny and he seemed just as needy for me as I was him.

We'd also keep this a secret too. After all, he worked in the public, so if his image was fucked, we'd both be fucked.

Even though I knew for a fact that it was wrong, that I'd get in trouble, I had my case here for these types of moments for the off chance that I'd get to explore this further, that I'd get to enjoy this too.

I watched him as he sat there, looking me in the eyes, and I could see that anticipation that was there. Then, before I knew it, I started to grab the container, bringing it in here.

The truth was, I was a dominatrix on the side. It was mostly when I was having a rough week in terms of bills. Guys would ask me to dominate them, and I'd do so for a price. And now, I'd get to finally experience this once again, and there was a thrill that came out of this.

The first thing that I did, was put on the blindfold. I also cuffed his hands. He sat there, gulping. I grabbed his chin, looking him in the eyes.

"So you want me to dominate you because you're too much of a little bitch to take control? What a pathetic sight," I said.

"Ahh yes. Please mistress," he said, already getting into the role.

That's what shocked me the most about this. It was the fact that he was already so into this, and I was just beginning.

"I didn't say you should talk. You only talk when spoken to. And only when I give you permission. Got it?" I snapped at him.

"Yes mistress," he said, obedient.

"Now, what should I do with your pathetic ass first. Perhaps I should step on your pathetic dick, that you can barely use," I said.

He let out a small gasp of pleasure as I moved my leg, rubbing it there against the obvious bulge in his pants. He was hard as a rock, and it surprised me that he was like this.

"Look at you, getting hard like the dog that you are," I said.

"Yes mistress, I'm a dog," he said.

"Bark."

He let out a half-assed bark, and I smiled. I enjoyed the way that he sounded, and the pleasure that came out of this.

I smiled, moving my foot against there, pressing against his cock with a bit more force. He let out a small gasp, and I smiled.

"What's the matter? You like it when my boot is against your cock?" I asked.

"Yes mistress. Please, crush me," he said.

I put a bit more force against there, hearing him groan.

"You're too fucking loud. Clean them," I said.

I shoved my boot in his face, and he quickly went to work, cleaning off all of the edges of my boots. I laughed, watching him finally shut up as he slurped and took care of my boots, making sure that they were cleaned.

"Very good. Well, I take it that you want this mistress to take care of you, to peg your pathetic hole, and make you whimper and cry?" I asked, grabbing his chin. He nodded.

"Yes. I'm nothing more than your toy, someone that you can use as you see fit," he said.

This guy was hells getting into it. In the past I've done this with guys, but most of the time, they were usually not all that focused on the play. But this guy here was definitely into it, and there was something thrilling about that.

"Very well. If that's what you see fit, then so be it. I'll make sure you whimper and cry," I said.

"Yes mistress. Anything," he insisted.

There was that sound of desperation that came out of his mouth as I smiled.

I pushed him so that he was on his stomach. I got onto his back, digging my boots into there. He let out a small cry of pain, and I pushed his head down.

"You need to stay quiet, or else I'll gag you," I said.

I continued to lightly walk on him, knowing damn well that this was more than enough for him. The sounds that he made were music to my ears, making me shiver and moan with delight as I continued to move my body there, getting on top of him, enjoying the fun that came from this.

He was such a goddamn mess., this was so fun, and there was something exciting about taking over this man, making him my bitch, and watching him slowly come undone.

"What's the matter? Can't take it?" I said.

"I-I can," I heard from the muffle.

I continued to step around for a second before getting off. I walked over to the kit that I had, grabbing of course the gag and putting it into his mouth.

In truth, I just didn't want the wrong people coming in. but most therapy sessions were done for the day, so I'd get to of course, have him all to myself. That's why I kept the kit in a small corner of my office, and it looked like a regular briefcase, so it wasn't like anyone could really go and ask about that.

That's what's so thrilling about this. The fact that I could do all of this, and I had this man of all people losing his mind as I took him and teased him.

I pushed his cheeks up, pulling off his pants and boxers, revealing his large, aching cock. While I'd normally be thinking of riding that, today I wanted to make him feel good. And if this would help with well...all of the problems that he had, then so be it.

"Look at you, hard as a rock already," I told him.

"Y-yes I am mistress," he said.

"Maybe I'll milk you later on, turn you into the pathetic little slut that you are," I said.

"please mistress," he replied.

All of his sounds were muffled due to the gag but I'd been doing this long enough that I could understand just what the hell he was looking for.

But that's when I moved to my next target.

His ass.

It was right there, up in the air. It was plump, but not too big. And when I touched it, he let out a small, hissing sound of pleasure.

Look at you. Already so turned on," I said to him.

"Y-yes mistress," he said.

"As you should be. Anyways…let's make some magic," I told him.

I grabbed the first thing that I sued. It was a typical paddle, but on one side were little metal spikes. They of course wouldn't be that hard on the person, but for someone who was already as sensitive as he was, it would make things a bit more painful. I decided to use the flat side first, spanking him with it. He let out a small cry, enjoying the touch of my hands.

"There you go. Look at you, already losing control and turned on by the mere touches of my hands," I told him.

"Yes," he said, breathing out slightly.

I soon started to hit him again and again, enjoying the feeling of this. I soon started to watch him tense up, moaning out loud and in pleasure, and I loved everything about this sort of thing. It was fun to see him squirm, and I enjoyed it.

I continued to paddle him, switching sides at one point, the little moans only growing a little bit louder as he did this. There was something exciting about this, and I loved it. I continued to paddle and tease him, enjoying the sounds of pleasure that escaped his mouth, the fun that this brought all of us.

For a little bit, I continued to tease him, until finally, I stopped, watching his bass twitch a little bit. I then moved towards the case again, getting something a little bit harder.

"There we go," I said to him.

I grabbed the little crop that I had. This one had a much harder bite to it, and I watched his eyes widen in surprise at the feeling of this.

"Holy shit," he said pout loud as I hit him once.

"You good?"

He nodded, and I hit him a few more times with this. The little yelps and sounds that were muffled by the gag were music to my ears of course, and there was something thrilling about all of this. But I wanted more, and seeing him twitch like this was quite fun.

"Look at my little pet here. All twitching and needy," I said.

He let out a whimper, and I soon reached over, grabbing the lube and one of the plugs that I used.

"Look at your little hole. All needy for me," I said.

"Yes mistress," he muttered into the pillow. I let out a chuckle, teasing the very edge of his pucker, watching him shiver and squirm in response to my actions.

"That's right. You like this don't you? I can see you twitching and squirming like the little bitch that you are," I said, teasing the very tip of his pucker with my hand. I didn't even get far, I just knew that this alone was enough to make him lose control and composure slightly, and there was something fun about this. I loved seeing him in this state, there was something fun about this. I continued my teasing, playing with him a little bit with my finger, enough to make him shiver and squirm in response to everything. He continued to let out a series of small grunts and moans, and I enjoyed hearing him like this. I continued to tease him, touching him slightly, and he soon let out a small gasp as I got right up against his pucker, moving my finger there, dancing it slightly.

"Yes," he said to himself.

I then lubed up my finger more, forcing it through there, hearing him letting out a series of small grunts and cries. He seemed to be in his own little world with this, and I loved it. I continued to touch, tease, and ply with him, watching his eyes widen, and his body react to the touches of my hand.

I loved seeing him come apart like this, and there was something at that was driving him crazy, and I wanted nothing more than to just take this whole and make him shiver and scream.

I continued to tease with one finger, and then two, then three fingers, but then I got bored. It was fun and all, but I really wanted to make him squirm, to make him really lose it.

That's when I grabbed the dildo that I had. It was only a little bit smaller than the one I used with my strap, but I pushed it in. To my surprise, it fit perfectly into his ass. I thrust it in there, giggling as I did so.

"Look at you, already turned on by this. Your ass takes so much like the little bitch it is," I said, plunging it in there. He let out a small whimper and cry, thrusting his hips upwards, enjoying the sensation of my hands there, and the toy teasing and titillating him. I then pressed the vibration function, watching him squirm there, and I couldn't help but love it. There was something thrilling about making a man like this lose it. And I was going to make him lose it and then some.

I continued the teasing for a little while, but then, I felt that urge for so much more. That crave, that need, that enticing desire for him. I soon moved the toy out of him, and I heard the little moan from his lips.

"Don't worry, you'll be filled with something even better soon," I purred.

He let out a small whimper, and I couldn't help but find this even more fun than I thought it'd be. I mean, he was here, like putty in my hands, and I couldn't help but love everything about this. It was only It was only a matter of time before I got myself together, getting the toy that I had and slowly pushing it into me. I let out a small gasp, and then, I moved towards him.

"There we go. Ready pet?" I asked.

The little whimper that I heard from him made me smile, and I felt excited about this. I soon got myself together, spreading his cheeks apart, pressing all the way into him.

I heard him tense up, and then cry out as I started plunging deep into him, watching him slowly lose all semblance of control as I moved myself deep into him. I watched his eyes widen, and the choked sobs that came out of him as I pushed myself deep within.

This was what I loved about domination. The feeling of control that this given to me through this was just...fun you know. I definitely enjoyed the feeling of this.

I began to thrust in and out, watching his body spasm in response to my touches. I then grabbed his hips, looking at him and chuckling.

"Wow, you're doing so damn well. I'm impressed with you," I told him.

He let out a small shudder, a moan of response, and I noticed his back began to arch slightly as I began to thrust in deeper and deeper, holding him there. I continued to pound him, hearing the sounds and whimpers.

I knew that he was getting close, and while it was fun just teasing him and watching him whimper, I knew that I had to end things off soonish.

I grabbed him, holding him against my body, thrusting upwards.

I grabbed his cock, milking him, and he let out a low, guttural sound, cumming against my hand. I shivered, feeling the strapon hit that one spot that made me shiver and cry out. not only after did I feel the force of my own orgasm hit me, but I pushed into him, causing him to let out a small, needy whimper of desire.

When I felt my orgasm hit me, I knew that this was definitely it. I finished up, pulling out, and I looked at him, seeing him there.

"Now you've been used my little pet. All used and neatly kept here," I said.

"Yes mistress," he said.

I soon got back to my normal type of state. While it was fun to tease him, I knew that I had to make sure I still kept an inkling of professionalism throughout all of this. I put my stuff back, took off the blindfold and gag, and I put the boots away. He laid there, still unable to say as word to me, just amazed by how good it felt. I for one didn't blame him. I mean, I knew I was good at what I did. The fact that men would come back to me even after seeing me a few times was proof alone.

But there was something else that was there, something that was bothering him.

"How are you feeling? Do you need anything?" I asked him.

He looked at me, shaking his head.

"No. not really," he admitted.

"What do you mean by that?" I asked him.

He paused, flushing crimson.

"Well it's more of...thanks for what you did. I really did like that you know," he said.

"You mean the fucking? I figured that's what you were looking for. A woman to dominate you. Consider it therapy, just don't mention it to anyone," I said.

Lord knows I'd be in deep shit if someone found out about this. William flushed, nodding.

"Yeah, I wouldn't dare. My career would be on the line. But thank you Nadine. You're kind of amazing you know," he said to me.

I flushed, nodding.

"Yeah, I feel this was good for both of us," I told him.

"Yeah, I'm really glad that I have you," he said to me.

I knew that he meant this. Deep down, everything seemed so perfect, so right, and I knew that he enjoyed this too. I sat there, thinking about the way things were.

"So I take it a part of your kisses stem from well...someone not giving you this kind of treatment?" I asked him.

"Yeah. My ex found it weird, and I never felt comfortable seeing a dominatrix about this, especially when I was with her. It was embarrassing, and I knew that it would've fixed itself so much faster if I just did. But you know how it is," he said.

"Yeah. You had the internalized desires but you were afraid of what someone else may think. I get that, and I know that you're struggling to truly understand everything. But I'm here for you, and I'm proud of you," I told him.

He nodded.

"Thank you doc. And yeah. I won't say a thing about this. But maybe we can...do this again sometime down the road?" he asked.

It was risky. He would have to sneak around, and I'd have to do the same thing just to get an inkling of this to work. But my lips curled into that of a smile.

"Sure. I wouldn't mind that. I'm sure we could arrange something good for both of us, something that benefits both parties," I told him.

The look on his face told me everything. The obvious smile, the look of pure, raw desire, and that ache that I could see in his eyes, it was so obvious that he was just as excited for this as I was.

It could be our little secret, a confidential ordeal between two people.

"Thank you. And I will make sure that this is kept under wraps," he said.

"You damn well better make sure. I know that otherwise it's not going to be good for either of us," I told him.

"You've got that right. Anyways, I hope that we can do this again. I should probably go back to work though," he said.

"Yeah, you've got a lot of people waiting on you," I admitted.

"Yeah I know. But I feel a lot better talking to you about this. Not just because of the sex. But well...everything. So thank you doctor," he said.

"Just call me Nadine," I replied.

His lips curled into that of a smile, one that said it all.

"Well thank you Nadine. I appreciate all that you've done for me, and everything that transpired," he replied.

I knew that he meant it. I just felt so nervous, especially given the fact that this was all happening like this. We parted ways, and while I did miss him, I knew that this was the start of something. I wasn't sure what, but I was ready to explore this.

He was the forbidden patient, the one I couldn't get out of my head.

Deeper than Mere Friendship

I waited for Jack to come over. He was my best friend, and we were going to spend the night together watching shitty horror movies and having a good time. At least, that's what he told me.

The ruth was, I wondered if there was something else there, something deeper than just the little friendship that we had. The truth was, I did have a crush on Jack, but I was scared to tell him.

I wanted to just admit it, and hope the feelings were reciprocated, but I didn't know. He'd been eying another woman, and there was something about that which set me off a little bit.

I didn't dare tell him though. That was the last thing I wanted. I didn't know what Jack thought about me, and honestly, I was scared to ask.

I heard the doorbell ring, and I quickly got myself together. I did straighten up my curly blonde hair, and put on some makeup. I opened the door, and there was Jack, with a six-pack in hand and a smile on his face.

"Hey there Vicky," he said.

"Hey! Excited for this movie night," I told him.

He grinned, but there was something about this which made me wonder things. I didn't know why. But I got a feeling that there was something different about Jack. Could not put my finger on it though.

I shrugged it off, ignoring the feeling that was there. I followed Jack inside to the living room, and as we sat on the couch together, he smiled.

"Sorry for being so late. I was kind of busy with a couple of things," he said.

"Oh it's fine. I just got everything set up," I told him.

"Great. I'm really excited for this movie night," he said.

I was too, but I also felt there was something different in the air tonight. He turned on the TV, putting in the monster movie, and soon, we began watching it.

Jack was my best friend, ever since we were kids. I felt like there was something hidden there, something missing, and I wanted to ask about it, but I didn't want to make him feel weird. But during the movie, I saw him move a little bit closer, inch by inch. I tried to ignore it, but I wondered if there was some sort of deeper meaning to that. Was he...trying to imply something? I didn't know for sure, but I felt like there was something deeper there that he refused to discuss.

When the movie was over and the credits rolled, I turned on the light. We looked at one another, the silence awkward.

'do you want me to put in another movie?" I asked him.

"Well...not really, " he said.

He didn't want to watch another movie? That shocked me.

"So what are you planning to do?" I asked him.

He smiled at me, a reassuring grin, and then I looked at him. He seemed different. There was obviously something else there.

"Say Vicky, you're not going to get offended if I...decide we should try something else, right?" he asked.

Something different? But Jack and I always watched movies together. Neither of us had drank a lot, so I don't know what he was getting at with this one.

That's what made me wonder.

"What the hell are you getting at Jack? What are you talking about?" I asked him.

I legit didn't know. It felt like there was some sort of embarrassing thing there that he was scared to tell me about, but he wouldn't just spit it out.

But then he flushed.

"It's a little embarrassing. Tell you what, why don't I just get the game out and if you want to play it, then great. If not, we can go back to the movies and such," he said.

I didn't know what the hell was going on. He was being so cryptic and it wasn't like him. I wanted him to just spit out whatever was bothering him, but I guess he didn't want to.

For some reason, he wanted to play the cryptic game. Well I guess two can play at that, or I'd get my answers eventually.

"Well get the game out then. We'll see what we can do," I said to him.

I didn't know what he had planned. But shortly afterwards he got out the cards. I looked at them, seeing the stick figures there.

"Deep—a game about getting to know the other person. But we're best friends Jack," I said.

"I know but...it may be fun. Something a little different from the normal bullshit, you know?" he said.

I didn't get it myself, and I thought that it was stupid, but also...I was curious. Did it have something to do with the awkwardness that Jack possessed.

"Sure, let's do this," I told him.

I wanted to find out what it was that he had planned, or even what this may mean. Jack smiled, and I felt a sudden rush of relief that he wasn't mad at me or anything.

"Good. Then it's simple. There's little cards and you put them in a few piles. There are three piles of course, and these cards determine your actions. When you get one, you can do the action, or pass, and then you have to pick another and do that action, or whatever is on the card," he said.

"And who wins?"

"Depends. I guess we'll see how this goes," he said.

I had no clue what he was trying to do with this. It seemed like a stupid ass game, and I had no clue what the endgame of any of this was. But I wanted to ease that tension that I felt in my bones, because of him. and I wanted to learn more about this.

So finally gave in, listening to him as he spread out the cards.

"I'll go first. Is that okay?" he asked.

"Y-yeah," I said, feeling my heart race.

He then grabbed a card, picking it up and reading it.

"Confess the secret that's on the tip of your tongue to them," he said.

"Is this some sort of truth or dare?" I asked Jack.

"No Vicky. It's something that has also some actions there. It brings people closer together. Well….I don't know. I'm nervous about mentioning this," he said.

"Come on man. Tell me," I told him.

He paused, flushing crimson. I didn't know why, but I felt like it had something to do with us. Something that was bigger than what we both thought.

"If I tell you…you don't plan on getting mad or anything, right?"

"Why would I get mad Jack. You've been acting weird for a bit," I said.

"Well I just want to make sure that it isn't weird or anything," he said.

I wasn't sure what was considered weird in this man's eyes. But I nodded.

"Don't worry, I'll make sure that this is all kept between us. I promise nobody else will find out about whatever it is that you are hiding," I said to him.

He looked into my eyes, obvious relief there. What was he holding back. Finally, he spoke.

"Well…what if I told you that I masturbated to you before?" he said.

I flushed. I wasn't expecting that. I mean, I thought that this was going to be him confessing he liked me or something. Which wasn't necessarily wrong. I got that vibe.

But this was different. My eyes widened, and my eyebrow raised.

"Really now," I said.

"Yeah. It was a couple of times. I feel a bit embarrassed about this," he said.

"Don't be. It's okay," I told him.

"Thanks. But yeah, I have. I guess that's a secret that I first thought about. Your turn," he said.

I picked the card, holding it.

"Give them a kiss on a body part," I read out loud.

I was red as a tomato. There was no way I was going to kiss Jack…right?"

"Well…you going to do it?" he asked me.

I looked at the options. I could get another card, and things could be worse. Or I could just do this.

"I'll take another card," I replied.

161

"Makes sense," he said, hiding the slight disappointment in his voice.

I took the next card, reading it out loud.

"Tell the other person a small sexy fact about yourself," I said.

God not another embarrassing one. Was this supposed to be sexual on purpose? I looked at Jack, realizing that there was no way I was getting out of this.

"Well…I have a vibrator I refuse to get rid of because it always hits that one spot. And well…I love being eaten out. my clit really likes the attention," I said.

Fuck this was embarrassing. But Jack smiled.

"What a secret. Two of them really," he teased.

I looked at him, realizing he liked this. Was this some sort of fucked up sex game that he found enjoyment in. I'd be lying if I said I didn't find this fun though. Even though it was indeed fucking embarrassing, I knew for a fact that what I was feeling definitely was a bit different.

It was both arousal, and of course…the urge for something more.

He picked the next card, reading it over.

"Kiss the other person's body part and lick it," he said.

"There's no way you're doing this, right?" I asked.

"Depends. I may want to take a risk with this. I don't want to give out more embarrassing secrets now do I?" he said.

God was this really how this was going to go? I don't know, but then I sighed.

"Fine. Where?" I asked.

"Give me your hand," he told me.

I looked at him, confused as to why he needed it, but I extended it. He grabbed my hand, kissing the tip of my finger, but then, he put the finger in his mouth, letting his tongue drag downwards against the bottom of it.

Okay that was hot. I felt my heart race, my body grow ragged with need, and a smile ghost his face once more.

"Getting kind of hot in here," he said.

"Y-yeah," I said.

Fuck it was my turn. I had no idea what in the world was going to happen. What other kinds of little secrets were there? I looked around, and then, I picked up the next card.

"Show your genitals to the other person," I said.

Was he fucking serious? I looked at Jack, and he smiled.

"If you're nervous about this, I can do this with you," he told me.

That only made things worse. The little crush that I had was starting to become more and more apparent. Did this guy just like teasing me like this? I wanted the answers, but then, I sighed.

"Fine. I'll do it," I said.

I started to undo my pants, sliding them off, and then, I removed my underwear.

I shaved, not because I thought this would be happening, but because I imagined it was getting a bit hairy and unkempt. He looked over, nodding.

"Very nice," he said.

"Don't make this embarrassing. Please," I told him.

"I'm not. In fact, I'll also hold up my end and show you," he said. He pulled his pants down, revealing his erection.

I immediately blushed. He was huge, fucking packing, and I knew that it would feel amazing inside me. but I didn't want to mention that.

And it didn't help that he was hard as a rock too. Fuck this was making the game even more awkward for the two of us.

"W-wow," I said.

"Not bad huh?" he teased.

"Yeah. Not at all," I told him, struggling to form words as I looked at the meaty member. This was getting harder to concentrate on. But I had to keep my wits about me, no matter what.

"Anyways, it's your turn," I finally said, putting everything aside.

I looked at him, and he grabbed a card.

"Stick a finger inside the other person," he said.

"Are you fucking serious?"

"Hey, I could just stick it in your ear if I wanted to," he joked.

I knew he wouldn't do that though. This was all a game, and this was making me lose it right then and there. I started to flush as he brought the finger closer to my pussy, spreading me apart as he plunged it in.

I let out a small cry. He just had to stick it in, but then he began to explore, fingering it. I felt my eyes roll to the back of my head, my body suddenly crave more of the touch, and the ache and pleasure that came out of this was only driving me crazier and crazier.

He continued to tease me, plunging his fingers deep into my pussy, and it was driving me mad., I started to feel my whole body tense up, the sudden feeling of my pussy begin to tighten, and I let out a small cry.

He pulled it out, licking it, looking me in the eyes with a surprised look.

"Wow, I didn't know you'd cum that fast," he said.

"I-it wasn't like I meant to be," I told him.

"Relax. Trust me, I know this game is helping us discover things. Just take it easy. Besides, it's your turn," he said.

I looked at him, still flushing from what had just occurred, and I grabbed the next card. This one was a lot easier than well the last few that I had.

"Lick their nipples," I said.

I looked at Jack, who weas laughing.

"That should've been mine," he said.

"Well it wasn't. I guess I can do that now," I told him.

I leaned in, taking the tip of one of the nipples into my mouth, sucking on the flesh there, making me suddenly feel hot and bothered by this. The groan that came out of his mouth made me feel turned on, in ways that I didn't expect. I started to suck and tease on it, flicking my tongue against the very tip of this, moving my other hand towards the other nipple, teasing it.

"Okay…I think that's more than enough," he said.

I did get lost in the teasing, turned on by the way that this felt. I looked at the cards. At this point, I felt like it was just a waste of time that this happened. I looked at them, and then he grabbed a card.

"Give them a kiss," he read.

"You mean like…."

"Yeah, a kiss-kiss," he said.

Well we were already half naked, and after what had just happened, I didn't think this game would be of much use for far too much longer.

"I guess…he goes nothing," I told him.

"Yeah. Here goes nothing," he said to me.

He leaned in, and we soon kissed slightly. At first, it was an awkward kiss, one that had a little bit of chastity to it, but then moments later, we both deepened the kiss, enjoying the feeling of one another, and the passion that this ignited.

I loved the way that this felt, and it was clear that he did too. We continued to make out for what felt like forever, and it was definitely making me lose my mind, making me want more from him.

We kissed for what felt like forever until he pulled away, looking me in the eyes.

"I don't think we need to play this game anymore," he said.

"What do you mean?"

"Well…we're kind of like this. Do you want to continue it?" he asked.

I mean I did. There was that ache inside of me that craved this. I soon nodded.

"Yeah, I'd love that," I told him.

He beamed, an obvious smile on his face.

"Good. Because I want that too," he said.

I grabbed another card, holding it there.

"Try missionary together," I said.

164

"I mean, we cand o that, but let's get to that point first. I want...I want to kiss you again," he said to me.

"You sure?" I asked. I didn't expect this to happen so suddenly with my best friend of all people. But he nodded.

"Yeah. I'd be lying if I didn't feel the same way about you Vicky. I brought this over because I thought it would be funny. But it's kinda...made me realize how much I fucking want you," he said to me.

I blushed crimson. I mean, I didn't want this to affect our friendship, but I didn't think it would do that. At least, that's not the vibes I was getting from this one.

"Are you sure? I don't want to make this weird for anyone," I said to him.

"No. I like this. I like you," he told me.

I beamed, and soon, we pressed our lips to one another, kissing passionately, enjoying the feeling of one another. This stupid little sex game ended up changing our lives forever, and it made me realize that there were unbridled feelings deep within me, that threatened to come the fuck out.

We continued to kiss for what felt like forever and soon, before I knew it, I felt a tongue snake out, meeting my own. This was different from earlier. There were any holds back anymore. I continued to kiss and make out with him, enjoying the touch that this made me feel, enjoying everything that came out of this. For a long time, we simply made out here enjoying one another, when finally, he pushed me into the couch.

"Now I get to see the rest of you," he told me.

I shivered, moaning slightly at the way his voice sounded. It was low and guttural and there was something about it which made me lose control, and there was clearly that need that only grew more so, and that unbridled need for one another.

He kissed down my neck, touching every single part of this, and as he kissed down every part of my neck, I started to shiver and cry out.

I loved this, and I knew that there was clearly a desire for more, a need that was unbridled, and that ache which made me shiver with delight.

He soon moved his lips to my collarbone, biting down on the flesh, making a small hickey appear there. I cried out, looking at him with mild annoyance.

"I didn't say to leave Marks," I muttered.

"Sorry, I just thought that your neck looked nice," I heard him say to me.

I flushed, but then nodded.

"Yeah, it is nice," I said.

"I just want to make you feel good. Because...you mean a lot to me Vicky," he said.

I blushed, and nodded.

"Yeah, you mean a lot to me too," I told him as well.

There was clearly a bit of tension that went along with this, and I felt embarrassed even admitting it, but he seemed to understand and there was something about the way that he treated me which made me feel better too.

He soon started to move his hands towards my shirt, pulling it off, grasping my breasts from over the confines of the bra.

"Wow," he said.

"You know you can take off the bra you know," I said.

"Yeah, I know. Let me have this moment please," he said.

He touched my breasts, massaging them, and even with the bra on, I moaned. There was something nice about a pair of hands that weren't your own touching, teasing, and playing with your titties. There was something exciting about the little touches too, and I couldn't help but enjoy the presence, and the moment that this gave me.

For a long time, he simply played with them, moving his hands to the back of my bra, pulling on the clasp, undoing this and letting them come out of the confines.

I shivered, moaning in pleasure as I started to feel his hands there, touching and playing with them. His hands moved towards my nipples, playing with them. I cried out, feeling my hands grip the couch as I felt the small, subtle touches. There was something different about these touches. They were nice, but I also could feel how close I was to losing it right then and there.

His hands moved against each of the tips of my nipples, pulling and tugging on them. I cried out, moaning as I bucked my hips upwards, shivering with delight at every single touch that came out of this. I started to feel his hands continue to move, touch, and tease there, and it was already driving me mad. I didn't know how much more of this I could take.

But then, his lips replaced one of the hands, touching the tip of it with small, subtle licks. The little licks and teases right then and there was enough to drive me insane. I let out a small moan, excited and turned on by this. He continued to lick and suck, pleasuring me there, and I lost all semblance of reality as I continued to feel this.

There was something thrilling about the way that he touched me, about the way that he teased me, and I couldn't help but feel like I was slowly coming undone. He flicked his tongue there, tugging on the other nipple, causing it to harden in response to his actions. I let out a cry, begging for more, aching for him.

That's when he pulled back, smiling at me, moving between my legs and pushing two fingers inside. His thumb moved right over the clit, just barely touching and teasing me there. I didn't know how much of this I could take. I wanted more, and I ached for him. I knew that I was close already, and that he knew this too.

He continued the teasing, every single motion and touch driving me crazy. After a brief second though, he pulled my hips upwards, his tongue coming out, exploring every part of me, touching my folders, teasing the nub of my clit, sucking on that.

I cried out, feeling my body instantly react to this. There was something about his lips that made me almost lose it there. I let out a guttural sound, one that was barely understood or distinguished, but I held onto the couch, moaning in response to his touches, his licks, and the sucking and pleasuring of every part of the flesh that he had.

That was something that I enjoyed. It was something that I ached and wanted to feel, that I desired more than anything else, and I knew that he was also getting into it in the same vein that I was. I knew that I was already close to my limit, enjoying the pleasure that came out of this.

He then pushed his tongue, exploring inside of me, pressing against each part of the moment, and it made me suddenly start to tense holding the couch.

But as soon as I felt the sudden onset of the orgasm hit me, it was gone. He pulled his mouth away, causing me to pout in response to his actions.

"Dammit," I muttered.

"Hey, I wasn't going to let you get away with that that easily," he teased.

"You motherfucker," I told him.

"I know that you enjoy this," he replied.

I rubbed Jack's blonde hair, looking into his blue eyes. He then moved himself so that his cock was right at my entrance.

I was nervous to say the least. I had no clue how this was going to feel, or if it would be good. But I wanted to trust him. I wanted this to be okay. and then, moments later, he pushed himself inside.

I cried out, feeling my whole body get filled up in an instance as I felt his cock all the way inside of there, buried within me. I felt my whole body suddenly tense up, and the moans that escaped my mouth drive me crazy. I began to hold onto the couch, moving my hips against him, letting out a series of cries.

This was so good, although he was filling me up pretty tightly. It did feel a little uncomfortable, but I didn't mind it. I started to feel his thrusts grow stronger, and as he looked into my eyes, I knew that there was that implicit desire for more, that need for all of this, and I couldn't help but feel the same way.

But then I stopped, looking over at the cards.

"Grab another," I said with a teasing smile.

He was confused, but then he did so.

"Get on top," he said.

"Don't mind if I do," I replied.

I pushed him down onto the couch, scrambling on top of him. when I finally got there, we locked eyes, my brown eyes looking into his blue ones, and there was clearly a feeling of excitement and need which came out of this too.

"There we go," I said.

I slid down on his cock, moaning as I felt him suddenly grip me, moving his cock deep in and out of me, making me shiver with delight, enjoying the feeling of all of this. There was something nice about this, something thrilling, and I wanted nothing more than to just enjoy the moment, embrace it, and love every single moment of this.

For a long time, I moved up and down. Then, two hands came forward, teasing my breasts, touching the tips of my nipples there, making me lose all semblance of control, enjoying the feel of the moment, the pleasure that came out of this, and the sounds of our bodies together.

It was a thrill that I didn't expect to enjoy so much, but when we locked eyes, there was clearly that unbridled desire that need for one another, and that need for more.

After a few more thrusts, he pulled me down, kissing me passionately as his fingers moved towards my clit, rubbing there, making me cry out, and then, he pulled my lips to his own, kissing me passionately.

For a second, we just kissed. He finished, and I suddenly felt my whole body lose it. I cried out, my orgasm hitting me to the core. I suddenly moved back, arching, and then, I finished.

When we were done, we looked at one another, neither of us saying a word for a moment. There was clearly something that needed to be said, but neither of us knew how to go about saying this.

All I knew was that Jack changed me. my best friend, someone who was always there by my side, now wanted...something more. And there was that feeling of desire, a need to also take the plunge and do this.

"Wow," I said to him as I moved out of him, sitting there. I grabbed a morning after pill and took it. I had one just in case. Never thought I'd use it in this situation.

When we got back to the couch, I sat next to him and tried to figure out what to say. Then, he spoke.

"You know I've wanted that for a while," he admitted.

"You mean like....for both of us," I asked him.

"Yeah. I've liked you for a long time Vicky. I just didn't want to make things weird. I brought this over to see what may happen. Maybe some sex games could help determine this. I never thought that it'd be something like that though," he said to me.

I didn't expect it either. I simply nodded, surprised by this.

"Yeah, you and me both," I told him.

"Anyways, I guess it's safe to say that it was a lot of fun, and I enjoyed that," he told me.

"Yeah, I did as well," I told him.

We looked at one another, and then for a long time, we didn't say a word. Finally, he sighed, trying to grapple with the obvious feelings that he had.

"Would you be against dating though? I didn't want to push my luck or anything, but if you'd like, we could—"

"I'd like that," I said. It was something I hadn't really thought all that much about, but now that we were here, in this moment together, there was clearly a desire for more, a desire for something together. He then nodded.

"Thank god you feel the same way. I was a little worried you didn't feel this way," he said.

"No I do. I'm really happy to have this chance though," I said.

"Me too. I didn't think it's work out like this. But it did, and I'm glad about that," he said.

"I am too," I replied.

I didn't think I was in love with him, but there was clearly a desire for more. As we kissed one another, I eagerly accepted this, enjoying the touch of his lips, and of him. we stayed like this for a long time, enjoying the touch of one another, and I knew that this was what I wanted to.

That night, he spent the night, even though we hadn't done that before. But I knew for a fact that Jack changed my feelings, made me realize what I'd been missing out on, and I knew that this was the beginning of something new, amazing, and something better than ever expected it to be.

I had a good feeling about the future, and about the desires which showed through that night, and brought us forward.

Her new Farmhands

"So you're the new ones?" I asked the two guys that walked on in.

They stepped over to me, smiling with little wry smiles.

"Sure am! My name is Toby," the blonde guy said.

"I'm Kenneth," the other guy, a tall, muscular guy with brown hair and subtle stubble on their faces said.

My eyes glazed over them, and I smiled in slight excitement.

"Yeah, my name's Mary. My dad hired you guys. But he'll be gone for the next week or so. So I'll be the one in charge for a bit," I said.

My name is Mary Lindback. My dad Craig Lindback owns this huge-ass dairy farm. Usually he'd run the whole thing himself but well...things don't always go as planned.

My dad ended up falling and breaking his leg. Shit hit the fan, and while I tried to keep up with everything, and my dad was a stubborn ass and continued to work, the doctor said he needed to take off some time, at least a week or two in order to recover so he didn't fuck up his leg further.

That of course led to my mom taking him to one of the nearby towns, where he'd get a "vacation" of sorts for a little bit. My mom insisted he take some damn time off, and it was obvious that he needed it.

But of course my dad is a stubborn ass, and I'd have to run the farm by myself. He told me he sent over some hands to help me with this. I was expecting family. Not two attractive guys that I never met till this point.

"Well....I guess it's time to get started then. I thought that your dad would be here. But I guess he really did hurt himself. Not just a rumor," Kenneth said.

"Well yeah, my dad doesn't fuck around with this. He's stubborn, so of course, if he ends up stopping his job, it's for a good reason," I said.

"Indeed. Anyways, can you show us around so we can get started? We'd love to help with some of the fields and such. It's a big ass farm. Can't believe he was doing this all on his own," Toby said.

"Yeah, I heard your dad was stubborn, but not like this," Kenneth added.

"Yeah well, he's gone so I've got to take care of this place. Anyways, my dad had it set up so you can stay in the guest house and such," I said.

Of course, in the bowels of my mind, I had an idea. I thought about...possibly letting them stay with me. but I didn't want things to get weird like that. It was the first time I'd been left alone like this, and I didn't want to fuck things up.

The truth was, my dad was a bit of straightedge, so that meant I rarely had the freedom to do what I wanted. And the fact that I was given this chance both excited me, and made me wonder how much of this I could get away with. I liked the idea of him possibly letting me do more, but also...I didn't know what else would happen now that well...we were here like this.

But I couldn't stop thinking about them. They were attractive as well, hot guys that I'd have to work with on the farm with. I moved my hands over to the guest house, grabbing the key and handing them over to them.

"Here you are," I told them.

"Well thanks," Kenneth said.

When our hands touched, I flushed crimson. I shouldn't be getting this excited over shit like this, but here we fucking were. I flushed thinking about the state of everything, and what this would mean for me. but then, moments later, I heard Kenneth speak,.

"Anyways, we can start with the farm work around here. If you want to show us anything, we can do it," he said.

I looked at the different places. They had to know at least a little bit about where the equipment was before I could let them on their own.

"Let me show you around the place a little bit. Fi that's okay of course," I told them.

"Sure as shit is. I'm glad we have such a cute guide like yourself," toby added with a wink.

I felt the heat burst through my body. I knew already these two would get me in so much trouble. But also…my parents weren't here, so it's not like they'd berate me or anything. If anything, they probably didn't care. Then again, they were kind of traditional.

But I was nineteen. I was old enough to make decisions like this on my own, so the prospect of having these two so close didn't feel like it was an accident. I mean, if my dad didn't want me to get into shit like this, they could've just had Billy come over. He's my cousin and a total oaf, but gets the work done.

But no…they did this. On purpose, and that made me realize the state of everything, and what was going on.

After a little bit of thinking, I walked with the two of them over to different parts of the farm, showing them how to use the milking machines.

"You sure know how to milk, don't you?" Kenneth said.

"Course. I'm an expert with milking," I teased.

I saw his eyes move down between my chest, and I flushed, putting my hands there.

"I mean…I've used them a lot," I said.

I felt like a fucking moron saying shit like that. I mean, how could I sound any more pathetic. But then….I heard them laugh. Instead of being upset, they laughed at my dumbass shit.

"No it's okay. I like that you know so much about milking. Very interesting," Toby said.

"Y-yeah," I replied, flushing crimson at the idea of this. For a long time, I didn't say anything, but then, I sighed.

"Anyways, I guess we should get started with this. I'll feed them while you guys make sure they're properly rounded up," I said to them.

"We can do that. We're good with wrangling," Toby said.

"Yeah, it's something fun we like to do," Kenneth said.

"I'm sure you're experts on wrangling," I teased.

That's when I flushed, realizing how sexual this was getting. I flushed at the realization of this. I knew that this flirting would get me in trouble eventually, but not like this.

However, I enjoyed the playful flirting that went on with these two. There was something fun about flirting with them that made it even more adventurous and fun. For a long time, we simply continue this flirting.

Over the next couple of days, I felt their eyes stare at me a little longer than usual. I flushed, realizing that they enjoyed this as much as I did. I liked it though, feeling like it was obvious that they were enjoying this as much as I was.

But I didn't want to make any weird moves or anything that would get me in trouble. After all, they were here for my dad, not for me of course.

But one day, I was working in the barn, getting the hay out. However, it was up on the top area of the barn. As I reached up to grab it, the little stool I was using to reach the top started to shake. I held myself, bracing myself for impact, when suddenly, I fell into something soft. I looked over, seeing Kenneth there, holding me in his arms.

"T-thanks for that," I said, turning as red as a tomato.

"You're most welcome. Don't want you to get hurt, right?" he said.

He was definitely correct about that. Didn't need two people in the Lindback family hurt.

"Anyways, I think I'll be going," I said, rushing out of there.

That night, when I laid in bed, I moved my hands between my legs, teasing my entrance. I let out a small sigh, pushing my hands deep into her. For a long time, I started to push them inside, two fingers, imagining it being Kenneth's dick inside of me. as I did that, I thumbed my clit, letting out a small sigh as I thought about toby against my breasts, teasing them while I was fucked.

"Ahh," I said, feeling my hips jerk forward. I began thrusting faster, touching myself, imagining them there, when suddenly, I heard the sound of rustling. I looked upwards, seeing that there was a shadow there.

Was it them? A part of me felt embarrassed if so, but if they ran into me during this, I certainly couldn't help but enjoy this. I didn't know what to say to them though if I did find them there.

One moment passed before I thought about it...about possibly seeing what they were up to. But I stopped myself.

I didn't want to seem like a desperate fuck or anything.

Over the next few days, I started to work closely with both Toby and Kenneth. They were interesting guys, not just two people my dad hired, and we were close.

"Say, do you guys want to come over for dinner tonight? I normally make it for my parents but...they're not here right now," I offered.

It may seem weird to some people, but I did enjoy taking care of people. They looked at one another and then nodded.

"I'd love to. I just don't want to be a damn bother or anything," Kenneth said.

"Oh you're far from that. In fact, you're a welcome distraction," I said to them.

They looked at one another, and then at me. we went back over to my place, where I had the dinner set up, and as we all sat down to eat, I could see their eyes lingering upon me.

"You guys like the food?" I asked.

"Yes. It's amazing. Definitely really good," Kenneth said.

I have to admit, you're certainly a star in the kitchen. You're not just fun to milk with," toby said.

I flushed realizing he meant something else. I then spoke.

"Yeah I try to be," I told them.

"Anyways, let's dig on in and finish up dessert. We had a long ass day," Kenneth said.

The conversation changed back to food, but I could sense the tension that was there, just screaming to finally come out. when all of this was said and done, they sat back, sighing.

"That was good," Kenneth said.

"Sure was. My compliments to Mary here though. She's amazing, and definitely handy in the kitchen," Toby said.

"Oh shucks. I'm just trying to give everyone a nice little experience. And I mean...you guys have helped a lot with all of the farm work around here. Kind of sucks it won't last forever," I told them.

"Indeed. By the way, any word on your dad coming back?" Kenneth asked.

"He said as early as tomorrow evening, but I doubt it," I said to them. I didn't think he'd come back that fast. But my dad is also a stubborn motherfucker, so I wouldn't be surprised.

That's when I saw their faces change. A smile ghosted Toby's face, and Kenneth nodded.

"Very well. Good to know. It makes things a bit easier for both of us then," he said.

"What do you mean?" I asked. I had no idea what they had planned, or even what they proposed to do.

They looked at one another, smiling excitedly, before moving towards me, looking me in the eyes.

"What's going on then guys?" I asked them.

"Oh, we wanted to give you a little present for all of the hard work. You're definitely a great boss Mary," Kenneth said.

"What do you mean?" I asked.

That's when it happened. I felt Kenneth's lips press against my own. I kissed him, feeling my body tense for a second, surprised that he even wanted this, but then I slowly relaxed. Kissing him felt nice. He had soft lips, and despite his rugged personality, I had a feeling I wouldn't be able to get enough of this if I wasn't careful.

For a long time, I started to feel my body grow nervous, but I also liked the feeling of his lips against my own, of the touch that was there, and as I kissed him, I relaxed, enjoying the sensation of it all. For a bit, we just stayed there kissing and exploring one another's lips.

But then, toby grabbed my chin, turning me so that I could face him, and then, our lips moved and touched against one another. His kisses were a bit more passionate, which surprised even me, making me shiver with delight and enjoy the feeling of all of this. For a bit, we stayed like this, and I didn't mind the excitement, need and desire that came out of this too. For a bit, we continued to make out, and then, shortly afterwards, he pulled back.

"But...why?" I asked them. I mean they were both super attractive, but I didn't know they felt the same way about me. did they?

172

"We wanted to give you a little something to remember us by. Especially if we have to leave tomorrow. You're pretty cute Mary, and good at milking," Kenneth said.

"Indeed. We wanted to make this fun for everyone, and Kenneth and I spoke. We thought about…giving you a fun time if that's what you're into. We can show you many things, since we know quite a bit," Toby purred.

I knew exactly what they were getting at, and I felt a little nervous about this. But then I nodded.

"Yeah. I'd like that," I told them.

They beamed, leaning in and giving me a kiss, staying like this and enjoying the sensation of the touch, the pleasure that came out of this, and for a second, I couldn't help but enjoy the touch and passion that came from it.

They then grabbed my waist, and Kenneth pulled me into his arms, carrying me bridal-style up the stairs to the bedroom I had. I was surprised that they knew where to go, but I guess they just assumed.

When they got up there, Kenneth put me on the bed, giving me a long, passionate kiss. I immediately melted into this, kissing him back, enjoying the feeling of this. His tongue snaked out, and I soon moved my own tongue to meet his, enjoying the sensation of everything that came out of this.

For a bit, we simply stayed like this, and I enjoyed the sensation of it too. But then moments later, he started to move down my body, kissing and touching my neck with the slightest of touches.

I purred, shivering with delight, enjoying the sensation of this. He soon lightly nibbled on my neck there. As Kenneth did this, toby moved his lips, brushing them against my own, and I quickly kissed him back, enjoying the feeling of his own lips. His were a bit rougher than Kenneth's, a different sensation, and there was something thrilling about the different touches, the feelings of such, and the pleasure that came out of this.

I soon started to move my hips, feeling that urge, that need, and that desire that started to push through me, making me enjoy this too.

I began to feel their lisp descend down my body, lightly touching and teasing the sides of my neck, pressing against there and nibbling on the flesh. I tensed up, bucking my hips and moving slightly, feeling the force and pleasure that came out of this drive me to the point of madness.

I enjoyed it, and I enjoyed the feeling of such. It was amazing, and it made me excited for a lot of things, and as he continued to press his lips towards the crook of my neck, biting and teasing the flesh there, I felt my whole body give in, and the pleasure grow.

I was enthralled. I was completely immersed in the feelings that came over me with this. I started to feel Kenneth's tongue move down further and further, nibbling in the wake of his touches, and then, before I knew it, he got in between my breasts, biting on my collarbone before he started to move his hands downwards, teasing the very tip of the fabric of my shirt.

Then, there was toby, who bit down against that part of my neck, lightly nibbling and touching the flesh there making me shiver and cry out with delight, enjoying the feeling of such. I then felt him press his lips there deeper and deeper, enjoying the sounds that came out of my lips.

He then moved towards the other part of the sweater, pulling it over my head.

Kenneth's hands were the first ones to explore my body, touching my breasts and teasing them from outside the cups. I shivered, moaning, and then toby's own hands moved to the tip of my nipple, playing with it there watching my eyes widen and my hips begin to move forward.

"Fuck," I said out loud, enjoying the feeling of this, loving the sensation that came with the touches. The little ghosts of touches against my breasts, nipples, and everything else made me enjoy the feeling, completely enraptured in the pleasure of the moment, and the delight that I felt.

For a long time, I just simply moaned, feeling like it was just taking over me. I wanted nothing more than to just completely lose control, to enjoy everything, and that's when I felt their hands move to the back of my bra, undoing the clasp, pulling it off, and my breasts came out of there.

I had a pretty sizable chest, so when they were exposed, I let out a small gasp, feeling a flush ghost my face. I moved my hand into my red hair, teasing the very edges of this, playing with the fringe there, and I looked at them, my eyes wide with lust and need.

Kenneth was the first to act, touching the very tip of my nipple, playing with them against his hand. As he did that, I suddenly felt my body grow hot, and I knew that this was something that I craved. He touched the very edge, causing the nipple to harden. As he did that, I felt toby's lips against the other nipple, touching it there. As they continued to tease and service me, I started to feel my whole body ache, growing strongly, and I felt like there was something more brewing within.

I started to feel the heat grow from within, touching and teasing every single aspect of them, enjoying the feeling of such. Both of them groaned as they heard my sounds, the little cries and moans of pleasure which came out of my mouth. It was then when, after a few more moments, Kenneth's hands moved towards both, teasing the very edges, making me shiver with delight, crying out loud, enjoying the feeling of all of this as time began to pass forward.

I ached for them. There was that deep-seated need for both of them to take me like this, and I knew that they enjoyed the feeling of this too. I could see them looking at me, the eyes of need obvious. Then, I felt their hands move downwards, until of course they got between my legs, touching the heat that was there against my jeans.

As they did so, I tensed up, moaning out loud and enjoying the feeling of this. The little touches against the heat of my entrance were only making my heart beat faster and faster, the ache and need growing within. They were just touching me slowly, making me feel turned on and teased from this. I was excited for more, and I craved more.

A pair of hands moved towards my jeans, touching them and then looking into my eyes. I simply nodded, needing them to do this, and then, I felt their hands slide the jeans off my body, getting them over my ass until they were down and then off to the side.

I shivered, realizing that this was the beginning of something more. I soon felt another hand move towards my clit, rubbing it from the outside. When I felt that I jumped, flushing.

"You okay there?" Toby asked.

"Yeah sorry. Just...a bit sensitive down there you know," I said with a blush.

"It's all good. I'll make sure that you're taken care of properly then," he said.

The reassurance in his voice made me smile, but not before he rubbed there, touching and teasing, and then, he started to move his hand to my panties, sliding them off. When his thumb encircled the clit, I shivered, moaning out loud, completely enraptured in the pleasure of the moment, the feeling this gave me, and everything good

that came out of this. He continued to tease, every single little touch driving me crazy, and I loved the way that this felt too.

For a long time, they just teased, and I felt a finger dip into me. it was large, and it filled me up. While toby did this, Kenneth moved towards my nipples, pressing his lips to them, teasing and touching them, making me lose all semblance of control and ache that grew within me.

They continued this, and for a long time, I felt like I was at my limit, that aching need driving me crazy, and I wanted to just lose it. But I was so close to the edge, and the two fingers that were within me started to move around, pressing up against that spot.

I was so close, I didn't know how much more of this I could take! But as soon as It happened, they pulled back, making me shiver.

"Come on, I need it," I said.

"You will get it. You've done this before, right?" Toby asked.

I shook my head, red as a tomato as they looked at me with widened eyes.

"You guys are my firsts. But I have…used toys and shit before," I said.

I wasn't a total virgin per se, but this would be a new experience for me. They looked at one another, smiling in excitement, and then looked back at me.

"Well then I guess it's safe to say that we'll be having a lot of fun with this," Kenneth said.

"We sure as shit will be," Toby added.

I flushed, but then nodded.

"Good. I'm excited for this," I told them.

"Yes, we'll make sure everything's properly taken care of then," Toby said.

He pushed another finger inside, making me gasp out in surprise, but as they pumped into me, I knew that I was getting to my limit.

He pulled back, making sure I was okay before reaching into his pocket, grabbing a condom and slipping it onto his cock.

It was much bigger than I thought it'd be, but I wasn't going to let that get me down. I looked into his eyes, and he nodded.

"There we go. That's good," he said to me.

As I watched him spread me apart, I started to flush. I knew it'd be big, but I didn't realize that he'd be so large. As he slid into me I closed my eyes, bit my lip, and then gasped as he got all the way inside me.

Toby looked me in the eyes, to make sure he was fine, and I nodded.

"Yes. Please keep going," I insisted.

I wanted to feel more of him, to feel him deep within me. He soon started to push in and out, pressing in deeply, holding me there as I looked into his eyes, letting out a small moan of pleasure as we started to hold one another.

For a long time, I started to hold onto him, feeling the pleasures of the moment, the ache and excitement which came from me, and then, after a few more moments, I felt something against my lips.

It was Kenneth. His cock was there, big and thick, twitching as I looked at it. I flushed, but then I opened my mouth, accepting him completely. I felt him push into my mouth, filling me up, making me shiver with delight, enjoying the sensation of this, feeling him groan as he pushed into my mouth. I suddenly felt his cock against the back of my throat, and I started to hold back from gagging, simply because I didn't want that embarrassment. But it felt nice., I liked how they used me, even though I felt a little bit nervous.

A pair of hands moved to my thighs, grasping them, holding them against their shoulders, and then I felt toby's cock deep within me. I shivered, crying out loud, enjoying the feeling of this. He gripped my thighs, holding them there as he pushed in deep, enjoying the feeling of my body against his. I moaned, completely enraptured by the feeling of his lips, moaning with need and desire, the ache and pleasure of it all driving me crazy.

For a long time, they continued this, each of them taking my holes, pushing in deep, causing me to feel a newfound pleasure. Then, I felt a pair of hands move towards my nipples, teasing the edges of them, making me shiver and cry out loud, completely immersed in the feelings of this. For a moment, they continued, and then, I felt something against my clit, lightly rubbing there. The smallest of touches made my body tense, and made me let out a small groan of pleasure, the aching need driving me crazy.

For a moment, they held me there, each of them keeping my holes properly taken care of, when suddenly, I felt toby push against me, a hand move to my clit to rub against me, and then he groaned, filling me with his seed. as he did that, he touched against that one spot. As he did so, I cried out, holding onto him, and then I suddenly released, the pleasure of the moment driving me insane.

For a long time, I didn't move. Then, a pair of hands moved to my head, pushing me in. what surprised me next was Kenneth's' seed.

It filled up my mouth, causing me to let out a gagging sensation. But I didn't want to spit it out. I kept it down, swallowing everything, enjoying the feeling of this as it flooded my mouth. For a long time, after Kenneth finished, he didn't move. We all stayed like this, all of us surprised by how good this felt, and the pleasure we all experienced.

It was a different feeling to say the least, and while I was a bit surprised myself, I certainly wasn't against it either.

After a brief moment, they pulled back and I sat there, completely amazed by how good this felt, the pleasure that they provided to me, and the excitement that came with it.

"Wow," I told them.

"You good?" Toby asked.

"More than good. That was just...wow. I should've asked you guys to bone me sooner," I replied.

It was something on the back of my mind, but I didn't realize just how utterly amazing this was going to feel. Both Kenneth and toby looked at one another, and then at me, surprised by the way I felt.

"Well I enjoyed this just as much as you did," Kenneth said.

"Yeah, me too," Toby replied.

I smiled.

"Yeah, I'm really glad that I got to share this moment with both of you," I admitted.

It was an exciting feeling, that's for sure, and I knew that there was a desire for more. I then moved, pushing my breasts together and smiling.

"Well, if you guys want to stick around for a bit, I'm sure that you can. I don't think my dad will be coming back tonight," I purred.

That's what excited me. I was alone with both of them, and they liked it just as much. They both beamed, looking at one another, and then at me.

"Well since you're asking so nicely, I certainly wouldn't mind it," Toby purred.

"Me too. We can keep this our little secret," Toby said.

I beamed, moving towards them, rubbing their cocks. They both groaned, hard once again, and I licked my lips.

I got between them, licking, teasing, and playing with their cocks. These two introduced me to a newfound life, something that I'd never experienced up till this point, and I couldn't help but enjoy it. I liked the idea of these two simply taking me, playing with me, pleasuring me completely. And I had a feeling that they enjoyed this too.

And that of course wasn't to say that they were going to deny this either. They wanted this as much as I did, and for the rest of the night, we were making love, feeling one another's bodies, and enjoying each other.

To say that this was a small little instance would be wrong. It awoke something in all of us. The next evening, my dad came home, asking me how things were. I of course told them it was great, and that the guys were a huge help.

"Do you think we could keep them around for a bit?" I asked him.

He pursed his lips, and then nodded.

"I think that could be arranged," he said.

I gave my dad an innocent smile, but of course, I knew what would come with this. We had a pretty good relationship already, the three of us, and this would only make things even better.

"Thanks dad," I said.

And that's how it began. How my dad hired two farmhands, and we ended up having quickies behind the barn while he was busy. My dad never found out, and it would be the secret I'd take to my grave, never telling a soul about.

The Billionaire's Secret

No way.

There was no way in hell that this was happening.

But as I read the contents of the message, my fingers shook, my body suddenly tightened, and a feeling of dread hit me.

I know your secret Amy. I know everything. And you'll need to keep me quiet. You know where to find me.

I knew who this was from.

That rat bastard Cody.

Cody was a guy that I knew from my college days, someone who I didn't want to ever remember. But unfortunately, I was in this shithole of a mess, unable to get out of this.

He knew my secret about the partying.

Little old me, perfectly innocent billionaire Amy Sanders was now at risk for being exposed. The innocent arc and attitude was there on purpose, and now…I had to worry about this bullshit.

That fucking dick! I didn't know what to do about any of this. I couldn't even tell my friends. The only people who knew about my clubbing and hobbies were of course my friends :Stacy and Stephanie, but they also weren't part of the elites.

That meant that if this was exposed, I'd be fucked.

"What do I do…." I told myself.

I had no idea what to say to him, or even what to respond with. Cody was of course, one of the rival billionaires and the son of my father's biggest rival Travis Gibbons.

Cody Gibbons always loved to create a shitload of trouble, no matter what it might be, and that of course was something that I hated, and something I very much disliked.

I wanted to cry. If this word got out…I'd be royally fucked, that's for sure. I guess the best thing for me to do at this time would be to find out if there was any way for me to keep this a secret.

If the press found out about this, it'd hurt my dad, and I didn't want that. My dad was a big part of my life, my rock. And to know that he was in danger because of this man…royally pissed me the hell off.

That's why I needed to handle this all in private. I didn't want to put my dad's company at risk.

But how do you begin with something like this? Where does someone begin? I can't necessarily threaten the bastard. He's the one who has me by the balls for fucks sake.

Or it would be tits in this case, since I'm a girl.

I knew where Cody lived. He was at a private home that was somewhat close to his dad's place. He somewhat ran the company, but not as much as his dad did. Either way, I'd be meeting him on his own turf, and I don't know how to feel about that.

I guess the proper response was worried? I don't really know how to feel about this, other than of course, worried about the future, and about what may transpire out of this.

The best thing for me to do of course, was to play it by ear, and of course to hope for the best., I didn't know what to tell him, other than to not fucking expose that or else.

What did he want from me though? I hope it wouldn't be something bad.

I sighed, heading out of my dad's place and making my way over to the car. As I went by, my dad asked me if anything was wrong. To which I flashed him a fake smile.

"Everything's okay dad. Trust me on this," I lied.

But I had to make sure nothing happened. I didn't want him to get in trouble.

"Okay sweetie. Holler if you need anything," he said.

Oh I would if I needed to. But I wasn't right now. I went over to Cody's house. When I got there, I buzzed the gate, waiting a brief moment. I heard the crackle of the speakers, but then, I heard him speak.

"Is that you Amy?"

"Yeah, why?"

"Oh, I was wondering if you got my little love note I left for you. I take it that you did," he teased.

That rat bastard. What a fucking dick. I clearly didn't like the way things were at this point, and I hated that this was happening. For a long time, I simply felt like I was at a loss.

"Well I want to talk about that," I said to him.

"Fine fine. Come on in. I'm in the living room. You know where to go," he said.

Of course I did. I came here plenty of times with my dad when I was younger. It'd been a little while though, simply because we weren't friends. I wouldn't necessarily say direct enemies, but that was my dad's rival, and I hated that this was happening.

I drove in, parking the car and then walking on inside. I saw him sitting there in the living room, looking at me with a smile on his face.

"There you are," he said with a smile.

"Let's cut the bullshit. What do you want? I don't want to make this a problem for either of us. And I don't want that getting out," I said.

"Oh? That I saw you at the club, dancing and doing coke? That you're not the good little girl that you pretend to be? How cute," he said.

I gritted my teeth. I hated this guy. But he was incredibly attractive. If he wasn't such a dick, he certainly would be someone I'd consider dating. Even if it meant merging the family businesses.

"Well what do you want? I don't take kindly to this bullshit," I said to him.

"That depends. Are you ready for what I want from you?" he asked me.

I pause, d confusion present on my face.

"Well I'm here. I'm not going to leave until you tell me," I said to him.

I didn't know what the hell his endgame was. Did he want to fuck? Was there some other sort of fucked up blackmail he wanted? Did he want me to tell my dad to pull out of the business deal?

Then, he simply chuckled, looking me up and down.

"I wouldn't mind arranging something privately with you," he said.

"Well tell me. I don't want to pussyfoot around. Please," I said.

My partying days would eventually bite me in the ass, but I didn't expect this. I just didn't want my dad to get in trouble or anything either.

He then chuckled.

"It's simple. I want your ass," he said to me.

"My...ass," I told him.

"Yeah. You've got an amazing ass there Amy. I see it when you're on tv. You've had one for a while, and I of course was curious about it. If you offer that to me, I'm sure we can just put this little mess aside," he said.

Why did he want this of all things? It surprised me that something so simple, yet it made me flush crimson. He was a simple guy with a strange bargain, that's for sure.

"And that's all you want...right? You're not going to lie to me or anything?" I asked him.

In truth, I didn't think he'd be into that of all things, but then he nodded.

"Yes. We don't have to have sex in any other ways. In fact, once this is over, we can pretend to not like each other like we always did. I just think it's...proper payment for what I'm trying to get here," he said.

Payment? Did he think I was some kind of commodity for sale? It pissed me the hell off knowing this. I bit my lip though, knowing for a fact that there was no way I could argue this one.

"Fine. You win," I said to him.

His eyes widened in surprise.

"Really now?" he asked me.

"Yeah. I'm not going to fuck around or anything else. I'm just....I just want that at least. It's not much...right," he said.

It really wasn't all that much, but it didn't make me any less apprehensive.

"Really?"

"Yes really. Just your ass. I just want to spank it, play around with it, you know. Maybe give it a bit of a tease," he said.

I mean, I wasn't a virgin or anything, but it was a very strange thing to ask of me. but I guess so long as he doesn't tell anyone about what happened, we should be fine…right?

"Fine," I finally said.

"You mean—"

"I'll do what you asked," I muttered, flushing crimson at the idea of this.

"Very well. I figured it wasn't much to ask of you. That way we can…have a little bit of fun with this," he said to me.

"Fine," I said.

There was an awkward pause, and I wondered what exactly he'd ask of me next. I mean…would we just do this here or….

"Let's go upstairs. Follow me," he said.

His house was huge, practically a mansion. What did he have up there. I followed him, flushing at the idea of this, but when we got up there, I followed him inside.

"This is—"

"Ding, ding, ding, you've got it," he said.

It was a dungeon. The man had a fucking sex dungeon in his own home. I don't know why, but there was something about this which felt different, but also…I couldn't necessarily complain or anything either.

"So what now?" I asked him.

"First, I want you to put this on," he said.

"But I thought that—"

'It's to get you more comfortable. Won't affect anything," he said.

He handed me some black lingerie. It was simple, but it made me flush.

"Fine," I muttered, grabbing it and going to the bathroom. I put it in, realizing it didn't cover much. Thankfully I didn't think he was filming this, so I didn't have to worry about that embarrassment.

"Okay…just tonight. You don't have to worry about anything else once this is over," I muttered to myself.

I made my way back to the room, seeing him there, a smile curled on his face.

"Wow. You look great," he said.

"Yeah, course I do. This thing is tiny as fuck though," I told him.

"Yeah, that's the fun of it. I'm sure that it'll be fun for you to indulge in of course," he said to me.

I didn't know how to feel. Other than slightly nervous, but also a bit aroused. I mean, I could see his eyes glazing over my body, specifically towards my butt. Even though this wasn't the type of circumstances I expected, there was a thrill in this…for some odd reason.

"Get on the bed, hands and knees," he instructed.

"Okay," I said with a nervous voice. I scrambled onto the bed, realizing the sheets were very soft and plushy. Even though this was embarrassing, and bordering on blackmail, there was something exciting about this. And like…it wasn't the worst thing that could happen.

He could've just straight told my dad, or fucked him over.

So why didn't he? I had no clue, but it wasn't like I was going to ask him right now. I was just relieved that I could get him to forget about this whole mess with well…my body and all.

I laid down, my butt in the air. I felt a hand grasp it, touching it there, and then the hand squeeze it a few times. I let out a small yelp of surprise, and then I heard Cody chuckle.

"Wow, surprised by me grabbing your ass? How cute," he said.

"I wasn't surprised. Just wasn't expecting that much force you know?" I told him.?

"I know. It's kind of cute to see you like this, all flustered and turned on. Now…where were we?" he asked.

He grabbed my butt, teasing the orbs, and while I felt embarrassed to be getting pleasure from this, I couldn't help but enjoy the touch of his hands there. He continued to massage and tease my body, making me shiver and tense up, enjoying the sensation of this.

"There we go. You have such a nice and fun butt. I can't wait to give it a few little Marks here and there," he said.

"Marks?" I said, surprised by this.

"Course. I said I was going to spank it," he said.

I'd never been spanked hard before. While it did make me nervous, there was something thrilling about the way his hands hovered over there.

His hands delicately moved against the edge of my butt, little touches that made me shiver and moan, a gasp of surprise emitting from my mouth when I felt his hand move downwards, just barely teasing my pucker.

I felt so embarrassed but that embarrassment turned into surprise when I felt the smack of his hand, the arch of my hips forward, and the moan that escaped me.

"Look at you. So aroused already," he said to me.

"I…I wasn't expecting that," I told him.

"Course you weren't. you shouldn't. you should learn to relax, and embrace what I have in store for you," he teased in my ear.

What did he have in store for me? I shivered, excitement and need growing within me. I started to feel his hands rest against there slightly, and then, he hit me again.

This time, instead of feeling pain, I suddenly moaned, surprised that it felt…so good. I suddenly bucked my hips a little bit, moaning slightly.

"What's that? You're enjoying this? How surprising and lewd," he said.

"I didn't mean to make a sound. I liked it. That's all," I told him.

"I know you're enjoying this. You can lie all you want, but I can tell that you like this," he said.

It was a little bit painful, but also…I liked the fact that he was teasing my ass like this. I started to feel the hands ghost against there again, smacking me hard once more, and then another gasping moan of pleasure and desire came out of my mouth.

"Holy shit," I said, suddenly jerked to reality by how arousing and nice this was.

"There we go. Look at you, all turned on by this. How cute," he said to me.

I shivered, suddenly feeling like all eyes were on me as he grasped my ass, touching and teasing it there, making me shiver out loud, moaning slightly at the sensation of this. It was then when, moments later, he then hit me once again, another garbling sound emitting from my mouth. He hit me again and again, each spank making me suddenly cry out in pleasure, enjoying the feeling of this. It was driving me insane, making me feel like I was losing control of myself, my mind, and everything in between.

That's when I felt the smack once more, causing me to let out a small gasp, a feeling of pleasure erupting from my body, making me ache for more.

He then moved his hands back, and I let out a small sigh of need. I didn't realize how much I liked his touches until well…he did this to me. but then he chuckled.

"Miss me already?"

"Maybe I did," I replied back.

He laughed once more.

"Well I have another surprise for you before we get to the fun stuff," he said to me.

What other surprise did he have? that's when I felt something graze against my cheeks once more. It felt like a flogger, or maybe a paddle. Either way the cold leather stimulated me, making me let out a small gasp. It felt exciting, but also a bit worrisome, mostly because I had no clue what would happen to me now.

Suddenly, I felt the whack of the flogger, hitting my ass cheeks directly. I let out a small yelp of surprise, mild pain, but also pleasure. He then chuckled, doing this again and again.

"There we go. Look at you, all turned on like this. I can't believe you're so aroused just by this alone," he said to me.

"Maybe I am," I told him.

"Good. As you should be," he said to me.

He continued to paddle me, hitting me hard, and every single point of contact was turning me on, making my ass arch, and my body crave more. My fleshy ass cheeks were soon growing red, and I felt like I was getting closer to my limit.

But, with one last smack, he pulled away, lightly rubbing the cheeks. I winced slightly, realizing just how raw this felt.

"Wow, I really did do a number on your ass. I love the way that it looks right here," he said.

I let out a small moan of surprise, realizing just how raw and sore it was. But I also craved more. Even though I knew that this was just payment for his silence, there was also that thrill of course of being his, of being taken by him, and of course used like this.

I never realized how much I needed a man to just take me and use me like this.

He grasped my ass, touching it slightly, and then, he moved back.

"I think that's enough for now. You're doing great. But I can also see that you're enjoying this too. Even though I know that you're trying to hold back," he said.

I blushed. Was it really that fucking obvious? I didn't expect him to see right through this, but I guess he did.

"So what is I am?"

"Then I'm doing something right. Very right in fact," he said with a purr.

I felt the growing need for more start to take over me. I didn't expect this to come about. But then, I heard him step away from my butt, rushing towards a drawer. He got out a few things, and then, he game over, lightly massaging the cheeks with some oil.

"That should help with the soreness," he said.

I let out a gasp of surprise at the cold texture of this, but also let out a relieved sigh as I felt the contents seep in. it did help with the sting from his touches.

"Thanks. I guess," I said.

"Hey, I could just leave you like this and smack you more. But I do appreciate how well you've been taking this. Maybe you're just a fan of someone playing with your ass after all," he replied.

"Maybe," I muttered.

But the truth was, I did enjoy this far more than I let on. The little massages against the raw, red skin felt nice, but I also was a bit surprised at how easily my body reacted to this. After a little bit, he pulled back, and then, I heard him uncap something else.

"What are you going to—"

Then, I felt it, a finger against my pucker. I suddenly tensed up, surprised by this.

"Now Amy, you don't want to be too tense. That'll ruin the fun," he said.

I knew that I had to relax. But it was such a...a different feeling that it was hard to. He danced his fingers against my pucker, and then two fingers rubbed my clit, causing me to let out a small gasp, a moan of surprise and need.

"There we go," he said, touching me there.

I let out a low moan of surprise, amazed by how nice this was. He continued to touch, tease, and play with me, getting me turned on and ready for more. He then slowly inserted the finger inside of me, which caused me to let out a small moan of surprise and a little wince of discomfort.

It was tight. Then again, I'd never really played much with myself down there. But he slowly got the first finger into me, causing me to let out a low, guttural sound, watching with widened eyes as he began to move his fingers in and out of me, touching, teasing and playing with me. I let out a low groan of surprise as he pushed the finger in deeper, making me aroused and turned on by the sheer feeling of this.

It didn't really hurt all that much either thank fuck. At first I thought it'd hurt the entire time. But it didn't. The discomfort started to go away, and that, combined with the fingers against my entrance and clit, made things a much more enjoyable experience.

He continued this for a little while, touching and teasing me, and it was then when, after a few mere moments, he then moved himself back a teeny bit, watching me with wide eyes and a smile of excitement.

"There we go," he said to me.

"W-what now?" I said to him.

"We add another finger of course. Just relax. I'm sure you'll enjoy it," he said.

I felt a little put on the spot, but I decided to humor him, laying down there. I felt the second finger start to push into me, and I let out a small gasp of surprise and discomfort. This was much tighter. But I felt something touch against the folds of my pussy, rubbing me there, causing me to let out a small moan, suddenly feeling my whole body begin to respond to him. I let out a low sound of need, a muttering moan that made me feel turned on and excited about all of this. He continued the touches, each and every single one causing me to let out a jolt of pleasure, enjoying the feeling of this.

He continued to insert another finger into me, pushing a finger into my pussy, causing me to let out a small moan of surprise, letting my body relax and take over the pleasuring feelings that were within me. even though I was a bit nervous about this, and I didn't know what would happen to me next, I still liked this feeling. It was then when, after a few more thrusts he pushed his fingers slightly upwards, causing me to let out a small cry of surprise.

The fingers in my pussy were pushed deep, hitting a spot within me that I didn't expect to experience like ever. I suddenly started to tense up, letting out a low, guttural sound of surprise, and then, moments later I suddenly felt my whole body just tense up, enjoying the sensation of this.

Moments later, I came hard, feeling my body grow ragged with need.

He pulled the fingers out, teasing one of them against his lips. I let out a sigh of surprise, realizing how good I felt at the present moment.

"Wow," I told him.

"You good?" he asked me.

"I think so," I told him.

"AS you should be. I think it's obvious that you're enjoying this. Well, I guess it's time for the main event," he said.

Oh yeah. He was going to fuck my ass. I felt a bit nervous, but as he pulled down his pants, revealing his cock, I felt a hunger and need.

He was pretty sizable, but I wanted to imagine that I could take it. I licked my lips as I moved my body so that I was closer to him.

"What you doing?" he asked.

"Giving you this," I said.

I opened my mouth, taking his cock into my mouth, letting it slide down my throat. He suddenly let out a low groan, suddenly holding my head there, skull fucking it, enjoying the feeling of this. I let out a gasp of surprise, and it was then when he started to push the cock in deeper, and I suddenly felt my whole body tense up.

He pulled away, making me gasp in surprise as he looked into my eyes.

"Are you ready? You can get on top you know," he said.

"You sure that's a good position? I can keep it like that you know," I offered.

I'm sure that made me sound more turned on and needy than I was, but he simply smiled.

"Well if you insist...."

He then pushed me down on the bed, and then, I felt his cock at the tip of my entrance. He slowly slid in, and I suddenly felt the pain of my ass being filled up. It was a little different from my pussy, and so much fucking tighter, but I started to feel him sink all the way into me, making me shiver, tense up, and enjoying the feeling of this.

When he got all the way in, he held me there, pushing himself inside. I let out a cry as I felt him in there, both turned on and a little bit shocked by how it all fit into there.

Then, he started to move. I clung to him for a moment, but then he pushed me into the sheets., I grasped those, holding onto them as he started to move his hips, thrusting in and out, holding me there as I started to let out a series of moans, enjoying the feeling.

Every single moan, every single touch, it was all just...amazing really.

It was such a turnon that I couldn't help but enjoy the way that this felt. I held onto the sheets, feeling him sink in and out of me, pushing in deep, holding me there, causing me to realize just how turned on I was by this.

He continued his large, harsh thrusts, holding me there, but then he grabbed my hips, thrusting in deep. As he did that, I suddenly tensed up, letting out a small cry of surprise and pleasure as he continued to push into me, holding me there as he thrust himself in.

His hands moved towards my front, teasing me there, and soon I felt two fingers inside, and a finger against my clit, rubbing it and holding onto me there.

As he pushed inside I tensed up, letting out a small cry of pleasure and surprise. I couldn't believe how good this felt, how amazing this was to me. it was only moments later that he finished up, letting out a low groan, and finishing inside of me.

I felt the power of my own orgasm completely overwhelm me, and as he finished inside, he then pulled away.

I fell onto the bed, amazed but also exhausted by this. I simply laid there, and he chuckled.

"Well, you okay there? Or did I KO you?" he asked with a smile.

I turned to him, giving him a small thumbs-up.

"I enjoyed it. Don't get the wrong idea," I said.

"Really now? You enjoyed getting fucked in the ass from your rival? How scandalous! Imagine if others found out and—"

"You won't tell anyone. Because it will also backfire on you," I said, giving him a small smile.

This was different from the revelations of my partying. This of course would also reflect on him. He paused, pursing his lips and then nodding.

"Course I won't say a damn thing. I don't want to get in trouble either. But I'd be lying if I said I didn't have a good time. And you more than paid off my silence on many things of course," he said.

I flushed, realizing that I didn't have to worry. So why did I feel the urge for…more.

"I see," I said.

"Well, I guess that's it. If you want to leave you can—"

I shook my head.

"I don't want to leave. I kind of liked it Cody. I had a good time. If you wanted to do this again, I wouldn't mind it. It's not really a punishment to me," I told him.

He looked at me with surprise on his face, and then he nodded.

"Wow. I see then. I guess that settles it," he told me.

"Yeah, I'm just…I'm glad that I had a good time with all of this," I told him.

"I'm glad that you did too. I don't think this was necessarily a total punishment for you either," he said.

It wasn't. it awoke something new within me though, a series of feelings that made me excited, and I craved more. But it also made me wonder if there was something more there, if there was a chance we could do this again.

"If you wanted to do this again…I wouldn't be against it," I teased.

His eyes widened for a second, and then he nodded.

"Really now?"

"Yeah. I really enjoyed it," I told him.

He chuckled, and I wondered what was so funny to him. but then he spoke.

"I didn't expect this to happen. But you know, I wouldn't mind it either. However, we don't tell our parents about this one. Got to keep the rivalry idea in place still," he said to me.

"You're right," I said to him.

"But…I can't wait for the next time we get to have something this fun happen. I'm sure it'll be good for both of us," he said.

"I'm sure it would be too," I replied.

He leaned in, giving me a kiss, much to my surprise. At first, I wanted to tell him to fuck off, but I kind of liked it. As soon as it happened, he pulled away.

"You know, I think this is the start of something fun Amy," he said.

I grinned.

"Yeah, I think so too," I replied.

It was the start of something alright. I had no clue what would happen now, or even what we'd have to do, but I also knew for a fact that this awoke something in both of us, something neither of us were expecting, but also…I liked it. I knew that this would change the way things would go, and I didn't regret anything that had happened either.

Erotic Sex Stories Collection For Adults- We Both Cum: Gangbangs, MILFs, BDSM, Hard Anal, Femdom, Tantra, Sex Games, Orgasmic Oral & 69, First Time Lesbian (Forbidden Fantasies Series)

By Rachael Richards

Table of Contents

Hannah sat alone in her two-bedroom apartment, wondering what she would do, and how everything had gotten so out of control. Boxes full of all her packed belongings surrounded her, despite having been in the apartment for almost a month now. She figured she had better leave her things packed up because unless things changed for her soon, she would have no other option but to move back home with her parents and her younger brother. She had just finished her last semester of college with a bachelor's degree in mass media. She was so proud to have gotten one step closer to her dream. She aspired to one day be an investigative journalist, and to use her job to have a positive impact on the world, but that dream had quickly begun looking increasingly bleak lately. Upon graduation, she used the last of her disbursement checks to get this little apartment, but now, after only a month, she is faced with the possibility of being evicted because she had no money to cover the second months' rent. Her eyes welled up with tears at the thought of having to return home in defeat. Her family had warned her about journalism being such a competitive work line, but Hannah had been determined to follow her dream. She was regretting that decision now. Hannah did not know what she was going to do with her life, but she knew that she needed something to survive. She did not have a job, and if she does not figure something out quickly, she will not even have a place to call home.

She furiously typed away on her phone, looking for any work she might be able to do. She reluctantly put applications in at retailers and restaurants that probably would not pay much more than minimum wage. There is no way these jobs could possibly pay the bills here, but at least it is something. Days of filling out job application after job application had seemingly led her nowhere, so she started looking into other possible avenues. She looked at everything from paid survey sites to participating in paid clinical trials. She tried to sign up to deliver food and to drive people around, but the speeding tickets she got last year cause every single one of the companies she applied for to deny her application. If only David had not tossed her away right before graduation. He had been her sugar daddy for two years and the second she got near graduation he discarded her like a used tissue, probably to get himself a newer model. She bitterly thought about David and hoped that his day was sucking as badly as hers was, but she doubted that was the case. She knew the internet held the key to thousands of lucrative options for her to come out of this on top, but she had no idea where to begin looking. After searching for hours and hours, she mistakenly stumbled her way onto a website that looked rather promising but required her to not only compromise her morals but also it would put her at risk of being heavily judged if anyone ever found out. There were pages of women to scroll through, both young and old, thin and thick, all types and seemingly from all walks of life. They were all advertising their services as escorts, and most were charging hundreds per hour. She was surprised by how classy and beautiful some of them appeared to be. A year ago, she would have never considered this an option, but now her livelihood was at stake.

As Hannah's plans for the future had begun to turn into a long shot, she steadily became increasingly desperate, and now with the rent's due date closing in on her, she was desperate enough to do almost anything to avoid having to return home with her tail tucked between her legs. She could not stand where she currently stood in life, it was incredibly embarrassing for her, and as a result she avoided her friend's. She missed going to college and living on a college campus. She missed the parties, and the activities, and clubs. Hell, she even missed going to classes. Probably most of all she missed her friends. She felt a pang of jealousy when she realized they were all probably starting their careers, while she was scared and alone wondering what to do. Fallon, she figured was probably taking advantage of her very practical, as her parents would say, paralegal degree. She was probably quickly offered a good-paying job, but the last thing Hannah wanted was a job as immoral as a lawyer's job was. Katie was probably getting prepared for medical school. Hannah did not envy her at all truthfully. Medical school sounded terrible to Hannah. Ella was probably enjoying a great internship at some prestigious company, no doubt that her sugar daddy helped her get.

She did not like how envious she felt in this moment. She was not normally like this as a matter of fact she normally would have celebrated the success of her friends. She tried to push the negative thoughts from her mind. She

focused on fixing the circumstances she has found herself in. She kept trying to tell her brain that would be a much better use of her memory. She hoped none of them would ever see her like this. She felt embarrassed by her desperate situation. As she walked down the hallway, she thought about her parents, and how they had tried to steer her into the medical field. It was then that she lost all the control that she had held onto for so long now and finally she burst into tears. She did not care about what others might think anymore, and it did not matter how bad it was or how many people hated her for it. Her emotions were too volatile and sad to cope with any other emotion, so she let the determination to fix this situation overcome her. She knew what she had to do, and she was not proud of her decision, but she was confident in it.

She curled up on the edge of her bed feeling exhausted by all the stress she had been enduring. She slept for longer than she had in what seems like ages. The next morning, she woke up feeling groggy, but still with a much clearer head than she had before the sleep. She grabbed her laptop from its bag and opened it on her lap. She opened her browser and navigated back to the No Games website she had found the night before, and then she clicked the sign-up button at the bottom of the page. She paused on the first box where it asked for her name. After a moment of staring off deep in thought, she decided that Lexi would be her name in this new world she was entering. For her own safety, she was careful not to give any of her real information throughout the sign-up process. It felt as though she were creating an entire new person, but that person was also her. Once she had signed up, she considered what her next step would be. Her ad was missing one vitally important thing. So before actually posting an ad, she got up, and began digging furiously through the boxes that sat in her living room. While looking through her third box she found what she had been searching for. She emerged from the box with her arms full of all kinds of lingerie and ran with it to her room, which was the only room in the house that looked decent enough for to be the background of a photo and had a mirror.

Hannah quickly threw on her favorite set of lingerie first thing, and then found herself some black thigh-high stockings to go with it. It was a leopard print bra and panty set with a matching garter. Her C-cup breasts fit snugly in the B-cup bra, making her boobs appear to be bigger. Her perfectly round nipples were just barely poking out of the top of her bra. The garter belt and lace stockings showed off her beautiful long tan legs, and her long blonde hair fell loosely over her shoulders creating a beautiful contrast against the dark orange, brown of the bra. She ran her fingers through her hair before running to the bathroom and using some dry shampoo to add some volume. She almost began applying make-up but quickly decided that it would be a waste of time because she was planning to blur her face out to protect her identity anyways. Hannah began posing for photos while she took them herself with her iPhone. She used her bed and a chair from the dining room as props. After taking pictures of every pose, she could think of and at every angle she could think of, she plopped down on her bed and began flipping through the pictures she had just taken. Majority of them, she did not like, and those got deleted but even she could see that the few she kept were stunning. She used an app to blur her face out of the photos and immediately added them to her ad. She sat up on her bed for hours looking at the computer screen and the pictures of herself on her new escort profile. She saw someone who was not Hannah, but Lexi instead, with her bare legs outstretched and her hair falling over her eyes. She could not take her eyes off her, and she could not believe she was doing it.

Her heart pounded hard in her chest and her hands shook as she clicked the button that would make her ad go public at last. Once it was done there was no going back. She stared off in a daze of mixed emotions as she tried to process her own actions and what they meant. It had not even been twenty minutes after posting her ad when her phone began to buzz off the hook. She could not even keep up with the flow of the incoming calls messages despite her best efforts to do sp. She sat there typing as fast as she could until she had found a potential client that she felt comfortable enough to have her first 'visit' with. Part of the reason she chose him was that he said that he was only interested in receiving oral, and she thought that sounded easy enough. She knew her skills in that department were exceptional, and that made her feel more confident. He also had agreed to pay the full

hour's rate without trying to barter her down like most were doing. After exchanging all the necessary details along with a few pictures, she had set the visit up for later that evening at her apartment.

Hannah looked at the clutter around her and shook her head in disapproval. She decided that she could not have company with the place in this condition. Plus, now that she had some hope that she might be able to pay her rent, she felt a little better about unpacking things. She went to work unpacking and setting up the furniture and any other big items. She unpacked a few of the boxes with home décor in them and began hanging pictures and artwork that she had acquired. She laid out a few rugs the had and she even put out her wax burners with fresh wax and tea candles. The place felt so much more like home when Hannah was done. She still had a couple hours before her client was supposed to arrive, so she began to shower, shave, and get herself completely ready. When she was done blow drying her hair she looked over in the corner of the room and saw her lingerie. She picked up the whole pile and shoved them all in a drawer, quickly grabbing one out, as she shut the door. She slipped it on and looked at herself and smiled. She was feeling nervous but luckily, she was also feeling confident and sexy, and she figured those feelings would carry her through this.

Hannah's first pay to play (oral story)

The loud knock at the door came abruptly and interrupted her deep thoughts. It startled Hannah to the point of nearly jumping out of her skin. She looked at the time and was surprised to see that it was in fact closing in on the time of her scheduled visit. It was amazing how quickly the last couple of hours had passed. She quietly crept over to the door, being careful not to make any noise just in case it was someone whom she did not want to answer the door to. She slowly leaned forward and looked through the peephole and there stood the same man from the photo she had received earlier in the day. He was an older man, most likely in his late 40s or maybe 50s. He had on a light blue button-up shirt and a pair of khakis. His disheveled hair was grey and so was his mustache and his beard. He was certainly not the most attractive man ever, but she did not anticipate that he would be. She noticed that he had very kind eyes. The kind of eyes that just shouted for you to trust them without question. Hannah quickly swung the door open and let him in. She closed it behind him as fast as possible so that no neighbors would see this older gentleman coming in her apartment. Once he was inside, he looked at Hannah with a surprised and happy expression.

"Woah, you really look just like your pics", he said in awe as he looked her up and down. "I'm Daryl by the way", he noted. Hannah giggled for a moment before introducing herself.

"I'm Lexi", she said politely. She was surprised by how calm and collected she was. She had anticipated that this would be so much more stressful than it was turning out to be. "You can come on back to my room", Hannah said sweetly while giving the man a friendly smile as she waved him down the hall and toward her bedroom.

"Alright miss", he said, with the awe still clearly in his voice, as he followed her into the first of the apartment's two bedrooms. He looked around the place, curiously peeking behind each door and into every room he could see. Hannah noticed his eyes wandering around the apartment almost frantically as if he were looking for something.

"Please excuse the mess, I just moved in", she said as she tried to figure out why he kept looking everywhere as if he expected a monster to be lurking somewhere waiting for the chance to attack.

"Oh, that's alright", he said, apparently satisfied as he brought his gaze back to his prize. Hannah apologized in advance to the man in case she starts seeming nervous. She explained to him that this was her first time ever doing anything like this and told him that she would likely have the first-time jitters. He gave her a look that let her know that he knew her struggles and he felt for her. He told her that he always gets nervous too. The kind understanding feeling between them turned to something a little confusing and hard for her to comprehend when he began undoing his belt with haste. As he unbuttoned and dropped his pants, Hannah stripped dutifully down to the lingerie she had hidden underneath her clothes. He nearly did a double take when he turned his attention back to her and saw her outfit. The see-through lace baby doll and matching thong she had on, had clearly impressed the man who stood patiently waiting for her. When she got close enough, he reached out his hands and began touching her body with an expression that indicated amazement. As she dropped down to the floor on her knees if front of the stranger his fingers slid lightly up her body, giving her chills which made goosebumps begin popping up all over her skin. She took his still flaccid cock, first into her hand for a brief moment, and then she looked up at his smiling face seductively and she teased his cock with her mouth for just a moment.

"Are you ready", she asked the stranger as she teased him by stroking her hand up and down his thick shaft.

"Yes, yes", he said breathlessly and with a slow intentional nod. She immediately began sucking on his stiffening cock. He gasped a little bit when Hannah began working his shaft, but he quickly began enjoying her work. She listened as his breathing got heavier. He reached down and started massaging her breasts gently, circling her nipples lightly with his fingertips. The sensual feeling made her nipples tingle and they hardened almost instantly as she let out a quiet moan. She quickly swirled her tongue around the smooth cock head and slowly began to suck the throbbing member harder, pulling it in and out of her mouth over and over.

"That feels so nice", he said softly as if he were in a dream. She acknowledged him with a gaze and a nod and began to gently suck on the head of his member. She momentarily licked his balls and he moaned in appreciation. After a few minutes she was back to working the man's cock with the ease of someone who was used to doing this. Then the man began to moan quietly as he looked into her eyes. She looked back at him seductively with her mouth stuffed full of his cock.

"I...it's...ohhhh, Lexi!" he cried out in great pleasure. She took him in deep and pulled out only to plunge her mouth quickly back onto his dick hard. She began to fall into a steady and constant rhythm. Her head bobbed up and down on his erect cock for quite some time. She began to wonder when he would cum as she had begun to grow impatient and bored after a while. She was brought out of her daze when she felt his fingers run through her hair and grab some of it at the top of her head. Her attention refocused and she began sucking him harder and more passionately as he kept his grip on her hair firm. The man moaned louder and began to thrust himself into her mouth harder and faster. She gagged a little bit when he pushed as deep as his cock could go, but she quickly followed up by locking her lips around the shaft with a deep suction. "I'm gonna cum baby", he warned. She continued to continue to gently bob her head up and down on his shaft. She stopped just before she felt him blow his load into her mouth. As he did, she heard him gasp in a breath of air. She pulled him out of her mouth and licked his shaft completely clean. "I'll be honest", he began. "I have been having some trouble lately. I did not think that was gonna happen. You have surprised me", he admitted in an almost as quiet a tone as her voice. Hannah gave him a sympathetic look. "Are you going to be in town a while?", he asked hopefully. Hannah laughed.

"You'll have other opportunities", she assured him as he pulled his pants back up and buckled his belt around his hips. "This is my place and I do not plan on going anywhere for a while", she said with a smile.

"You really have not done this before have you", he asked looking doubtful. Hannah shook her head no. He asked if he could tell her a few things he knows by being a client. Hannah told him that she would be grateful for any knowledge he could offer. She explained to him that she started all on her own, with no help or knowledge of how it works. He told Hannah that she should be careful giving her address out like that. He explained to her how most girls just give a general area and direct the to the right place. Hannah listened intently and nodded. She wondered why she had not considered that. Probably due to the nerves she shrugged. He also told her that in the future she should not begin to provide services until they place the money on a table or another surface in plain view. He told her that most girls will not touch the money until the services are rendered. This all made sense to Hannah as he said it. He saw her eyes look around the room to see if he had placed the money somewhere already.

He noticed and began pulling his wallet out of his pocket. He opened it an pulled out a wad. A thoughtful looked flashed across his face and he quickly opened his wallet again to pull out another bill to add to the pile. Hannah hesitated for a moment unsure of what she should do. He nodded his head in the direction of the cash letting her know that it was okay to pick it up. She began counting it and excitement welled up in her belly in response when she realized he has left three hundred which was one hundred more than they had agreed on. She smiled and thanked the man for his generous tip. He thanked her as well and assured Hannah that he would be back if she would have him. Before walking out the door he stopped and turned back to her.

"I would suggest you contact some of the other girls on the site. Maybe someone will show you the ropes, besides you could probably use a friend being that you just moved", he suggested. Her eyes widened and she smiled.

"What a fantastic idea", she exclaimed excitedly. They wished each other a great evening as he left her apartment as swiftly as he could.

Hannah sat in her room and pondered the likelihood of Daryl's suggestion working out in her favor. She knew she needed some tips so that she could make doing this as safe as possible for herself, but she was so nervous about reaching out to these girls considering all the negative stereotypes about the girls who work in this industry. She did not want to make herself seem desperate or weak to them, so that they could come to the conclusion that she would be easy to take advantage of. All of a sudden, she realized that she could at least reach out to a few of the girls from the website, without ever revealing who she was, or taking any risks. She did not have to reveal her real identity, or her newly acquired escort identity, unless she felt comfortable doing so. This would allow her to test the waters before completely jumping in. She downloaded a second messaging app to keep herself anonymous when contacting these girls, she navigated to the find escorts section of the No Games website. Hours after she has sent texts out to quite a few of the girls who advertised on this site, she finally received a response. Hannah then, without giving any details as to her motives, asked the girl if she could take a quick phone call. When the girl responded with a yes, Hannah wasted no time dialing her number. She impatiently tapped her nails onto the counter as the phone rang.

"Hello? This is Kayla", said the girl from the escort website. Hannah noticed how smooth and sultry the girl's voice was.

"Um, hi", Hannah responded taking care to avoid using her name or any other identifiable details.

"Hmmm, that's not at all the voice I was expecting to hear", Kayla said in a suspicious but teasing tone, "Are you calling about my...um..services?". Hannah's heart was pounding fast and hard in her chest, but she just let it all spill out in one long frustrated sentence, without any details of course. She told the girl about her struggles, and how she needed someone to help her get started safely. When she finished there was radio silence on the other line. "Are you there?", Hannah asked tentatively.

"Yeah", said the girl, "Send me your address and I'll come by later to talk", Kayla said before ending the call. She did not give Hannah the chance to agree or to say anything at all. Hannah found that to ve incredibly rude, but at least she was not told no. She hesitated and wondered if sending this girl her address was safe or smart. In the end she decided that there was not any reason for this girl to want to harm her, so it was worth the risk. Then, before she could change her mind, she typed the address into a text message and hit the send key. Hannah began nervously pacing about her apartment, as she did anytime, she was feeling stressed or impatient. She began wondering if she had made the right decision. She decided that there was not anything she could do to change the situation at this point, so she decided to pass the time, and distract herself by unpacking more of her things. The entire time she had spent unpacking she kept checking her phone obsessively, every five minutes or so. It was driving her crazy not having any clue when this Kayla girl would show up. She decided to ignore the messages from potential clients for a while until she had an opportunity to work this out, so she muted the app she used for client's messages. She just finished breaking down the third box that she had finished unpacking and putting the contents away. She heard a faint ding and ran to check her phone.

"OTW", the message said simply. After some deliberation, Hannah responded with an okay, before she began walking around her home and hiding anything with her real name on it, and anything of value that she thought someone might want to steal. Right as she was finishing hiding all the stuff she wanted hidden her phone dinged again. It was Kayla again, only this time she was announcing her arrival. Hannah peered out her living room window which looked out to the building's main entrance. She had made it to the window just in time to see a

glimpse of a woman who appeared to be in her late twenties coming in the doors of the apartment building. Moments later there was a light knock on the door, Hannah opened the door and there stood Kayla, the girl who's arrival Hannah had been anxiously awaiting all day.

"Come on in", Hannah said smiling as she held the door open for Kayla. She walked in and took a seat on the couch. Hannah first noticed how pretty Kayla was. She was a bit older than Hannah, but she was far from the stereotypical prostitute that Hannah had imagined this girl would be in her mind. Kayla was definitely a far cry from that. She was a healthy-looking, tall, brunette with an hourglass figure. She had thick thighs and an extremely healthy bust as well. Her beautiful olive skin-tone was a perfect complement to her bright green eyes. Her long straight hair almost made it down to her hips. Hannah thanked her for coming, and Kayla just quietly nodded as she looked around the place.

"So, you need some help getting started, right?", Kayla asked. Hannah nodded. "I would be happy to give you all the help you need", Kayla said. "I remember starting out, it's hard with no one on your side, and us working girls, we gotta stick together", Kayla smiled at Hannah. Hannah could not help but to be suspicious of Kayla's kindness. She wondered why this girl was being so nice to her, what could this girl possibly want from her? She hoped it was genuine, but she somehow doubted it would turn out that way.

"Is this where you plan to work?", Kayla asked. Hannah nodded in affirmation. "You know not to ever give your address, right?", she asked. Without giving Hannah a chance to answer, Kayla began speaking again, "just give a general area, or a nearby landmark that is viewable from inside your apartment, when they say they've arrived look out your window and get a good look at them. Make sure there are no suspicious vehicles surrounding them. Once you see them, you can then invite them up if they look safe". She went on to explain that she always asked for a photo so she could compare it to the person that gets out of the car. Hannah sat quietly taking it all in as Kayla continued with tons of useful information. Every now and then Hannah would take out her phone so that she could take note of the things she did not think she would be able to remember.

"How do you know if someone is a cop?", Hannah asked. Kayla then taught her how to check a person for wires inconspicuously by hugging them. She also taught her other ques that someone could potentially be a cop. Hannah had no idea how much necessary information she was missing, and she came to realize that without Kayla's help, this venture could have easily turned into a nightmare. There were so many little technicalities to remember like the one about touching the money. As Kayla continued to reveal piece after piece of valuable information, Hannah began to let her guard down very slowly. She finally had decided to introduce herself to Kayla as Lexi. The two girls spent hours going over the various ways to make things safer for themselves, a few times their conversations had accidentally veered off into their personal lives, but by this point Hannah did not mind in the least. Kayla had a kind and nurturing spirit and Hannah felt that she could trust this girl, so she had begun to throw away her caution.

Kayla looked over Hannah's online ad and helped her make many important improvements. They also did a rn down of typical ling or slang words that were exclusive to the escort world. When she offered to take some better pictures of Hannah for the ad, Hannah started to blush a little. Other than her mom, Hannah had always been very modest and timid about being naked in front of other women. Although Hannah did think she could use some better-quality photos for her ad. After some careful deliberation she accepted Kayla's offer, and offered to return the favor as well. First Hannah knew she would need a good strong drink to help her relax. She offered Kayla one as well, which she happily accepted. So Hannah went to the kitchen and mixed each of them up a delicious tasting coconut drink with cherries in it. Plus, it was extraordinarily strong which Hannah was certain she needed at the moment. The girls were awfully close to being the same size, so they both began sorting through Hannah's lingerie, trying things on, and taking sexy photos of each other for the ads. They were having a great time hanging out together, and they clicked so naturally and instantly. After quite a few drinks Hannah offered to

let Kayla stay overnight so she did not have to take the risk of getting a DUI by trying to drive home. It felt as if the two were already becoming best friends. They cuddled up in bed together and eventually fell asleep while watching one of Hannah's favorite television shows.

The next morning, when Hannah woke up the first thing, she noticed was her viciously head pounding with a hangover as a result of the previous night's festivities. She slowly sat up in bed and noticed something else peculiar. There was the delicious smell of cooking food coming from the kitchen. Hannah's stomach growled angrily, demanding to be fed. All of a sudden, the events of the night before came back to her in a flood, and she remembered how her, and Kayla had become fast friends. Hannah walked into the kitchen excited to see her new best friend. There was a huge breakfast made that Kayla was just sitting out on the table waiting to be eaten.

"I really hope you don't mind me cooking breakfast", Kayla said. "I did not use any of your food, I went to the grocery store and got stuff to make breakfast", Kayla explained. She then sat two champagne flutes and a carafe full of something orange on the table. "I got stuff for mimosas too", Kayla said excitedly. Hannah thanked Kayla and gulped down half of her glass of mimosa in a single gulp. The two girls had a great breakfast. Afterwards Kayla said that she would have to leave soon because she had plans with a client later that day. She gave another rundown of some of the safety measures they had spoken about the night before.

"How long have you been doing this?", Hannah asked.

"A long time", replied Kayla. "Honestly, I love it", Kayla admitted sheepishly. It took me a long time to admit that openly. "I have never been appreciated in any other job, relationship, or any other role in life, the way I am appreciated in this job", Kayla explained. She went on to explain how the perks of getting pampered, getting to take luxurious vacations, and in general just being doted on in every way. Hannah did not quite understand what she meant yet, but Kayla knew she would soon enough. Kayla could see the confusion cross Hannah's face, so she decided to try to explain it in a different way. Kayla had a story that she was sure would help shine some light on the situation. what she was talking about using a true story about when she had discovered that she really loved doing this job.

Kayla gets spoiled (69 Story)

Kayla grabbed her bags as she disembarked the plane. A client had flown her out to New York for a weekend visit. Kayla was exhausted from the flight. She had not expected there to be snow, and she had not packed with the expectation of snow, so she was shivering in her light jacket as she waited outside the airport for Tate to come pick her up. When he finally pulled up, she tossed her bags into the back seat and hurried into the passenger side where she huddled close to the vent to get as much heat from it as she possibly could. Tate parked in the parking garage and then they entered the neighboring apartment building. They took the elevator up to the thirty-sixth floor and made their way to an adorable studio apartment that had a beautiful view of the city. Kayla tucked her bags beneath the bed. Once she got her things put away, Tate was already laying in the bed beckoning for Kayla to come join him. She was exhausted so Tate rearranged their schedule, so they had the time to take a nap.

When she woke up Tate informed her that they only had a couple hours before they had to be at Aska, which is one of the nicest restaurants in New York City. She was delighted to discover that while she had been sleeping, Tate took the liberty of visiting a few of the designer stores a couple blocks over and he returned with a stunning cocktail dress for her to wear to Aska. When he pulled it out of the shopping bag she smiled and looped her arms around his neck and kissed him. She tried on the dress right there in front of him. She looked in the mirror at the way the dress brought out all her favorite parts of her body. He reminded her that they did not have much time to make their reservations at Aska, so she quickly did her make-up and then called to Tate to inform him that she was ready to go. They made it to the restaurant with little time to spare. They were shown to their table immediately by the nicely dressed hostess. She began looking for the menu when Tate informed her that there was no need. He made the reservations for them to have the tasting menu. She could see the chefs cooking in the nearby kitched and was amazed by their focus and deliberation throughout the entire process.

The waitress suddenly appeared with a bottle of wine. She began explaining the bottle, but it was gibberish to Kayla, who knew nothing about wine. The waitress poured them each a glass before sitting the bottle gently on the table. Moments later a plate was brought out. On it was what looked like a bundle of sticks. Even Tate was confused on how to eat the dish. Once they had figured it out, they found that it was remarkably delicious. That course was followed by eleven more artistically beautiful and stunningly tasty dishes and three more bottles of wine. Luckily, each course had a fairly small portion so that by time they were done, they were both comfortably full and sufficiently intoxicated. Tate took her to a high-end lingerie shop on the way back to the apartment. She picked a few things she liked, and he paid for the steep bill. They made one last stop on the way back to get a massage in a Chinatown shop. Kayla spent the entire time taking in all the sights of New York in amazement. Each street looked vastly different from the last, and each one was crowded with so many people from all different walks of life. They finally made it back to the apartment and Kayla went straight to the bathroom with her bag of lingerie in hand. She tried each one on and picked her favorite to wear for Tate. It was a lacy see-through romper. It was blue and had an adorable pink bow that tied around the waist. When she came out of the bathroom Tate looked at her with desire in his eyes.

"You look beautiful.", he said dreamily.

"Thank you, I'm so glad you like them." She smiled at him.

"I want to see you in all of them.", he said hopefully.

His big blue eyes shone with excitement. He ran his hands through his wavy blonde hair. She wondered why he had to resort to seeing escorts when he was such a good-looking man who also happened to be very wealthy. She decided it did not matter to her. She loved the way he doted on her, spoiled her, and tried to give her everything that caught her eye. He pulled her towards him and kissed her passionately on her beautiful plump lips. He pulled out a long white envelope from his pocket. It was half full of cash, her payment for the weekend. He brought it to her face, and she could smell the strong odor of cocaine. He smiled at her with anticipation as she pulled the small bag of white powder from the envelope.

"Just a little something extra I threw in", he said coolly. She smiled back at him and dumped a little on the table beside them and began breaking it up with a dollar bill and a paper weight that was sitting on the table. They each did a line and then laid back to let the drugs take effect. She could feel him pressing her head down to his chest, while he unzipped her romper.

"Are you alright? Do you want me to stop?", he asked softly with concern.

"No, I like it.", she said timidly as her nerves seemingly began coming to life.

"Alright, if you're sure.", he said smiling, and then he continued with his business. She could feel the fabric sliding down her back. Once he got it around her feet the held it over the bed and they watched as the fabric fell to the floor. He grabbed her by the shoulders and pulled her in close, so that she was straddling him. His hands now were rubbing her pussy. She did not have to do much to make her body respond to the stimulus. She was already very aroused and ready to go thanks to the euphoria caused by the cocaine. He slid his hand up to her chest and massaged her tits for a moment before sliding it back down to rub her bare pussy. Then fueled by the wine and cocaine, she began rubbing her tits and arching her pussy forward, pressing herself against his boner. He slid two fingers into her pussy and she moaned in response and then she felt him flip her onto her back in a single swift motion, and just like that his face was buried between her legs.

"Oh, God", she said in a heavy voice, letting her head fall back, as she felt his tongue rubbing her pussy. Her head lolled back, but it did not help the pull of the tongue. It felt as though her head was going to roll off her shoulders. His tongue was circling around her pussy lips and he could not resist the taste of her juices. He stuck his tongue as far inside her as it would go. She squirmed with ecstasy as her pussy tried to keep his tongue out. He had to have some of her, as much of her as he could get. He shoved his tongue all the way in and then brought it out and he began licking at her clit. She cried out in ecstasy. Her orgasm was quickly approaching, and she could feel the beads of sweat forming on her forehead. When he finally did bring her to her first orgasm, she grabbed his head and his hair and screamed as she shot her whole body into an out of control orgasm. She pulled his face to her pussy and forced him to continue licking and sucking. When her orgasm subsided, she took his head into her hands and looked him in the eyes.

"I am not done yet!", she said excitedly as she pulled herself up to her hands and knees. She pulled his pants off him and discarded them to the floor. Then she did the same thing with his boxers. She took his entire member into her mouth, chocking a little as she plunged all the way down forcing his cock into her throat. When he felt it enter her throat he felt as if he were about to explode with pleasure. He could not help himself. He gripped the hair on the back of her head and forced himself down into her throat a few more times. He moaned loudly as he felt the muscles constricting tightly around his cock. He kept thrusting his hips forward, moaning in appreciation. "I want to taste you again", he groaned as she continued to work his cock with her tongue. She slowly and carefully scooted her knees towards the head of the bed and threw her leg over so that she was straddling hi face. Her mouth did not stop bobbing up and down on his cock a single time. He pressed his mouth against her pussy as she took his balls in her hand and began licking them softly. He was in heaven. He knew his dick was going to cum soon if he did not slow her down. The way she kept sliding her mouth up and down his dick was just too good. He

could not bear to bring himself to stop her. He managed to will himself to not come for the time being, as he began to circle her clit with his tongue again making her press her hips harder against his face. He thought about how amazing she tasted and he hoped he could make her come in his face again before this was over. He plunged two of his fingers deep into her tight little hole while she sucked hard on his cocked. She moaned in pleasure, so he continued pulling his fingers out and pushing them back in repeatedly.

"Oh my", she mumbled. It was barely understandable with his cock in her mouth. He reached to the back of her head and grabbed her hair, pulling her face away from his cock.

"Didn't your daddy teach you not to talk with your mouth full?", he asked before slamming her face back down so that his cock reached the back of her throat again. Her legs began to quiver, letting him know that she was close to another orgasm. So, he pushed his fingers back inside her and repeatedly slid them in and out of the dripping wet hole. First a slight tricked of cum dripped into his mouth,

"Yes", he said as he enjoyed the taste of her cum. Then, she suddenly gushed her juices as she straddled his face. He had to hold his breath to keep from inhaling it but he did not care. He was just trying to lap up as much of her come as he could. Her legs were shaking hard and quivering as she pulled her pussy away from his mouth.

"I can't take anymore", she said breathlessly. "Just let me take care of you now", she suggested. He nodded at her and smiled. He felt accomplished at making her cum so hard. She felt her soft lips lock around his cock once more. He felt her tongue rubbing against the sensitive spot right beneath the head of his cock as she gripped his balls with her hand. He loved the feeling of her mouth on his cock. He explored her entire body with his hands and watched her lips move up and down the length of his shaft.

"She is a persistent little thing", he thought with adoration as he realized that she had been going at it for some time now. He pulled lightly at her nipple with one hand as the other cupped her ass firmly. "Do you think you can handle this?", he asked as he pulled one of those high-powered wands from a bag beside the bed. She had never gotten the opportunity to use one of those, and she was curious.

"Yes baby, I want it", she cried out. He flipped the switch and the wand roared to life. She could tell that this was going to be a wild experience. He gently used his fingers to spread her pussy open and he spit on it so that it was good and lubricated. The moment the wand touched her clit she began bucking her hips forward and shaking and moaning loudly with her mouth still around his cock. It took some effort but she managed to refocus her attention on pleasing him. Seeing her experiencing that much pleasure got him closer to coming than she could have imagined. He knew he would soon come. He began using his hips to thrust his cock harder into her mouth again as he held the wand against her pussy.. The cum felt as if it were slowly making its way to the head of his cock. He knew this would be a huge load, as he had not had anything but his hand to relieve this tension in months. He felt her fingers lightly caressing his balls as he still continued to thrust his cock into her mouth. He did not want to come yet, not until he absolutely could not hold it back any longer. The look on her face made him think she was very closeto coming again as well. The feeling of his cock being at the back of her throat, it was enough to send him over the edge, and she went swiftly with him. He bucked his hips forward as they both lost all control. He began spurting all of his cum into her mouth, and a warm sweet stream began to gush from her pussy as she was hungrily swallowing every drop of his cum with greed. She sucked it all in, swallowing it in full gulps, cleaning the remnants of his load from her throat as she looked up at him.

"Oh, my that was amazing", he said leaning back against the pillows at the head of the bed. She licked her lips and nodded as she crawled towards him to lay her head on his chest.

"I was so nervous to come here", she admitted. "I am so glad I did though", she said smiling.

"I'm happy you did too", he agreed. "Hey, that worked up an appetite for me, Are you hungry?", he asked.

"Yeah, actually I am", she said. He said he knew the perfect place to take her. New York is famous for pizza, so they went to his favorite pizza spot and they got a few slices to share. She was shocked at how big they were when he brought them to the table. They were delicious though and between the two of them, they ate almost every bite. He remembered her mentioning wanting to get some souvenirs to bring back for her daughter, so next he took her to a nearby street that was lined with souvenir shops. She ended up loading her arms with things that she liked, and he paid for it all despite her telling him that she could cover it.

"If you play your cards right, some of these men will absolutely spoil you rotten", Kayla said to Hannah as she finished telling her story. Hannah had sat quietly, listening intently as Kayla explained why she loved this job so much. Hannah understood everything Kayla had said pretty well, and she knew exactly what Kayla was talking about. She remembered the rush she felt when her sugar daddy doted on her and gave her anything that she wanted without questioning it or even looking at the price tag. She remembered how powerful it made her feel, how important she felt when he would put her on that pedestal. Even just the attention he gave her was enough to give her some of the fulfillment she was now craving to have again. The way he would ignore even the most important clients to give her his undivided attention. She doubted that most wives got this kind of treatment from their husbands.

"How do you make that happen?", Hannah asked with curiosity. She was determined to get that feeling back. Hearing Kayla's story reawakened Hannah's desire to have that feeling again. The feeling had begun to swell up inside her chest, a feeling of excitement. It felt the way someone might feel if they had won the lottery.

"It doesn't always happen, some men will be very professional about their interactions with you, and you likely will not be able to get that out of those ones. With other's it can be really simple and easy actually", Kayla began to explain as Hannah leaned forward listening with interest. "Learn their names and take a genuine interest in them. It makes them feel special, and then they want to make you feel special in return". Hannah nodded at this thoughtfully. For the first time since she had graduated and left the college campus, she felt truly optimistic about her future and her financial well-being. She looked around at her apartment and instead of feeling stressed and anxious, she felt as if she could take on the whole world and win. Suddenly, she thought about how she had begun to feel about the man who was supposed to be just a sugar daddy, how she had begun to see him differently. This thought sparked an important question in her mind.

"Do you ever catch feelings for these guys?", she asked as she considered her own feelings for her former sugar daddy.

"I have a few times", Kayla answered honestly and without hesitation. With this question a few of her former clients came to mind, and she realized that this had happened to her more times than she would like to admit.

"How do you manage that", Hannah questioned. Kayla explained that she just had to keep it in the front of her mind that the feelings would eventually dwindle and subside. She had to remind herself that she was absolutely free and living a life most women could only dream of living, and that to give that up for an exclusive relationship with one man was completely insane, especially when she could still have that man in all the best ways without having to give everything up to commit herself to him. Hannah made a mental note to remind herself of that if ever she felt the desire to emotionally attach herself to a client. She knew she had a tendency to be a highly emotional individual, and that could be difficult to manage at times. So, she could foresee the possibility of this type of thing happening to her at some point. It almost seemed inevitable in this type of job. An opposing though occurred to her as she considered how the job could also make her not want any type of attachment to any person. It was just as likely that she could become overwhelmed with having to fake interest and attachment with people she may not particularly like.

"Does sex ever begin to feel like work to you? I mean do you stop enjoying it due to it being your job?", Hannah asked. Kayla thought this over for a moment and then she began telling Hannah that thinking about the money she was making always turned her on. So even if she did not necessarily enjoy the sex with that particular client, she could still get herself turned on by thinking about the cash she would be walking away with. Luckily, there had almost always been at least one client with whom she genuinely enjoyed having sex with. She did however go through a period of time when she had begun to lose interest in sex. Thankfully, it was only temporary, and it turned out to be a rather easy fix. She just had to engage in some sexual activity that was not related to her work. The first time she did this, she did not do it with intention, and in fact she engaged in some pretty high-risk sexual behavior as a result, but it taught her an important lesson about how to, and how not to handle those situations. Luckily on her first instance of this she was able to emerge from it unscathed. However, she considered herself lucky because it very well could have easily turned out much different for her.

Kayla pondered whether she should tell this story to Hannah or not. It was a somewhat embarrassing story to tell, and she had not told many people at all for fear it could come back to bite her. It was actually fairly recent in fact and she unfortunately had to worry constantly about the possibility of it coming out into the open. She was surprised at how much she already trusted Hannah already. This girl had just stumbled into Kayla's life, and Kayla was not even completely sure why she had agreed to take on the huge job of mentoring her, and without even asking for payment in any form. She brushed it off when she recognized how good it made her feel. She wanted to help this girl empower herself. Kayla threw all caution to the wind and decided to tell Hannah the story despite how embarrassed she felt about doing so.

"I need to let you in on a few things before I tell you this story", she said to Hannah. First she made Hannah promise to remain tight-lipped about this one. She explained that it had the potential to have consequences on her relationship with her daughter. Hannah felt honored that Kayla was willing to share this clearly personal story with her. She had heard Kayla mention getting souvenirs for her daughter in the last story but decided not to ask and questions about it due to the personal nature of the topic, not that she was not curious. Kayla then revealed that at the time she had been experiencing some sort of crisis that had made her act out of character. Hannah assured her that she understood what it was like to go through that sort of thing, she had many coming of age crises in her teenage years. So, Kayla took a deep breath to calm her nerves and began at the beginning of the story.

A Naughty MILF (MILF Story)

"I should mention that I became a wife and mother at the young age of eighteen. So, I have a daughter who is now in her preteens", she admitted. She explained that she had lost custody of her daughter when she got divorced, and the court ordered that she only got to see her child when her ex-husband allowed it from then on. Her former husband eventually remarried, moved across the country and now Kayla's daughter had a stepmother and a stepbrother. Kayla tried not to complain much because they were incredibly good to her Pheobe, and she realized that the situation could be much worse. They gave her daughter an excellent life and provided her with everything she would possibly need and then some. She knew her daughter was happy where she was, despite the fact that they both wished they could see one another more often. One evening her daughter called her as she usually did each night before her bedtime. When Kayla answered the phone, her daughter's voice boomed loudly through the Phone. She could tell that Phoebe was excited but could hardly understand what she was saying at first. When Phoebe finally calmed down enough so that Kayla could understand her, she became just as excited as her daughter was. She would soon get to spend some quality time with her daughter.

Kayla was excited to be going to visit her ten-year-old daughter after more than a year had passed without seeing her. She got off the plane and met Phoebe, who was accompanied to the airport by her eighteen-year-old stepbrother, who politely introduced himself as Justin. Phoebe's father, Gerald, and stepmother, Karen were going on a vacation with Karen's family for a few days and Justin had already made plans to leave town to go on a road trip with some of his friends from school, so they asked Kayla if she would like to come baby sit for them. Kayla was happy they had asked, and she quickly agreed, she was not going to miss this rare opportunity to spend quality time with her daughter for anything. When Kayla got off the plane, Phoebe stood waiting with a bouquet of flowers in one hand and a homemade card in the other. When Kayla approached, they both had tears welling up in their eyes. Phoebe held both of her arms out to her mother with the gifts she had brought her and excitement shining in her eyes. They stopped a few times on the way out of the airport to take a few selfies together, as well as to pick up the rental car Kayla had booked for the trip. Phoebe asked her brother Justin time and time again if she could ride along with Kayla. He looked at Kayla apologetically as he explained that his mother instructed him to drive Phoebe home himself.

Kayla calmed her upset daughter, assuring her that she would be following right behind her in the rental car the entire way back. Phoebe remained a little pouty after that but did not put up much more of a fuss. Upon arriving at their house, Justin, who was a skinny young man with dirty blonde hair, dutifully turned on the oven to prepare a casserole his mother had made in preparation for Kayla's arrival. It smelled delicious and when it was done Kayla made all three of them a plate and sat them at the table. The all sat down and ate together at the dining room table as Justin went over the extensive instructions his mom, Karen had left for Kayla. Kayla felt a little overwhelmed, and even Justin had indicated that he recognized how ridiculous his mother was being. Karen had practically planned the entire week for her and Phoebe. She was thrilled and grateful to be able to spend the time with her daughter, but she was really hoping to take her to do some things that she thought they would enjoy doing together. Once everyone had eaten everything on their plates, Kayla watched television as she sat on the floor and colored with Phoebe for a while before putting her to bed at the time Karen had instructed her to do so. With Phoebe asleep and Justin up in his room, began searching the kitchen for some wine or anything else to help her relax. She looked in every cabinet, the fridge, and even the pantry, but found no trace of anything to help her take the edge off her jetlag.

"Looking for this?", a voice came suddenly from behind her. She jumped and turned to see Justin standing behind her with an unopened bottle of wine in one hand. "I won't tell if you won't", he said looking at her smiling. She breathed a sigh of relief and smiled back at Justin.

"You scared me half to death", Kayla responded as she turned to retrieve two wine glasses and a corkscrew from the cabinet. Justin took the corkscrew from Kayla, carefully opened the bottle and poured them each a glass of the wine pouring it exactly as a professional would have. "Are you old enough to be drinking?", she asked even though she already knew the answer. He just at her and shrugged as if it did not matter.

"Have you ever played spades?", he asked Kayla as he retrieved a deck of cards from his back pocket. Kayla agreed to play because spades was one of her favorite games, but she had not played it in years. They sat down at the table and Justin began shuffling the deck. She could tell he played sports. He was not as scrawny as she had first thought. Just toned and fairly thin. He had striking gray eyes and an incredibly handsome smile. Time flew as they got playfully competitive over the game. About three games in the wine bottle was empty. "I'll go grab another", Justin said nonchalantly.

"But what if", Kayla began, but Justin quickly cut her off.

"Trust me, my mom would never notice even if we drank twenty bottles. Her wine cellar has hundreds of bottles in it", he explained. "Come on I'll show you", he said as he waved her in the direction of the door that led down to the basement. At the bottom of the stairs there was a big open den like area, through one of the two doors down there was a massive wine cellar that was fully stocked with an enormous collection of wine.

"Woah", explained Kayla.

"Go on, pick any one you like", Justin urged. Kayla selected a sweet white wine that caught her eye. Justin popped it open and they settled on the couch in the den. Justin put some music on the surround sound system. Both of their heads were buzzing from the wine. They were having a thought provoking and deep conversation about Justin's romantic life. When he asked about her love life, she told him there was not much to tell. He got a thoughtful expression on his face and then leaned in towards her. Everything in her was screaming to put a stop to this. Something stopped her. Maybe it was the wine or how cute and sweet Justin was, or maybe it was her anger at Karen and her ex that she had kept submerged all these years, but when his lips met hers, she kissed him back. She knew it was wrong but once it began, she felt as if she were powerless to stop it. His tongue gently pried her lips apart and made its way inside, pressing gently against the inside of her cheeks. She clumsily pressed her tongue back against his. He was careful and tactful, never pushing too hard so that she could come to her senses and put a stop to this madness. Her insides felt as if they were a molten lava pool ready to erupt at any moment. Justin's arms went around her and rested at her waist as they kissed.

She could feel his penis press against her thigh. He moved his lips to her neck for a moment and then kissed her on the lips again. As if she were in a trance, she mindlessly let her hand glide slowly up from his thigh, stopping at the waistband of his shorts. It was uncomfortable, and she was not sure why she kept moving forward but she did. She felt the warmth of his body as she slid her hand down to his penis. It was still partially limp, just slightly chubby, most likely as a result of his nerves. He pushed the bottom of her tank top up slightly and pinched her nipples lightly. Her head was spinning with misplaced desire that likely stemmed from the forbidden nature of what she was doing. She still had a dry mouth and no breath to give. She took another gulp of the wine that was still flowing freely through her causing her inhibitions to falter. Justin massaged her shoulders as he left a trail of kisses up her neck. Each one left a tingling sensation behind. She had gone from being shocked and disgusted with herself and what was taking place to euphoric within a matter of mere seconds. He gave her a quick but lingering kiss on the lips. Kayla scrambled to her feet unsure of what to do next. She had never wanted to be naked with anyone this bad before, but the thought simultaneously turned her stomach, or maybe it was the wine doing that.

Justin was sitting on the couch and was watching her with intensity. His hand went between his legs and he rubbed himself. Kayla reached over and placed her hand on his dick. It was soft before but now he was rock hard. She was stunned by the size of his erect cock.

Kayla did not know why, but she just could not resist touching him. She slid her hand down the length of his shaft, over his balls and then on to his taint. She did not think much about it because she was completely hammered by this point. It felt amazing for both of them and she giggled out loud at this outrageous situation she had found herself in. It was at that point that Justin slowly moved in front of her. His eyes were downcast as he had her turn around so that she was sitting between his legs, facing him. He then reached over and took her hand and placed it on his dick. Kayla jumped up, momentarily coming to her senses and looked over her shoulder.

"Justin, what are you doing?", she asked

"I need this," he stated. "I need to feel your touch." Kayla succumbed slowly stroked his penis until it was as hard as a rock again. Kayla was unsure what to do next. She knew she needed to get out of there, but Justin had her fully turned around. Justin put his arms around her and began kissing her neck, and then slowly down her chest. He stopped just at her chest and stared at her nipples for a few moments. He looked her in the eyes, winked, and slowly lowered his mouth to her left nipple and took it in his mouth. Kayla's nipples were extremely sensitive, which was not a good thing when she was drunk. Her body began to tingle, and she wanted to reach over and rub herself, but was unsure of what to do or how to do it. Justin continued sucking on her nipples as he continued tracing a line around her belly button with his fingers. Kayla felt one of his fingers tickling her belly button. She could feel the warming sensation travel up into her belly. As he continued his attention to her breasts, he began pushing the other finger inside her. Kayla quickly found that she loved his fingers. She felt like her vagina was on fire. He took his finger out of her pussy and her it immediately returned to feeling normal. He put his hand between her knees, spreading her legs open wider and ran his finger slowly from her clitoris up to her anus. This was unexpected, and Kayla let out a loud yelp of surprise. Justin remained unfazed and continued to touch her as if nothing out of the ordinary had happened.

She pushed him back and he leaned back onto the couch. He then moved back in closer to her. Both Kayla's excitement and fear intensified all at once. He bent down toward her and kissed her deeply and passionately. He felt her breath become heavy as she almost began to pant, and felt every muscle in her body tensing up. She realized she was about to give in to her desire completely and she could do nothing to stop it. He gently removed his belt and lowered his pants. He gripped her hips and gently pushed himself into her. Justin slowly slid inside her as he held her hips in his hands and stared down at her face. Kayla began to relax as he slowly slid in and out of her body. He grabbed her hips and began pumping faster. She let out a loud moan as he hit her g-spot with every thrust. Justin was now fully inside her, and he began thrusting even harder. Kayla felt as if her insides were burning up with an intense sensation as she neared an orgasm, and soon she was on fire. Her head was spinning as the pleasure completely overcame her. She wanted to tell him to stop, but for some unknown reason she needed this badly. He looked up at her as he continued to thrust inside her and smiled.

"You look beautiful like that," he said to her. He began thrusting harder and harder, pounding himself into her with all the force he could muster up.

"Justin," she said suddenly. Then she weakly murmured, "please don't stop", she silently cussed herself as she knew she had meant to tell him to stop. He could see the worried expression on her face.

"Don't worry", he said comfortingly as he smiled at her and began thrusting faster into her wet pussy. After a few more minutes, he let out a loud moan, and Kayla felt his body shake violently as he came inside her. She could feel his cum gushing out and filling her with his seed. The trance she had been in was broken immediately. She ran to the bathroom and tried to clean as much of his cum out of her pussy as she could. When Kayla walked out

of the bathroom, she saw that Justin had made himself comfortable on the couch and had fallen asleep. He still had no clothes on so Kayla put a blanket over him and quietly crept upstairs to the guest bedroom where she should have been all along. She curled up in bed and tried to make sense of what she had just done. When she could not make sense of it, she began thinking up ways that she could ensure that no one ever found out about what had just happened. Then she cried herself to sleep, hoping that this would not come between her and her daughter

After finishing her story, Kayla was already late meeting her client, so she had to rush off quickly, leaving Hannah alone to ponder everything Kayla had covered throughout the last couple days. Hannah did not judge Kayla for any of the things she told her, in fact she looked up to her even more for having overcame the obstacles she had to face. Taking in all that new information must have worn her out because Hannah felt insanely tired all of a sudden. She laid down, curled up in her bed and fell straight into a deep sleep. Hannah woke up a couple hours later feeling as refreshed as she would have if she had gotten a full night's rest. She got straight up and jumped into a hot shower. When she got out and dried off, she grabbed her phone to see if she had missed anything during her nap. She saw a missed call from Kayla from about thirty minutes prior so she immediately pressed the call button to see what she had called about.

"Hey", Kayla said cheerfully. "What are you doing?", she asked.

"Not much", Hannah replied trying to get the sleepiness out of her voice.

"Well, I realized that I desperately need to get my nails done, and I thought I would invite you to come along with me. My treat!", she said to Hannah in a persuasive tone. Hannah needed no persuasion though. She agreed immediately and with no hesitation and thanked Kayla for inviting her along. Kayla told her she would be there in about twenty minutes and Hannah told her that she would be ready. They said their goodbyes and hung up the phone so that Kayla could focus on driving and Hannah could finish getting ready. Once she was off the phone, Hannah ran to the restroom to blow dry her hair and fix her make-up before Kayla arrived. About a half hour later Hannah got a text from Kayla letting her know that she was pulling up to the apartment building. Hannah was already ready and waiting downstairs. She hopped into the passenger seat, sat her purse down in the floorboard, and fastened her seatbelt. The salon where Kayla got her nails done was conveniently right down the road from Hannah's apartment. The bell dinged as they opened the front door of the nail salon to go inside a were immediately sat side by side on the area of the salon that was dedicated to manicures. They were offered a glass of wine which they both accepted graciously.

After discussing a few different colors and designs and getting one another's opinions. They both settled on what they wanted done to their nails. Kayla was getting a simple elegant design with fed paint and gold glitter swirls. Hannah had a tendency to be a bit quirkier and more expressive, so she got an adorable design with lip prints for Valentine's Day which was just around the corner. A little over an hour later, Hannah and Kayla were washing their hands and showing each other their nails proudly. Once they got back into the car the conversations about their job resumed since they no longer had to worry about their conversation being overheard by patrons or the salon staff.

"Where do you live and work?", Hannah asked Kayla noticing that Kayla had never mentioned anything about this before.

"I stay in hotels", Kayla stated.

"That must be expensive! How do you carry all your stuff around all the time like that?", Hannah asked with a concerned expression. Kayla explained that hotels were the norm for working girls. She realized as she thought about it that she had actually never met an escort who had a permanent residence. She then assured Hannah

that it should be fine, better actually, than jumping from one hotel room to the next. She told Hannah that she just did not keep more than she needed, which made it easier to move frequently. Hannah frowned at this, thinking that Kayla would probably be much happier with the stability of having a place to call home. Hannah pointed out her favorite sushi spot as they drove past.

"Oh I love that place", she exclaimed.

"Sushi?", Kayla asked making a disgusted face. Kayla looked surprised.

"You don't like sushi?", she asked.

"I've never actually had it", Kayla said. Hannah insisted that the go get some so Kayla pulled into the sushi bar. They went inside and both ordered a drink called oriental water, which had sake and some fruity mixers. Hannah ordered for the both of them. When the waitress brought out the sushi, Kayla admired how pretty it looked but admitted that she was nervous to taste it. Hannah showed her which to try first. She was amazed by how delicious it was, and she liked every one that Hannah had ordered for them. They ended the meal with some green tea ice cream and then Hannah paid the bill. They left excitedly talking about how great the food was. The girls had become close friends and rather quickly. It all felt very natural to them both.

Kayla dropped Hannah off at her apartment so that she could go back to her room and work. Hannah decided to finish getting her place set up and ready for her to work. She unpacked the rest of her boxes and organized everything. She looked around in the spare bedroom and wondered what she would use it for. When she got done getting her place the way she wanted it she poured herself a glass of wine and sat down to go over the things Kayla had taught her, and to reflect on her friendship with Kayla. She loved how naturally they clicked. Kayla really was a truly kind person, and Hannah was not sure what she would have done without her. She decided she probably would have landed herself into some massive trouble. She began considering ways she could repay Kayla for her kindness and help.

The following morning Hannah awoke to her phone ringing. She had been hearing it ring for a while, but she was unable to bring herself to get up until now. She rolled over and grabbed her phone from her nightstand and squinted her eyes at the screen to see who was calling her. It was Kayla, so she bolted upright and answered her phone as quickly as possible.

"Hello?", she said with the grogginess still apparent in her voice.

"Hey", Kayla said on the other line, "Sorry I didn't mean to wake you up but it is sort of important".

"It's fine", Hannah replied. "I was about to get up anyways", she lied. Kayla explained to Hannah that one of her best clients had come to see her the night before. She had been telling him all about Hannah and their friendship. Then this morning she woke up to a message from him requesting to see them both. He said that he did not actually want to fuck both of them. He wanted to take them out to a nice dinner and afterwards he wanted to watch Hannah and Kayla fuck each other. Hannah was silent on the other line as she took this all in. She had never done anything with a girl before and the idea was very intimidating. Hannah could not help but to be incredibly nervous about this proposal and she was not sure if she would even be able to go through with it.

"Hannah?", Kayla's voice called, breaking through Hannah's daze.

"Yeah, I'm still here", Hannah replied.

"So, what do you think?", Kayla asked. Hannah paused for a moment trying to figure out the least embarrassing way to tell Kayla the truth. She stumbled over her words for a moment.

"Have you ever been with a girl before?", Kayla chimed in.

"No", Hannah replied. Kayla assured Hannah that everything would be fine. She said that they really just needed to put on a show for the client. She told Hannah just how lucrative this could be. She also assured Hannah that she would help her along and make sure she knew what she was doing. "Okay", Hannah said, finally agreeing tentatively.

"Awesome, I'll be over in a bit to start your training young Jedi", Kayla replied jokingly.

Hannah got out of bed and went straight to the shower. She was not sure what Kala had meant by training, so she wanted to be clean just in case. After scrubbing herself to her satisfaction and shaving her legs, underarms and pussy, she stood under the almost scalding hot water until it ran cold. When she got out of the shower, she wrapped her hair in a towel and wrapped another around her body and headed towards her room to get herself dressed. As she stepped into the hallway, Kayla busted into her living room without knocking startling Hannah.

"Oh, sorry I didn't mean to scare you", she said. "You left your door unlocked", she shrugged her shoulders and then smiled at Hannah. Hannah told her that she was going to get dressed and she would be right back out. Hannah ran to her room and threw on the cutest underwear in her drawer, the first pair of jeans she could find, and a crop top she grabbed from her closet. She spritzed herself with some perfume before going to meet Kayla in the living room. Kayla was sitting on the couch seemingly captivated by whatever she was doing on her phone. Hannah sat beside her and Kayla showed her the screen on her phone. It was playing porn from a porn website Hannah had heard of once or twice before but had never visited. Predictably, Kayla had lesbian porn playing, Hannah leaned in to watch, silently telling herself that it was solely for the purpose of research. They watched the screen as the two girls went from kissing one another to fingering each other, then one girl began eating the other's pussy, and then that girls pulled a rabbit toy seemingly from thin air and began thrusting it into the pussy of the girl who was eating her out. The girls sat side by side, watching and saying nothing, both felt awkward knowing that they would probably be doing these things with each other soon.

"So, I spoke to Jason, that's the clients name, about when he wants to do this and he leaves town tomorrow, so we have to do it this evening", Hannah's jaw nearly dropped. She had not been expecting it to move so quickly. Kayla looked at her apologetically.

"Okay", Hannah replied apprehensively.

"He's paying us five hundred dollars each", Kayla said looking at Hannah intensely. Hannah thought of how much five hundred dollars would help her right now, and it would only take a couple hours of her time. She knew she needed to do this. Plus having her new best friend with her should provide her with some much-needed comfort.

"I'm in", Hannah said more decisively this time. Kayla sent Hannah a few links for some videos to watch that demonstrated what she had in mind. Hannah agreed to watch them. Then Kayla learned in and kissed Hannah on the mouth. Hannah kissed her back, feeling shockingly passionate in the moment. Hannah was surprised to find that she enjoyed the kiss so much she felt herself start to get wet. Kayla looked at Hannah and smiled victoriously.

"We've so got this", she said confidently as Hannah was still trying to regain her composure from the dizzying kiss they had just shared. Hannah smiled back at her feeling a little awkward. Kayla began excitedly rambling about doing a two-girl special if this went well. She seemed excited about the earning potential this had so Hannah figured it must be pretty in demand. Kayla told Hannah she would see her later and they hugged before Kayla left the apartment. Hannah locked the door behind her and once alone her eyes went wide as she took in what had just happened. She had never felt attracted to a girl before, but the kiss she had just shared with Kayla had left her craving more. She found herself looking forward to that evening. She was still incredibly nervous, maybe even more so now, but at least there was now some excitement mixed in too. Hannah made her way back to the bathroom to do her makeup and her hair. Kayla had texted her to tell her she would be back around five to pick

Hannah up so they could meet Jason at the restaurant. Then she sent a pic of herself in the lingerie she planned to wear. She had on a black bra and pantie set, a matching garter belt, and some stockings. She suggested that Hannah wear the similar set she had in red. Hannah texted her back to say that she would.

Hannah passed the time by watching the videos Kayla had recommended. She was glad to be watching them alone. The few moments she had spent watching porn with Kayla had been very awkward and uncomfortable. However, the kiss they had shared made it much easier, and much more exciting to imagine doing those things with Kayla. Hannah got a little wet watching the first video, and by the end of the second she was squirming. She tried to curb her libido as much as she could, but she eventually had to get her clit sucker toy from her dresser drawer. This thing was incredibly quick and straight to the point and Hannah liked that. The moment it latched onto her clit her entire body began to shake and twitch. Within moments she was gushing. Luckily, she had the foresight to put a towel beneath the lower portion of her body before getting the toy. Otherwise, there would have been a terrible mess for her to clean. Hannah glanced at the time on her phone. She had about an hour before Kayla would be arriving to pick her up. Hannah decided it was time that she get up and get herself done up for this dinner date. She grabbed a classy yet sexy cocktail dress from her closet and slipped it on. Then she went to the restroom to freshen up and touch-up her makeup. About the time she finished getting ready, she heard Kayla banging on her door. Hannah grabbed her purse and hurried out the door. Once outside Kayla looped her arm around Hannah's.

Hannah's First Girl (First Time Lesbian Story)

"Ready?", she looked at Hannah with an adorably mischievous smile. Hannah could not help but smile back as she nodded her head. The ride to the restaurant was spent jamming to their favorite songs. They took turns blaring their favorite songs through the car's speakers. They both sang along to every song they knew as the bobbed their heads to the music. Kayla exchanged a few texts as they pulled into the area where the restaurant was so she could find out where Jason had parked. She pulled up directly beside his huge black Toyota. They got out of the car and there stood Jason. He was a medium height, older gentleman who was not bad looking by any means. He smiled brightly and hugged Kayla first, and the hugging Hannah as he introduced himself to her. He escorted them into the restaurant where they were quickly seated at a table near the bar.

"She's every bit as stunning as you said she would be", Jason said to Kayla. He glanced in Hannah's direction and winked at her flirtatiously.

"I know isn't she", Kayla said touching Hannah's face clearly putting it on extra thick for her client. Hannah looked into Kayla's eyes lustfully to let her know she understood the role they were to play. Hannah wondered how much of it was really them playing a role and how much of it was real. Hannah could feel the chemistry between her and her friend since they had kissed, she wondered if Kayla was feeling it to. They sat and chatted and flirted with one another constantly throughout their meal. They ended up just sharing a few appetizers and having a couple drinks each.

"Would you ladies care to ride with me?", Jason asked. "I can drive you back here to your car once we finish up at my place", he offered.

"Sure", Kayla responded in a bubbly tone. "That's okay with you right Lexi?", Hannah had nearly forgotten to respond to her escort name.

"Of course, it is", she said trying to imitate Kayla's level of enthusiasm.

Kayla climbed into the passenger seat beside Jason, and Hannah got into the seat behind Kayla. It was a short ride, which Hannah mostly spent listening to the light conversation that was taking place between Kayla and Jason. They pulled in and parked in front of an enormous house. Hannah looked over the place taking in the massiveness of it. She wondered if Jason had family here or if he lived alone. If it were the latter, she did not know how he could stand to live alone in such a huge place. She marveled at the beautiful design of the place. Each detail was clearly intentional. Hannah thought briefly of her old friend Ella, from college. She had graduated with a degree in design and would have loved to have seen this stunning place. The thought made her feel a pang of sadness as she realized how much she missed the dorms. Having friends around her all the time had made living alone quite the adjustment, Hannah frequently got lonely and often had trouble sleeping as a result.

"What a beautiful place you've got", Hannah said as she turned her attention back towards Jason and Kayla.

"You haven't seen the best of it yet", he exclaimed. "I think a tour is in order", he said as he began leading the ladies through the house. Hannah noticed that Jason loved showing off. She was careful to frequently give him complements because she had already gathered that was the best way to win his favor. Jason had been momentarily distracted when Kayla gave her an expression of excitement and a thumbs up. Even though she had quickly grown bored of the tour, Hannah acted as if she were wowed by every single room for the purpose of stroking Jason's clearly enormous ego. Jason passed her a drink which she took and thanked him. He then escorted

them to a room with a huge bed in the center of it. Adjacent to that room there was a lounge area which appeared to have formerly been a walk-in-closet. The lounge area had small windows that one could look through to see into the bedroom without being seen themselves. Hannah thought that was rather odd, but she made no mention of it because she did not want to be rude.

"This is where we do our thing", Kayla said to Hannah flirtatiously and with an exaggerated excitement. Hannah followed along smiling back at Kayla mischievously.

"I've been waiting patiently for this all day, and I don't know if I can stand waiting much longer", she said seductively back to Kayla. Jason quietly excused himself to the lounge, leaving Hannah and Kayla alone together.

"I brought us all kinds of fun things to play with Lexi my dear", Kayla said as she slowly unzipped the purple duffel bag she had brought along for the date. She began to pull out vibrators of various shapes and sizes, a few different dildos, a strap-on, a large bottle of toy friendly lubricant, and even a few butt plugs. She laid each item neatly on the small table that was right beside the bed so that everything was within their reach. Hannah watched with interest and responded to each item as Kayla pulled it out of the bag with various oohhs and aahhs. When she was finished laying the toys out, Kayla walked across the room to where Hannah stood and began kissing her on the mouth passionately and deeply just as they had done earlier at Hannah's apartment. Just like it had been before it was instantly dizzying to Hannah. "So, do you like that?", she asked Hannah pulling away slightly so that she could gaze seductively into her eyes.

"Yes, I do like it. It's pretty nice", Hannah answered with slight bashfulness.

"Well, we should definitely start off with something that is pretty nice", Kayla said with a laugh as she pulled Hannah's jacket off her shoulders and placed it out of the way on the corner of the bed.

"You're not going to take my dress off of me, are you?" Hannah asked in a sarcastic tone.

"Now look who's being the demure one?", Kayla joked while rubbing her hand lightly up Hannah's inner thigh. She then pushed the skirt of Hannah's dress up past her plump ass and looked appreciatively at the lingerie underneath without ever touching her skin.

"So, you don't want to play with me now huh?", Hannah said in slight mock disappointment.

"Well, I thought my sweetie may want to spend a little time with me to get him going", Kayla said gesturing over to the lounge where Jason sat alone. "But you might be lucky enough to have some hands-on fun with me afterwards", Kayla said coyly.

"Can I trust you to keep that promise?", Hannah teased her, raising her eyebrows suggestively. Kayla shrugged with a playful smirk. Jason was accustomed to being the man in charge in most situations. He loved that role and anything else caused him to feel anxiousness, so Kayla wanted to take the time to make sure he felt that he was the one calling the shots. She walked over to him with the lace of her thigh-high stockings showing just beneath her dress, and as she had expected he would do, he told her he would rather spend time with her after he got to watch the two ladies have their fun, and that he had really been looking forward to his private show, so Kayla returned to Hannah with an eager smile.

"You're in luck, I guess he wants his show first after all", Kayla said looking as if she were a feline about to pounce on Hannah. Hannah was nearly shaking with nervousness, but so far, she had hidden it well. She decided to calm her nerves by taking control of the situation, so before Kayla could make the first move, Hannah stopped her by grabbing Hannah by the arm and leaning in close to her, placing her lips right above Kayla's ear.

"I want to please you first", she whispered despite her nervousness. She carefully unzipped Kayla's dress, letting it fall straight to the hardwood floor. "It's the least I can do for the girl who got me out of my terrible funk", Hannah said with a wink. The expression on Kayla's face showed her surprise and delightedness at Hannah's unexpectedly bold behavior. Hannah then started to finger Kayla's pussy, delighting in the strong and sweet smell of her desire. "It's not going to take very long sweetie", Hannah promised her, while looking into her eyes.

"I suppose it isn't like you want me to, I'm sure", Kayla said.

"Is that so?" Hannah asked expectantly as she pulled her fingers out and began to lightly flick her fingertips across Kayla's swollen clit.

"It sure looks that way", Kayla said with a giggle.

As Hannah continued to play with Kayla's clit, Kayla moaned and occasionally jerked slightly. She took her hand and softly rubbed it lightly up and down Hannah's thighs and arms, as Kayla started to moan in pleasure. Hannah then began to rub her fingers between Kayla's labia lips, as she parted them and inserted a finger back inside Kayla's wet ready pussy.

"Oh baby, that feels so good", Kayla moaned, enticing Hannah into inserting a second finger inside Kayla's waiting pussy. She began to rapidly finger fuck Kayla with just the two fingers as she kissed her passionately on the lips.

"I think I'm ready", Hannah said to Kayla with a sexy confident smile.

"For what?" Kayla asked coyly, looking into Hannah's bright eyes.

"For you to take me, right here, right now!", Hannah said in a whisper.

"I hope you are ready", Kayla said seductively. Then she suddenly pushed Hannah down hard on the bed and climbed on top of her pinning her down. She grabbed the bottom of Hannah's dress and pulled it over her head and threw it across the room. Together they looked like a montage of good and evil. They had on matching bra and panty sets, each had a garter belt and stockings that went with it as well. Hannah's was white, and Kayla's was deep red. Behind the glass of one of the small windows, Jason was watching as he began to slowly stroke his own cock. Kayla fastened the strap-on tightly around herself and then carefully selected the dildo she wanted to use with it. As she rubbed lubricant on the one that she had decided to use, she kept her eyes intensely locked with Hannah's.

"Oh fuck!", Hannah cried out with pleasure as Kayla thrust her hips forward pushing the dildo deep into Hannah's pussy. Kayla pulled back and thrusted her hips forward again, making Hannah moan, then she grabbed a handful of Hannah's hair and did it a few more times. Hannah reacted more intensely with each thrust.

"Do you like it when I fuck you?", Kayla asked. Hannah nodded to let Kayla know she liked it. Kayla smiled down at her with a handful of Kayla's hair still in her hand. Kayla leaned back, pulled her panties to the side, and forced Hannah to taste her wet pussy.

"Taste it", Kayla demanded, and Hannah obediently extended her tongue and began licking Kayla's pussy tentatively at first and then slowly speeding up. Before long, Hannah had begun licking it hungrily and Kayla leaned back in pleasure and moaned, nearly closing her eyes. Hannah reached to the table and grabbed the first vibrator that caught her eye. She felt it begin to buzz in her hand when she pushed the first button she saw. She pressed it firmly against Kayla's swollen clitoris. Kayla began bucking her hips forward violently and shaking involuntarily and then suddenly she was sent completely over the edge and she began to gush cum from her tight pussy. Hannah caught some of Kayla's sweet juices in her mouth and spit the cum into Kayla's open mouth, then shoving

her tongue into her mouth behind it. When Kayla was done coming, she lay there panting as she regained her composure.

"Is that all you got?", Hannah said challenging Kayla. Kayla was suddenly motivated, and she bolted upright and pushed Kayla down onto her hands and knees. She firmly gripped Hannah's soft and perky tits and began plowing into her young tight little hole. She grabbed a small butt plug from the table and eased it into Hannah's ass as she fucked her pussy. The resulting sensation was almost too intense. Hannah began to moan louder and louder till they had nearly become screams. Hannah screamed out one final time as she experienced the most intense pleasure of her entire life. She began to squirt relentlessly, soaking the bed they were on in the process. The sight of this nearly caused Jason to come. He sat stroking his penis as he watched the beautiful ladies, he had hired to give him a show. They were definitely giving him a good one.

The girls collapsed in a hot, wet, pile panting and both in a daze. They were stunned at what had just happened between them. That was not anything like what they had planned. It was not even comparable to the pornography videos from which they had watched for inspiration. Their sexual chemistry paved the way for this to become the hot mess it now was. Neither of the ladies were mad though. Kayla was just hoping that Jason did not get to upset about the bedding they had just soaked. She silently hoped that he had a mattress cover on this thing.

"Oh yes", Jason said as he replayed what had just happened with his imagination. He was remarkably close to coming. Suddenly both girls appeared in the doorway. He let then know he was close to coming so that they were not surprised or caught off guard if it happened. He was pleasantly surprised when both ladies dropped to their knees in front of him ready to take his cum. The sight of them waiting for it sent him over the edge. It was a record-breaking sized load. There was plenty for both of the women to get a cum facial. He loved how they looked with his jizz on their faces. He appreciated the sight for just a moment before giving them each a hand towel to clean their faces with.

Tantric Discovery (Tantra Story)

Hannah and Kayla got themselves cleaned up, dressed, and ready to go. Kayla had planned to take Hannah back to her apartment, and then come right back to Jason's house for a private date. Hannah had another scheduled appointment with Daryl, who had been her first ever client, later that evening. Hannah was in a bit of a hurry to get home so that she had time to shower and do everything else it takes to get herself ready for another date. She grabbed the envelope, which was thick with cash, that Jason had left sitting in the foyer with her escort name, Lexi written across it in red ink. On the drive home they excitedly recapped the events that had just taken place and ranted about how well it had gone. They highlighted all their favorite parts and agreed to get together to celebrate later. Kayla even suggested that they post an ad for a two-girl show and start doing doubles as often as clients come seeking. Upon arriving home, she said bye as she hugged Kayla, and then ran straight to her apartment and to the shower. She was too limited on time to eat or do anything else besides get ready, so she rushed through her shower, rubbing the sudsy loofah across her entire body as quickly as possible and leaning around the water to avoid wetting her hair as much as she could. When she got out, she immediately turned on the blow dryer and dried the parts of her hair that got splashed with the water so that her hair would not become frizzy. She had to clean the streaks of eyeliner from her face which she accidently caused when she rubbed her face with her wet soapy hands. She then redid her make-up, sprayed some perfume all over herself and then went to her room to put on some lingerie. She barely had time to get some music going when she heard the anticipated knock at the door. She peeked out the small peephole and saw Daryl standing there patiently. She opened the door and invited him inside hiding her mostly naked body behind the door in case someone was to walk down the hallway.

"Hello beautiful", he said as he looked at her in appreciation at the strappy black teddy and fishnet stockings she had on.

"Hey babe, thank you", she said back to him with a sweet smile. "How are you today?", she asked him with bubbliness in her voice.

"Oh, I'm doing well", he said back to her cheerfully. When he had first reached out to her to set up a time to come see her again, he had mentioned wanting to try something new with her this time. She asked what it was, but he said he would prefer to discuss that in person if that was alright with her, and she said it was. Daryl seemed like a pretty normal and respectful guy so she doubted his request would be anything so strange that she would feel too uncomfortable to go through with it.

"So, what was it that you wanted to try?", she asked him curiously as she adjusted one of the straps on her teddy in the full-length mirror.

"Tantra", he responded plainly. Hannah just looked back at him with her head slightly tilted to the side and a confused look on her face.

"I'm not sure what that is", Hannah admitted. Daryl began to explain it to her. He said it was like a cross between meditation and sex, and that they would be having sex in different positions with the goal of creating a deep intimate connection between them, while reaching some sort of spiritual enlightenment. Hannah thought it sounded interesting and fun, she liked the idea of combining spirituality and sex. Hannah tried to imagine what the positions would be like as she told Daryl that she would be happy to have this experience with him. She imagined something along the lines of yoga and began to feel a little intimidated by this idea, but it was not too

crazy of a request, so she agreed to give it a try. Daryl paid her for several hours of her time because he wanted ti to ensure that they had the time needed to fully experience Tantric sex. He was not particularly familiar with exactly how it was done either, so they had to do a Google search to search for some inspiration and guidance. They learned that the practice usually involved getting to know their own bodies as well as partner's body. According to the research they had done, they would have the best experience if they took the time to get familiar with each other's body prior to getting started, so they decided to begin by exchanging full-body massages.

"Ladies go first of course", Daryl said as he gestured for Hannah to lie down on the bed in front of where he was sitting. She grabbed a jar of coconut oil from her dresser as she slowly lowered herself onto the bed facing downwards. Hannah had been abnormally sore and tense lately and knew she was probably in dire need of a proper massage, but she honestly doubted Daryl was going to be able to really provide that. Her seemed very clumsy and awkward in the way he carried himself, and massages sometimes required grace and sureness in your movements, so she doubted he had the finesse that would be required of a professional masseuse. When he first gripped the back of her neck, she was impressed by how firm and steady his hands felt against the muscles as they began to work the soreness out of her neck. She felt him unzip the back of her teddy completely and he laid both sides of it open on the bed and out of his way. He worked his way slowly but firmly down her body as he let the path his hands took be guided by the natural grooves and curves of her body. She groaned in pleasure when his hands got to that persistently sore spot in the center of her back. She took deep breaths and cleared her mind so that she could focus on enjoying the feeling of his strong hands against her naked body. He massaged all the way down her back, then to her butt cheeks, which he rubbed in a circular motion. She let out a sigh at how amazing it was feeling as he made his way across her thighs and calves. He paid special attention to her feet which he for last.

"Would you please roll onto your back for me now?", he asked in a quietly calming tone. Hannah rolled over, leaving her unzipped teddy lying flat of the bed, and exposing her bare chest and freshly shaved pussy. She looked at him unapologetically and smiled as Daryl marveled at the breath-taking sight of her naked body. He returned his attention to his work and began rubbing the front of her feet with both of his hands, and then he slowly massaged his hands up the front of her body much like how he had done with the back side. He stopped once when he reached her pussy, to lightly brush his fingertips across Hannah's exposed clit for a brief moment before he continued. She felt her pussy begin to tingle and get moist in response to his touch.

"Mmmm", she moaned barely loud enough for Daryl to hear it. When he had finished with her massage, she took her time stretching her muscles out and experiencing the relaxed state her muscles were in as she prepared to swap roles with Daryl. Suddenly she had an idea come to mind. It was something she had been taught by her former sugar daddy.

"Have you ever had a Nuru massage?", Hannah asked Daryl. She was so grateful for the massage he had just given her, and she wanted to make sure Daryl had an equally good experience with his massage in return.

"No, I have not, what's that?", he asked. Hannah explained it in detail and Daryl readily agreed, even mentioning that the idea might also be beneficial to the tantra part of it as well. Hannah prepared by blowing up an air mattress she kept in the hallway closet for guests, then she heated the coconut oil up in her microwave oven, just long enough for it to be melted but being careful to not get it too hot to be used on the skin. Then she gestured for Daryl to follow her into the bathroom to get their skin wet. She turned the shower on and together, they both got in long enough to get enough water on their skin so that the oil would easily spread across their skin and become slippery. Without drying off Daryl laid face-down and naked on the air mattress. Hannah grabbed the coconut oil from the top of her dresser and poured a generous amount over him, and then she poured some over her own wet and naked body. After nearly emptying the entire jar of oil onto their bodies, he began massaging his neck with her hands as she rubbed her tits against his upper-back and simultaneously used her knees to

215

massage his thighs. Her skin glided across his with ease as she moved the various parts of her body against his. She pressed her tits hard against his back and made a circular motion against his thighs using her knees. Suddenly she flipped over so that her back faced his and turned around so that she was sitting in the crease of his lower-back. Her ass cheeks were sliding back and forth smoothly across his back as she used the heels of her feet to massage his tired and achy calf muscles.

"Does it feel good to you?", she asked Daryl who laid there with his eyes closed and a relaxed smile on his face.

"mmmhmm", he replied, dragging the word out to emphasis how much he was enjoying his Nuru massage. She straddled his butt cheeks between her thick thighs and began clenching them together and letting them spread them open just enough so that her pussy barely touched him. She did this over and over quite a few times, which resulted in her thighs firmly massaging both of his butt cheeks and the outer part of his hips. Once she was sure she had thoroughly rubbed every part of the back of his body with at least one part of hers, she politely requested that he turn over so that she could work on the front half of his body. When he did, she smiled at the sight of his penis standing strong and thick and fully hard. It waved back-and-forth a few times as if it were beckoning for her to come play with it. She ignored the beckoning of his cock at first so that she could focus her attention on massaging the front of his legs with her arms. Her knees rubbed against his arms so that her legs were spread open across his chest, giving him a wonderful view of her pussy. Once his arms were free, he reached between her legs and began lightly flicking his finger against her clit as she continued to slide her oiled-up body over the entire front of his body, leaving only his erect penis unmassaged. Then she took her tits and squeezed them together tightly around his cock. She used her hands to bounce her boobs up and down a few times, giving his dick a good tug. Daryl moaned in appreciation as he admired Hannah's body which was shiny from the coconut oil. Once she had finished with his massage, Daryl suggested the start by practicing the breathing technique. They started by sitting on the floor facing each other. They each placed their hand gently on the other's chest and quietly focused on synchronizing their breathing with their eyed closed. After a while, they both felt ready to begin, so Hannah climbed on top of Daryl's crossed legs and slid her still oiled body against his chest as she slipped her pussy down onto his erect cock slowly. She bounced up and down on his member as his hands explored her body. Suddenly she felt him moving his legs.

"My leg is cramping up a bit", Daryl complained. Then he began to straighten both of his legs out underneath her. As he did, he held Hannah's hips in place on his cock, so that she remained where he wanted her to be as he adjusted his position. He moved one of his hands to her chest and cupped the other behind her back to support her. Then he squeezed one of her boobs in his hand as he used it to push her body backwards so that her head was resting on the floor in between the lower half of his legs. He grabbed her hips and used them to slide her pussy up and down his rock-hard cock. They both moaned together in unison. Hannah reached down and began slowly massaging her clit with her fingertips as Daryl slid her pussy up and down the length of his shaft. He pushed himself up onto his knees and put her legs in the air so that her toes were pointed up at the ceiling. She laid on her back as he began thrusting himself deeper into her pussy. She wanted to watch him fucking her, so she pushed herself up so that she was propped up on her elbows. She looked down at her pussy, enjoying the view of his cock going in and out of her tight tiny hole. They both could feel their orgasms beginning to build, and Daryl began to thrust his hips forward harder and faster, slamming himself hard into her pussy. Hannah's eyes rolled back as an orgasm began to crash over her knocking her back like an ocean's wave. Her orgasm was intensified by Daryl's cum, as it began to fill her pussy with a huge load of his hot cum. She thrusted her hips upward momentarily allowing his cock to get even deeper inside of her as they both enjoyed their shared orgasm. As they finished, they both began to relax their bodies feeling completely satisfied.

"Oh, that was amazing. Thank you, babe,", Daryl said as he carefully pulled his cock out of her. Hannah found herself in a bit of a daze from the spectacular orgasm she had just experienced. She decided that she was really

impressed by Daryl's performance. She certainly did not expect him to have her legs trembling the way they were. She noticed he seemed to have enjoyed it as much as she had, and she wondered if they had experienced the same levels of intensity. Daryl had only taken up two of the three hours that he had paid for at the beginning of their time together, yet he still left her a forty-dollar tip. As soon as he left, she got out the envelope she had got from Jason and combined it with the cash Daryl had given her. She nearly gasped when she realized that she had made nearly a thousand dollars in a single day.

She thought about how grateful she was to Kayla for teaching her how to earn this kind of money, then she wondered what Kayla was doing so she sent her a text asking her if she was done at Jason's. While she waited for a response an idea about how to repay Kayla for her help came to her suddenly and she could not wait for Kayla to respond so she could tell her all about it. It took Kayla about an hour to respond to Hannah's message, in her response she informed Hannah that she was done at Jason's. Hannah responded by simply telling her to come over as soon as she could and that she had some big news. Within an hour Kayla was banging on the door of Hannah's apartment, curious to know what was going on. When Hannah opened it, she was grinning ear-to ear and hardly able to contain herself.

"Hey what's up?", Kayla asked, curious about Hannah's giddy behavior.

"I was thinking", Hannah began excitedly, "I have an extra bedroom here and I get lonely being here by myself all the time. I was going to ask if you wanted to take the extra bedroom?". Kayla looked a little shocked at first then she smiled back at Hannah with a playful expression.

"I know I'm good, but we only slept together once and you're asking me to move in?", she asked with a smirk as she winked at her friend. Hannah rolled her eyes and laughed along with Kayla. "I mean, I would love to", Kayla finally said with a grateful smile. Hannah began on a rant about how much easier it would be for them to work together, and how much fun they would have. Kayla agreed when she pointed out that splitting the apartment's rent would be much cheaper than having to pay for a hotel every day. They talked about it for a couple hours and went over how things would work and how they would split bills and chores. Hannah told her that she was welcome to sleep on the couch tonight and they could go get her a bed tomorrow if she wanted. Kayla agreed but she had to return to the hotel to get her things, so Hannah decided to ride along with her. She had never been to the hotel Kayla stayed at and she wondered why she had never been invited over, so she had been curious to see what it was like for a while now.

Hannah was shocked and a little nervous by the scene before her when they pulled up to the place her friend had been staying. It was in a part of town she had never been to. The rundown looking motel, which was across from the airport, was befittingly called The Airport Inn. There were plastic chairs outside of many of the rooms where people sat with forty-ounce beers or cigarettes or both in their hands. It felt dangerous to Hannah, and it made her feel even better about her decision to ask Kayla to move in. Kayla's room was on the second floor. She instructed Hannah to stay in the car while she ran up and grabbed her things and said bye to a couple of friends. Hannah did as she was told and was grateful when Hannah locked her in the car. Just a few minutes later Kayla was back in the car and they were on the way to the safety of the apartment. Hannah decided not to say anything about the conditions at the hotel because she did not want to offend Kayla or say anything to hurt her feelings. When they got back Hannah poured them each a strong drink and they piled up in Hannah's bed to watch a funny movie.

The following morning Hannah got out of bed. Kayla was still sleeping peacefully so Hannah decided to let her be. It was almost two in the afternoon when she finally made her way out of bed. At Hannah's request they got ready and made their way to the furniture store to get a bed for Kayla's room. They did not spend but a few minutes inside the small furniture store Kayla decided to check out. She was very quick to pick one of the least expensive

bed frames the place had in stock. The salesman had barely managed to talk her into getting a mattress that was slightly better than their least expensive option. After taking the money and adding it to the cash register, he scheduled for the bed to be delivered directly to the apartment the following day since it was not going to fit in Kayla's small car. On their way back to the apartment they stopped and got some Chinese food takeout. Kayla and Hannah discussed that they would keep a shared schedule so they could schedule their appointments to see clients around each other. Kayla often went to her client's homes to see them so that made the scheduling much more convenient for them both. Everything seemed to work out perfectly and the girls were both feeling good about their decision to move in together.

"What are you doing up so early?", Hannah asked Kayla groggily as Kayla hurriedly was getting herself ready for something. Hannah saw that she was wearing a skirt that went past her knees which was something she had never seen before.

"I'm getting ready for church", she said hurriedly as she finished throwing her hair into a neat ponytail.

"Church?", Hannah asked clearly confused.

"Every Sunday", Kayla clipped back. Hannah watched silently as Kayla finished getting ready and rushed out the door. She had heard Kayla say some religious things before, but she still did not think she was the type to go to church every Sunday. Hannah was quite surprised by this new information, but she decided that it was probably a good thing. Hannah was not a believer herself, but she appreciated how it drove people to have strong morals and to treat others well. When Kayla returned a few hours later Hannah had decided to go on without mentioning it. She was somewhat curious about what inspired her friend to go to church, but she figured her friend would tell her when and if she felt like it. The bed was delivered that afternoon and the girls set it up together. The instructions were a little confusing, but they had fun figuring it out together. When it was done Hannah pushed the extra nightstand that she had into Kayla's room so that she had a couple drawers for her socks and underwear, and anything else she could not hang up.

"Hey, I might have a client over tomorrow if you don't already have plans", Kayla said once they had finished getting the bed together.

"Sure, okay. Just be sure to update the schedule on your phone. It will automatically block out any times that I have plans", Hannah reminded her. Kayla asked for Hannah's help doing that and they blocked out the time that her client was wanting to come by.

A special request (Anal Story)

"Could I ask you something? It's kind of embarrassing but I need to ask", Hannah said looking timidly at Kayla. Kayla reminded her that they were close enough that most things should not be embarrassing to talk about. She used their experience at Jason's house as an example to prove her point. Hannah asked if Kayla had ever done anal for a client. She told her that she had a potential client who was offering a pretty large sum of cash for it, and Hannah felt tempted.

"Yes, I actually do pretty regularly", she answered, "Have you ever done it at all?". Hannah said she had a boyfriend who had been really into it her first year of college, so she had done it plenty of times, she just did not know if it was a common request or if it was okay to agree to do something like that with a client, the potential mess she pointed out as an example. Kayla explained that Hannah could do it, but she would probably want to take some measures to prevent any embarrassing incidents. She took Hannah to the adult store and helped her get the necessary supplies. When they got back to the apartment Hannah texted her client to set up a time. He seemed incredibly eager to make it happen and decided to schedule it for the following day. Hannah was nervous but wanted to get it done with, so she agreed to it despite it being so soon. She exchanged a few photos with the

client, who's name was Tyler, and was surprised to find that he was a very good-looking guy. He looked young, maybe in his late twenties at most, and he had dirty blonde hair and bright blue eyes. She was not sure if that increased or decreased her level of nervousness, but she was sure that it would make the whole thing a little more enjoyable. The following morning Hannah got things in her room so that she would not have to leave it for a couple hours while Kayla took her date. Kayla assured her that this was a regular client and would be no trouble, and Hannah responded by telling her not to worry about it.

"I'm not worried at all, I trust you", she told Kayla with a confident smile as she closed her bedroom door. Kayla sat down and put the television on. She heard a knock not long after and Kayla opened the front door and invited the client in. By the way he talked, she figured this was a client from the motel Kayla had been staying at. This made Hannah nervous, but she told herself that she needed to trust Kayla and decided that she would not say anything or make a fuss about it unless it became a real issue. Once they had went to Kayla's room. She did not hear anything else until Kayla and her client said bye and she walked him out, but about ten minutes before the date ended, she did begin to smell the unrecognizable scent of marijuana seeping into her room. Hannah did not want to mess up Kayla's date so she decided to talk to her about it once he was gone, but she could swear she remembered telling Kayla that they were not allowed to smoke in the apartment and that it could get them kicked out if they were caught. So, she sat there, alone in her room and the more and the longer she smelled the stink of the weed, the more upset she started feeling at Kayla's disregard for the rules.

"What in the world was that?", Hannah asked as soon as she opened her door. Kayla looked at her with a confused expression and asked what Hannah was talking about.

"It reeks of weed in here", Hannah said as she crossed her arms and eyed Kayla with a stern expression. Kayla acted as if she were surprised that Hannah was upset about her smoking weed inside the apartment.

"I don't remember us talking about not smoking weed in here but it won't happen again", Kayla said with a scowl. Hannah reminded her of the no smoking conversation, to which Kayla said she assumed that Hannah had been referring to cigarettes.

"Any kind of smoke", Hannah clarified still a little annoyed. Kayla apologized and assured Hannah that it would not happen again, so Hannah decided to let it go and went back to her room to cool off and start getting ready for her upcoming date. Once she felt totally calm again, she asked Kayla for one more explanation on how to use the supplies they had gotten from the adult store the day before. Kayla gave her a final detailed explanation and Hannah listened intently and mentally repeated each instruction back to herself so that she remembered every detail. When she was done getting ready, she still had at least thirty minutes before Tyler was supposed to arrive, so she decided to hang out with Kayla in the meantime. Hannah apologized for getting so upset about smelling the weed.

"That's okay, I get it", Kayla said before apologizing for not initially understanding what Hannah had meant when they talked about smoking in the apartment. They sat and talked until a few minutes before Hannah's new client was set to arrive. She got up to check herself in the mirror one last time before he got there. The incoming call she had been expecting finally came through. When she answered it, a smooth deep voice came through the line asking her where he should park. She stood at the window until she saw him get out of the car. Hannah quickly identified him as the guy from the photo and he certainly did not disappoint. He was tall but not too tall, and he was in shape too. When he made it to the door Hannah already had it cracked ready to welcome him inside. As he walked through the door, she could not help but notice the large bulge in the front of his khaki pants. He was clearly very well endowed, which made Hannah feel suddenly nervous about what was about to happen. She managed to bring her attention up to his face.

"Hey babe, come on back to my room", she said keeping a straight face. He smiled and nodded and followed her back to her bedroom. Once inside he immediately removed his shoes. Hannah stripped down to the lingerie she had on underneath her clothes. She could hear him behind her following her lead and stripping off his pants and shirts. She turned around and without realizing how close behind her he was she nearly ran into him.

"Woah", she said looking down. She was not necessarily saying that because she had nearly ran into him. It was because she now could see exactly how well-endowed he was now that he had nothing left on but his boxers. When he followed her gaze to his member he looked at her apologetically.

"I probably should have mentioned…", he said trailing off, unsure of how to finish his sentence. Hannah felt a little bad for him, clearly, he got this reaction quite often.

"No, it's fine, or it should be", Hannah said with an unmistakable doubt in her voice.

"You look stunning", he offered as if it would help the situation.

"Thank you", Hannah said as she made her way over to him. He touched her waist, looking at her as if wondering if this were okay. "I have a few butt plugs", she said without making eye contact with him, "do you suppose we could start with those and work our way up to it".

"Of course,", he said looking relieved that she was even willing to try. She grabbed two butt plugs and some anal lubricant from her dresser drawer, the first was a medium sized silicone one with a red heart at the tip, and the other was exceptionally large, it was made of metal and it had a round pink gem on it. She had never used that one. It was too big for her, but she figured now would be the time to get used to it. She bent over in front of him and pushed the smaller one of the two slowly into her butt. She made a face when the thickest part of it entered, it caught her off guard, but she found it was surprisingly comfortable. He grabbed the end that stuck out and moved it around and she arched her back out in response to the feeling of him pushing it deeper into her ass. "Do you think you can take the larger one?", he asked eagerly.

"I think so", she responded questioningly. She gasped as he pulled the smaller one out of her ass. She felt the pressure from the larger one against her hole within moments. She let out a whimper as it began to push into her bottom. The girth of it almost made her lose her balance, but she braced herself against her bed post and managed to remain standing.

"Just relax", he told her after several minutes of her struggling with it.

"I'm trying", she snapped, but in reality, she was really enjoying herself.

"Relax and stay put", he firmly instructed as he applied some more lubricant around the plug, "It'll hurt a little bit, but I won't let you fall". She quickly acquiesced, but she made sure not to let the plug end of it out. The larger one fit much more comfortably now, but the pressure of it resting inside her made her gulp down a few quick breaths. She was going to try to do this, so she tried not to freak out. "Don't move, alright?", he asked.

"I won't", she grumbled, but she did relax her body as the rest of it slid in. After several minutes, she could feel the pressure subside a little as it settled into place.

"Good. Now that it is all the way in, I'm going to move it around a bit before taking it out.", he informed her. She did not answer. She simply moved her hips back slightly, so that it pushed as far into her as it could go. He pushed her further into the bed as he applied a bit more pressure. She grunted out a sigh when she felt the tip go deep into her bottom. She felt it begin to stretch her asshole as he wriggled it around inside of her. Once he was satisfied, she began to feel the pressure of him pulling on the butt plug. She could not help but to clench her ass tightly holding it inside of her. "Relax", he reminded her gently. She refocused her mind and forced her body to

relax so he could get the huge butt plug out of her tight little asshole. She felt it slowly being pulled out of her. He applied some more lubricant around the edge of it to help it along before he kept pulling. After a moment of an intense feeling that made her hold her breath, she felt it pop out and she sighed as she relaxed herself on the bed.

"Okay", she sighed, "I think I'm ready". Her heart began to pound as he pressed his huge cock against her asshole.

"You are ready for this?", he asked.

"Uh-huh", she responded, "I'm still a bit nervous. I've never taken a cock this big in my ass, so please try to take it easy on me", she requested, as she reached up to run her fingers through her hair, pushing it out of her face as she waited for his big cock to make its way into her ass.

"Okay baby, I'll try not to hurt you too bad.", he said, smiling at her before pushing his massive cock into her tight asshole. He could feel her tight ring stretch to accommodate his shaft and when the head broke past her sphincter, he froze. "It's still a bit tight, I think we need to get it a bit looser.", he stated, before slowly pushing it in further. He did not want to get too aggressive with her asshole just yet, since he did not want to end up having to stop if he caused her too much pain. After pushing his cock deeper and further into her until she felt it lodge against her sphincter muscle, he let out a loud groan and began to pump his cock in and out of her slowly.

"Oh shit… that is the tightest ass I've ever had.", he exclaimed, continuing to pump his cock into her, "damn, it feels so good". He began to get increase his pace with each of his strokes and he had to wrap his hands under her legs and ass to keep her from rising and hitting her head against the headboard. He continued to pump his cock in and out of her as she began to pant and moan. He started to fuck her faster, punching her small but firm little butt as hard as he could as he slammed into her tight asshole.

"Oh god, I'm gonna come!", he told her in between rapid thrusts.

"Ughh. Oh god, yeah!", she responded with a moan, reaching up and grabbing his balls in both hands as his cock pumped in and out of her tiny butt hole.

"Yeah, yeah, yeah! Give me that ass bitch!", he encouraged, thrusting harder as he reached his peak. He felt his cock twinge as he felt the first blast of cum shoot into her small asshole.

"Ooooooohhhhhhhhhhhhhhhhh", she moaned in pleasure, as she squeezed his dick with her ass. The thought of his massive cock filling up her tiny ass with his cum was too much for him and he came several more times filling her little butt up with his spunk. He gently pulled his dick out of her ass and her little butt hole slowly opened up and then closed again. He slid his hands up her little ass to hold on to her ass cheeks to make sure his cum remained inside of her.

"Yeah… that was good.", he said, laughing. He started to grab his boxers to slide them back on and she slowly began getting dressed too. "Can I come back and see you sometime?", he asked as he sat a white envelope on her dresser. She smiled at him flirtatiously and said he could, and he knew that she had enjoyed it as much as he had.

"Thank you, hopefully I'll see you again soon", she said politely and cheerfully as she showed him out. She closed and locked the door behind him and went straight back to her room as the day's events sunk in. She had an uncomfortable feeling of guilt as she often did after seeing most of the clients. She had felt it for the first time after she had first met Daryl and sucked him off. She felt it again when she had her first lesbian experience with Kayla at Jason's house. She even felt it when Kayla would explain to her how her dates went and describe the events that took place. She was not sure what made her feel this way, and despite trying, she could not make sense of it. She did not think she had any hidden moral issues with what she was doing. She did not feel she was

hurting anyone by escorting. In fact, most of the time she felt empowered by it. It is her body, and she was proud to be resourceful enough to use it to provide for herself. She also felt it might even be able to be considered a good deed because she brought joy to these men, many of which seemed to need it badly. She sat alone in her room and contemplated her reasons for feeling so down after most of her dates but came to no conclusion. Suddenly she heard a light tap at her bedroom door.

"Are you awake Hannah?", Kayla called in from the hallway in what was barely more than a whisper. Hannah felt instantly annoyed by the interruption and had almost snapped at Kayla for invading her privacy. She barely caught herself just in time knowing that Kayla was not trying to do that at all.

"I'm up", she called back through the door, "Just having a bit of a moment". Kayla kindly asked her if she thought some food might help improve her mood. Hannah realized she had not eaten at all that day and she felt her stomach grumble angrily at the mere thought of food. Hannah told her friend that she was starving, and she would be out in just a moment so they could figure out what to do for dinner.

"Alright", Kayla responded. Hannah could hear the concern in her friend's voice, but she brushed it off for now figuring that Kayla would see her move improve when they got food and it would resolve itself. She could not help but to wonder if she just was not cut out to be an escort. The feeling of despair was intense and on the way to the restaurant they had chosen to eat at, she broke down and told Kayla all about how she had been feeling. Kayla listened and nodded with an understanding but sad expression that made Hannah wonder if she had experienced the same thing at some point. Kayla suggested that Hannah go to church with her the following Sunday. She said being involved in something like that, something that is about the greater good, helped her feel a sense of normalcy and strengthened her morals. Hannah felt very doubtful that church would be the solution to her problems, but she reluctantly agreed to go after Kayla had pushed a few times, insisting that it could not hurt to try it. Kayla found an outfit that was church appropriate and laid it out when she got home. She was surprised that she had found something appropriate. She asked Kayla if she could help remind her to iron the wrinkles out of it the night before they go, and shortly after both girls went to their own rooms.

Over the next few days both girls saw quite a few clients. Hannah began to hope that church would in fact offer her some sort of reprieve from her turmoil. She was growing tired of having to deal with this sinking feeling of depression each time she worked. Even Kayla could see how badly it was impacting Hannah, and she tried to help however she could, but her every effort only seemed to make the problem worse. Hannah had begun to become short-tempered and snappy with her, and more and more she stopped trying to help and began avoiding Hannah instead. On Saturday night Kayla was surprised to hear that Hannah was still planning to accompany her to church. Kayla explained a few important things about Catholic churches to Hannah and reminded her to iron her dress as she had requested. When they were both ready, they bid one another a good night, and each went to their rooms and went to bed.

"Hannah, it's time to get up", Kayla called sweetly through the door. Hannah sat upright wondering why she was being woken up, then she remembered that she was supposed to be going along with Kayla to church today.

"Okay, I'm up", she called back to Kayla. Hannah felt nervous and considered backing out, but something inside her was urging her to go, and she could not ignore it. Maybe it was self-loathing or morbid curiosity, but regardless, Hannah got herself ready as quickly as possible and made herself a quick breakfast before her and Kayla headed out the door. When they arrived, Hannah noticed that the outside of the church was breath-takingly pretty. It was a huge brick building, of which some parts of were as high as four stories. One of the largest towers had an enormous clock with roman numerals, and most of the windows had unique shapes that made the place look incredibly old, and there were some statures which Hannah found to be quite creepy, and she had avoided walking near them. It all looked like something that belonged in Europe. The inside of the church was somehow

even prettier than the outside. Hannah looked in awe at the stained-glass windows which depicted incredibly detailed images and scenes that were famously described in the bible. There were beautiful and elegant gold arches lining every doorway in sight, and the warm lighting casted some remarkable shadows that made the place look magical. They slid their way quietly into an empty pew and waited patiently for the church service to start as everyone else took their seats.

Hannah sat and listened intently throughout the entire service, which seemed to last for hours, she stood when everyone else did, put a generous sum of money in the collections plate when it came around to her, and she ate the bread and wine that had been distributed during the service. Kayla looked over at her with a curious expression periodically and silently wondered what she was thinking. Hannah just sat quietly taking it all in. After the service she followed close behind Kayla, who spoke to a few people she knew briefly, and she returned any greeting that had been extended to her. She then followed Kayla over to the confessional box.

"Do you want to go first?", she asked Hannah gesturing to the box.

"No, after you", Hannah replied shaking her head. When Kayla was done, Hannah went into the box and sat down as her heart pounded.

"I don't know how to do this", she confessed to the mysterious figure she could barely make out sitting on the other side of the box. She heard a chuckle from the other side and felt a little embarrassed, but when he spoke again her embarrassment subsided because of the kindness and wisdom she could hear in the man's voice.

"That's quite alright", he said with a smile that she could almost hear. Then he walked her through the steps of confessing patiently and with a tone that made her feel safe and loved. Hannah was not sure why, but she felt so comfortable that she openly admitted everything without holding back. She found it strange because she was normally so reserved. She felt relieved when she was done and out of the box. She wondered how much time she had spent in there. She walked out and her and Kayla went to the car in a peaceful silence. She still did not consider herself a religious person, but she had to admit that it had felt good to confess all her wrongdoings. She felt refreshed and renewed as she returned home with Kayla.

"What did you think?", Kayla asked probingly.

"I don't know", Hannah replied with genuine cluelessness, "I still don't buy into it, but it felt strangely refreshing regardless". Kayla asked if she wanted to keep going back, and Kayla responded by saying that she probably would not go back anytime soon. Kayla was a little disappointed that Hannah did not want to keep going but she decided to not push the issue because she feared it would drive a wedge between them. Thankfully, Hannah's attitude seemed to improve greatly over the next few days. She still had the same uncomfortable feeling after seeing her clients, but she was able to handle it better now. She had gotten caught up and even ahead on her rent. It was especially easy with Kayla's help. The two girls even spent an evening bonding over some drinks, a movie, and conversation like they did when Kayla had first moved in. Everything felt nice and relaxed around the house again. This was a great relief to Kayla who had started to wonder how much longer she was going to have a place to stay. She had a client who had made a request some time back, but Kayla did not feel comfortable asking Hannah about it. With everything seemingly getting back to normal she began to consider asking Hannah about her client's inquiry.

The More the Merrier (Gangbang Story)

"Hannah, can you come in here for a second? I wanted to ask you a question", Kayla called loudly from her room. Moments later the door to Kayla's room swung open. Hannah stood there with a bottle of wine in her hand.

"What's up? Want some?", she asked gesturing to the bottle in her hand.

"You know I do", Kayla replied enthusiastically. Hannah ran to the kitchen to pour two glasses of the wine. She returned with the glasses and the rest of the bottle in tow. She plopped down on the bed beside Kayla.

"You wanted to ask me something?", she reminded Kayla. Kayla looked at Hannah with a serious expression and told her she had a client who was wanting to see them both. Hannah looked at Kayla with a quizzical expression. "You made it sound like it was going to be something bigger than that", she questioned.

"Oh, it is", Kayla insisted. "The client has a few friends who want to participate as well", she murmured quietly almost hoping that Hannah had not heard her.

"What?", Hannah exclaimed, "Not way I'm doing that, how many friends?". Kayla said that her client was wanting for three of his friends to participate. Hannah thought this over and came to the conclusion that with four guys and two of them, it would not be that hard to handle. It should be like having a threesome basically. "How much?", Hannah queried, doubting they would be paying enough. Kayla leaned in close and whispered to her that they would be getting two thousand each. Kayla's mouth fell open and her eyes went wide. She smiled at Kayla excitedly.

"So, you're in?", Kayla implored.

"Oh, I'm in", Hannah replied with a grin. They both began screaming excitedly at the prospect of making four thousand dollars in just a couple hours. Hannah leaned over Kayla's shoulder as she texted a client whose name was Alfie. They both kept glancing at her phone as the drank wine and enthusiastically chatted about the ordeal.

"Oh my god, I got a message", Kayla screamed. Hannah leaned in close to see what it said. He was wanting to set it up for Friday, in the early afternoon or evening. Both girls had open schedules on Friday, so they were happy to agree. They planned to meet at four in the evening at a really nice hotel. Hannah was happy they were getting a room because she was not sure about having that many people in the apartment at once. They spent the remainder of the night celebrating and after finishing the wine off and putting dents in two fresh bottles of liquor, they both got quite drunk. They passed out together in Kayla's bed as they were playing a funny card game. They both had a great night and had begun feeling like things were finally getting back to normal between them.

Kayla woke up and looked around Kayla's room groggily. There was a card stuck to her face and her back was hurting badly from sleeping on Kayla's shitty mattress. She began to recall the events that took place the night before. A pit formed in her stomach when she remembered what she had agreed to. The idea of participating in a gangbang made her feel sick to her stomach. She got out of the bed and crept to her room and tried to watch some television to distract herself. After over an hour of watching the television, she realized that she was very thirsty. She made her way to the kitchen to get herself something to drink. She was pouring some apple juice into a glass when she suddenly was startled by someone behind her.

"Is there any coffee made yet", Kayla muttered.

"Fuck!", Hannah screamed angrily, "Don't fucking sneak up o n me like that. Kayla shrunk back, shocked by Hannah's aggressive response.

"I'm sorry", Kayla whispered as she tried to remember if she had done something to upset Hannah. She could not remember if she had but she was obnoxiously drunk last night, so she did not really know. "Did I do something wrong?", she asked.

"Just don't sneak up on me like that anymore", Hannah barked. The rest of the next few days continued on this way. Kayla wondered what had caused Hannah's sudden change. She tried to avoid her as much as she possibly could, and she returned to wondering if she would need to get a new place soon. Friday rolled around before they knew it. Kayla almost dreaded the day because she knew it meant interacting with Hannah more. They began getting ready around one in the afternoon. They picked some lingerie that matched well and threw some cute outfits on over the lingerie. Alfie texted her the address of the hotel. She looked it up and saw it was one of the nicest hotels in town. She went to show Hannah hoping this might bring her out of her funk and get her excited.

"Look at this hotel", Kayla began, "Isn't it stunning?". Hannah looked at the picture on Kayla's phone.

"It's nice", she answered without any enthusiasm.

"What is wrong with you?", Kayla blurted. Hannah looked at her for a moment.

"I'm really sorry. I have not been sleeping well at all and it's been putting me in a mood", Hannah whined. She sat down on the edge of Kayla's bed. "I'll get better before the date I promise", she offered. Kayla nodded an agreeance and they finished getting themselves ready in silence. At around three-fifteen they got in Kayla's car and made their way over to the hotel. Alfie sent Kayla the room number once they got to the hotel. The room was up on the twenty-sixth floor of the beautiful and eloquently decorated skyrise hotel. They felt as though they were in the elevator for ages as it stopped to pick people up and to drop others off at different floors of the hotel on their way up. The button with the number twenty-six finally lit up and the elevator made a dinging noise. When the doors opened, they both stepped out of the elevator quickly. They followed the signs on the wall to room two six five nine, Kayla tapped on the door lightly. A stocky man with a big curly brown beard answered the door and greeted them.

"Alfie!", Kayla shouted as she wrapped her arms around the big man. He returned her hug.

"You must be Lexi", he spoke looking at Hannah. Hannah nodded politely and smiled up at him. "Come on in", he added as he gestured them inside. They noticed the three other men sitting in chairs around a computer. All three immediately got up and greeted the girls as Alfie introduced them. The first had short brown hair and glasses, he was clean cut and wore a button up. "This is Brandon", Alfie announced. He tried to offer his hand for them to shake but both gave him a hug instead. The next guy was clearly athletic. His muscles almost ripped through his t-shirt. There was no way he did not lift weights. Alfie introduced him as Calvin. When they hugged him, they could feel the hardness of his entire body. The last guy was thin and tall, he had tattoos covering almost every visible piece of skin on his body and his ears had some huge gauges in them. "Finally, this is Frank", Alfie proclaimed. Hannah noticed the enticing smell of Frank's cologne. Alfie introduced the ladies next, and then Kayla excused herself to the restroom dragging Hannah along. Once inside they stripped down to their lingerie and spritzed themselves with some perfume with pheromones that Kayla had bought them at the adult store.

"We have got this", Kayla assured Hannah. Hannah closed her eyes and breathed deeply for a moment.

"Alright, here we go", Hannah chirped. When they walked back through the door all the men's eyes fell on them and remained locked onto them a each of them examined them both thoroughly. There were practically foaming at the mouth.

"oo, oo, oo", Alfie chirruped, "just because we're an odd group doesn't mean shit". The other men began to nod in agreement as Alfie spoke. "We aren't gonna take it easy on you", Alfie swore. At this point Hannah had already gotten herself completely into character.

"I would be disappointed if you did", she flirted. A couple of the guys chuckled and then Frank walked up to Hannah and grabbed her.

"This is gonna be fun", Frank proclaimed. Frank's breath smelled of vodka. He poured himself another shot and offered one to Hannah. She took it graciously. She threw the shot back and he grabbed the glass from her and sat it on the table. Then he grabbed her wrists and pinned her down on the bed.

"Are you ready slut?", he challenged with a smirk on his face.

"Good question," she replied coolly. Suddenly it was not just Frank who stood over her, Brandon was there too and they both began pawing at her. She whimpered as she felt her tit getting squeezed hard. She could not help it; her pussy became involuntarily wet. Before she knew it Frank was pounding his cock into her tight little pussy, and she was gagging on Brandon's huge cock at the same time.

"Mmmmmm", Kayla moaned as Alfie carefully eased his boner into her tight asshole. Calvin grabbed her by the hair and shoved his dick deep into her mouth.

"Jesus Christ, she's good!", Calvin remarked as she sucked him hard. Alfie wrapped his arms around Kayla's waist and pinned her down with his massive cock between her legs.

"Suck that cock bitch!", Brandon demanded. Hannah looked at Frank and then up at Brandon. Both men looked down on her pitiful body and smiled as they shoved their cocks into her various holes. Frank was thoroughly enjoying fucking Hannah, slowly moving his massive cock in and out of her tight pussy as Bryson leaned over her and sucked on one of her tits. His hard cock was sliding in and out of her gagging mouth like it had been born to be there.

Calvin was licking up and down Kayla's neck. His tongue moved up to her ear lobe and down to her soft tits. The feeling of his tongue on her nipples caused Kayla to squeal with delight. She leaned her head back and closed her eyes as his lips began to work their magic. He began kissing his way down her belly.

"Fuck yeah," Alfie growled as he pounded himself into her. Alfie continued fucking Kayla, grabbing her long dark hair and holding her head back so he could slam himself into her tight pussy as she gagged on Calvin's cock and moaned loudly. Calvin straddled her face and groaned loudly as he fucked it hard. Suddenly cum spurted out of his cock and into Kayla's mouth.

"Fuck yeah!", he called out as he kept pumping his cock in her mouth till all the cum was out. Kayla excused herself to the restroom so she could get a drink and rinse the cum out of her mouth. While she was away all four men advanced on Hannah.

"Can you lick my dick clean bitch?", Calvin asked her.

"Yeah," Hannah replied instantly and took Calvin's huge thick cock in her mouth. Hannah sucked Calvin's cock hard, taking all the cum off of it and licking it all off her lips.

"That's the way," Calvin declared as he pulled his cock from her mouth.

"It's my turn now", Alfie demanded. He grabbed Hannah's hair and forcefully pulled her head back so he could shove his cock into her mouth and go at it. Hannah gagged as his huge cock filled her throat. She gagged again when his balls touched her nose. While Alfie face fucked her Frank was busy ponding his cock into her pussy and

Brandon was fucking her tight little ass. Brandon began panting as he used all the force that he could gather to push himself deeper and deeper into her ass.

"I'm gonna cum in your slut hole", Brandon screamed as he pumped himself into her as hard as he could. He let out a loud groan and Hannah began to feel her asshole being filled with his cum. He kept pumping and it kept squirting out in bursts. When he was done, he pulled his cock out gently and patted her on the cheek. "Good job my little slut", he said. Kayla came out of the restroom and Alfie abruptly quit fucking Hannah's mouth and ran to Kayla. He grabbed her by the arm and pulled her over to where Hannah was.

"I wanna see you two fuck each other now", Alfie declared.

"What a great idea', Frank said to Alfie as he pulled his cock out of Hannah. They ordered Kayla to lick Hannah's pussy. Alfie grabbed her by the hair and pulled her down to her knees. She stuck her tongue out and began flicking it against Hannah's clit. Hannah moaned and arched her back. Frank grabbed Hannah by the waist and turned her onto all fours. Alfie shoved Kayla's face into Hannah's wet pussy. Frank grabbed Hannah's ass cheeks and spread them apart to show off her open asshole and the cum that was left inside. Kayla kept licking Hannah's clit until Hannah began to shake and moan. She came hard as Alfie shoved Kayla's face into her pussy.

"Now it's time to please me whore", Alfie said as he pulled Kayla to her feet. He bent her over the back of the couch and pounded his cock into her ass until he came hard into her. As he came in her, Kayla began to cry out as she felt an orgasm overcome her. "Fuck, that pussy is so good", Alfie announced as he emptied the last of his cum in her.

"Fuck me, bitch", Frank yelled as he pulled Hannah back by her hips, slamming her hard into his cock as she remained on all fours in front of him. He kept ramming his cock harder into her swollen pussy. Hannah knew she was going to cum again, she panted and moaned as Frank kept slamming himself into her sore pussy. "Don't worry babe, I'm gonna cum soon", he assured her. He pumped his cock into her a few more times before his huge load emptied into Hannah's pussy. She moaned loudly and pushed herself back onto his cock harder. She moaned and squealed as he emptied every bit of his seed into her. Then she suddenly felt his body relax and she knew he had finished.

"Good girl", he said as he smacked her hard on the bare ass. "You girls sure were a treat", he said as he turned to walk towards the bathroom. The other men all agreed in unison and began giving both girls celebratory slaps on their asses. Hannah went to the bathroom and got herself cleaned up a little and dressed. Kayla came in about halfway through and started getting herself dressed and presentable as well. There was an awkward tension between the two that Kayla could not explain. Hannah seemed upset about something, but Kayla was not sure what it could be. As soon as she finished getting ready Hannah left the bathroom without saying a word to Kayla, and when Kayla came out the guys said that she had already went down to the car. Kayla said goodbye to the guys and followed Hannah down to the car.

"Hey, What's up?", Kayla asked Hannah as she got into the car and started it.

"What do you mean?", Hannah scowled at Kayla.

"Well, you seem pretty upset", she suggested.

"Did you know that all four of them were on me the entire time you spent in the bathroom?", Hannah asked accusingly.

"I am sorry. I started my period unexpectedly and I had to go take care of the situation", Kayla explained.

"Yeah, well that really sucked for me", Hannah said clearly not letting up. Kayla drove them home as they sat in silence. Once there Hannah went straight to her room and shut the door behind her. She took out the envelope the men had given her and counted the money. It was exactly two thousand dollars. She knew she had not been fair about the situation. Kayla could not help it that her body picked the worst possible time to start bleeding. She felt a twinge of guilt underneath the anger but in the end anger won. She was pissed that she had been left to deal with all four of those men alone. On top of that Hannah was feeling the familiar unrest that she felt after seeing a client. She could not handle the intensity of the emotions that bubbled up inside of her. She felt as though she were about to explode with anger. She got up and stormed out of her room. She stomped down the hallway to Kayla's closed door. Hannah pounded on it with her fist a few times before throwing it open.

"I want you to move out immediately", She screamed at Kayla who sat there looking stunned and confused. Hannah did not wait for a response. She slammed the door closed again and stormed out of the apartment. She felt a desperate need to get as far from there as she could. She went walking down the street with no specific destination in mind. There was a small shopping center with a restaurant, an insurance place, and three small stores. She was far from hungry and had no need for any insurance, so she walked right past those two places. The first store was a cute boutique that sold women's clothes. A door chime dinged loudly as she pulled the door open. A lady greeted Hannah as she walked inside, Hannah just nodded in her direction. She walked around the store, quietly examining anything that caught her attention. She filled her arms with things she liked and then piled it on the counter beside the register. The lady had to type the price of each item into the old resister individually. When she was done, she pressed a few more buttons and then looked up at Hannah.

"That'll be two-hundred and sixteen dollars and twenty-seven cents", she said before adding, "I gave you a five percent discount since you are buying so many items". She smiled at Hannah and Hannah pulled the envelope from her pocket as she thanked the lady for the discount. She took three of the one-hundred-dollar bills and threw them on the counter in front of the woman. The lady told Hannah that she had to go to the back to get her change and Hannah just nodded at her. After a few moments, the woman returned with Hannah's change and counted it out for her on the counter. Hannah left the store with three bags full of clothes on her arm. When she got outside, Hannah looked at the second store to see what they sold. It was a home décor place. Through the window she could see an adorable lamp that she thought would look perfect on her bedside table. Hannah went inside and spent almost three hundred more. The third store was a shop that sold baby clothes, which she had no use for, so she walked past it and back to the sidewalk. The bags were starting to feel quite heavy, and Hannah kept having to shift the weight of it. She was thinking about turning around and walking back when she saw the church that her and Kayla had gone to. She decided she would go to the church to sit down for a moment and rest her arms before walking home because her arms sere burning from the weight of the bags. She looked around still in awe of the places beauty as she walked in. It was much emptier than it had been last time. There were a few people praying amongst the pews but not many. Hannah slid into one of the pews and sat her bags down. She stretched her arms out and looked around for a moment before picking up a bible out of the back of the pew in front of her. She opened it and began flipping through it mindlessly. She felt a light tap on her shoulder and looked up to see the priest standing there looking at her.

"You were here with Kayla a couple weeks ago were you not?", she asked her with a friendly smile.

"Um, yeah I was actually", Hannah responded.

"I've known Kayla for quite some time now", he stated before a concerned look came across his face. "Are you okay? I was just sensing that there might be something troubling you", he questioned Hannah.

"I had an argument with Kayla actually, and I went walking, then I bought some things, and they were getting really heavy, so I had to stop to rest", Hannah blurted. She was not sure why she had been so honest and had

given so much detail to this man who she hardly knew. She felt immediately embarrassed. He looked at Hannah with a look of understanding.

"Well, I don't want to be a bother, but if you would like, you are more than welcome to come talk to me anytime, and about anything. I can't tell you what to do but I can listen give you an understanding ear and possibly some guidance or suggestions", he offered kindly. Hannah nodded and he began to walk away. He had just made it a few pews down when Hannah looked up and called out to him. Her turned around and looked at her as if he had known that was going to happen.

"Can I actually take you up on that now?", Hannah asked him as she shifted nervously in her seat. When he nodded and gestured for her to follow along, she stood up and followed behind him to an office a short walk from the doorway that led out to the podium where the priest stood to give his sermons. He took his seat behind his desk as she sat in the one across from him. She was not sure why but she trusted this man, she did not think he would look down on her or judge her no matter what. She wanted to tell him the whole story but did not know where to begin. She stumbled over her words for a moment as the priest waited patiently. 1210 He placed his hands on the desk in from on him.

"I know about Kayla's lifestyle", he said, "It is actually how I met her". Hannah just looked at him and wondered if he had meant what she was thinking. "I spoke to her a few weeks ago and she told me she was moving in with a friend who did the same thing. I'm assuming that you are that friend.", he looked at Hannah as if expecting a response. She nodded her head quickly, feeling as if she were being scolded. He assured her that it was okay and told her that he was not here to judge her. Hannah relaxed in her seat. She began telling the priest about the argument and how it happened, leaving out the gory details of course. She explained the things that had happened leading up to the argument even going weeks back. She sat there talking to the priest for hours, and he listened the entire time with a look of understanding. Hannah had been a little surprised when she had finished and realized that none of it seemed to have shocked him or made him veer from his look of calm understanding. Hannah waited for his response as he sat there for a moment looking deep in though. Finally she broke the silence.

"What are you thinking about?", she asked him.

"I'm wondering what you are wanting to do about it", he said. She thought for a moment.

"Well, I want to make up with Kayla. She has been a good friend to me and I would like to tell her not to move out after all", Hannah said

"Is that going to be enough?", asked the priest. Hannah looked at him confused as she wondered what he had meant by that. "There's a root cause to the problem that I think will still be there even if you make things right with Kayla", he explained. She thought this over for a moment.

"The escorting makes me feel uncomfortable", Hannah finally said, admitting it to herself for the very first time. The priest took a deep breath and nodded.

"But what would I do about my money situation?", she asked him, feeling a little panicked by the idea. He smiled and nodded.

"There are so many options", he said, "and you are young, so all of them are available to you, and if push ever came to shove, you could always come here for help". She thought this over. She realized she did have plenty of options, she could start a business, find work online, keep looking for a job, or maybe even go back to school for an even higher degree. She began to see that she had not exhausted all her options and escorting is not, in fact, her only option. She smiled brightly at this thought. She did not want to be too hasty and quit immediately though. She decided it might be a good idea to wait a couple weeks and make another plan before she completely stopped

working as an escort, but just the thought that she would soon be done with it was enough to make her so happy that she almost felt like crying. She thanked him profusely for helping her sort out her thoughts and issues.

"Is there anything else you would like to talk about?", he asked her.

"No", Hannah said, "but if something comes up, I will certainly be back".

"Do you need a ride home? If so, I think I can certainly find you one", he offered.

"Oh, yes thank you so much", she said, grateful that she would not have to walk back with all those bags on her arms. They both stood to leave. As she picked her bags up off the floor, he opened the door and held it for her. On their way out he stopped and spoke to a lady who was cleaning the church. He came back over to Hannah and the lady followed behind him.

"Mrs. Vero is willing to take you home", he said to Hannah gently. Hannah thanked her and the lady said that it was not problem, she was happy to be getting the rest of the day off to spend with her husband who had been extremely ill lately. The priest smiled at Hannah before telling her goodbye for now.

"Goodbye, and thank you", she responded.

Hannah returned home to find that Kayla and all of her things were gone. She tried to call her immediately and got no answer, so she sent an apology in a text message. Ten minutes after she sent the message, Kayla had still not responded, Hannah went to her room to lay down and take a nap. She was completely exhausted from the walk with all the bags of things she had bought, and from the emotional toll her conversation with the priest had taken on her, so she ended up sleeping through the entire night. She woke up to the light shining through the window. The clock by her bed said it was six in the morning. She checked her phone and was disappointed and saddened to see that she had no new messages or missed phone calls. After looking at her schedule she realized she had an appointment with a client later that day. She wanted to cancel the appointment so bad, but with Kayla gone she knew she could not afford to do that if she wanted to keep her apartment. She did not know how she was going to get through the appointment, but she got up and began getting ready, and while she did, she focused on getting into character.

The client she was seeing today had requested a female domination experience which Hannah felt nervous about. She had never been a dom before, so she watched plenty of online porn to gather inspiration, but she was still nervous because she did not see herself as the type of girl who was suited for that kind of thing. She kept the porn in mind as she selected her lingerie for the date. She picked a black bodysuit. It was made from a leather-like material and had straps that went around her thighs. It snapped in the crotch to make her pussy more accessible with the suit on. She took a long shower and shaved before putting the bodysuit on. She loved the plunging neckline that exposed a great deal of cleavage. After blow-drying her hair, she found a pair of stockings and a black pair of stilettos that matched her outfit. Before doing her make-up, she checked her phone in hopes that Kayla had finally texted her back but the only message she had was her client letting her know that he was on the way. Her heart sank even lower, and she tried to put it out of her mind as she put on the finishing touches. She pretended she was applying warpaint instead of makeup, as she took on the tough and unbreakable mentality that she knew she would need to get through the next couple hours. She finally felt ready and even optimistic that this might in fact be beneficial by helping to relieve some of the tension she was feeling. When her phone rang, she answered it and guided the man to her apartment. When she opened the door, a slim dark-skinned guy who looked to be barely in his twenties walked through the door.

Mistress Hannah (FemDom Story)

"Hey there", she said flirtatiously to the guy who stood before her, "so you're the guy who needs some discipline huh?". When he looked at her an expression of excitement and satisfaction came across his face as he nodded his head in eager agreement.

"Yes, I believe I do", he said eagerly.

"To my room, now", she demanded. He followed close behind her and when she pointed in the doorway he went in the room obediently. "What's your name?", Hannah asked him.

"I'm Donny, ma'am", he replied. She began to circle him as if I were a predator ready to strike as she started feeling more in tune with the character she was playing.

"Donny? What kind of fucking name is that? Sissy boy Donny", she teased. He looked down at his feet with embarrassment and whimpered a little. "I am your mistress Donny", she introduced herself before asking, "Do you understand?".

"Yes", he hurriedly replied.

"Yes What?", she demanded.

"Yes, mistress", he quickly corrected.

"You belong to me now Donny", she snapped sternly.

"Yes, mistress", he repeated.

"Do you understand?", she demanded as she walked over and sat on the edge of her bed eyeing him the whole way.

"Yes, mistress", he uttered.

"Now get down on your hands and knees and come here, my Donny. I want to discipline you now.", she declared.

Donny dropped down to the ground onto his hands and knees, quickly crawling over to the edge of the bed where she sat. She gently patted the bed beside her, and he climbed up onto it. "Now kneel over here Donny", she commanded.

As he did as she ordered him to do, she then pulled out a black collar with silver spikes and fastened it tightly around his neck and then clipped on a matching leash. She turned him around to face her and stared deeply into his eyes, with a look of contempt. "You're a bad, bad boy Donny, how should I punish you?", she asked him.

"Severely", he responded with lust in her eyes as he reached up timidly to touch her.

"Don't touch me you dirty slut", she yelled smacking his hand away from her. He pulled back, looking wounded. "Take your pants off", she ordered coyly. He did as he was told as quickly as he could. She took his cock in her hand and squeezed it hard. Her well-manicured nails dug into the soft flesh leaving small red half-moon shapes. He whimpered and she slowly began to stroke his rock-hard dick. She stared up at him with contempt on her face.

"Thank you, mistress", he said gratefully with a wavering voice.

"Do you like that slut?" she sneered.

"Yes, mistress", he admitted with a soft tone.

"You better not cum, not until I give you my permission to", she ordered. He grimaced but told her that he would not. She continued to stroke his cock with her hand and slowly his moans became louder and louder. She could feel his body getting increasingly tense as he struggled to hold back his desire to cum.

"Oh, please mistress", he began to beg. She loved it when they begged. "Please don't make me wait any longer", he choked out.

"I'll tell you when", she smiled. Suddenly, and without any warning, she slapped him hard across the face with the flat part of her hand. He did not even flinch. She continued to do it two more times and then one final time. "Don't you fucking dare cum", she snapped at him, "That was not permission." As he looked at her with tears in his eyes he was filled with shame.

"Yes, mistress" he said again.

"I'll tell you when," she said sternly, as she smiled sweetly.

"Ok, mistress, I understand", he replied.

"Yes, that's what you fucking think", she replied, slapping him again. He could smell her distinctive scent all over the room and his arousal began to grow even more. It was all he could do not to touch her, not to beg her for permission. He did not know how much longer he would be able to hold back the cum. His resolve had begun to break.

"Please don't make me wait any longer", he said in a pleading tone. She just stared at him without a hint of emotion on her face. After a few minutes she slowly began to stroke him faster and faster.

"Alright Donny, my good slut, you may come", she slowly said, deliberately dragging out every word.

"Thank you, mistress", he breathed. He groaned as he came hard into her hand. She felt his tense muscles begin to relax as he finished. She held her hand beneath his nose.

"Well, would you just look at that", she said shoving it close to his face.

"I'm sorry mistress", he cried out.

"Lick it up", she demanded as she looked down at him. He stuck out his tongue and began to lap up the cum on her hand and she began to pet his head. "Good boy, you clean the messes you make", she softly cooed. He nodded at her to let her know he understood. Once he had most of it up, she shoved him backwards onto the bed so that he was looking up at the ceiling.

"Thank you, mistress" he said with tears of shame streaming down his face. She grabbed his face hard in her hands and brought her face close to his. "Now you will please me, my slut", he nodded unable to speak as she threw her leg over him straddling his face. She moved her hips back, pulled her pussy away from his mouth, looked down at him and told him to open his mouth. He did as he had been instructed and she spat directly into his mouth.

"Thank you, mistress", he said with a smile of gratitude as she buried his face back into her pussy and began to rock her hips back and forth. He stuck his tongue out and she moaned at the feeling of his hot wet tongue on her wet pussy. She grabbed a handful of his hair and used it to pull his face harder against her pussy and she positioned herself on top of his face so that he could not breathe. She used the leash to pull him even harder against her.

She remained there for a moment. When she pulled away and gave him access to air he gasped for breath as she began riding his face again. He looked up at her appreciatively. "You like that don't you?", she asked with a smile. He nodded his head at her as he held his tongue out continuing to taste her sweet pussy.

"I love it, my mistress", he confirmed. She looked down at him with disdain and rode his face harder, using his face for her own pleasure. She began to moan a little as he flicked his tongue against her clit.

"Mmmm, yes my slut. That feels so good", she said. He moaned at the affirmation he had given her, and he began to flick his tongue against her clit even faster. Suddenly she felt pleasure and warmth overcome her as she began to come hard against his face. He moaned loudly and began to cry out in pleasure at the taste of her come. When she was done, she ordered for him to stop. "You did good slut", she said as she looked at him approvingly. "Have you ever been owned by a mistress before?", she asked.

"No, mistress", he responded shyly. She thought this over for a moment before instructing him to get back on the floor and on his knees. She did as he was told without a word. She looked down at him and raised her foot up to his eye level, dangling it in front od his face as if it were a prize. He reached out to touch it, but she snatched it away with a laugh. She pressed a toe against his lips as he kept his hands down at his side. He opened his mouth and let her toes slide in. She noticed his eyes were shut tight.

"Look at me slut", she said calmly. He opened his eyes wide and looked at his mistress feeling his hot desire rushing back to him. She saw his cock begin to grow and become hard once again and laughed at the sight. With her foot still in his mouth she began to speak. "Do you understand what being my sub means?", she asked. She removed her foot and placed it back onto the floor. As she did he looked at it as if he were a dog and she was taking his treat.

"I think so mistress", he said. She went on to explain to him that she would cause him pain, but that in turn would give him pleasure.

"Do you love me, slut?", she questioned.

"Yes, mistress", he answered. She picked up a riding crop from her dresser and smacked him hard with it on his thigh. "No slut", she said, "You do not love me, in fact slut you do not know me", she sternly stated as she hit his thigh again with the crop. He winced a little at the sting and he agreed.

"I understand mistress, I do not love you", he said.

"Good slut", she said patting his head affectionately. "Now, who do you belong to bitch", she asked as she rested her heel on his thigh and began to press her weight down as the heel sank into his thigh.

"You do my mistress, I am your worthless slut", he said looking at her as the pain became apparent on her face. His cock was now fully erect.

"Do you want to stick that filthy thing in me, slut?", she asked him as she gestured to his dick.

"I would love to slut, but only if it pleases you", he responded with a hopeful look.

"That will never please me, you disgusting slut", she scoffed. He looked away from her and she dug her heel even deeper. "Don't look away from me", she demanded. He snapped his eyes back and locked his gaze with hers.

"Mistress?", he said cautiously.

"What do you want, slut?", she asked.

"May I please stroke my cock?", he asked her.

"Yes, I'll allow it", she said. She watched as he gripped his cock and started pumping his hand up and down the shaft. "Faster slut, but do not come without asking", she reminded.

"Yes, mistress", he said as he began to pick up the pace.

"Does it feel good?", she asked him. He nodded and she saw his muscles begin to twitch. She had no intention on letting him come that fast. She demanded him to stop, and he obediently took his hand away from his cock. She began to slowly rub her foot across his cock, and he whimpered as he tried to hold back his urge to come. She gazed down at him unenthusiastically as she continued stroking him with her foot. "You can come now slut", she chimed. And she immediately did. It spurted out all over her foot. She looked at him with disgust.

"Now clean it up", she commanded. He immediately did as he was told. Once her foot was clean, she put it back into her shoe. "You've been a good slut today", she said with a smile. "Now it is time for you to leave. Mistress is tired now", she said. He began to object but she cut him off before he could get it out. "You will do as you're told", she screamed. He whimpered and got up. He gathered his clothes and put them on. When he was done, he shyly sat an envelope on the table beside her bed. He kept his head down like a wounded animal as he left, not saying another word to his new mistress.

She breathed a heavy sigh of relief once he left. She was surprised to find that this was one of the rare occasions that she did not feel uneasy after a date. She glanced at her phone and saw a text from Daryl. He was the only other client that she did not feel uncomfortable with. He requested to see both Hannah and the friend she had told him about. He explained that he had bought a game that required at least three players, and he wanted to play it. He clarified that it was a sex game that he had picked up at the porn store. Hannah felt hopeful that this might be her ticket to get Kayla to talk to her again. He offered them each five hundred and Hannah told him that she would see if she could make it happen. She immediately texted Kayla about it but did not hear anything back. Hannah fell asleep waiting for a response from Kayla. Hannah woke up to a loud bang on the door. She rolled out of bed and groggily made her way to the door and opened it. When she saw Kayla standing there her eyes went wide.

"Sorry for waking you up, I had to come by to let you know that I want to do that date. I broke my phone, and I can read your messages, but I can't respond. I get my replacement tomorrow", Kayla explained.

"I'm really sorry", Hannah began. Kayla flicked her wrist in a gesture that meant it's no big deal. When Hannah asked her to come back, Kayla looked at her with an unsure expression.

"Let's just see how things go, okay?", Kayla said. Hannah felt terrible about her being back at the hotel, but she understood Kayla's apprehensiveness. The two girls sat and talked for a bit and Hannah messaged Daryl and set the appointment for a few days out. Hannah told Kayla all about her talk with the priest and how she figured out that escorting was not right for her.

"He even told me that if it came down to it, I could come to him for help", Hannah said.

"Watch out, he might be trying to turn you into a nun", Kayla joked. Hannah told her that she had been considering her options.

"I could probably find work if I tried a little harder", she said, "but, I don't know, it might be easier to just find a wealthy guy who is not too bad on the eyes and get him to marry me". She told Kayla that she had also considered going back to school but said she doubted she would. She felt done with that part of her life and wanted to move on from it. Kayla suggested that Hannah also consider doing webcam modeling or something like that, but Hannah doubted she would be able to do that. She could hardly manage to keep up with her Facebook account. Keeping up with getting on the webcam every day seemed like an impossible task for her. They discussed a few ideas

Hannah had for businesses she had considered starting up as well, but she was not sure how she would be able to get the money she needed for stat-up costs.

"I just know I can not do much more of this escorting thing. I'm just not cut out for it", Hannah finished.

"I guess it's to the cloister with ya then", Kayla said laughing.

"I do love to go from one extreme to the next", Hannah admitted. Kayla stood to leave, and Hannah began to object.

"I've really got to run a few errands", Kayla insisted. Hannah hugged her tight and gave her one last apology before letting Kayla walk away.

"I'll see you in a few days for the appointment with Daryl?", she asked.

"Of course, I'll be here right at three", Kayla promised. Hannah closed and locked the door behind Kayla when she left and sat of the couch. She kept going through the options in her head. She considered the possibility of dating one of her clients. She thought through them and it seemed to her that many of them liked her enough that they would probably be happy to date her. She thought a few of them would probably even agree to marry her out the gate, but she did not know for sure if that would be much better than her current situation. She made herself a drink and went to her room, vowing to put it out of her mind for the night. After taking a moment to appreciate the fact that Kayla, did not hate her as she had been beginning to think, she grabbed the remote and switched the television on and began flipping through some channels. She finally settled on a lifetime movie, which she quickly fell asleep to.

The next few days Kayla spent considering and continuing to research all of her available options. She even stumbled across some loans and grants for business start-ups, that she felt she had a fairly good chance of being able to get. She got lonely and texted Kayla a few times, but she seemed to be staying busy most of the time, all-of-a-sudden. Which made Hannah question whether she might actually be somewhat angry at her. She decided that she would discuss it with Hannah either before or after their upcoming date with Daryl. Hannah was actually beginning to look forward to that date, sitting around the apartment by herself was no fun at all, especially after being so used to having Kayla around all the time.

The day of the appointment finally came. Kayla had her new phone finally working right so Hannah was able to send her a message to ask when she would be coming. Around ten in the morning Kayla responded saying that she was on her way and that she was going to come early so they could get ready together. When she read the text, Hannah squealed with excitement. She missed her friend and was ready to spend some time with her and try to get things back to normal between them. Hannah jumped in the shower before Kayla arrived so that she would not have to take the time to do it while she was there. Then she went ahead and pre-made a couple of drinks for them to sip on before Daryl arrived. She texted him to confirm the time and he responded saying that he would be there. Hannah left the door unlocked as she blow-dried her hair so that if she did not hear the knock, Kayla could just walk in. As Hannah expected she would she did walk in. So, when she came out the bathroom, Kayla accidentally startled Hannah. They drank and got caught up on all the recent happenings. Hannah did a lot more listening than talking because her last few days had been spent at home not doing much at all. Kayla told Hannah about how the woman who had brought her home from the church that day, Mrs. Vero, had unfortunately lost her husband to cancer. Hannah felt terrible and decided to send flowers to the upcoming funeral.

Game Night (Sex Game Story)

It was getting close to time for Daryl to arrive so both Hannah and Kayla got on some lingerie and took care of all the last-minute details they needed to do before he arrived. The knock on the door came a little earlier than expected and Kayla had to answer the door and keep Daryl busy for a moment so Hannah could finish getting ready. When she joined them in the living room Daryl was excitedly showing Kayla the game that he was wanting them to play with him and Kayla was listening intently as he explained it.

"Hey guys, what's up?", Kayla asked as she walked into the room.

"Just checking out this game that Daryl brought for us to play", Kayla responded.

"What's the game called?", Hannah asked as looked down at the cards on the table.

"Dirty Deeds", Daryl said with an unmistakable excitement in his voice. Hannah offered Daryl a drink, and he said he could have just one, so she quickly made three mixed drinks and they sat in a circle around the coffee table as Daryl shuffled the cards.

"The player to the left of the dealer goes first so Kayla it's your go", Daryl said once he got the cards shuffled. Kayla picked a card from the stack and read it.

"Who do I do it to?", Kayla asked.

"It's your choice", Daryl responded. Kayla began reading her card aloud.

"Wait so how do we declare a winner?", Kayla asked.

"How about whoever gets Daryl's come wins?", Hannah suggested with a mischievous grin.

"Okay", Kayla said, feeling confident that she could make Daryl come faster than Hannah could.

"Alright", said Daryl, "But I get to pick one of your cards for you ladies to work on each other.

"Kiss your lover from head to toe for five minutes", she said. Then she made a thinking face and smiled over at Daryl. His cheeks tuned slightly red as she kissed the top of his head. She made a trail of kisses down to the collar of his shirt. She began unbuttoning the shirt leaving a kiss where each button had been. She unbuttoned his pants and kissed her way down his cock as she pulled off his pants and boxers. She kissed all the way down his legs and the tops of his feet. She left one final kiss on the tip of his pinky toe and then smiled up at him. They all three laughed and then Kayla turned to Hannah.

"It's your turn", she said to Hannah smiling. Hannah selected a card from the top of the pile and turned it over and read it to herself.

"I have to give one of you oral for twenty-five minutes", Hannah said smiling. Daryl quickly pointed to Kayla and Hannah smiled at him. "Does that mean you are using what might be your one chance to see some girl-on-girl action?", she asked him teasingly.

"Yes I am. This one is for you and Kayla", Daryl declared with a playful smile as he decided to use his ability to make one of the girls chose the other.

"Kayla get those panties out of my way", Hannah said winking at Daryl playfully. She got down onto her knees in the floor between Kayla's legs and began softly began kissing up her thigh as she slowly made her way over to her clit, then she began flicking it with her tongue. Hannah lightly nibbled at her clit before she plunged her tongue into Kayla's tight hole. She enjoyed the taste of Kayla's arousal on her tongue. Hannah really began to get into it as she vivaciously licked all over Kayla's wet pussy. She knew she only had twenty-five minutes and she wanted to make Kayla come. Kayla began to squirm and move her hips pushing herself eagerly against Hannah's warm wet tongue. She threw her head back and then moaned loudly as Hannah sucked gently on her clit.

"Oh fuck, yes, lick my pussy," Kayla said, holding her hand on the top of Hannah's head. Hannah briefly looked up and saw Daryl standing there watching her longingly as he rubbed his cock at the sight of them. The twenty-five minutes were nearly up so Hannah picked up her pace. She licked and sucked at Kayla's swollen wet pussy with everything she had. When Kayla's legs began to shake and tremble, she flicked her tongue against faster against Kayla's clit knowing that she was getting close to her climax. Warm sweet liquid suddenly began gushing out of Kayla's pussy just in time. When she finished coming, there was quite a mess left behind. Hannah had just enough time remaining to lick up her sweet juices as she moaned and trembled. Then Kayla's body went limp as she relaxed her muscles, and she began to pant, and she tried to catch her breathe. Hannah looked up at Kayla with a proud expression.

"Do I get Bonus points for that?", she asked jokingly. Daryl and Kayla both busted out laughing at Hannah's question. As Hannah wiped her mouth clean and took a sip from her drink. Hannah then had to quickly run to the restroom so that she could pee because the alcohol was filling her bladder quickly.

"You should! Oh my, that was good", Kayla breathed. "You've been holding out on me bitch", she half joked as she struggled to regain her composure. They all three laughed in unison as they returned to their seats around the coffee table to resume the game. Daryl rubbed his hands together for luck before picking up a card up. He took a sip of his drink and then looked at his card. Both girls looked at him expectantly as he immediately read the card aloud.

"Tease one player's nipples for five minutes.", he said shrugging clearly unimpressed by the card he had drawn. He looked over at Kayla who was still trying to catch her breathe from the intense orgasm she had just experienced, "I'll give you a rest my dear", he said kindly before making his way over to where Hannah was sitting looking as if she were getting bored. "You look like you could use some excitement", he said to Hannah who quickly nodded her head and smiled in response. He pulled the bralette of her lingerie set out of his way and began to circle her nipples lightly with the tip of his tongue. He made each circle smaller and smaller until the tip of his tongue touched the very tip of her perky little nipples. Hannah moaned, feeling her pussy tingle with excitement as if it were linked to her nipples. She moaned as he nibbled and sucked on her hard ready nipples. Kayla touched Daryl's cock and she noticed that it was fully erect and harder than she had ever felt it. She could not help but stroke it a few times as he teased Hannah's nipples. He could feel how badly she wanted to be fucked by him and he wanted to fuck her just as badly. He wanted to touch and play with that hot wet pussy and he was having a tough time struggling to resist the urge. Suddenly, the timer went off loudly reminding them that their time was up, and Hannah looked at him and bit her lip seductively. Daryl had trouble pulling himself away, but he did regardless. It was now Kayla's turn again, so she grabbed a card from the deck. She looked at the card with confusion and then she lowered it so everyone could see why she looked so confused.

"It just has a pair of handcuffs on it, with no words", she said unsure of what that meant. Daryl remembered that he had forgotten to explain this part of the game, and he pulled his bag close to him and he took out eight items that were typically used for sexual purposes and laid them all out in front of them. He explained that she did not have to take a turn now, and that getting that card meant that the next task that she was to select, had to be done with the handcuffs somehow being used. Daryl picked up the pair of handcuffs. They were lined with black

fur to make them more comfortable for the person wearing them. He sat them on the table close to Kayla so that she had them in her reach when it came time to use them. Hannah picked up a card slowly to build suspense. She peeked at it for a moment and made eye contact with both Kayla, and then Daryl before beginning to read it aloud.

"Give one player a five-minute lap dance", she read with a smile. Hannah turned up the volume on the music and began to seductively grind her mostly nude body against Daryl. She felt his hard cock rubbing against her ass as she danced. The feeling of it made her pussy get very wet. He could feel the wetness when he ran his hand across her pussy. She turned to face him, and he felt her breath against his ear as she lightly nibbled it. As she moved her body with the music, he explored every inch of her skin with his hands. He stared at the way her body moved as if he were in a trance. He wanted to do terrible things to her. He imagined himself licking her, touching her, and fucking her. The timer went off and to Daryl's dismay, she was done He clapped his hands together a few times slowly to show his appreciation. Hannah loved the impressed look on his face. Daryl did not say a word before he selected a card from the pile on the table.

"Spank a player for five minutes", Daryl read as if he were still deciding. "Kayla, you really have been being such a bad girl tonight", he said as he gestured for Kayla to come over to him. She crawled over to him without any objections and obediently bent herself over his knee as she braced herself for the first blow. Daryl pulled her panties down to her knees, exposing her bare ass cheeks, which were begging to be spanked. He smacked her hard on her ass and she moaned a response. He began slapping her plump bottom repeatedly, using more strength with each blow. After a minute Kayla winced with every smack as she felt his hand beginning to sting against her ass, badly. After two minutes Daryl noticed her ass was getting red and welted. This only made him want to smack her harder. Three minutes in her ass was hot to the touch, and she was groaning with a mix of pleasure and fiery pain. At four minutes in she was on fire and tears began coming from her eyes. Kayla whimpered through the last few blows Daryl delivered. When he was done, he complemented Kayla on withstanding that pain. Kayla did not mind; she had loved every second of it. She was feeling a bit overstimulated, so she called for a much-needed break so using the excuse that she was thirsty and needed to get them some fresh drinks. Daryl refused to drink any more alcohol because he had to drive home, so Kayla came back with just two mixed drinks and a bottle of water, which Daryl graciously accepted. She cautiously picked a card up and read it out loud to the group.

"Fuck one player for twenty fine minutes", she said looking around as if she did not know who she should pick. "So, I have to use the handcuffs during this, right?", she clarified.

"That's right", Daryl said nodding. Kayla asked Daryl to lay down, flat on his back. He smiled with a knowing expression and did as he was instructed to do. "I'm not going to make this easy for you", he promised with a devilish smile.

"Nor will I make it easy for you", she said with a calm confidence as she straddled his cock, running her pussy against it seductively where it was resting between her long tan legs. She grabbed his hands and raised them above his head forcefully. He gazed at her as if challenging her to give it her all. She used the handcuffs to lock his hands securely around the leg of the coffee table so that he could not touch her. Then she took hold of his cock with both of her hands and began to slide the thick cock straight into her tight wet pussy. He moaned in satisfaction as he felt his member being squeezed hard by her pussy. He liked the helpless feeling he got from being cuffed and she embraced the feeling of control that came from Daryl being restrained and unable to do anything to stop her, not that he wanted to. She rocked her hips back and forth slowly easing his cock deeper and deeper inside of her tiny hole.

"Oh Yeah, that feels so fucking good", Daryl said with a growl as he admired her perky beautiful tits. He loved how they bounced vigorously up and down with the force of her fucking him. Each time she sped up and began to fuck him harder they began bouncing with even more force than before. He had almost forgotten that Hannah was in the room. He glanced over at Hannah who was sitting on the couch watching them intently and reminded himself to resist any urges to come. He knew the urge would probably begin to surface soon, so he braced himself for it and tried to prepare so that he would not let himself come in Kayla's ready pussy. This cum belongs to Hannah, he said trying to convince his body to hold back. As Kayla bounced up and down on his cock, he felt his orgasm building despite his attempts to stifle it. Suddenly, the timer began to ding, and Daryl breathed a sigh of relief at having been able to hold himself back from his orgasm. Kayla looked slightly disappointed by this, and Daryl writhed with sexual frustration, because of the fact that he had gotten so close, but did not get to come, but he know it would soon happen. He found solace in the knowledge that he would probably have another opportunity very soon, so he convinced himself that he was not too worried about it. Kayla slowly opened the locks of the handcuffs to release Daryl. Everyone settled back around the coffee table without talking much. Both ladies were plotting attempting to devise a plan that would assist them in winning this game. As they contemplated strategies, Hannah felt hopeful as she picked up her next card and read it. First to herself, then to everyone else. She flipped her card over with a disappointed expression. On the card there was a vibrator. Which meant she did not get a turn this round. Daryl looked at her apologetically as he flipped the next card.

"Make out with any player for five minutes", he scowled a little and rolled his eyes at the card. Daryl pointed over to Hannah to let her know that he had selected her. He was disappointed by his card. He figured that there was no way Hannah could make him come by making out with him. They began passionately kissing, and the timer was dinging before they knew it. Kayla selected a card and revealed that it had a paddle on it. Her shoulders slumped a little as she realized she was not getting a turn this round.

"Damn, I so thought I had this", Kayla said with a disappointed tone, "You really didn't make it easy on me did you Daryl?", she said. Hannah eagerly picked her next card up. She smiled when she saw what it said.

"Sixty-nine with another player for ten minutes", She read with a triumphant smile. She had already made Daryl come many times before with her mouth, and she knew exactly what she had to do and how he liked his cock licked, but ten minutes is not much time at all, so she knew that she had to be on her best game and perform fast to get it done before the timer began to. Hannah pointed at Daryl and seductively motioned for him to come to her. He laid down on the floor flat on his back and took in the view as Hannah positioned herself on top of him. His cock was still hard from the last round, and he felt ready to come at any moment.

"I love all this attention I'm getting, Thanks so much, ladies", he said smiling at both girls. "Thank you both for playing this game with me, and with so much enthusiasm. You girls are amazing.", he said affectionately and as if the game had already ended. Both girls agreed that they were having a great time with this adventurous little card game, and they had both gotten to be competitive with it. Hannah crawled on top of Daryl and took his entire cock into her mouth as she straddled his face. He tasted her sweet pussy and moaned. She bobbed her head up and down on his cock, pushing it far back into her throat.

"Mmmm baby, you are delicious", he said to Hannah appreciatively. She felt his cock twinge in her mouth, and she knew he would soon be coming.

"Thank you", she said smiling up at Daryl with appreciation. "I love sucking your fat cock", she enthusiastically stated before plunging his cock into the back of her throat. She circled the tip of his head with her tongue, and he moaned and arched his back as he felt the come building up inside of him. She sucked on it hard as she ran her tongue up and down the entire length of his cock. He buried his face into her pussy and moaned loudly into it. She heard his moans become louder and she looked up at the expression of pure ecstasy on his face. He looked

back down at her and he suddenly felt himself beginning to erupt inside of her mouth. It came out hard and fast and she hungrily swallowed it in full gulps as it did. When she knew she had sucked his cock completely dry, she saved the last little bit of his come in her mouth and stuck her tongue out to show Kayla that she had won the game. Daryl said goodbye to each of the girls, hugged them each tightly, and thanked them both for a wonderful time.

"I hope I get to see you again", Kayla flirted as she pushed a strand of hair out of her face.

"I definitely think you will", Daryl responded with a wink in her direction.

"That was actually really fun", Hannah exclaimed after Daryl had left and she had closed the door. She turned to look at Kayla excitedly thinking that they could maybe hang out for the night.

"I had a blast", Kayla agreed. "But now I'm tired, and I really need to get to bed", Kayla said yawning. She began to gather her things to get ready to leave. Hannah wanted to protest, but she decided it would be best not to do that, despite the pit she felt deep in her stomach. They said their goodbyes and hugged one another, and when Kayla left, Hannah looked around her big empty apartment feeling lonely. She had a lot of fun tonight with Kayla and Daryl. She did not have those awful feelings that typically followed Hannah's dates, but regardless; she knew that this was a rare exception, and she could not bear to continue doing this to herself. She felt stuck and bound by her financial needs. She remained unsure of what to do to escape this life that had begun to wear her down. She got out her laptop and began doing research again to try to find a solution. After searching the web for various options for a couple of hours she somehow ended up on the catholic church's website. She knew Kayla had just been kidding when she suggested that Hannah become a nun, but she was curious about it. The church had an admirable set of values, and to her it seemed it might be one her quickest, easiest and safest option out of this deplorable life she had found herself living. She knew she desired a life with strong values and morals, and to her this option seemed like it was perfectly aligned with what she wanted out of life. She was also afraid that she would fall back into escorting if ever she started to struggle with money, and being a nun seemed like a solid way of mitigating that risk.

She fell asleep in front of her computer with a web page on the typical processes of becoming a nun pulled up in front of her. She snapped awake still at her computer. She got up and threw on some of the most modest clothes she had and made her way down to the church on foot. When she got there, she walked inside the building and she was overcome with a homey feeling that made her feel as though she belonged there. She immediately saw the priest at the front of the room, hovering over some papers at his podium and she walked directly up to him.

"Oh, what a nice surprise", he said smiling at Hannah with a bright smile.

"Hey father, can I please have a word with you in private?", she asked him quietly.

"Of course,", he responded kindly. He immediately put down the papers that he had been working on filling out and he led Hannah back to his office where they had spoken for the first time not so long ago. Once there they both sat down in the exact spots they had been in for their last conversation, facing each other. Hannah took on a thoughtful expression, and the priest patiently waited as she gathered her words and tried to carefully chose them.

"What is the process of becoming a nun?", she plainly asked, unsure of how to more tactfully ease into the conversation. The priest looked at her lovingly as he thought about her question and considered how to best answer it.

"That's a huge commitment", he began, "but if you are really serious, I would be honored to help you get there". They sat and spoke about it for a while. He gave her a brief rundown of the steps involved in becoming a nun. He

told her that technically, she was too young to join the nuns, but then he told her that with his recommendation, they would likely make an exception for her. Hannah was thrilled to hear this. He just said that she needed to prove to him that she really was committed to it. She began trying to convince the priest that she was completely committed immediately. She began to spend most of her free time volunteering at the church and she even began learning the scripture from the bible. At her core she still did not honestly have the unwavering faith and belief that most of the church goers seemed to possess, but she loved the values and character of the church and that is what drove her to take this path. She was excited about the prospect of doing services for her community and helping others. She had always felt great anytime she was doing something kind for someone else. The other thing that drover her was the idea of being free of the worries of money and sex and the many other things that were considered a sin. She was at the church volunteering, working with the children in the community one day when Kayla happened to stop by the church and had spotted her. She called out to Hannah to get her attention but Hannah could not hear her over all the kids yelling excitedly.

"What is she doing here?", she asked herself. She finally got Hannah's attention. "Hey, what are you doing?", she asked as she approached Hannah.

"I'm just helping out", Hannah replied.

"I thought you did not like it here", Kayla inquired.

"I didn't say I didn't like it. I just felt out of place. Lately I have begun to feel more like I belong", she explained. Kayla nodded in agreement. Hannah did not mention to Kayla that she was trying to join the nuns.

"Do you want to hang out later?", Kayla asked Hannah nonchalantly.

"Sure", Kayla responded, "I will be done here in about an hour then I was planning to head back home". Kayla looked at her with a curious expression for a moment before turning to walk away. A few hours later she texted Hannah to see if she had made it back home. Kayla had some news to give Hannah that she thought she would be thrilled to hear. When Hannah responded saying that she was in fact home, Kayla headed straight over to her apartment. On the way there she pondered reasons why Hannah would have suddenly become interested in the church.

"Hey", Hannah said to Kayla as she opened the door.

"Hey", Kayla responded. "Are you okay?", Kayla asked with concern apparent on her face.

"Of course, why? What is up?", Hannah inquired.

"I'm just wondering about your sudden interest in the church", Kayla said quizzically as she probed for answers.

"It's just that the church has a lot of resources that could help me out of my current situation. You know how much I cannot stand escorting and I like the values they carry at the church", Hannah added. Kayla nodded slowly.

"Anyway, I noticed you took your ad down", Kayla said.

"Yeah, I'm only seeing my regulars now", Hannah said without stating any reasons.

"I have a client who has been interested in seeing you for a while. I showed him a picture of you and ever since he keeps asking about you every time, I see him", Kayla mentioned. "Should I send him your way or are you not taking on any new clients at all?", Kayla asked. Hannah thought it over.

"I don't mind seeing him", Hannah said trying to hide her reluctance. She knew she needed the money badly, so she agreed despite her feeling of repulsion by the notion. She was already getting behind on rent again after just getting completely caught up.

"Also, I would consider moving back in if you wanted", Kayla suggested. Hannah agreed excitedly asnd told Kayla that she could do so immediately.

"It's been really lonely around here since you left", she explained. Kayla went back to her hotel and got her stuff and Hannah stayed this time, remembering how scared she had been the last time she went. Kayla quickly moved back into the apartment the following day after making Hannah promise that she would not try to kick Kayla out again without giving her adequate notice. Kayla went ahead and paid her half of the month since she knew that Hannah was behind and struggling to get caught up on all of the bills by herself. Kayla set the date with her client up a few days out for Hannah. Hannah was glad she had because she had not been working much lately, so she felt that she needed the time to prepare for the date mentally. Those few days went by incredibly fast especially since she now had Kayla around again. Hannah liked the relief from the loneliness that Kayla provided. They were back to spending most of their free time hanging out, and drinking and watching movies, which was not very much since Hannah has so many commitments to the church now. On the day of the date, Hannah was relaxing in her room after just waking up when she suddenly heard Kayla banging hard on her bedroom door.

Daddy's Little Girl (BDSM)

"What?", Hannah called wondering why Kayla felt the need to pound on her door so early in the morning. She felt frustrated by it but tried to hold it back so that she did not get snappy or mean with Kayla. She took a few calming breaths and waited for Kayla to respond.

"Did you forget about the client coming?", Kayla urgently called through the door. Hannah looked at the time and began to panic.

"Oh, shit", she grumbled. Then she called out to Kayla that she was getting ready as fast as she could. She asked Kayla to send the client a text to ask him to push the appointment back an hour or so. Luckily, the client was fine with pushing back the appointment by a half hour. This gave Hannah just enough time to get herself ready. She quickly ran across the hall and got straight in the shower. She rushed through the entire process of shaving, washing, doing her hair and make-up, and getting herself dressed, but at the end she was satisfied with the outcome as she looked at herself in the mirror. She picked a cute body harness that she had recently bought to wear since she knew that this client was interested in BDSM. Hannah knew she was good at being a sub, and she was much more comfortable with that than she was with being a dom, so she definitely felt more comfortable with this date. She finished getting ready just in time and ran to the door to let the client inside. Kayla left to run some errands so her and this new client had the apartment to themselves. He came inside with a duffle bag over his shoulder and did not say a word when Hannah greeted him. She quickly became nervous due to his silent and tough demeanor and began to ramble on about senseless things.

"Silence!", he ordered loudly having apparently had enough of her talking. Hannah abruptly stopped talking and watched him with a shocked, wide-eyed expression as he dropped his bag to the floor with a thud. He pulled out a ball gag and walked over to Hannah holding it out. When he put it up to her mouth, she opened wide and let him fasten it around her head. He walked back to his bag and pulled some restraints our of it. He made his way back over to Hannah and fastened thick leather straps to each of her wrists, and then to each of her ankles. He clipped the wrist straps to the back of her body harness so that her hands were secured tightly behind her back. He looked at her directly in her eyes. "When you address me, you will call me daddy, do you understand?", he said sternly as he looked her in the eyes. He removed the gag from her mouth long enough for her to answer him.

"Yes daddy", she said sweetly. Her pussy got wet just from saying those words to this strange man. He replaced the ball gag then walked back over to his bag. He came back with a paddle in one hand, and his fist closed around something else. He saw Hannah looking at his hand curiously, so he held his hand out in front of her. When he unclenched his fist, Hannah saw two nipple clamps in his hand. One at a time, he fastened them both to her nipples. Then he yanked the first one off. Hannah yelped at the pain, and the man smiled sadistically at Hannah. He clamped it back onto her nipple before bending her over his knee and smacking her hard on the ass with the wooden paddle a few times. She whimpered and her ass felt as if it had been set on fire as he delivered each blow with all his might. Suddenly he was grabbing her hair and forcing her to her knees. He held onto her hair as he unbuttoned his pants and took out his cock. Then he shoved his long hard cock deep into Hannah's throat so that she gagged on it. He used her hair to fuck her in the mouth. She gagged so hard tears began streaking down her cheeks leaving a trail of black eyeliner and mascara all the way down. When he was satisfied, he pulled her to her feet. He went back to his bag and pulled something rather large from it. It was a board, and it had clips on it to fasten her restraints to. He pulled Hannah over to the board and began attaching her restraints in various places. When he was happy with the position she was in, he slid his cock into her groaning as he entered her dripping

wet pussy. For a moment he fucked her hard. Without any warning he reached up and yanked one of the nipples clamps off.

"Ouch", she cried out in pain. She winced as she felt her nipple becoming harder from the pain of the clamp being ripped carelessly from her soft tiny nipple. A tear rand down her cheek and he wiped it off with his hand.

"Calm down slut," he responded. "This is just a little reminder of who's in control. Don't forget to call me daddy." He thrust his cock in and out of her pussy, as he did, he pulled the nipple other clamp off her. She screamed in pain, and he vigorously slammed his cock into her pussy over and over. He pulled his cock out and unclipped the restraints so he could flip Hannah onto her back. "I want you to come now", he said as he lowered his face down into her eager pussy.

"Yes daddy", she responded. He began to lick her pussy. He flicked his tongue back and forth across her clit as she moaned. He ate her pussy so good she came within minutes. She squirted hot come from her pussy. He kept licking her and she continued to come for several minutes. When she was done, he flipped her onto her hands and knees and fastened her into position on the board. He resumed slamming his cock into her now soaked pussy. He began to pant harder and harder, and his moans got increasingly loud. Her tight pussy made his cock begin to spasm and not long after that he reached his orgasm despite his attempts to hold it back. He filled her pussy with his hot cum. He leaned over her and took the time to catch his breath. He did not want to be done. He decided he was not done.

"Lick it clean", he ordered as he positioned his cock directly in front of her face. She opened her mouth and he thrusted himself inside. She began sucking his cock again and did so eagerly. Her hands reached up and she began rubbing her swollen clit. It was only a minute before she screamed out in pure ecstasy. She arched her back as waves of orgasmic pleasure gripped her body. She continued moaning loudly and her body continued to spasm in what seemed like wave after wave of pleasure, almost too much to handle. He pulled out of her soaked pussy and stood up. He sat on the board and reached around her, grabbing her arms and pulling her down until her shoulders rested on the board. She was completely exposed, and at his mercy. He positioned his cock at the entrance to her pussy and began to slowly slide it into her soaking wet, dripping cunt. She was completely wet and ready for him to fuck her. She screamed out and again begged him to fuck her harder. He pushed even deeper inside her. She was almost aching to be filled by his cock. He continued sliding his cock into her slowly. She clenched her eyes closed, only vaguely aware of the waves of pleasure that were starting to overwhelm her body. He could feel her pussy walls begin to clamp down on his cock, wanting his cock to fill them to the brim. He moved his hands up her arms and wrapped them around her neck. He placed his hands on her shoulders and began pushing even harder into her pussy. She begged him to fuck her harder. She could feel him lift on his toes and was pretty sure he could feel her wet, tight pussy engulfing his cock. He began to slam his cock deeper and deeper into her pussy.

"Oh God yes", she screamed. He began to gasp, and this body jerked involuntarily as he felt his orgasm getting close. He grabbed her tits and squeezed them hard. She squealed in pain and pleasure as he pulled her tits back and forth as he continued to fuck her. It seemed like he had fucked her harder and longer than she had ever been fucked before, and she could not believe he was still going. As the last wave of orgasmic pleasure washed over her, he started to come so hard within her that it almost felt as if he had been fucking her nonstop for hours.

"That's it daddy, fuck your baby girl's pussy. Fuck her pussy! I can feel it!" she cried out with delight. He could feel himself pumping his thick cum into her as he tried to thrust every last drop into her tiny pussy. He could feel her pussy grabbing at his cock and taking it inside of her again. He felt the last flood of his cum fill her up as if he had exploded in her pussy. She screamed out in pleasure. Then they both collapsed on the board, panting hard as the room spun around them.

"That's my good girl", he whispered in her ear as he softly petted her head and continued to lay there trying to catch his breathe. She whimpered beneath him feeling utterly exhausted as the shame of what she had just done began to take hold. She silently wished he would leave, but he took his time. He finished catching his breath, and then went straight to the bathroom to clean himself up without saying a word to her or acknowledging her in any way. Then he slowly and methodically packed all of his things into the duffel bag he had arrived with. He lightly kissed her forehead before he walked out of the apartment door. Hannah quickly jumped up and locked the door behind him. She went to her room and began to cry into her pillow until she fell into a deep sleep. Her eyes were swollen and puffy from crying when she woke up. She realized she was nearly late for an important event at the church that the priest had asked her to attend.

"Shit", she cussed under her breathe as she got up and jumped in the shower. Every step she took was a painful reminder of what had happened before she went to sleep thanks to her sore and swollen pussy. She tried to ignore it as she finished getting herself ready. She heard Kayla come in the door and so Hannah asked her for a ride down to the church. Kayla said she would take her, and Hannah thanked her. Hannah quickly finished getting ready and then the girls got into the car. Kayla decided to stay at the church for the event, which neither of them were sure exactly what the purpose for it was. The pews were filled with people as the priest walked to the front of the room. He began speaking about celebrating life and having gratitude for our blessings. Hannah periodically nodded her head in agreement. She almost did not hear it when he called out her name. He was looking at her expectantly and so was half the people in the room. He gestured for her to come up to the stage, so she slowly stood. Suddenly she realized what he had said before her name. Sister, he had said Sister Hannah. Her mouth fell open as the realization struck her. That meant she finally had been accepted into the ranks of the nuns. She looked back at Kayla's shocked and confused expression, but she could not help but beam with pride at the news. She blushed when she realized the room was clapping loudly for her. Not long after, as she stood in a group of her new sisters, as people began to file out of the room. She approached the priest to ask if she could go speak to Kayla for a moment. He nodded an affirmation and so she ran down the aisle to where her friend stood waiting.

"I was kidding when I suggested you become a nun, but you actually did it", she blurted out in a mix of tears and laughter. Hannah shrugged and began to explain that she had wanted so bad to be free of the worries that had begun plaguing her since she had left college and became an escort. She expressed her desire to do good for the world and told Kayla that she felt that this life had been calling out to her for some time now. The shock did not leave Kayla's face, but she nodded realizing that she had no choice but to accept her friend's decision. Kayla burst out in sobs and tears, sobbing as she hugged Hannah tight as if she would never see her again. Hannah assured her that it would all be okay.

"I will be right here whenever you need me", she cooed softly to her friend, "you are welcome to come see me anytime". Kayla nodded her head in agreement and her tears began to subside. Hannah informed her that she had signed the apartment over to her. The hugged each other tight before Hannah returned to her place among the other sisters. At last she felt at peace knowing that she was leaving that life that she was so unhappy with, behind her.

Women's Orgasmic & Erotic Sex Stories:

Threesomes, BDSM, Gangbangs, Oral Orgasms, First Time Lesbian, Rough Anal, Sex Toys & Games, Spanking, Tantra & More

(Forbidden Fantasies Series)

By Rachael Richards

Table of Contents

Our Dirty Little Secret

"A young job applicant is desperate to get a position with a prestigious company. She's willing to do anything her new boss asks of her. But will it be enough to secure the position?"

I squirm in my seat as I look at the other women who are sitting in the waiting room around me. They all look like something off a catwalk, skinny, pretty, and perfectly dressed in their designer clothes. I look down at myself and my neat, but unbranded clothes, and I feel self-conscious.

Jesus, I need this job.

I've just left college and I really don't want to have to go back home. My parents are what I would call 'tiger parents' - they have always been so very strict with me and have tried to control my entire life. This is my chance to escape. If I can get a good job at a prestigious law firm in New York, then I won't have to go home since I have a 'proper job'. It's either become a lawyer, or become a doctor, and honestly, just the thought of needles makes me feel queasy so Law School it was. I'm hoping that coming top of my class is going to give me some kind of advantage against these women. The position is for a Personal Assistant and I know that this will be a good step for me into the company.

I wait nervously until eventually, they call my name.

"Emma Taylor."

For some reason, I still look around as if there is another Emma Taylor here as well. I resist rolling my eyes at my anxious behavior.

I need to be in control. I need to be confident.

The words are my mantra as I follow the woman down the long, blindingly white corridor and to the double doors at the end. She turns and smiles at me. Somehow I return it. She knocks on the door three times and then opens the large door on the right. I expect her to follow me inside but she doesn't. Before I know it, I'm standing in a large office by myself as the door closes behind me.

"Good morning," a deep voice greets me from across the room.

I turn my attention to the sound and find a man sitting at a large table that is central to the room. The nameplate on his desk reads 'Erik Reed' and my eyes widen. Reed and Reed is the name of the law firm. This must be one of the owners of the company.

He is not what I expected at all. I had kind of pictured a balding old man who would be overweight and dressed in a suit that was too small for him. The man at the desk - Erik - is definitely none of those things.

"G-good morning," I stutter back as I try to gather myself. Unsurely, I take a step forward and begin the walk over to the chair which is empty in the room. "Thank you for seeing me this morning."

I hold out my hand as I arrive to shake the man's hand and I give him a smile. I hope he can't tell how nervous I am. I have a habit of embarrassing myself and I really don't have time for that right now. I need this.

Thankfully, the man stands and takes my hand with a grin that makes me weak at the knees before he gestures for me to sit. I do as I am told, place my bag onto the floor and take a seat slowly. I pull my dress down as it rides up and self-consciously my attention zeros in on it as I realize just how short it is.

"Emma, my name is Erik Reed, and I am one of the partners for Reed and Reed. How are you?" He straightens his jacket and then sits back down.

"I'm good, thank you. How are you?" I reply on autopilot, making eye contact with him. He has sharp green eyes and mousy hair and he's clean-shaven and smart. I can feel myself blushing as I look at him.

Get a grip, Emma, I remind myself sharply.

"I'm very well, thanks," he replies before he leans and grabs the laptop that sits to the left of him. "So, Emma, tell me a little about yourself."

It's such an open question... I'm not really sure what he wants to hear but I think back to all the interview prep that I have done. "Well, I'm twenty-one, single, and just moved to the area. I graduated with honors just this year."

"And that was from New York?" he asks, looking at the screen.

I nod in response. "Yes. I've been volunteering at several charities for the past two years assisting with pro bono cases. I like helping people so that's been a lot of fun but now I'm looking for something secure so I can settle here."

He snaps the laptop closed and turns his attention fully to me. "Good. Law is all about helping out clients. The type of cases that we get here are pretty complex, so we're looking for someone with excellent attention to detail. You need to have fantastic communication skills, be confident with office skills. It's not easy. The hours are long and even with your degree, it's going to be hard for you. A lot of girls your ages just can't hack it."

I try not to feel intimidated by his words.

"I'm happiest when I'm working hard. I'm the kind of person who rises to a challenge. I'm not afraid of things being hard. I'm not looking for the type of job where I can sail through without any real effort." I look into those green eyes as I speak, trying to show him how sincere I am. How serious I am about this.

Reeds and Reeds is a prestigious law firm and my parents would accept nothing less than the best. I either get a job here or I'll be forced to go home.

He stares at me curiously for a while, clearly thinking about what to do next.

Under the desk, I cross my fingers.

"I was impressed by your application. And you've kept yourself busy which shows your work ethic. You've got some excellent letters of recommendation. I won't lie, Emma, you're among the top candidates for this job. I think the position would suit you. But tell me, what sets you apart from the other girls? They're just as qualified and want this as much as you do."

The question has me reeling. "Mr. Reed… I… I promise you that I'll do whatever it takes. I have no prior commitments and I plan to give this job one-hundred and ten percent of my efforts and time. I'm happy to start immediately and assist you with whatever you require. As I said, I have been working for non-profit organizations for the past 26 months, so I've accumulated a good amount of experience editing and proofing, researching and verifying, and developing my practical legal knowledge alongside my degree. I feel I would be a strong asset to you and your team." I'm not sure where the words are coming from, but they just pour from me. I'm so desperate for the position that I just say whatever I feel will help Mr. Reed to like me.

"Well, you certainly are convincing," he replies, and I let myself feel hopeful for a moment that I have actually said something right. "But are you sure you can handle the other things that I might need? I have a very specific taste with everything I do, so things have to be perfect. I like things to be done on a strict schedule. I expect my assistant to be with me wherever I am, and to work alongside me. So if I decide to work at home until 3 am on a Saturday, then you'll be there with me." It's a lot of information to take in at once. He looks at me curiously, judging my reaction to his words. Honestly, though, I don't feel phased at the expectations. I expected as much.

"For such good company benefits, I would expect nothing less."

The job is something out of a dream. It's no wonder that there are so many women (and a couple of men) crowding the waiting room outside. 65k starting salary, company car, pension and insurance including dental, free lunches and 28 days paid vacation… I didn't expect the work to be a walk in the park. Stepping into a job like this will have me set for life. Even if I somehow don't pass the bar exam which I should be taking next year, then the position is good enough that I can continue to do it without my parenting bearing down on me and pressuring me to do more with myself.

I stare at him determinedly. I need him to know that I will do anything to get this position. It actually scares me a little about how far I'm willing to go.

He grins at me as he thinks and I watch as his eye drop downwards slightly. I follow his gaze and I realize that he's staring at my breasts through my dress. I should shy away and be disgusted… I should storm out and give him a piece of my mind - I am not a piece of meat to be gawked at! Yet, his focus has me approaching a new tactic.

I'm not experienced when it comes to men… in fact, I've only ever had short relationships and I've never admitted it to my friends, but I'm actually still a virgin. It's embarrassing but I just haven't had the

time to explore that side of me. I've been laser-focused on my education… it's not like I've had any other option with the way my parents are...

I shrug my jacket off and fold it over my handbag, I try to make it look as if I'm just getting comfortable and I lean back in my chair, when in fact, I want to expose myself further to him. I might not be the prettiest girl, but I do have something that I know men just can't resist about me - my breasts. When God was handing them out I must have been at the front of the line because I've always had large perky breasts. No matter what I wear they are visible through my clothing and stand out as one of my prominent features.

"Plus," I continue, "I'm sure that there will be other benefits of having me around. I'm a very good listener and I'm fantastic at following instructions. I can do anything that you ask me to do promptly and with little guidance." I shift in my seat and this time when my dress rides up, instead of feeling self-conscious, I leave it to ride up my thighs and expose several more inches of my bare legs.

Mr. Reed raises an eyebrow at me, but he also smirks and I know that I've got his attention. He is taking the bait. "Seems that you're very willing to do wherever it takes," he tells me. "But I don't go just on words. You need to have the ability to back it up."

"I can do that. I can do anything that you need me to," I insist eagerly, and I smile at him in a way that I hope is pretty.

I am willing to see where this goes. A part of me is terrified. After all, Mr. Reed is clearly older than me, though not by too much. He is very attractive. I'm not so stupid to think that I will be the only employee that he ever fucks.

"I can do anything you want me to." I try to sound confident but there is a waver in my voice. I don't let it affect my focus and dedication to what I'm about to do.

Mr. Reed stands and slowly he walks around the desk and stops in front of me. He leans back, his ass at the edge of the desk. The way he towers over me has me feeling nervous and shaky inside but there's also a thrill that I want more of. I want to explore what it is that has me feeling like this: flushed and curious, and oh so willing to do anything that this man says.

"Go on then," he challenges me.

I hesitate but it only takes a few seconds for me to gather my courage. I instantly drop to my knees. I kneel in front of him obediently. The floor feels hard where it digs into my knees but I ignore the discomfort in favor of concentrating on the task at hand. I reach for his belt. The leather feels smooth in my hands and it easily slips through the buckle, effectively releasing the buckle.

Oh my God, this is actually happening... I'm really going to suck this guy off for a chance at a job for working for him.

Even if I don't get the position, at least I will have this. I finally get to pop my cherry. I get to do something naughty and reckless. It makes me feel dirty. Like a little slut. It's a role I've never had to play before and I'm excited to step into it.

I look up at him, seeking encouragement to continue as I'm face to face with his Armani boxers. I can see the long, fat line of his cock through the material. It has me feeling dizzy that I've been able to turn him on so simply. I want to see what else I can do.

His expression is cocky as he looks down at me. Like he knows that he has some kind of power over me. That he can control me. It makes arousal twist in my stomach and I clench my thighs.

I actually like this. What I'm doing is making me feel hot inside.

With trembling hands, I reach for the waistband of his boxers and slowly pull them down. I softly gasp as his cock is released and exposed to me for the first time. It's long and thick and cut, his pubic hair short and neat. I'm surprised at how little I'm intimidated by it. In fact, I'm actually attracted to it. I waste no time as I reach forward and I wrap my fingers around it.

Fuck... there's no backing out now... and I don't want to. I want this.

I lean forward and wrap my lips around the head. I lick the slit and he tastes clean and musky and I find that I like it.

Mr. Reed's hand grabs my hair and holds me in place as he sinks his cock deeper into my mouth. It's an odd sensation but one that I learn I like. I struggle to keep up as suddenly I can feel it pressing at the back of my throat.

"Shhh, good girl," he tells me and I look up at him with wide eyes and nod slightly. I seal my lips around his cock and suck.

I let him take control and it takes a few minutes to get used to the sensation as he stays in control. I'm powerless to do anything but take every inch that he shoves into my mouth and down my throat. I try not to splutter and a whimper falls from my lips. From then on, I can't help the sounds that fall from my lips. I find myself moaning and gasping as I feel myself growing wet. My pussy throbs and I ache, clenching against nothing and for a second I think about what his cock might feel like inside me.

Would I really let this guy fuck me? Take my virginity? My mind tells me *yes*.

Suddenly, his cock is pulled from my mouth and saliva drips from my mouth messily. Pain erupts in my scalp and I'm shocked as I'm pulled to my feet. A tingly feeling trickles down my scalp and down my neck in its wake.

"Bend over the desk," Mr. Reed orders me.

Immediately, I do as I am told. "Yes, sir," I reply and I bend, my top half laying on his desk and my tits pressed against the wood.

My dress is suddenly pulled up at the back and I feel suddenly bare, my panties dropping to the floor. I spread my legs.

"Please, more," I tell him.

I feel filthy as he looks at me; his hands on my ass and then spreading my pussy. My face flames. He can see me. All of me. I can do nothing but twitch and leak, desperate for him to do something, anything to me.

I groan long and loud as his fingers slip through my hot needy cunt and with no warning, they plunge inside me deeply as he starts to fuck me with them. It sounds obscene. I'm so wet that I can hear the sound of my pussy squelching under his attention. It feels like nothing that I've ever experienced. Nothing like how it is when I finger myself.

"Oh, God. Mr. Reed. Please. Fuck me," I beg.

Instead of fucking me more, his fingers disappear and behind me he tuts. "Very bossy, Emma," he scolds me.

My face flames. "I'm sorry," I gasp, ashamed at how greedy and out of control I'm starting to feel. "But it feels so good. I can't help it." I'm pathetic the way I beg.

"You said you could do anything that I needed…" he tells me and then pauses, waiting for a response.

"Yes. Yes, I'll do anything," I assure him, nodding eagerly against the table.

I shudder as I feel his fingers move to my asshole. I tense but then remember his words. *I can do this, I can be anything that he wants.* I can do everything that he needs. Even this. I feel the intrusion and I tense again. It's odd. His fingers feel large inside of me and I struggle to relax. I'm so turned on and I'm enjoying being wanted for the first time in my life. I shouldn't like it but I do. His fingers are wet from my juices and he drags the wetness from my pussy, using it to open me up.

His fingers are inside my ass, fucking me there and I hear and feel him spit on me, making me slick. I can't help it. I cry out loudly as he presses against my sensitive insides. My ass and pussy throbs and I feel like I might come from his expert touches. He's pushing me higher and higher and I can't stop it. I feel ashamed but at the same time, I feel empowered. I never realized that I liked this, that someone could want me this way.

They're going to hear me outside. They're all going to know what a little slut I am, that I'm letting Mr. Reed do whatever he wants to me…

"Look at you… You're being such a good girl for me," he praises and I nod again.

"Yes," I agree and my words cut off as I cry out again. His fingers are deep inside me and it's addictive. I need more. I need his cock in me. "Please, fuck me," I manage to gasp out. I'm so desperate that I don't even care which hole he abuses. I just need him inside me. I need it so badly that I'm squirming and panting against the desk.

"Demanding again, aren't you?" he tells me, his voice is deep and gravelly in his arousal. I squeal, the sound of it echoing around the large room as there is a sudden sharp pain on my left ass cheek and it takes me a second to realize that he's spanked me.

I whimper, my eyes watering from the humiliation and the arousal. But he spanks me again and again. I feel my ass burning and I push it back into the touch. I'm humiliated as I realize I like it. I like this man spanking my ass, I like him hurting me.

I take his rough treatment as a sign to obey him so I try my best to do as I am told. So I take some deep, shuddering breaths and try to still myself under his attention.

"Good," he says.

He rewards me by pressing the hot, blunt head of his cock against my pussy. He runs it over my labia, rubbing it in circles on my hot, swollen clit before he drags it over my quivering hole and then to my ass. I tense, my eyes squeezed shut in anticipation.

Oh, fuck, this is it. I'm going to lose my virginity to this man. And God, he's going to fuck me in my ass. It's so dirty... I can't believe that I like this so much...

I cry out as his cock presses against my asshole and then pushes inside, opening me up in a place that I've never even dared to touch. I feel full. So impossibly full. I'm stretched to my limit and I think that I can't possibly take anymore but then I feel Mr. Reed's hips press flush against me. He's completely inside me. His cock is bare and it should scare me but I can't possibly feel scared when everything feels so amazing.

He doesn't mess around. He fucks me hard from the start and I scramble to grip at the desk to steady myself. He hits something inside me that I don't understand and wave upon wave of pleasure seems to hit me all over. It feels good in a way that I didn't think was possible. It's hot and fast and hard and I feel like I'm spiraling. I can't stop it. Everything feels so much and I can't do anything as I begin to tremble and my ass and pussy clench and throb as I come. He fucks me through it as I feel drops of my own come hitting my thighs and my toes curl.

He reaches down and I feel his fingers bump against my clit and suddenly it's as if all the hair on my body has stood up. Pleasure blooms around my clit and flows downwards in my pussy and towards my empty hole as it throbs.

"Fuck, fuuuuck," I cry out, powerless as he continues to fuck me with a rhythm that seems punishing. I'm pinned against the table, my tits being crushed as he uses my body. I can't stop it. Even though he's fucking me so brutally inside my asshole, my pussy feels so good. I can't help but get off on the feel of him doing something so depraved to me. I love every moment. It isn't long before I am screaming and then I'm humiliated as he shoves into me roughly, and suddenly pleasure is exploding from inside me. I can feel the spray of my pussy juices and I hide my face.

It's too much. It feels so good. I don't want him to stop.

Over and over he makes me come until I'm crying, sobbing against the wood of the desk. I feel hot and sweaty and I'm sure my makeup is ruined, smudged, and cried off messily as tears pour from me.

I don't know how long we stay like this. Time seems to slow down and there's nothing in the world but me and him until I finally feel him tense up. I gasp, my eyes wide as I feel my ass suddenly flood with hot and wet come.

I feel in shock.

What's just happened?

I lie there still until he moves away from me. His cock slipping from me and his come splattering to the floor. Unsteadily I stand up, my eyes flitting down to the floor and I can see the white drops at my feet. I feel dirty but instead of being embarrassed or regretting it, it feels exhilarating.

I immediately reach for my underwear and pull my panties back up. I look at him unsurely as I straighten my clothes.

I hope this was good enough, that I get to experience this again.

"Very good, Emma. I'll get you to sign your contract today. You start now."

I can't stop smiling.

Love Games

"Recently divorced from a boring marriage, a lonely woman is more than ready to try something new. So when she sees the description on an App - "Rich, Male, 30, looking for Female Plaything - 18-30" she applies on a whim. It's not like he'll choose her. Right?"

It starts with an App.

My work friend Tina tells me about it, whispering to me one day on our work lunch break.

"It's exactly what you need. You just meet up and spend the night together, then do *your thing*. Then that's it. No expectations."

I look at her, not convinced. I'm not even sure if she's being serious right now. It wouldn't be the first time she has played a joke on me.

"Are… are you joking?" I ask her suspiciously, and I can feel my face going red just from talking about something like this in public - where anyone could be listening in and hear us.

"No, honestly. Here, I have it on my phone." She unlocks her iPhone and then clicks an App in the menu. To my surprise, a dating-style app opens and it looks exactly as she has described. "Look, here are my matches. They base it on keywords and location."

"Keywords?" I ask her, already curious now I realize that she's being serious.

"Yeah, so my keywords are: *SugarBaby*, *Spanking*, and *FootFetish*."

I balk. She says it so casually. I hurry to shush her. "Oh my God, Tina." I gesture for her to be quiet. "What does that even mean? Have you actually been on one of these dates?"

She grins at me. "Of course. I'd be crazy not to." She shrugs.

I think about it for a moment and take her phone from her. I scroll through her matches and see what she means, the pictures of men on there have similar keywords: *SugarDaddy*, *Rich*, *FootFetish*. It's then that I glance down at Tina's shoes, and it clicks. I was wondering how she could afford such an expensive habit on our wage. My mouth drops open in surprise as I pointedly look at her shoes with a brow raised.

"Yep," Tina agrees with a nod and looking pretty snug.

"So… So you what? Meet up with these guys and let them buy you things and then… what?" I ask. It's obvious that they must want something in return. Surely they don't just give her a pair of Prada shoes for free.

"Depends," she says, a little mysteriously.

"On what?" I dare to ask.

"The client, obviously."

"Well, what did you do for those?" I ask, and gesture down at her pretty shoes longingly. They are gorgeous compared to my cheap, worn heels. I don't think I've ever brought myself a decent pair of heels in my entire life. Especially since I'd spent the last 10 years married to an asshole. But the less about that the better.

"Well… this guy wanted to… you know… *finish* on my feet while I wore them. And he liked pictures. He recorded himself doing it."

I'm in shock. I don't know what I was expecting. I'm not sure if it's better or worse… But to be honest with myself, it doesn't sound like the worst thing in the world. "And then, you just take the shoes and you're allowed to keep them?"

"Yeah, took about an hour. These shoes were $900. They still had the price on the box."

I'm honestly gobsmacked but we don't have any more time to talk about it. It's almost the end of our lunch hour, so I grab what's left of my latte and we head back up to the office.

***

I don't think about it again until I'm lying in bed that night, feeling lonely in my silent apartment. I find my thumb hovering over the icon in the App Store. Do I really want to do this?

It's been 6 months since I left my husband. It hasn't been easy, but the more time that passes, I know that I've made the right decision. I didn't realize how bad things had gotten. Being miserable became my normal and I just got tired of it. I couldn't do it anymore. And now… it's all over. I can be happy. I want to start living again.

Before I can change my mind, I'm downloading the App and paying for the registration fee, then setting up a profile for myself. I try to find a photo where I look decent and it takes me a few minutes, but I do find one from last year's Christmas party. I'm dressed up nicely. I actually bothered to do something with my hair for once. I'm wearing a pretty red dress. It's not really a pleasant memory associated with the picture because my husband didn't want me to go that night. But in the picture, I look so happy. I think it was at that moment that I realized that I didn't want us to be together anymore.

I retouch the picture by adding a few filters because I'm not feeling too confident compared to the other woman that are on this App. When I'm finally finished, I set up a bio for myself and write: *Learning to love life. Learn with me?*

Am I actually going to do this? I think to myself. *Surely it can't hurt…* Tina made it seem so easy. Plus, I guess that if I change my mind, I can always just uninstall it and forget it ever happened. No-one will know.

It takes me 5/10 minutes to set up my profile completely. When that finally is done, it immediately asks me what I'm interested in. I think back too to Tina's profile.

What are *you interested in?* I ask myself.

That's an interesting question because if I'm honest with myself, I don't really know. You would think that my age I'd have things sorted out, that I'd know who I was as a person. But honestly, I have no clue.

I scroll through the different categories: *Anal, RolePlaying, Group Sex, Bondage, Voyeurism…* The list goes on and on and I don't even understand what most of it means. I decide to go with something plain and click a few things that seem on the vanilla side of things that I think I will be comfortable with.

Once all of that is done, I can scroll through some profiles that have similar interests to mine. One, in particular, stands out to me: *Rich, Male, 30, looking for Female Plaything - 18-30.*

Female plaything? What does that mean? I click into it and I am sent to a messenger app that says 'Send a Wink' at the top. I click it and it deducts from my balance. I mean, what harm can it do? He probably won't respond. After all, I'm on the older end of that, I am 30 this year… He'll probably pick someone younger with kinkier interests than me.

I click on his profile. He looks handsome from what I can see of his face. Except none of the pictures have his full profile. Just parts. From what I can tell, he's nothing like my ex. In fact, he looks the polar opposite and that makes him even more attractive to me. I scroll through his photos, he has a few on there. One shows off just his sharp arctic blue eyes. His current profile picture is mysterious and has me curious. His face is slightly cut off, but at the center of the picture, his finger to his mouth shushing. He is dressed in a sharp black suit. The whole thing has a strange appeal to it. I click out of it.

Is it shallow if I want to spend time with someone rich? I hope not. My husband was definitely not in that category. He was very selfish with his money and I spent all of mine on the bills, so because of that I feel like it would be nice if I could have someone treat me or take care of me. Even if it is just for a few hours…

I let my mind run away with me for a moment. I think about having a nice expensive dinner at a restaurant with a gentleman who is tall, dark and handsome. Someone who wants to spend time with me. Who is talking to me and actually interested in every word that I say. I would be dressed in a pretty dress, my hair done up, and my face made up in glamourous-looking makeup. I'll be wearing a pretty pair of Prada shoes like Tina's. It's a fantasy that feels so far away.

It isn't long before I let my mind wander and I find myself getting lost in the little fantasy that I have created in my mind. The guy would be handsome, more handsome than anything I dare to believe that I deserve. He'd be funny too. He makes me laugh and be happy. For a moment I can feel beautiful.

I start to feel warm in my stomach. It's a familiar feeling at the moment, one I've learned to deal with by myself. Even so, I still look around me feeling self-conscious as a slip my hand downwards and into panties. I pet myself for a moment, just stroking across my lips before I teasingly slip a finger into the wet slit. I stroke myself, rubbing circles over my clit as I let myself sink back into the bed, relaxed, and my mind racing of all the possibilities.

The nameless and faceless man is there, lusting after me and treating me like a princess. He kisses me deeply, his hands all over me, and he touches me in ways that I've never experienced. It isn't long until I'm tipping over the edge, soft moans falling from my lips as I climax and then happy, I let myself fall asleep.

***

It's the very next day that I start to get messages. An unfamiliar notification sounds while I'm working and I frown. Across the room, Tina immediately spins and gives me a look. She knows exactly what I did last night. From the look on her face and a quick glance to my phone screen, I realize what it is.

Shit, I curse myself. I forgot to put my phone on silent. I reach into my bag and turn it onto vibrate before any other messages come through. But I find myself unable to resist and I grab my phone mid-morning and unlock it underneath the table.

It's the guy I winked at last night! My eyes are wide in surprise. I didn't think that he would entertain me. Curious, I open the message.

Gabriel has sent you a Wink.

Hi. Still looking for someone to learn with?

Gabriel. His name is Gabriel... For a moment I wonder what he means by his message, but then I remember what my profile bio says – looking to learn. I click into the profile again and check that it is in fact the man that I looked at last night and not just some randomer. It is. The familiar profile picture appears and I see his post that connected us. I return to the message.

Yes... I think so... I type out. I'm not really sure what to say.

I watch the screen as a little loading icon dances at the bottom. I can see that he's typing back to me and I wonder what he's going to say.

Good, I can probably teach you a few things. But only if you are interested. ;)

The words have my heart palpitating in my chest. I'm instantly excited at the possibilities.

I'm definitely interested. You'll have to tell me what to do though... This is all new to me.

As long as you can do as you are told, then we will get on. You can be a good girl for me, can't you?

I gasp softly at the reply. I look up and around me, ensuring that no-one has noticed that I am texting underneath the table. I've never done this. I've never dirty talked with anyone or 'sexted'. I feel like that's where this is going. Instead of being nervous about it, it excites me.

Yes. I can be a good girl.

It's then that I feel a hand on my shoulder. I jump out of my skin and my phone drops from my hand, falling to the floor. I scramble to pick it up before anyone can see what I'm doing.

"Kinky," Tina tells me and she catches a glimpse of the screen before I can lock it and shove it into my bag. I groan. I really don't want to have this conversation with her. It's embarrassing. "I see you took my advice…"

"Um... yes," I reply, my face flaming.

"Come on, tell me about it on lunch."

I glance towards my computer screen and I realize it's our allocated lunch break. I eagerly stand and grab my bag, following her downstairs and to our usual Starbucks. Once I've ordered my coffee and mac and cheese, we sit together in the crowded coffee room and squeeze into the corner.

My phone pings again from my bag and I purposefully ignore it. Tina wiggles her eyebrows at me.

"So, I take it you found someone then?" she asks me, not beating around the bush at all.

"Oh, God no. Nothing like that," I hurry to tell her. "I just made a profile last night and winked at some guy I matched with. That's all. He just winked back." I don't know why I don't tell her that we have just started talking. I guess because it's such early days. Nothing is likely to come from this anyway. He'll probably flirt with me for a few hours and then that will be it. Plus, it feels nice to have a little secret.

"Good for you," she tells me. "It's about time that you start doing things for yourself. You're allowed to move on. You do whatever makes you happy."

The words empower me and I smile at her, feeling thankful. She is such a good friend. I don't know what I would do without her. "Thanks, Tina." Her words make me smile. It's then that I notice she's wearing yet another new pair of shoes. Suddenly, my interest is piqued and I want to know the story behind them. She proceeds to delve into telling me about her evening – one that's far more interesting than I am ever going to experience.

It's twenty minutes later, when we are back at work and I am wasting the last of my lunch break sitting in the toilet cubical that I check my phone. I'm happy to see another message.

How about we start with something simple. Send me a picture of you wearing something sexy and I'll give you a reward.

I stare at the words for a moment. Can I really send this stranger a sexy picture? *...Is it even possible for me to be sexy?* an unhelpful voice pipes up in the back of my mind.

What kind of reward? I ask him. I don't know how this works. How any of this works.

PayPal? he replies.

There's no way this man is going to send me money for no reason. Life just doesn't work this way. But I give him the benefit of doubt and I send him my PayPal details. I almost drop my phone when a notification pops up at the top of my phone and informs me that I have received $100. I have to open the App just to believe it. But there, in black and white, I read that the money has been added to my balance.

Immediately, I hurriedly open the messenger app to reply to this man, Gabriel. *I got your gift. What can I do for you? I'm at work at the moment. I'm almost due off my lunch break but let me know and I'll message you back when I can.*

I want to do something for him in return. I can hardly believe that his man has just sent me money for no reason. I reopen my PayPal again just to double-check, convinced that it will vanish but no, it's still there.

Send me a pretty picture of your tits.

My face burns. I've never sent a nude picture in my life. But this guy has given me a hundred dollars. I guess I could send him one without my face in…

Okay. I'll send you one when I get home.

I close the App, ready to prepare to go back to work. I reach for my lipstick to reapply it in my pocket mirror. By the time I'm done, another message beeps.

I want it now.

A strange feeling bubbles inside me. It feels like a demand. Something twists pleasantly in my stomach at doing as I am told. I can hear someone else in the ladies' bathroom with me. I can hear her fiddling with something, no doubt reapplying her own makeup. She's oblivious to me, sitting talking to this stranger mere feet from her behind the locked door.

Can I really take a picture of my tits while I'm at work? I think to myself. *God, that's… that's so filthy.*

The idea of doing it turns me on and I realize that I'm growing wet. I clench my thighs. I open my camera app and before I even realize what I'm doing, I'm pulling my work blouse open and then snapping a picture of my breasts in my black bra. I look at it and have to admit that it looks good. My breasts full. It's the first time I feel pretty in a long time. Then before I can chicken out, I pull my tits from my bra and expose them to the air. I snap another picture and look at that one too. It looks like something you'd see on a porn site.

I hit send and then hurry to tidy myself up. Then I stuff my phone in my bag and return to work. Purposefully ignoring my phone for the rest of the day.

By the time the clock ticks around to 5 pm, I can think of nothing but Gabriel. I'm surprised that I managed to get any work done today at all, but by some miracle, my boss didn't notice. I know he's probably not messaged now that he got what he wanted. I'm not naive. But he gave me a powerful feeling, a rush of pride and I want to experience it again. Except, when I do open the App when I get into my car, he has messaged me again. This time, with an invitation.

I see you really are a good girl.

You deserve something special.

How about dinner? 7 pm tonight.

He attaches a link to a local high-end restaurant, and I click on it. I know where this is, it's just on the other side of town. Maybe a ten-minute drive from my apartment.

Immediately, I call Tina despite only just having seen her. She answers on the third ring.

"Forget something?" she asks me.

"The guy I was talking to invited me for dinner," I blurt out. If anyone knows what to do, then it's going to be her.

"Oh, fuck. Is he hot?"

I laugh. My nerves relax a little. "I hope so," I tell her. "I have no idea what I'm going to wear," I lament. I don't have anything remotely suitable for this restaurant. It looks like a nice place from what I can see on the website. Plus, when I've driven past it, I've always had the impression it was one of those fancy places that I would never be able to afford.

"Best get your ass to mine then. I'm sure I'll have something you can wear. You can even borrow those Prada shoes you're so in love with if you like."

I'm flooded with appreciation for her. The sound of one night where I can dress up and go on a date with a sexy man is amazing. "Are you sure?" I ask her.

"Duh," she replies, and I know her so well that from the tone of her voice I can basically hear that she's rolling her eyes at me.

I grin and then make my way to hers.

For the first time in my life, I'm feeling pretty as I look at myself in the mirror. I don't recognize my reflection. Don't get me wrong, it's not like I've had a facelift or anything dramatic– I'm still me. But

I just feel different. It's like finally my ex's words have evaporated and I'm learning my worth. The girl who looks back at me is pretty. Strong. Confident. I can do this. Excited, I make my way to the restaurant.

***

My jaw drops as I'm approached by a tall, handsome man with sharp blue eyes and instantly, I know that it's Gabriel. It's the man from the pictures. He walks towards me with a strong and confident stance and honestly, I hadn't expected anything less.

Oh, wow, he's real, I think to myself.

It's not like I thought he was lying about his identity, but I just expected that maybe the pictures were from when he was younger, or photoshopped in some way. But no, he stands before me, looking very much like he has stepped out of some kind of fantasy.

"Hi," I tell him shyly and my cheeks grow warm. The reality that I have sent this man a picture of my tits catches up with me. It feels naughty and I learn that I like that. I want to feel more of it. Something tells me that he's going to be a lot of fun.

"Hello," he replies, and I gulp. His voice is deep and gravelly, soothing. He looks like he's devouring me, his eyes are all over my body, my face and then down to my cleavage, to my bare thighs which are exposed from the dress I've borrowed from Tina… I grin. It's clear that he likes what he sees. No-one has ever looked at me like this.

"Shall we?" he asks me, and then offers his arm. I take it and then follow him into the restaurant.

"Welcome," we're greeted by a smartly dressed Maître D' that seems to recognize him. He takes us to our reserved seats and then bows to us before leaving us. I can't stop looking around.

"This place is lovely," I say as I take in the high ceilings and beautiful artwork. The place is lushly dressed and the table we have been led to is more private than the others. We are slightly around the corner on a raised section of the restaurant. It is less crowded and seems quieter. We are hidden away from the prying eyes which is nice. We might get to actually talk properly. It's nice to know we can have a little privacy.

"I'm glad. I came here on a business lunch not too long ago and it was great. I thought of bringing you here right away after chatting with you this afternoon."

Chatting. *Well, if you could call it chatting.* I'd basically spoken to him for a few minutes and then shown him my tits.

"Thank you for inviting me. I was surprised at a dinner invitation if I'm honest."

We take our seats opposite each other and the two of us order. I worry for a moment since there aren't prices on anything, but then I remember that Gabriel sent me $100 earlier that day. So if for some reason I need to pay I will have enough. I don't want to assume that he's going to pay for me. I like to think that I'm a modern girl.

Both both make our orders and I go for the salmon. He chooses the steak. Once the waitress leaves to get our drinks, I realize I'm starving. I haven't eaten since my Starbucks at lunch which seems like forever ago. I hope he can't hear my tummy rumbling…

"So, tell me about yourself," he tells me and I'm diverted from my inner monologue.

I feel shy. There isn't much interesting about me. Well, I don't think so… "Well. I'm a Virgo," I say with a little laugh, because it seems to be the kind of cliched things that you say when you go on a date. It gets a small smile from him. But I get the feeling he wants something a little more personal. "Um… I just moved into the city and started working for a company called PowerCore. I like it so far, I've made a few friends. It seems like a really ethical company which is important to me, so I think I'm happy."

He looks at me oddly for a minute, a little smirk playing on his lips. "PowerCore?" he asks, and I nod.

"Oh, have you heard of it?" I ask him. It's a newer company that's just gaining popularity. It's been in social media a lot lately so I guess he must have heard of it.

"Oh, yes I have." He looks at me amused and I wonder what I've said that could be so funny.

His smile is infectious and I find myself smiling too, even if I'm not really sure why. "What about yourself?" I ask him, eager to learn more about him. I essentially know nothing about him. This is a bit like a blind date guess, except I have set it up myself…

"A bit of this and that," he replies vaguely. "I'm more interested in you." He looks at me like he's undressing me with his eyes.

The words have me stuttering and my face must be bright red. "Ohh… Well… thank you. I think."

Gabriel stands, and for a moment I wonder what he is doing. He grabs his chair and with purpose, he moves closer it closer to me and then sits so that we are almost side by side. "You don't mind, do you?" he asks me, though I suspect that he doesn't want me to answer anything but no. "I find it better for us to be closer while we are getting to know each other. It's more intimate."

I can't help but agree with him. His voice is a little bit hypnotizing. He reaches for me and touches my hair. He is very charming. He seems to make me blush with such ease. I feel younger. As if I have no experience at all. I'm 29. I shouldn't have butterflies in my stomach like this. My hands shouldn't be trembling.

It's as if he is playing a game, and I have to admit, I want to play too.

"Why did you pick me on that App?" I ask him, feeling that if he can be direct then I can too.

"You stood out to me. Your red hair is very pretty. I have a thing for redheads."

"Ohhh, I…" I'm suddenly shy. I've always been self-conscious of it. I've been teased for it most of my life. Plus, my ex-husband used to tell me that it looked better blond. He hated when I would let the highlights grow out. After I left, I cut most of the blond out, opting for a slightly shorter more layered

hairstyle. I like it how it is now. To be complimented for it has me weak at the knees. He's taken my biggest insecurity and made me feel desirable for it. "Thank you."

"You're very modest. I like that too," he tells me and I feel his hand on my leg. I glance downwards but I don't move away. I like that he's touching me. I lick my lips. "I enjoyed the picture you sent me this afternoon." His hand dances upwards and takes my dress with it but then he pauses.

"It was exciting," I admit. "Like right now. I've never done something like this before." My words are hushed. A secret between us. I glance towards the openness to the side of us, but we are essentially alone.

"There's plenty of things that I can do that will excite you," he rebukes, and the hand on my thigh encourages me to open my legs. I can't believe it, but with a shaky breath, I lock eyes with him, and then I follow his touch, submitting to him.

"I think I'd like that," I admit.

The waitress returns and I stiffen. I expect his hand to retreat, but it's the opposite. He gives me a smirk and his movements become surer. He brushes against my panties as our drinks are filled. I can't believe that he's doing this here. The waitress flits around us, oblivious to what is happening right underneath her nose. I eagerly reach for my wine as soon as we are alone again. I gulp it down, feeling like I need the Dutch courage to survive this, to gather the confidence to be the person I want to be around Gabriel.

He lets out a chuckle. "You like this?" he asks me.

I do. It's exhilarating. Fun. Daring. All the things that I have never been in my life.

My hand trembles as I place my wine glass down. I let out a whimper and bite into my lip as his fingers brush over me addictively until my panties are soaked and my knuckles are white on the edge of the table. I nod my head. It's been a very long time – years – since I've been touched like this and his movements have me trembling and red hot within minutes. I never thought I had to capability to do this, but I'm learning that I do. I would do this and more.

"Shhhhh, quiet, sweetheart," he tells me, leaning ever closer. "You don't want anyone to realize what we are doing…" he warns me.

I nod my head obediently and let out a steady shaky breath. I feel my panties pull to the side and I gasp softly. His fingers tease me. They slip inside my wet pussy and then slowly push inside of me. I lean back, my legs falling open.

Oh, God. What am I doing? I must have gone completely insane. I lock eyes with him as I gnaw on my lip and try to remain quiet.

"I think you're going to be perfect for me," he tells me, and I wonder what he means but I haven't got the words to try and form an eloquent sentence while he plays with me, finger fucking me mere meters from where others are sat and eating their dinner. "I'm looking for someone to keep me company," he continues, his voice steady as if he's not completely reducing me to madness with his expert touches. "I

like to play games and I'm looking for a playmate. For someone who likes to have fun just as much as me."

I nod unsteadily, my breath coming in pants as pleasure swirls in my stomach. Right now, I feel like I could be that person. I want this. I want him to do these filthy things to me. I want even more.

"Now, I think that can be you. Something just told me that you were going to be the perfect little slut."

I'm going to come. I can't help it. His words… the way he's talking to me… all of it has me on edge. It's too much. He looks at me like he knows. Like he can see right into my mind.

When I think I can't keep quiet any longer, that it's completely impossible as his fingers rub against me insistently, he shocks me even more.

Gabriel kisses me. His lips are firm against me, but his kiss gentle. It's enough to have me tipping over the edge, my pussy clenching around his fingers as pleasure rushes through me. I haven't ever come so hard. Ever. Not with another person, and not by myself. It's probably the combination of Gabriel's whole demeanor and the situation I've found myself in.

I'm almost glad when his fingers finally slip from me. I'm allowed to catch my breath and it gives me a chance for me to catch up with what's just happened. My heart is soaring in my chest, my legs splayed like a whore and I'm slightly slouched in my seat.

Gabriel chuckles again and he brings his hand to his mouth, sucking at his wet fingers and licking them clean. My mouth drops open. I've never seen someone do something so dirty but something raw and primal inside of me keens at the gesture.

"So, are you interested, sweetheart?"

I hear the click of heels and know that the waitress is approaching. I hurriedly snap my legs closed. I could be caught any moment. The idea that someone is going just walk over and see what a whore I am turns me on even more. I straighten my clothes and then smile politely as soon as I see her. Gabriel and I share a secret look while she serves us our food.

As soon as we are alone again, I ask him, "So, what game do you want to play next?"

A Teacher's Forbidden Desire

A normally sensible teacher lets her hair down when a new student transfers to her class. The age difference should stop her - but actually, it just makes her want it more.

I'm going to hell.

It's the only thing that I can think of as I stare at the young man who has just walked into my English lit class. One minute I'm staring into my triple shot latte and counting down the minutes until I can leave, and the next my eyes are zeroing in on the door. Because the hottest guy I have ever seen has just walked through the door. He's like something out of a naughty magazine – obscenely cute, floppy hair and ripped. I'm pretty sure his arm muscles are bigger than my head. Even under his sensible clothes, it's impossible not to notice that this guy must put in some serious gym time. I've never seen him before. I wonder why he's wandered into my classroom and if he's lost. I can't help it as my eyes are all over him. I'm not sure why but I just get a good feeling as soon as he's looking towards me, looking happy to have found a teacher.

It's a mixed class, but it's mainly girls who tend to take this course. It's about a 70/30 split of girls and boys, and the guys who do take this class are usually either complete dorks or being forced to take it by their parents and have no interest. A lot of the guys are messing around, jumping all over each other, and ready to leave for the day – not thinking about the lesson ahead of them. Whereas this guy seems more reserved. Quiet. He doesn't look like he fits in with this crowd at all. There's just something about him that I can't put my finger on that instantly attracts me to him. He's also taller than his peers, a respectable 6 foot something and he can't be any older than 20 at the very most. It kind of feels like lust at first sight.

Everyone piles in and settles into their usual seats aside from him. He walks confidently up towards my desk and introduces himself.

"Hey, I'm Troy," he greets me and gives me a smile that makes me feel like I'm the teenager in this situation and not the other way round. "I've just transferred onto this course."

"Oh." Now that I hadn't expected. I look him up and down again. I'd obviously judged him too quickly. "Hi," I mutter, my eyes fluttering to my laptop and to my open staff mail then back again. "Troy…?" I can't see anything about a new student in the email but it wouldn't be the first time. It's not exactly Harvard here.

"Jensen. Troy Jensen," he replies instantly. "I was taking an online class before but I wasn't any good at studying by myself. I decided to try here. I'm more of a people person," he tells me with a grin.

I sit up straight as I take in his words. "That's great. Welcome to your 'English Lit through the Ages' unit. Have you got the course material?" I ask. I know nothing about his guy. I don't know what course he's doing, his student ID, nothing. I guess I'll have to wait to speak to the office or the head of the department since it's a 5 pm class on a Friday. They won't be back in now until Monday so it's going to have to wait.

Why do these things always happen on a Friday?

"Ermm… No?" He looks at me unsurely, his expression apologetic.

What a sweetheart.

"I was supposed to get an email about it to let me know which books I needed, but I never received it and then I tried to call the office and they said there would be a call-back," he hurries to explain himself.

"Let me guess, they never called?" I ask him. It's a story I've heard over and over. I've been working here now for 3 years and it's always the same. It's a load of teachers walking around blindly and praying that everything is done well enough that these kids can pass their course.

"How did you know?" he asks; his hair is all floppy and adorable. I feel my heart skip in my chest. It falls into his eyes and I watch transfixed as he brushes it back. His large hands and long fingers brush his bangs back, exposing those arm muscles and I feel like I'm about to have a heart attack.

Jesus, I never knew that I could get so thirsty from looking at a guy's arms.

"Just a guess, happens all the time," I reply, trying to pull my focus from his arms and to this guy's education.

Illegal, I remind myself as well. *Probably half my age…* yet the thought doesn't seem to deter me, and I hate myself a little bit for how creepy I'm probably being right now.

"You can borrow my spares until you can get your own," I offer, I have plenty. People forget their books all the time. There's this kind of assumption that all English teachers are dicks so I try my best not to be.

"That would be great," he says, looking relieved and I wonder if he's nervous for his first class. For a well-built, masculine man, he seems like he doesn't fit the stereotype – he's in an English class for a start.

"If you stay behind, I can get your details and send them as a PDF - save you a couple of hundred bucks."

It's a terrible idea. I don't know why I suggest it. Putting the two of us alone together in my office is the exact opposite of what I should be doing right now. I know that I shouldn't do it because it feels like I'm being totally unprofessional. My thoughts are running away with me and I should probably keep my distance from him to stop things from being awkward – namely me. I'll probably end up embarrassing myself.

"Aww, Miss, thanks," he tells me, looking grateful and he gives me a stunning smile. My stomach twists pleasantly and yet again I remind myself that this is wrong. I don't know why I'm feeling like this. This has never happened before. Normally I'm a very sensible person. But there's just something about him that has me feeling like I have butterflies.

You're gonna get fired for lusting after college boys. Fuck.

"No problem, take a seat and I'll find what you need for today." I'm happy to put a bit of distance between us as I push back in my chair and then stand. I compose myself as I disappear into my office which is literally a small room connected to the classroom because the English department here doesn't give a crap. We're an arts school and most of our funding goes into the art departments. Shakespeare isn't so popular here.

I grab the books that I'm looking for: *Othello* and a copy of our Introduction to English Literature textbook which is the one we're using at the moment. He's chosen a good time to start, it's only been a month or so since the beginning of term – 6 weeks to be exact - so he's only missed one paper. He should probably be able to redo it at the end of the term. I guess he can do it now and get it out of the way so it would mean less marking for me at the end of the year when I'm usually flooded with essays. I take another moment to remind myself to get a grip before I head back out and into the chaos.

It takes a few minutes for the class to settle but I'm used to it. It's always the same on a Friday. I quickly fall into teacher mode, forgetting about Troy and his irresistible cuteness as I start my lesson of the evening. I'm glad that he's chosen to sit towards the back of the class, so I don't have to see him in my direct line of fight.

As usual, it's the same faces that participate in the class, but I am shocked when the new guy raises his hands and confidently talks. I didn't expect him to know anything about Othello, it's not usually on a teenager's read list, but I guess he must have studied it at high school or something. He speaks about the plot in-depth, quoting chapters and paragraphs like it's easy and he gets more than a few stares from his classmates for that.

I feel like my heart is going to skip from my chest at any moment.

This is bad. Very bad...

He's cute and he clearly loves reading... It's not really a combination that I find very often with men my own age. I have had exactly zero success in finding a man who can keep up with my references. But Troy... he even laughs when I make a joke that seems to go over everyone else's heads.

Oh God, he's a total dork hiding in the body of a football quarterback...

The lesson doesn't seem to last long. That in itself is a surprise because this is the one lesson of the week that I pulled a short straw on against the rest of the English department. It's the one lesson that nobody wants to do because of how badly it drags and how little focus everyone seems to have. I know when the clock has ticked around to six pm because people are standing from their seats and packing their bags before I can even finish my sentence. Everyone but Troy. I glance towards the clock and sure enough, it reads that it's time to go home.

Troy stays sitting at his desk and then grins at me as I sarcastically announce, "Class over, guys," to their backs, "feel free to head home!" But they're already gone and have all completely ignored me. "Huh, not sure whether to take it personally," I joke, and then turn to Troy giving him a little smile.

"I doubt it," he replies, "they're all eager to head out tonight. No doubt off to Kelly Parker's party – whoever that is." He looks like he's not bothered though. I wonder why he's not rushing off with them. He's attractive, cool… there's no doubt that he's been invited to this party whether or not he knows Kelly personally.

"Long blond hair… wears a bright pink bag," I describe, trying to prompt his memory. There's a lot of girls at this school and it's his first week after all. I'm sure to leave out that Kelly is probably one of the prettiest girls in the class and seems to attract pretty much anything that walks. For some reason, I don't want him thinking about her that way.

I must be turning into a bitter woman. Jealous of my students... It's a new low.

"Oh, I haven't noticed her. Maybe we haven't met," he says with a shrug.

I raise an eyebrow at him. "You were sitting next to her." It makes me smile. For someone so smart, he seems kind of oblivious.

He looks at me cluelessly and then shrugs. "I was concentrating on more important things." He looks at me with a cheeky grin as he says it.

My heart stops and I have to scold myself again. I shouldn't be acting like this – feeling loopy since he clearly enjoyed my lesson. You'd think I was desperate.

I am desperate... My brain supplies me unhelpfully and I feel betrayed by my own thoughts, though I know I'm only being honest with myself. It's been a long time since I hooked up with anyone. Months. And the last time I slept with someone he was obnoxious afterward and I couldn't wait to get out of his apartment. It soured the whole experience. Plus, the sex hadn't been that good (at all). It was very one-sided. I had blown the guy and jerked him off and then when he fucked me, he hadn't bothered to warm me up. He just kind of just put it in and then... it had been over very quickly… Maybe because there just wasn't much chemistry between us… I hadn't attempted to try since.

Troy stands, his bag hanging from his shoulder. He walks to the front and then hands me the borrowed textbooks. "Thanks for letting me borrow these," he tells me with a grin and then he stands waiting.

"Oh, yes," I remember and then lead him into my office to collect the books that Troy will need. The office door bangs shut behind us.

"So, you like Shakespeare?" I ask him because he had seemed pretty entranced in the lesson. "You seem pretty into *Othello*?" That's an understatement, it was clear that he had a really good knowledge of the book. It was something that I wasn't used to seeing unless people were super into Shakespeare. But I could be wrong, he could have recently done a paper on it or something.

"Yes, actually, I loved theatre in Highschool. I started as one of those annoying drama kids, but I just realized that I loved reading Shakespeare's scripts instead of acting them out. I just love how we analyze everything so intricately, but really, it all comes down to violence and dick jokes."

I laugh. I hadn't expected him to say that. It's true, of course. "Ah, a true connoisseur," I joke with a grin because he clearly understands a lot more than most people.

"Something like that," he replies.

It's hard to picture him as a theatre kid though, but I guess looks can be deceiving and I shouldn't judge a book by its cover as they say.

"You did AP English?" I ask, just trying to get a feel for his knowledge, because from his performance in class today, I know that he can get a really good grade for this unit. Discussing literature seems to come naturally to him.

"Yes, I loved it."

"You went to Greenwell?" It's a private school which is famous in this district.

"No, actually, I went to Willow."

The knowledge surprises me. I'd assumed he had gone to Greenwell because he seemed to know his stuff. They had an excellent English department and had a very good student GPA.

"Oh, sorry. I went to Willow as well actually."

Though there is probably over ten years difference in our graduation dates…

"I enjoyed it. I wanted to go. My mom's actually an English teacher too. She works at Greenwell."

"Ah, makes sense, that's why you didn't want to go and went to Willow instead."

"Yeah, that last thing I wanted was to have mom be my teacher." I cringe. I have to agree with him. It sounds like a nightmare. Kids are brutal these days, he would have probably been bullied, no matter how attractive he was. "But as you can tell, she's kind of rubbed off on me anyway."

"I can tell," I tell him as I shoot him a smile and sit at my desk. I gesture for him to sit down next to me as well in the spare chair that I keep for my students. I open my laptop and boot it up so I can find the files that he needs. It'll take me a few minutes to find them, I should be more organized but hey, nobody is perfect. I'm one of those people that I name things terribly and then I can never find anything.

"So, we have a reading list," I explain. "I have a few of the files here so you can get started if you like, but you'll have plenty of time to read each book closer to the time. I normally give a couple of weeks' notice." I don't like to drop things on people's heads.

"That's great. I'll probably have most of them at home. I've been reading a lot of Jane Austin lately, but I enjoy most of the classics."

"Oh, fantastic. We'll be doing *Emma* at the end of the year and *Pride and Prejudice* in the new year." I give him a smile.

"I have them both, thanks," he tells me, but I'm not surprised. He'll probably have most of these books if his mom's a teacher. It will just be the specific books written for the college that he'll need, but they're still overpriced and cost a fortune when they're all bought together.

"Great." I locate the files for him and then attach them all to an email. I slide the laptop across the table to him so he can type in his address.

"You look young for an English teacher," he comments as he is typing. It catches me by surprise. I don't feel young. I'm racing towards my middle-aged years without much to show for it. I'm still saving up for my first house, I still drive a crappy car, and I spend most of my days at the college. I don't really have much of a life outside of school.

"Not really," I reply. I know that he's trying to be polite.

He scoffs. "What, you think just cause I'm younger than you that I can't see how good you look for your age?"

My face flames and I turn to him in shock. I can't believe the words that have just come out of his mouth. I've never had a student speak to me like that. I'm not really sure what to say in response. I end up opening and closing my mouth a few times.

Great, now I probably look like a fish. I snap my mouth closed and then look away; my words lost for the moment.

I know that all I've done is think about my desire for this guy, but I'm not stupid enough to think that he will ever reciprocate any of my feelings. It's just the silly thoughts of an English teacher who desperately needs to get laid.

"Funny," I reply because he's got to be joking. I don't know how else to take his words, aside from assuming that I've been too obvious with my feelings and that he is teasing me.

"Wasn't a joke," he replies, sharp as a pin, and then turns and grins at me, that soft floppy hair falling into his eyes again. I feel my knees grow week and I'm glad that I'm sitting down.

"Don't be silly," I tell him, "I must be ten years older than you. I'm sure you have a pretty girl who would be interested in someone like you. Plenty, probably," I mutter.

"Well, Miss, I was actually hoping that would be you."

He's certainly smooth, that's for sure.

"Only if I want to lose my job," I reply and I find enough courage to stare at him. *I'm the elder here*, I remind myself.

"I wouldn't say that," he replies, hitting enter on the keyboard, sending the email to himself. "It's not like anyone will know." He leans his elbow on the table, his chin in his hand as he grins at me, taking

273

in my appearance. He isn't sly about it. He looks at my face, and my curly dark hair which is loose around my face, and then his gaze drops down to my dress. I'm dressed in a pretty black dress. I don't ever dress up for work, but I do take pride in my appearance. I like to think that I look okay.

"What?" I ask him. Troy is odd. He seems different to guys his age and I'm curious as to why he would be interested in someone like me. I'm older. I pale in comparison to the girls in his class. I'm barely wearing any makeup. I'm just me. I'm not anything special.

"Just looking," he tells me softly.

"Oh, well don't," I reply, trying to be firm with him. "I'm your teacher," I tell him explanation because that should be enough for us to stop whatever it is that's happening right now.

He shrugs. "So?" he says as if it's really that simple. Over the last 10 years, I've learned that nothing is simple.

I give him a firm look again. I'm not sure what he's trying to do here. "I… What does that even mean? What are you trying to accomplish here?"

My hands are sweating and I try to discretely wipe them on my dress. I feel on edge. I'm flattered yet confused. My emotions are always all over the place. I never get like this and I'm not sure why Troy is having such an effect on me.

"I don't know, as much as you'll let me get away with," he replies cheekily and he gives me a grin.

There is a moment between us where I'm not really sure if he's being serious. I feel in disbelief. "Nothing, obviously," I reply quickly, and I hope that he doesn't see through my lies.

"I don't really believe that," he says and he gives me a look as if he knows otherwise.

I blush. I can't help it. What can I possibly reply to that? "I… We shouldn't. You don't want me, you're just being ridiculous." I don't even believe the words myself, so I don't know how I expect him to. It doesn't sound like I mean it at all.

"I think I'm old enough to make my own choices," he refutes, and he looks at me like he knows how weak I am, that I don't mean anything that is coming out of my mouth right now.

"I'm thirty-two," I admit to him, "I'm too old for you."

I should probably just stand and tell him to leave, but a naughty part of me wants to stay. I want to see how this will play out. If he's actually going to make a move or if he is simply teasing me.

He shrugs in response, not phased at my admission. I expected him to recoil. To leave. But if anything, he's looking at me like he knows that he's winning this battle. I glance down at his lips. They look soft and I wonder what his lips will taste like.

"I don't know why you're fighting this. I saw the way you were looking at me. You want me. I know you do."

I'm nervous.

This isn't happening... I shouldn't want this.

Except... I really do. Even the idea of kissing Troy is making me hot inside. I feel desperate and out of control. No man has ever been so direct, or shown such an interest in me. I want this. For the first time in my life, I'm tempted to be selfish.

Troy is young and hot. He's so attractive that I can barely function at the idea that he wants me.

"But..." I try to fight it, but I lose my words.

His grin has my heart fluttering and I know that I'm lost. He's leaning forwards and then his strong hand is reaching for me and then he's touching me - cupping my face. There's no stopping this - I don't want to.

Oh, fuck. He's kissing me...

Suddenly he's in my space, his lips soft and insistent as they caress against my own. I slip into bliss. I can't stop this from happening. I don't want to. Oh, God. I want more, so much more. Troy's simple kiss seems to unravel my sanity and self-control. I can't help it. I'm shuffling closer in my seat and returning his kiss insistently.

I can feel him smirking against me. It does nothing but turn me on more. His tongue touches my lip and I open my mouth eagerly, letting him kiss me deeply. I feel something shift between us and his hands are on my waist, encouraging me closer. Then I find myself being pulled into his lap.

I can feel his cock press against me and I gasp. I can hardly believe it. I've hardly touched him – how is he so hard already?

He isn't shy. He's kissing me firmer, his hands gripping at my hips and then holding me in place. He is fully taking advantage of the situation and I can't blame him because honestly, I am doing the same. His hands slip down to cup my ass, pulling me closer to him so that I'm straddling him, my chests flush together and I moan as I feel myself unintentionally grind against his cock. It feels hot and large against me and instantly I want it inside me.

A thrill of pleasure runs through me. I can't help it as I do it again, my hips out of control as I start to grind against him. I'm in heaven. It's been so long since I've felt so good. My whole body is trembling and hot, burning from the inside.

"Oh, fuck. Troy," I moan, my words hot against his lips.

He lets out a chuckle and then his lips are tearing away from me and are at my neck. I submit to him, baring my neck so he can continue his assault of it. Arousal is curling in my stomach and my pussy starts to ache, throbbing and growing wet. I press insistently against his cock, rubbing my sensitive clit against him until I'm panting and my hands are gripping at him roughly, my nails digging into his ripped arms.

My head falls back and I push my chest out towards him but my dress is in the way. I grow frustrated. I think for a second, trying to find a way around this problem. I try to think logically, but Troy beats me to it. He grabs my dress and rips it upwards, pulling it over my head and leaving me sitting on him in my bra and panties.

I should feel self-conscious, but instead, I moan at being exposed like this. I arch my back, pushing my tits into his face and he doesn't hesitate. He pulls at my bra, my breasts bouncing out, my nipples swollen and begging to be sucked.

Troy cups my tits, his mouth sucking my nipple into his eager mouth and I cry out, my hips frantic as I rub my pussy against him.

Oh, fuck. I'm going to fuck him in my office.

The realization should make me stop. But I want it more. I try to keep my mouth shut, to stop the words that want to pour from me but I don't know how to. I'm out of control.

"I want your cock," I gasp, "please, I want it in me."

He chuckles again and his lips are at my neck again. "Suck it and I'll think about fucking you."

The order has me nodding eagerly. At this point, I'll do anything for this young, hot man. I climb off him and sink to the floor, sitting underneath my own desk. At any other time, I might find this amusing but right now I can't do anything but basically gag for his cock.

My hands are on his pants, and I pull his cock from his boxers, my mouth watering at the sight of it. It's long and thick and cut and just perfect. My hand grips at it and I don't hesitate to suck the fat head into my mouth. I instantly moan. It turns me on how much it makes me feel like a little slut to be doing this with one of my students. I could get caught. I could get fired… but I don't care. All I care about is sucking his cock deep into my mouth and choking on it. I've never sucked on something so large in my life so I treasure this, memorizing the feel of it filling my mouth and stretching my throat. I struggle to relax as it presses deep into my throat. But it's all worth it as I look up through watering eyes.

Troy is looking down at me in awe. His hands shaking and I can tell that although he's probably had plenty of girls blow him. No-one has ever been so eager or rough with him. I swallow him down eagerly, over and over as I force more and more into my mouth and down my throat.

I grab his hand and place it on my head, inviting him to fuck my mouth. I moan like a whore as he grabs me and his hips thrust up. I can't move. His cock shoved down my throat and I'm powerless. He grows in confidence and soon he's moaning. The sound goes straight to my pussy. Troy is confident and greedy. He fucks my throat until I'm spluttering and sore.

Suddenly, his grip is painful and his hips snap forward brutally. My eyes are wide and my mouth suddenly floods with his hot creamy come and I am forced to swallow it. I splutter and moan, and as he finally pulls out and I have some relief, I lick my lips.

He leans down and kisses me and I'm shocked, frozen. I've never had a man kiss me after he's come in my mouth. It's filthy and it turns me on. I try not to feel disappointed that this is already over.

"On the table," he snaps at me, pulling me up from under the desk and I'm confused for a moment.

"Whaaa…?"

I find myself pulled to my feet and my panties ripped down. Troy pushes me back so I'm sitting on my desk and then suddenly my legs are pushed apart and my pussy is on display. My face flames. No-one has ever done this. No-one has ever looked at me this way. I must look like a whore. My hair is a mess, my tits out my bra and my nipples swollen and pointing to the ceiling, and my legs wide, my pussy exposed for Troy to look at.

I wonder what he's going to do to me. He's already come so I'm not sure what he has planned for me.

"Relax," he says. He stays sitting in my chair but pulls it forward so he's sitting between my legs, face to face with my pussy. He leans forward and then kisses the side of my left knee. I instantly melt as tingles tickle through me.

Is he…?

I don't have time to wonder because suddenly his mouth is hot on me. His tongue is licking gently at my clit. I flop back on the table, my eyes falling closed because I physically can't do anything but lie there and let Troy do as he pleases. His touches are inexperienced but eager, he is very enthusiastic as he licks, kisses, and sucks my pussy.

I ache and tremble at his touches. Pleasure curls in my stomach and I can't keep quiet as his tongue licks inside me, fucking me sloppily and making me powerless. My legs twitch. I kick my shoes off and rest my heels on the edge of the desk so I can thrust up into his mouth. I grind my greedy cunt against him, my hands slipping into his hair as I groan and writhe on the table.

"I'm gonna come," I gasp out because I can't stop it. My pussy is red hot and the way he's licking rhythmically at my clit has me feeling super sensitive. No one has ever paid this kind of attention to my pussy before and in a role reversal, I find myself feeling inexperienced instead of the other way around.

"Troy, please," I beg, "please fuck me."

But he ignores my request, instead, licking harder and more persistently, lapping at my cunt as if he can't get enough.

My eyes roll into the back of my head. I can't stop it. The pleasure inside me builds and builds until suddenly it's all falling down. My pussy throbs and the pleasure that explodes from me is like nothing I've ever felt. I scream out. "Fuck, oh, God. Troy, I… I… Please, it… It feels so good. Please give me your cock."

I want it in me. I'm desperate for him to fuck me. I need his cock like I need air. I want his big fat dick inside me bare, fucking me raw and wrecking my tight pussy. I can't stop thinking about it. About him pushing inside me, of him using me and his hot young body taking advantage of me. I want his come inside me and filling me up…

I realize I'm sobbing, sucking in the air desperately.

He hasn't stopped, instead, he spreads my pussy with his fingers, exposing my swollen clit and hole and I try to spread my legs further. I want him to look at me like this.

"I don't think you can make demands," he tells me, and then leans forward again, his tongue licking into my hole and then slowly dragging upwards to my clit. He circles it and I feel like I might go insane. I feel so on edge. Like I'm just about to come again.

"I think it's only fair that you come again. I'm being so nice to you."

He is. He's being so so nice. I can't do anything but agree with him. I nod. "Yes, it feels so good. Please don't stop." I'm greedy. I want to come again. So like a whore I rub my cunt against his face, getting off on the idea that Troy is my student. That I have a hot twenty-something worshipping my pussy.

I can't help it. I'm throbbing again and I feel my pussy gush. I look down and watch as he licks me through my orgasm, lapping at my juicy cunt and it makes me come harder, another wave of pleasure rushing through me.

"Yes, oh, fuck, yes. Eat my pussy," I beg and my hands come to my breasts playing with my own nipples, pulling and pinching them. Troy licks up my come, looking like the cat that got the cream.

Finally, I'm allowed to catch my breath, but I'm foolish if I think that's the end of it. Troy is gripping at my thighs and standing up. His cock in his hand as he lines up and then pushes it inside me.

He places his hand over my mouth firmly as I cry out, and he manages to muffle my scream as he begins to fuck me. His cock is opening me up, brutally stretching my tight pussy as he snaps his hips forward, filling me up and making me quiver and cry from the stimulation. I have never been fucked like this. He's fucking me hard and selfishly, but at the same time, he's hitting me in all the right places. I'm already so sensitive that it only takes minutes before I'm falling over the edge and I'm throbbing, squeezing his cock, and come flooding from me, spraying all over his cock and thighs.

I'm shaking. I'm held down on that table, his strong hand over my face and his cock inside me for what feels like forever. He forces me to come over and over. I'm over-sensitive and sore. My pussy feels raw and I'm sure that I can't possibly come again but somehow, he forces it out of me. My swollen pussy squirts, soaking him and it seems to only spur him on more.

"Smmmhhhh," I try to call, but my words are muffled, and tears fall from my eyes as I stare at him helplessly.

"Shhhh," he hushes me, "you don't want any of the cleaners hearing you…" He's right. I have no idea what time it is, but the cleaners will be here and tidying up and I try to nod obediently, trying my best to remains quiet.

As if I cue, there is a knock on my office door. The two of us freeze. The door isn't locked. Whoever it is could just walk inside right now and see me spread naked on the table, Troy fucking me. I expect him to stop, to pull out and let me up, but he doesn't, he simply frees my mouth.

"One minute, I'm in a meeting, can you come back later?" I call out, my voice shaking and my throat sore from moaning so much.

"Do you need me to clean your office?" It's a male voice from behind the door and I'm very aware that Troy is buried deep inside me still. A thrill runs through me and I struggle to hold it together.

"No, thank you, I've got it. You can skip my classroom."

"Sure, no problem!"

Troy takes this as an invitation to circle his hips and now it's me that covers my mouth with my hands in an attempt to stifle any sounds that try to slip out. We both listen to the sound of retreating footsteps until finally, after a minute or so, we can only hear silence. I remove my hands and then glare at Troy.

"You fucker," I tell him, but I'm grinning. I've never done something so exciting in my entire life.

"Don't act like you don't love it, *Miss*," he tells me, emphasizing my title. He then grinds his hips against me. "I never thought that you'd be such a little slut, but here you are. Letting me fuck you with no condom on, while the janitor works in the hallway… God, you must really fucking love my cock."

He starts to fuck me again and I groan in relief. I never knew how much I needed him to move again. "Yes," I cry out, and I try to fuck back hard against him, to meet him halfway, "yes, I do. I love your cock so much, Troy. It's so big and feels so good inside my pussy. I need it. I need your come inside me. I love being a slut for you. Only you, Troy." I don't know where the words come from. But they seem to pour from me. From a place inside me that I didn't know existed. I don't care how desperate I sound, because every word is true. I don't know how I will survive now I have experienced this. I want Troy to use me like this every day. My mind runs away with me, the idea of us sneaking around, of him fucking me like this every day, of him just grabbing me and doing whatever he wants to me… I want it.

"Good girl. I know you can't resist it. I'm gonna fuck you like that whenever I want," he tells me and I nod. I can't do anything but agree with him as he pounds into my pussy. The table shakes and my tits are bouncing from the force. He reaches forward and squeezes one. I watch him through lidded eyes and the whole situation seems surreal. How is it that I am completely naked, and he is still fully dressed?

My eyes close again. I'm tired and overwhelmed. I feel almost feverish. The sound of my pussy squelching from being so wet has me cringing embarrassed, but the feeling turns me on even more.

Since when have I been so dirty? Why does something so naughty make me so hot? I really don't have the answer.

Troy pulls out of me unexpectedly and I feel like I might cry. "No, no, no!" I tell him, looking up at him desperately. "Troy, please, I want your come!" I try to convince him. "Please, my pussy needs it. You can do whatever you want to me, I'll do whatever you like, just please fill me with your come. I wanna feel it."

I'm disgusting. A whore. What kind of teacher speaks to a student like this? But I can't help it. I'm not in control.

"Turn over," he demands.

I scramble, bending over the desk. I grab my ass cheeks and in a dirty display of desperation, I spread them with my hands and show him my wet pussy. "Please, put it back in."

I cry when I feel him push back inside me. "Thank you. Thank you," I sob, tears spilling over my eyes and onto the table.

I feel him touch my asshole, his fingers teasing it and that's it, I'm tumbling over the edge again, my cunt squeezing and throbbing around his long hard cock. I cry out into the table, sobbing because everything feels so perfect. And then I feel Troy tense and I'm in heaven. His cock is throbbing inside me and I feel his come start to fill me, flooding me full. It's hot and wet and there's so much of it. I push back against the feeling, crying from the feeling.

"Troy, Troy, yesss, fuck…"

Finally, after a few minutes, we separate.

My lungs are working hard, desperately trying to drag in some air. It's then that I start laughing.

Troy laughs too. "What?" he asks, sounding amused. "What's so funny?" But he still laughs along with me, the sound infectious between us as we separate.

"I just let you fuck me," I say, dumbly stating the obvious.

"Yeah," he agrees, and he's out of breath too. "Yeah, you did. And I loved it." He licks his lips and then tidies himself up, tucking his dick back into his clothes.

I realize I'm still leaning against the desk, only wearing my bra which has been dragged down to my hips. I grab it and put my tits away, straightening the straps.

"Want to do it again?" he asks, and that cocky look is back again.

I blush. The butterflies are still here.

"Yeah, sure. I mean, I can give you my number," I tell him, and I reach for my dress.

"I meant tonight."

I look up from my dress.

Is he crazy? How can he even be thinking of fucking me right now? He's just made me come so many times that I…

I have no idea what time it is. I have no idea how long he's fucked me for, or how many times he has made me come.

"I mean, yeah, no time like the present. You live far from here?"

I'm wide-eyed at the suggestion but I find myself nodding. "I guess we can head back to my place…"

Troy grins, and he looks happy that he has gotten his own way. I suspect that this won't be the last time. Something tells me that this college year is gonna be a lot of fun.

All Eyes On Me

"Busy ER nurse Chloe makes no time for herself. Her friends promise to show her a good time by taking her to a BDSM club to let her hair down. Nothing could have prepared her for a party like this."

As I walk toward the building, I can't believe my eyes. This is not what I was expecting. At all. But I guess I did say that I wanted something a little different and wow, my friends sure know how to deliver. The nondescript building is lined with security at the entrance door and it's more than a little intimidating. But Anne promises me it's fine.

It's a Saturday night and it's the first weekend that I've had off in God-knows how long. I work as a nurse in my local ER department so my days off are few and far between. Tonight, I'm here with one of the younger colleagues, Tiffany, my best friend Anne, and her girlfriend Sarah. None of us have been out together before but we all have something in common: we are all attracted to women.

Well. The others are a lot more open about it than me. If it wasn't for them, I would never have the confidence to come somewhere like this. I am 24, single and I've never had a proper relationship in my entire life. I've not really had time. Studying to be a nurse is hard. Actually being a nurse is even harder. I need to find the right work/life balance, otherwise I'm going to end up a spinster with 10 cats.

Now, I'm not saying that I think I'm a lesbian because I don't. But I also don't think I'm straight either. I've messed around with a few guys here and there. But really nothing has ever been mind-blowing. I think my problem is that I live in my head too much and I expect something like fireworks to go off when on with someone. But that's never happened. And I'm not sure it really will. That's just for romance books and in the movies, right?

So here we are, lining up to get into what Anne promises me is one of the best-kept secrets in New York.

"I told you, you just need to relax," Anne tells me. But that's easier said than done when I'm surrounded by people that I know want the exact same thing as me. There are no pretenses. There is no acting. There are no false expectations. We are all here for the same thing: we want to get laid.

"I know, I know. But you know me, I'm an anxious mess."

"I promise there is nothing to be anxious about, I've never had a bad experience here."

'Here' is at a sex club – somewhere that I never thought I would take a step into. Yet here I am, dressed up to the nines and ready to make a connection with someone – anyone – so I can have a good time and let my hair down.

I look around nervously as I'm let in and the guy at the door stares at my ID suspiciously before scanning it and then asking to see inside my bag. I look toward Anne and pull a face that I hope says "what the hell is happening right now" but she just gives me an encouraging smile. I do as I'm told, let the guys check me over with a metal detector and then wait for my friends on the other side. I pay the fee which is so expensive that I physically cringe as I enter my card's PIN.

It feels like forever before my friends join me and then we are going into the club and walking down the stairs. My legs tremble in my heels. It's been a long time since I've walked down a flight of stairs in 5-inch heels.

The walls around us are painted black and there is explicit artwork painted onto the walls, and the different LGBT flags hang from the high ceilings. I never knew that there were so many.

"Yeah, sure," Tiff tells me, "gay, bisexual, pansexual, allosexual…" she lists them off and points at each one pretty flags.

Huh, you learn something new every day.

We arrive at the bottom of the steps and there is a woman stood outside. "Hey, guys. You want to play in the masquerade? Tonight, we are holding our very first masquerade! Everyone who plays get a free shot and all their drinks can be upgraded to doubles for free."

I look down at the table to the side of her and she has hundreds of different masks on display and other items of clothing and accessories to play dress up.

"Ohhhh, this is awesome!" Sarah reaches for a mask and pulls it on, admiring herself in the freestanding mirror that is there. It's bright and beautiful and decorated with pink, blue and yellow feathers and glitter. She also reaches for some glow-in-the-dark bracelets and then hands the cash over.

It is tempting. Plus, there is something appealing about hiding my identity a little, even though no one here will know who I am. We are far, far away from the hospital where I work. I decide to play too, and I find a pretty black glittery mask to match my tight black dress. I also pick up some glowing accessories for my hair. When I look in the mirror, I look like I fit in. I belong. I smile at my reflection and then hand over the cash. I'm already feeling much more relaxed than I was 10 minutes ago.

"Let me stamp you guys so you can get back in, because you're in the masquerade it's free," the girl tells us with a grin and reaches for our hands. I hold out my hand and I'm stamped with a large heart. It's good to know, a lot of clubs around here have a rule that once you're outside, you have to pay to get back in and I do not want to pay that eyewatering fee again.

All of us decide to dress up and we look fantastic.

"Do you want me to take a photo of you guys? You look super cute!"

It'll be nice to have something to remember the first night I've ever been to a BDSM club... I have a feeling I'm going to be drinking a lot, so having the reminder would be cool just in case my memories are misty.

"Ohhh, yes please!" Sarah replies, grabbing us all together. We stand in front of the artwork on the wall, underneath the name of the club. The girl then snaps a picture for us all. I have to admit, we look awesome.

"Have a nice night, guys!" she tells us before she greets the next group of people that begin to walk down the stairs. We push through the heavy double door and instantly, the room is darker than what I expected.

The light is dim, but we are surrounded by glow-in-the-dark lights and what I assume are false floating candles that are hovering from the ceiling. It's a large room, and everything is decorated in dark colors, making it harder to see. The music is a deep and dirty base and immediately I feel it in my bones and creeping into my soul. I look around and feel good, comforted at the surroundings. I kind of expected strippers or something but there isn't anything tacky or in your face like that.

I feel a slender hand slot into my own and I recognize it as Anne's. She gives me a smile and then leads me towards the bar which is lit up at the back of the room.

"Come on, let's get our free shots!"

I nod at her eagerly and follow, taking in everything around me. We walk past an archway and I glance through it. I almost fall over when I catch a glimpse of what is going on inside. I look back towards Anne and she bursts into laughter at the expression on my face.

She leans close to me, and then she yells, "We will get you a few drinks before we go over there!"

It's like nothing I've ever seen before. I have to admit, I don't even know what I've just seen. A lot of leather. A half-naked woman wearing only a thong and a pair of thigh-high leather boots and carrying a whip. A guy on his knees and wrapped in ropes...

I need a drink...

We arrive at the bar and the staff are all dressed up scantily and they greet us with friendly smiles, already grabbing shot glasses and lining them up on the bar as soon as they see us.

"Thank you!" I say, and with a big smile, I grab one and down it. I cough. It's been a few months since I have drunk anything, but I know that tonight I am going to do whatever I want. I'm not going to overthink anything. If it's fun, then it's going to happen. With that in mind, I order another shot and an espresso martini because yay for coffee and alcohol. I down the shot and then hold my cocktail. When I take a sip, it's strong but delicious and I know it's probably going to be one of many.

We make our way over to a corner of the room where there is a large booth with a black marble table in the center. We settle there for now and I shrug my black jacket off but I keep my clutch bag on with the silver strap across my shoulders so I can't lose it.

"So… what actually goes on here?" I ask everyone, speaking loudly to the girls so my voice carries over the music.

Sarah laughs. "What *doesn't* happen here?" she says and the other girls laugh. "A bit of everything, really. You can have a bit of tame fun, or you can do something a bit more exciting."

You look innocently between your friends. "More exciting? What like… spanking?" It's the first thing that comes into your head.

"Yeah, sure! There's a lot of really experienced staff here so they make sure that everyone is playing safe. You know… just in case."

The implications make me take another drink from my martini. I'm already starting to feel pleasantly buzzed from the alcohol and I find myself swaying to the music. It's hypnotic. By the time I'm halfway through my drink I'm already feeling the hum of alcohol under my skin and I'm smiling, enjoying myself.

I turn to Tiff who's sat to the left of me. I haven't known her very long, I met her when I was at college and we both did our nursing residents' place at the same hospital, so we've become close over the past few years. "So, do you ever go in that room?" I ask her, a little nosily, but I'm curious.

She nods. "I've been a couple of times. I've even hooked up with a few people here."

The idea of hooking up with someone here is still a little embarrassing, but it's because I'm not really confident about all of this. But I know my friends wouldn't bring me here if they didn't think I would enjoy it.

"You have?" I ask her. I'm not sure why I'm surprised. I guess it's because at work she is so professional. It's hard to think of her that way. But the thought it a pleasant one. I'd be crazy if I wasn't attracted to her.

Tiff grins at me, a little flirty. "So, do you think that you want to do try something like that?" she asks me. "We could have some fun if you like. A secret."

My mouth drops open at the suggestion. *Is she really asking to hook up with me?* I blush, surprised. "You'd… do that with me?" I ask her, a little shy but the alcohol gives me some courage.

I'm not stupid, Tiff is stunning. She's beautiful and funny and hardworking. She looks so pretty tonight. Of course, I'm used to seeing her in nurse uniform, but tonight she is swearing a pink shimmery dress, her hair curled into spirals and her face made up prettily. Her lips are pale matte pink, and they look plump and kissable.

"Oh, haha, you flatterer, you," I tell her with a smile. I take another sip of my drink but I realize that it's empty. My head is becoming a little fuzzy and my body feels lighter. I place my glass back down and then turn to her. "A secret?" I ask, repeating her words as I process them.

She nods and leans a little closer to me and she's in my space. I can smell her perfume and there is something attractive about a girl being so close to me. It's intoxicating. I'm excited at the prospect of

her kissing me. She's sitting so close. "Yes, of course," she promises, and then she presses a closed-mouth kiss against my lips.

I inhale softly as I feel my friends' lips on my own. It makes me feel a little dizzy and it's exhilarating. It feels good. So, I lean back in and I kiss her back, my lips moving softly against hers.

"Woohooooo!" I jump at the sound which is followed by a wolf whistle. We break away as Anne and Sarah catcall us and instantly, we are pulling away and then dissolving into giggles.

I can't believe I just kissed Tiff.

We exchange a look, the two of us so close that I can still feel her breath, but instead of feeling awkward, it feels amazing.

"Oh, shush you two!" I tell them.

Tiff stands. "Dance with me?" she asks and I nod.

I stand, straighten my dress and then follow her to the dance floor.

We take each other's hands and then slip close to each other, all smiles as we get comfortable in each other's space. I end up close to her, arms around her neck and her hands on my hips as we grind together to the deep and dirty base. I look around me. To the mix of the crowd and we're surrounded by people – some alone, and others paired off. My eyes focus on a girl who is sandwiched between another girl and a guy. Both of them are kissing and caressing her, their hands all over her. Arousal twists in my stomach. I want that. I want someone touching me. I want their hands on my breasts, their lips on my neck. Something runs through me and I follow my instincts.

I look at Tiff and then she kisses me. This time her tongue licks against my bottom lip and I open my mouth to her, letting her kiss me deeply. I moan into her mouth and I feel her moan back. I like it. I like that I can hear that I'm turning her on. I want more. I bite her lip playfully and wonder where this might go, but for now I am enjoying myself, so I continue. To two of us move together, kissing for a long time, our bodies swaying to the music and stuck together.

I feel a tap on my shoulder and I break apart from Tiff. I grin. It's Anne and Sarah and they hand us both another drink, urging us to drink up. We move into a circle, dancing together wildly, smiles on our faces.

"I love it here, it's a super nice atmosphere for… you know…"

"A sex club," Sarah finishes for me and we all laugh.

"Well, yeah."

"You haven't seen anything yet," Anne tells me and then wiggles her eyebrows at me.

I'm excited and my cheeks feel flushed from the alcohol. I really want to know what secrets are hiding in this club. We dance a little longer until Anne and Sarah suggest that I go with them to the

other rooms. I nod eagerly even though I'm not sure what to expect. We all hold hands as we walk through the room and towards the archway I had looked into before.

We step inside and there are lots of people sitting in comfortable chairs. People are kissing, making out all around us – men with other men, and women with other women, and even a group of four people who are all over each other, kissing and touching each other intimately. It makes my curiosity pique.

I glance towards Tiff and I wonder if she still wants to explore with me. My question is answered when we find a space to sit down. Anne and Sarah settled and immediately begin kissing. I'm a little shocked. I've known Anne for a long time, she's been my best friend for years. But I've never seen her kiss someone like this before. I've seen quick pecks here and there, and affectionate cuddles. But this is nothing like that. This is passionate as the two of them grasp each other tightly, their mouths eager on each other. The kiss is deep and steamy and not something that they would share in public. But this isn't 'public', we're in a sex club, and they let their passion for each other be shown to everyone around them.

If I'm honest, it turns me on a little. I want that. I want what they have.

Tiff scoots close to me and she's smiling and she watches my eyes transfixed on Anne and Sarah. "They're hot, aren't they?"

I shouldn't think such thoughts about my best friend, but I can't help it. She is young and attractive and seeing her like this has my temperature soaring. I nod because she's right. She is hot and I let myself take in her appearance. The sight of their hot bodies close. Anne's hand is on Sarah's thigh, pushing her dress up and I can't stop watching.

I softly gasp in surprise. Sarah's hand has cupped Anne's breast and suddenly he grabs the cup of her dress and pulls it down. Anne's breast is exposed to the room and I lick my lips. Anne bares her neck, relaxing back into the soft chair as Sarah begins to kiss down her neck. Anne looks up and she locks eyes with me. I expect her to look away, to stop what she is doing but she doesn't. She grins at me and pulls at her dress, showing me both of her tits.

Instantly, Sarah is on her, sucking one of Anne's nipples and kissing over her perky breasts. Anne bites into her bottom lip and her eyes slip closed.

I gulp and I look towards Tiff, not able to stop the look of shock on my face. I end up grinning and then Tiff reaches for me, in my space and her lips are on mine. It's addictive. She tastes of her sweet cocktail and I moan, wanting more. I find my confidence and I kick my heels off and climb into Tiff's lap.

She grins at me as our mouths break apart. "Naughty," she comments, and it encourages me. I settle there and then cup her face, making out with her again. We both get lost in the feel of each other until I feel someone sit down to the next of us. I feel like I'm waking from a dream as I turn to whoever it is. It's a young man, probably my age.

"Victor!" Tiff exclaims and she's excited as she sees him. "I didn't know you were going to be here tonight."

"Well, I saw your selfies and I thought I'd come to say hello." I wonder what he means but then I remember we took photos for our Instagram. He must follow Tiff.

"Chloe, this is Victor. A very good friend of mine. Victor, this is Chloe."

Victor grins at me and his eyes drag over my body. I feel hot. Caught in my position from where I'm sitting in Tiff's lap. I hesitate, not sure if I should move. I'm not used to showing affection like this in public. Even something so simple feels forbidden.

"Oh, don't mind me," he tells me, "you stay nice and comfy and I'll enjoy the view."

A burst of laughter erupts from me. He's so direct in the way he talks.

"He's a sweet talker," she tells me.

"No, because I normally follow through with what I'm saying. I only speak the truth," he replies cockily with a grin. "Sweet talkers tend to be full of false promises."

"See what I mean?" she replies with an affectionate roll of her eyes.

"You love it," he says before he stands and then leans over and grips her face, placing a kiss to her lips right in front of my face. I lick my lips. Nobody has ever kissed so closely to me before and I can see everything. My stomach shifts in arousal.

He turns and looks at me, a grin on his face. I look at him, my heart pounding.

Is he going to kiss me?

I glance down at his lips and then I find my confidence. Instead of waiting for him I lean up and kiss him.

"Nice to meet you," I tell him as we pull apart, "but I'll believe your claims when I see it."

"Ohhhh," he exclaims, his face lighting up in glee, "I like her," he tells Tiff before he straightens up.

"Drinks?" he asks the small group of us, making a gesture of him drinking as since he has stood, we can not hear him as well.

We all nod eagerly. "A cocktail?" I ask him, wondering if that's okay. The club isn't exactly cheap, but he nods, not phased as he collects the other orders and then disappears towards the bar. I watch him go, looking at his ass as he leaves.

"He's so cute," I gush to Tiff and I finally climb from her lap.

"Hey, I didn't say you could leave," she tells me with a pout.

I laugh and then settle back in the seat, but I give her another kiss in apology. We wait for Victor to come back and I focus my attention on Sarah and Anne. They seem lost in each other. I can't stop

looking. I can see that Sarah's hand is underneath Anne's dress and it takes me a minute, but I realize that she is fingering her, mere meters away from me. Anne's relaxed back and moaning softly as Sarah ravishes her neck and continues to play with her tits. They are oblivious to everything happening around them. I watch them until Victor returns and I snap out of my trance.

"Thank you," I tell him as I reach for the offered drink and I eagerly drink it down.

I glance back towards Anne again and Victor follows my gaze. He places his drink back onto the table. He reaches for me and then kisses the side of my face, then the line of my jaw. I move into the caress as he begins to kiss down my neck. I don't realize that my eyes have fallen shut until I feel Tiff's mouth on me too.

Fuck, it's so much all at once. It's like nothing that I have ever experienced and it's easy to lose track of who is touching me where. But it doesn't matter. I don't care, I just know that I want more of this. I want Tiff and Victor to continue their touches and to see where this goes. The alcohol lowers my inhibitions, and it makes me desperate.

I shouldn't want this, this is my work friend, and I don't even know this man Victor. If anything, I want this more.

I lay there, the alcohol a pleasant hum under my skin as tingles and pleasure runs through me from the attention. I can feel lips on the back of my neck, and hands gripping my breasts and fondling them. I open my eyes to peer towards Anne. Her legs are open wide and her dress at her waist and she's completely exposed, right next to me. I can see everything. I can see her wet pussy and Sarah's fingers delving inside over and over. The beat of the music is loud but I can just make out the sound of her moaning and crying out from her girlfriends' touches.

"More, please I need more," I beg. I turn towards Tiff and I look at her desperately. She kisses me again and I moan against her lips.

My shoes are uncomfortable, so I kick them off and bend my legs, resting my heels on the edge of the booth seat. My legs splayed open in invitation; my panties are on display for anyone who wants to look.

I can hear Victor chuckling in my ear and his touch is firm as he reaches between my legs and teasingly rubs on the sensitive insides of my legs. I squirm as arousal hits me full force. My pussy throbs and I know for sure that my panties must be sticky and wet.

"Yes," I moan, desperate for Victor to be inside me. "Please…"

I turn the other way, looking towards Tiff, and then her hands are there too. She pulls my panties to the side and I can't help the heat that seems to consume me. I'm sat in this club, my shaven cunt on display for anyone who looks this way.

I look down, and Tiff and Victor's fingers breach me, two slipping inside my aching hole and another two rubbing my swollen clit. They finger me like that until I can't take it anymore, and I feel myself coming, an orgasm ripping through me and making me tremble and shake.

"Fuck, oh, fuck," I cry out and I expect them to stop but they don't. They hold my legs open as they play with my pussy and I realize that there's a phone pointing at me. It's Anne. She's moved and she's on her knees in front of me.

When did she...?

But I have no time to think. Wave after wave of pleasure is taking over me and I can't stop myself as I'm taken too far. I can feel wetness spray from me and I scramble to grip at Victor and Tiff. I'm screaming from the pleasure and I know people must be able to hear me, they must be watching me.

Anna's phone light is on and she's recording me. She reaches for me, pulling my tits from my dress and I'm completely naked, still coming as my friends watch, the evidence of what I've let them do being saved onto Anne's phone.

I'm suddenly the center of attention and I like it.

"Look at you," Anna says, sounding impressed and proud of me. "Wave for the camera," she says and I grin and weakly manage to do as she has requested.

She hands her phone to Sarah and then she's suddenly between my thighs and looking up at me through thick lashes as she leans forwards. I can't look away as she licks a broad stripe up my pussy.

"Oh, god."

My pussy is so sensitive. I have only just come and I feel slightly swollen. I'm not used to being touched again so soon afterward. I'm overstimulated and already so high that I feel seconds away from tipping over the edge again. I can't believe my best friend is doing this to me. It feels amazing and I can't stop watching. She keeps licking at my clit softly until I'm orgasming again and Tiff and Victor have to hold my legs so they don't snap closed as an orgasm hits me.

I look around me, at my friends – Anne, Sarah and Tiff, and then to Victor and they are all smiling at me, clearly turned on at my slutty behavior.

Victor nips at my ear. "Do you need my cock?" he asks me.

I nod. I want it. I want to take advantage of this situation. All the eyes on me only turn me on more. The mysterious masked faces make the experience surreal, like something out of a mythical dream.

Victor stands and undoes his belt and I stare, interested at what is in store for me. It isn't long before his cock is exposed, and Tiff is leaving my side and sinking to her knees in front of him. I follow her, my dress still askew as I copy her. He's fiddling, applying a condom for a few seconds before he eventually lets us have it. His cock is a good size, and my mouth is watering. Tiff grips it in her left hand I can tell that's she familiar with Victor because she starts to jerk him in a way that he seems to like. I lean forward and start to lick and suck at his balls. I want to make him feel as good as he has made me feel. So as soon as I can, I'm licking the length of his dick and Tiff joins me. I find that I enjoy this, having someone else with me to make Victor feel good.

We take it in turns sucking him until he's had enough and he's pulling us up. He gestures for me to sit back down and I relax back and bring my knees up to my chest, holding them open and resting my ass on the edge of the seat.

Victor kisses me and mutters against my lips, "Still want me?"

I nod, looking into his eyes. They are a deep brown and captivate me. I bite into my lip in anticipation as I wait. I can feel him lining up, the blunt head pressing between my slick lips before lining up and then pushing inside me.

Anne is still here, moving to my side with her phone and kissing down my neck and recording everything. It touches something inside me, satisfying a part of me that I don't really understand but I know that I like it.

Victor feels hot inside of me, stretching me and hitting something deep in me that has me crying out and desperate. He fucks me hard and it takes me to new heights of pleasure. The fact that I can feel people's eyes on me only makes it feel even better. I know that this is the start of something for me. Everything feels so amazing and I'm so happy that Anne and Tiff told me about this and invited me along.

"Oh, God, fuck," I moan, and my hands grip at Victor's shoulders, my nails digging into him and that's all I can do until I can feel his cock throbbing and filling the condom with come.

When he's finished, he pulls out and finally I'm given some rest and I feel a relief that I didn't know that I needed. I'm shaking as Anne grins at me, putting her phone down and then helps me tidy my clothes.

Cheekily, Victor picks up my underwear and puts it in his jeans pocket as he tidies himself up. I find the humor in it and I shake my head at him. I feel amazing and I can't stop smiling. I have a feeling that I'm going to be back again.

Silencing the Man Next Door

"A new guy moves into the vacant apartment next door. Everything is fine until night falls."

I'm in too much of a rush as I leave my apartment that Saturday morning. I'm already late and as I run out, my attention is on my handbag instead of where I am going. I realize too late that I'm not alone. I go crashing into a guy holding a largish tan box and the two of us go tumbling to the floor. I know I've fucked up when I hear the sound of glass smashing.

"Shit!" I exclaim as I land on my ass. Thankfully, I don't seem to have hurt myself.

"Crap!" I hear echoed back and I wince. I don't recognize the deep tone of the man that I've apparently assaulted.

I hurry to get my bearings and stand. "I am so sorry!" I exclaim and wonder what the hell I've broken. I manage to straighten my clothes and take in the sight before me. A handsome, well-built man is picking up the box. He has dark hair and eyes, and a neatly trimmed beard. For a second I'm frozen as he stands to his full height. He towers over my puny 5 foot 2. I can't help it, I've always had a thing for tall men, and this man is huge.

"It's okay, these things happen," he replies, sounding completely reasonable and I snap out of my thoughts.

"Were you making a delivery?" I ask him. He must be lost on this floor. I've been living by myself on the second floor of this simple two-floor apartment for over six months now. For some reason, people don't tend to settle in this small apartment block. I've been living here since I moved in 6 years ago and they never stay.

"No, eh, I've just moved into number 3." He grins down at me and it's then I notice the box he is holding has 'kitchen' scribbled on it on a black Sharpie.

It's the apartment next door to mine. I'm surprised and instantly interested in this man and how I've just broken something that belongs to my new neighbor. Nothing says welcome to the neighborhood like destroying their property. I glance down at my Michael Korrs watch and I see that another 3 minutes have passed since I last checked. I'm gonna get my ass kicked if I'm late for work again.

"Oh, great, um… It's really nice to meet, you. I'm sorry for your…" I gesture to his box.

"It's just some cups and glasses. I'm sure I'll live," he tells me.

He looks like he's going to say more but I can't help it. I have to go. "I'm so sorry! I've gotta run!" I really can't help it and I feel terrible. "I've got to head to work, I finish at 5! I'll see you later!" With

that, I'm giving him an apologetic smile and then running past him, hoping that I don't miss my train again this morning.

***

I end up finishing at 6. It's so typical. I won't get paid for it. As usual. But I won't get into that. As soon as I'm out of my office, I'm pulling my coat on and taking the elevator down to escape my building. There's a target not far from where I work so I head there. I haven't stopped thinking about my new neighbor all day. I was so rude to him this morning. And he was so good about me breaking his stuff. I'm not sure how I would have reacted if our positions were reversed, but I'm sure it would have involved a lot of colorful language.

I grab my groceries for the weekend and then I head over to the home department with the intention of buying some replacement cups and glasses. I know that he wasn't mad, so the kitchenware couldn't have been expensive or sentimental. So I buy some reasonably priced, decent-looking things and a 'sorry card'. I hesitate for a moment, I don't want to wrap it because I'm pretty excited, so I grab a gift bag to shove it all into as well.

By the time I'm on the subway and making my way home it's gone 7 o'clock. When I eventually get home, Penny is at the door and waiting for me, meowing and telling me off that her dinner time has been delayed by an entire hour and that she might die if she's not given some wet food immediately. I lean down and pet her affectionately, and like the whipped pet owner that I am, I'm straight to the kitchen and doing as I am told. I put some dinner in the oven, and go for my evening shower as I wait for it to cook.

I eat alone as I do every night. I haven't got any family, and what friends I do have are now living across state and married, living happy lives with husbands. I'm not bitter about it, but I do sometimes wonder when my turn will be. My mind drifts to the man next door again.

I wonder if he's single…?

I glance at the Target bag. I should really drop that around…

By the time I make it to next door, it's almost 9 o'clock. I wonder if it's rude to knock this late but I come with gifts so I don't think he'll mind. Plus, he had seemed so nice this morning, I don't think he'd be rude about it.

I knock on the door sharply 3 times and then I step back waiting to see if he answers. It's a few moments and I hear nothing from inside. He could be working… He might work nights. I have no idea. I know nothing about this man. I don't overthink it though. Instead, I place the bag to the left of his door and leave it there for him tomorrow.

I go through my usual routine. I lock my door, I drink some tea and eat some snacks, and then I click my TV on as I walk into my room and it instantly picks up where I last watched on Netflix.

As soon as I snuggle into bed and get comfortable, Penny curls up to the side of me and I sigh in contentment. I'm so glad to have her. I never liked cats before Penny, but she was left here by the previous

tenant. She had been locked outside the apartment and it took a couple of days for me to find out that she was trying to get into my apartment. It's sad. I could never imagine leaving an animal behind. But I don't know the circumstances so I try not to judge. Instead, I let myself feel lucky that she came into my life. She's good company for me. She's not a person, but I do class her as my little friend.

After an hour of watching FRIENDS, my eyes start to droop and I'm yawning. I know it's only 10 o'clock but I work 6 days a week (sometimes 7 because my boss hates me) so I'm always exhausted. I click the TV off as I like to sleep in the dark. I instantly realize why my neighbor didn't answer the door to me.

"Oh, fuck, fuck! Yes, fuck me…" a loud shrill voice cries out from behind my wall.

I freeze.

Is that…? …No! Surely… It must be the TV. It's the only explanation.

"Oh, harder, fuck me. Please!"

That is not *the TV. He's at home, alright. And he's got company…*

I might be wrong, but I always thought that the room that backed onto my bedroom was the lounge, but I guess he could have swapped them around. Or, you know, they are having sex in the living room.

Not everyone is as boring as me, my brain unhelpfully reminds me. My experience of sex is confined to the missionary position in the dark. I've never been confident enough to explore more than that. Though over the last year or so I have begun to get more comfortable with myself. I haven't really had a choice since I'm single.

Even though I'm alone in my apartment, I feel the heat fill my face. I've never had this problem before. The guy next door is loudly, and very explicitly having sex. Of course, he hadn't mentioned that he had a partner, I only met him for a few seconds. I feel a little embarrassed that I've been lusting over him when he's already taken. Ashamed, I tuck myself under the bedsheets and turn the TV back on. It helps. Marginally. Even with that, I can hear the noise.

"Oh, Derek, fuck me!"

Well, at least I know his name now.

I feel the beginnings of arousal stirring inside me and I know I shouldn't. Eavesdropping on my next-door neighbors private time is not appropriate. I'm not that kind of woman. I pull my pillow over my head in an attempt to muffle the sound but it takes a long time to fall asleep.

***

In the morning I am exhausted. My next-door neighbors carried on long into the night. Jesus. I wasn't even aware that it was possible to do it for so long… I end up snoozing my alarm unknowingly. I shock awake properly once I realize what I've been doing. I curse myself.

How the hell do they have any energy for the next day? I feel like a zombie.

I drag myself out of bed and I'm not surprised that I'm already running behind. Everything goes wrong. I fall over Penny. I realize I've run out of mouthwash. I burn myself with the curling iron and poke myself in the eye with my eyeliner. I feel like I haven't slept a wink. I am not coping well with the lack of sleep.

I run out of the door.

Damn it.

I'm late again.

***

The day is long and I spend most of it yawning over my computer. I drink a ton of coffee but it doesn't really help. *I need my beauty sleep*, I complain in my head childishly and debate whether it's professional to have a nap on my lunch break. I manage to resist but by the time I'm sat on the subway, I feel like I'm being rocked to sleep as I stare out the window. I have to concentrate on not falling asleep and ending up several stops away from home.

I almost feel like crying in relief when I see my crappy apartment. I've never been so happy to be home. I check my mail out of habit and then realize that it's a Sunday. I roll my eyes at myself. The stairs feel like hell as I sluggishly take them one by one. But finally, I'm at my door and shoving my key in the lock.

I almost jump out of my skin when I'm greeted from behind.

"Hey! I got your gifts!"

I'm just about to walk into the apartment when he appears – Derek, I remind myself, that's the name that I heard chanted over and over last night. The reminder isn't helpful at all and the memories of the previous night flood back to me. I'm brought back to reality as I immediately slam my door in fear of Penny darting out. I don't want her getting downstairs and into the neighbors apartments. They don't like cats and I don't want any problems with them. I'm always been a little bitter that they left Penny out in the cold for those few days that I didn't know she had been abandoned. I try to avoid them if possible.

"Oh, hey!" I greet. I turn and *woah*… I had forgotten how tall and handsome he is. "I'm glad! It was just a little something to say sorry. I didn't mean to smash your stuff and then disappear."

I smile at him, feeling a little awkward. I can't stop thinking about what I heard last night. The way the woman was moaning and screaming… I have never heard something like that before.

The man is a giant and I gulp, my body instantly reacting to his close proximity.

"It's fine. I didn't think that. I get it. A lot of people work 9-5." The way he says it makes it sound like he doesn't and I'm curious for a second and I want to know more. But I shouldn't ask. I don't want to start an in-depth conversation with him after last night. I might need a few days to get the thoughts out of my head. My body is betraying me and I can feel butterflies in my stomach.

He's spoken for. I am not a homewrecker… I don't want this, no matter what my body is telling me.

"Well, I appreciate you being so great about it," I tell him. "Sorry again." I smile politely and then I open my door and step inside. I shut the door behind me and then lean against it for a second as I try to catch my breath and come to my senses. I'm not sure why I'm so interested in him, even knowing that he is spoken for isn't enough to stop the strange feelings inside of me.

Penny meows and looks up at me.

"I know, I know," I tell her, "at least I'm on time today."

I sigh. I'm so exhausted, and I can't wait to get into bed tonight.

***

I'm freshly showered, my nightclothes on, and a towel twisted onto my head when I step into my bedroom. I'm immediately wide-eyed.

"Oh, yes, fuck me harder!"

"You've got to be kidding me," I mutter to myself. "Do these two not sleep?" I glance towards the clock and it reads 21:15. It's not exactly late, but since I have no life it's already past my bedtime. I'm also still exhausted from missing sleep last night. I was looking forward to getting some sleep.

I look towards the offending sound. Tonight, it's even *worse*, I can hear the squeak of the bedsprings. I groan. Even Penny looks towards the wall as she follows me inside. I have no idea how I'm going to sleep through this again. They just had sex last night, so they can't want to do it again for hours on end, right? I cling to some kind of logic. Anything that will mean that I get some sleep.

Without a choice, I climb into bed and then try and get comfortable and settled. But the insistent squeaking and moaning instantly has me squirming in bed. The butterflies are back in my stomach and I can feel arousal start to seep under my skin as I lay in the dark, the loud sounds of love-making invading my bedroom.

I shouldn't. I must be a complete pervert to want to do this, but I try not to feel bad as I slip my hands into my panties. *They won't know...* I think to myself.

I sigh quietly as I rub myself softly. I don't want them to hear me so I focus on trying to stay quiet as I'm pretty sure that if I can hear them, then they can hear me. I tease myself for a few minutes and I can feel the sticky heat start to radiate from my pussy as I grow wet. I rub circles against my clit and I'm shaking as it feels like my neighbors are putting on a show for me. I can hear every gasp and moan. I can imagine the tall, muscled man from next door fucking a faceless woman. I imagine everything about it, how he would feel and what he would say. I can hear them talking, moaning, and gasping. I can't hear what he is saying, I can just hear the deep rumble of his voice, but my mind fills in the blanks.

As I slip my fingers inside myself, my eyes flutter closed, and I try to listen to what's happening. I try to put the sounds to actions and play out a scene in the darkness in my mind. But this time, instead of the faceless woman it's me, I'm underneath him and he's inside me, fucking me into the mattress.

My fingers thrust deeper inside myself, my body following an instinct and greedy for pleasure as I get off to whatever is happening merely meters away from me. I add one more, three of my fingers rubbing against the sensitive walls of my pussy as I grow wetter.

Oh, God, I bet he's so strong, he could probably pin me down and hold me in place. He could do anything he wants to me…

The thoughts don't stop. It's like my mind is out of control. My usually reserved personality is being overtaken by a desperately horny persona. Something inside of me is out of control and it makes me need more and more.

Very quickly, my fingers are not enough and I grow frustrated with myself. I sit up and open my bedside cabinet in search for my vibrator. It's a recent purchase. I've always been a reserved and quiet woman with a low sex drive. But I took the plunge and brought myself a treat last year. It's a simple rabbit vibrator, purple in color and 6 inches in length. I don't use it very often, but tonight, I feel like I'm going to need it. I find it within a few minutes, grab a condom from the packet I leave in my dresser, and then apply it to the silicone. I relax back and spread my legs, letting the sounds of my neighbors loud fucking spur me on as I line up the toy and then push it inside myself.

Oh. Fuck…

I always forget how good it feels. It feels cool and big inside me. I can feel it stretching my tight pussy. It must have been longer than I thought since I last used it because it feels massive inside of me and as I start to find a rhythm, I struggle to keep quiet. A few moans start to tumble from my lips and I spread my legs wider. Naughtily, I look down and watch the toy disappear inside myself. It's something that has always turned me on, I love watching myself get fucked. I think about Derek next door, about his cock splitting me open.

I bet he's got a huge cock…

I lick my lips as I think about it. I know it's such a stereotype, but I am weak to a tall, muscled man with a big dick and Derek is one hell of a man.

I start to fuck myself harder with the toy and it already feels so good. It's like I've got my own personal show. I quickly get too hot and I pull my clothes off. I lay on top of the bed, completely naked and turn on the toy. Goosebumps spring up on my body as the tiny vibrations massage my sensitive insides.

I cry out, I can't help it. It's impossible to keep quiet when I feel so good. My entire body feels like it's on fire as pleasure runs through me.

"Oh, fuck, ohhh!" The voice next door seems to be getting louder and I try to muffle my own cries as I fuck myself harder with the vibrator. I can't stop myself as I feel the telltale signs of an orgasm. I quicken the pace, slamming the vibrator into myself over and over until I am shaking. I can feel my pussy clench and squeeze the toy, gripping around it a powerful orgasm rips through me.

"Oh, yes, that's it. Darren!"

I flop back against the sheets, the sticky vibrator still buzzing next to me.

Wait… I thought his name was Derek?

The next morning, I put it down to not having enough sleep. I must have misheard. Or maybe he has a roommate?

Hmmm, I doubt it, I think to myself.

I'm so sure that next door is only a one-bed the same as mine. But hey, I don't judge. It could be anything.

Last night wasn't as bad as what I thought it was going to be. It carried on for another hour or so and then calmed down. But I think my orgasm definitely helps with my opinion on this. Despite it being a bit shorter of a session than the night before, it was louder! I really really hope that tonight is not the same. I'm not sure that I can put up with this if it's going to be an everyday occurrence. Having to knock on the door and complain will be humiliating, but if it means that I can actually get a decent night's sleep, then I am willing to do it.

I'm not sure when my next day off is. There's a couple of girls in the office who are on vacation at the moment, and since I'm not in my bosses' graces, I've been taking on the extra workload.

So by the time I'm home on the third night and it's happening again, I know that I'm going to have to say something but the idea of knocking the wall or actually going to their front door has me cringing. I lay in bed and think about the best way to approach the situation.

Huh. I'm gonna have to invest in some earplugs.

***

I take my chance on Friday when I finally get my day off. It's been over a week since I've had any time to myself. I go to a spin class, I buy something nice for my dinner, and then I come home ready to cuddle up with Penny. It's almost been a full week since Derek/Darren/David/Dylan has moved in and I'm confused as hell. Each night it has been a different name and so far I haven't run into his mystery girlfriend. Every night that I've come home, as soon as it gets to around 9 or 10 pm, it starts. Sometimes it only lasts a couple of hours, but like on Tuesday, it feels like it's all night. I feel like it's ruining my life. I'm so embarrassed. I have run into the downstairs neighbors a couple of times this week, and I think about asking them about it but I don't know how to approach it, plus I don't really want to make a big deal out of nothing. It's just two people having sex. I'm not a prude, I just want a good night's sleep!

I try by knocking on the door in the morning, but I wait around and no-one is at home. So I try again later after I've been to the gym and I've had my shower. I'm nervous, my hands shaking as I rehearse what I'm going to say in my head.

I'm shocked when the door opens. I gulp. There is no escaping it now. There he is, all 6 foot something looking down at me with a grin.

"Oh, hey! You okay?" he asks me and I nod, giving me a nervous smile. "I didn't actually catch your name, you know," he tells me, and then he holds out his hand, "I'm Daniel."

Daniel?! I'm pretty sure that I haven't heard Daniel all week. I can't help but look at him bewildered.

"I thought your name was… something different," I tell him, feeling more than suspicious.

"Nope, I've always been Daniel," he replies, but something on his face gives him away.

"I'm Katie," I tell him eventually, as I realize I haven't introduced myself properly either.

"You wanna come in, Katie?" he asks me, his thumb pointing behind himself and into his apartment. "You can try out these new mugs that my awesome neighbor brought me. I have coffee."

I find myself nodding, hypnotized by his easy charm. I follow him inside and he kicks the door closed behind him. I follow him to the kitchen and my suspicions are confirmed as I discreetly look into the open doors in the apartment. His bedroom is against mine.

His bed must be against mine too, that's why it's so loud.

"Have you been living here long?" he asks me as I enter the kitchen.

I sit down at the table and he prepares coffee at the coffee machine. I watch him flawlessly use the complicated machine and I realize that this guy must run off coffee.

It would be good if I could have my own unlimited coffee too, I think to myself as I watch him steam milk and prepare the coffee beans. *Maybe I should start asking for coffee from him in the morning when he keeps me up all night. As if.*

"About 6 years now. It's home at this point."

"Oh, nice. Do you have sugar?" he asks.

"Please," I reply. I shouldn't, I've been trying to cut down, but it's nice to have a treat sometimes.

The two of us are soon sat opposite each other and I'm taking a sip out of one of the cups I have brought him. I have to admit, the coffee is delicious. I have no idea how I am going to breach the subject when he is being so friendly to me. He seems like a genuinely nice person. As I look around, I can see that he must have been busy, he's already completely unpacked everything and the place is immaculate.

"So, you seem to be settling in. How are you finding it?" I ask him. "I hope downstairs aren't giving you any trouble."

"No, no, everyone's been really nice. Do you have a cat by the way?" he asks me.

"Yeah, her name's Penny." I wonder if he's about to complain about her like downstairs do… I hope not, because I have something to complain about first.

"Aww, cute, I thought I could hear a cat sometimes in the mornings. I love cats. I'd love to meet her."

He's very different from what I expected and I find myself nodding.

"Sure," I tell him. "She's kind of my baby." I probably sound pathetic so I don't care. I love my cat.

He smiles at me. "So, eh, was there a reason you came around, or did you just want a chat? It's nice. I'm such a social person so you're welcome around any time. I hate living by myself."

I almost choke on my coffee. "You live by yourself?"

"Yep, just me. Maybe I should get a cat too, huh."

"I thought…" My face is flushing and I lose my words.

Oh god, he's going to see right through me.

Daniel looks at me confused and lets out a little laugh. "What?"

I'm going to have to just come out and say it.

"Um… I actually come around here for a reason. This is really embarrassing but… I don't really know how to say this… I can hear you…"

He continues to look at me a little cluelessly.

"At night," I continue, trying to explain what I'm saying without actually saying *I can hear you fucking someone every night.*

I see the moment it clicks and he bursts out laughing, his face flushing. "Oh, Jesus, I am so sorry!" He covers his mouth with his hand, obviously embarrassed but amused. "I… I'll try and keep it down."

My face is flaming too and his laughter is infectious and I find myself laughing too. Being around Daniel is easy, and I find his company pleasant. He's very easy to talk to and I feel much better now that everything is a little bit easier.

"Thank you," I tell him sincerely. "Like Jeeze, when do you sleep?" I affectionately roll my eyes at him.

"I don't really," he explains, "I've always struggled which is why I…" He trails off and I'm grateful because if he said the words I would probably spontaneously combust. This guy is red hot.

"Oh, that sucks. I kind of just… pass out when I go to bed. I love my sleep," I say, giving him a big smile.

"Well, I hope I haven't been keeping you up," he says with a laugh.

I freeze, not sure whether to explain how many sleepless nights he has already caused me this week. I don't want him to feel bad. He already looks so embarrassed about it. But I can't hide it, my face must give me away.

"Oh, man, you must think I'm the worse neighbor—"

"No, no," I hurry to assure him, "not at all. You didn't know and I've been at work all week, I just didn't have a chance to come and let you know. If anything I'm kinda impressed now I know you're single. Is... is it rude for me to ask…? Has it been a different girl every night? I kinda heard you being called a lot of different names."

He looks away for a moment, his cheeks rosy. "Uh, yeah actually. I use Tinder a lot. I've been struggling to find someone long-term. It would be nice if I could find someone interested in more than just sex, but people on Tinder are superficial. I mean, I always used to ask for a second date, but I got sick of being turned down all the time. It's a blow to the ego… So now I just kinda, hook up with girls and stick to one-night stands." He sighs and actually sounds a little depressed about it which is odd.

"So… are you looking for someone then?" I ask him. I'm not sure how we've managed to get onto the subject so quickly. Maybe now that I know that there isn't a special someone my mind is actually letting me think that I might have a chance.

"I mean, who isn't? No-one wants to be alone."

I stare at him for a moment. He's right. I feel alone all the time. I only see people at work, and then I come home and see Penny. To be honest, this is the first time I've had a conversation with another adult that isn't the superficial, 'Hi, how are you?'.

"Yes, I think so too," I answer him honestly.

"What about you? Have you got someone?" he asks me, and it sounds kind, as if he hopes that I'm not as lonely as him.

I give him a sad smile. "Just me and Penny."

There's a silence between us for a few moments and I'm not sure what else to say. The atmosphere is comfortable despite the subject and this being our first real conversation. If nothing else, I'm pretty sure that I've at least made a friend.

"Do you want to meet her?" I blurt out, not very sure where it's come from. Penny makes me so happy, and if Daniel really does like cats, I hope that she can make him happy too.

"Sure!" he says and he stands, instantly perking up. "Is she home now?"

I stand too, my coffee still in my hands. "Yeah, she's a house cat, she doesn't really like it outdoors. Her owner abandoned her so she was in the cold for a while. I think that's why she doesn't like it. She seems afraid that she won't be allowed back in."

"Aww, that's awful. Was she a stray or did you get her from a shelter?"

"She actually belonged to the previous tenant. She kind of came with the apartment." I've never thought about it that way before, and it makes me smile.

The two of us carry on chatting and we make our way over to my apartment instead. We step inside and I call out for Penny, though I guess that she's sleeping in my room. Daniel follows me and as expected, she's curled up on my duvet.

"Oh, I see why it's been such as issue. Our bedrooms are back to back."

I nod shyly and then sit down on the bed, scooping Penny into my lap. Daniel comes to sit next to me. Our coffees are forgotten on my dresser.

Penny is instantly curious about the newcomer. I don't really have visitors very often, so I can understand why she is so friendly to him, eager to make a new friend. The way she climbs into his lap so readily gives me a good feeling. It's as if she approves of my secret crush – or whatever the hell this is. Daniel strokes her right away and is gentle with her, and I'm glad that he was honest about liking cats. It's an attractive quality to me and it only makes me like him even more.

"Why is it that you don't use your real name?" It's such a personal question, but it's weighing on my mind. It feels suspicious. It's the one thing that is stopping me from asking him if he would want to go on a date and taking a chance.

He shrugs. "They don't really like me. They like the persona that I put on. So it's a bit of a defense mechanism I think. I know they only want to sleep with me." He doesn't sound like he's lying.

"Oh, I see."

"Do you think it's wrong of me?" he asks.

Why would he care what I think?

"Not really," I tell him. "Though I guess I'm kind of special then if I know your real name," I tease him. "Unless you're pretending with me too?" I raise an eyebrow at me. "Are you sure you haven't got some kind of old-fashioned name like Escobar?" It's the first thing that comes into my mind.

Daniel laughs. "You're funny," he comments, "I like it."

I'm pleased. "Well, I like you – whoever you are. Albert," I guess.

He laughs again and I like the sound. "Am I ever going to live this down?" he asks me and I can't help but laugh too.

"Never," I confirm and I realize that I mean it. I really like Daniel and it shocks me how much. I glance to him nervously.

"Look, I know this is crazy but… would you maybe want to go on a date with me?" he turns to me and asks.

I almost fall off the bed. I had not expected him to ask that at all. "Like an actual date, or one of your one-night stands?" I ask him, but I'm still smiling as I talk to him, showing him that really I don't mind what the answer is.

"Well, which would you prefer?"

I pretend to think about it for a moment, "Hmm, I don't know, Nathaniel," I say, deliberately using the wrong name again. "What's in it for me?" I ask cheekily.

Daniel narrows his eyes at me playfully. "Well, you heard those women," he says, a smirk on his face and Penny chooses this time to jump down and leave the two of us alone.

Traitor, I think to her as I watch her disappear, her tail swishing as she goes.

Daniel takes this opportunity to lean in close to me, and it's clear that he knows I like him, and now, I know that he likes me too. There seems to be a chemistry between us that I've never felt before.

"You'll just have to show me what I'm missing out on then."

He smiles as he kisses me, and the two of us kiss for a few minutes before he pulls away. "You don't seem like those other women," he tells me.

"I'll take that as a compliment then," I say before I lean in and kiss him this time. I can feel the scratch of his beard on my face and it tickles a little. I like it. I hope that he's going to live up to his words. He's right, I want to know what had those women moaning and begging so much.

His hands cup my face and they feel huge against me. It reminds me how big he is; the fact that he is an absolute giant next to me. I should be afraid but I'm excited. Electricity is buzzing under my skin

and I'm eager. I know he must think I'm slut by the way I open my mouth to him, letting him fuck me with his tongue but I really can't help it. I'm desperate for him to touch me after listening to him wreck all those women for the last week. Now it's my turn and I want to take advantage of it.

"You don't have to be gentle with me," I tell him.

He takes it as an invitation and grabs me, pulling me into his lap. "How's that?" he asks.

I can feel the hot, hard line of his dick and I rub myself against it. I'm not really in control. I feel crazy, like I'm under some kind of love spell. I let out a shaky breath, and for the first time in a week, I don't have to be quiet in my pleasure. I let my head fall back as I groan and he takes full advantage. I feel his lips agianst my neck and then his teeth.

"Yes," I moan, "mark me up, I want to remember." I mean it. I want to look in the mirror tomorrow and see his teeth marks on me. I want my body to show the evidence of our night together so if it's just the once that he wants this, then I will have something to remind me of it for as long as I can. Then I can relive it, over and over.

"Steady," he tells me, and he grabs my hips, his fingers squeezing hard enough to bruise.

I can't. I can't keep still when he is here in my room and touching me. How can I? I ignore his words, and if anything, I rub my clothed pussy against him harder as his sharp kisses are on my neck.

"I wanna ride you," I whisper. I want to show him how good I can be for him. I want him to come back for more. Not like those other women. I want him.

I can tell my words have an effect on him because he lets out a shuddering breath and then he nods. "Fuck, yes," he agrees and then tugs on my clothes, stripping me of my shirt and then unclipping my bra expertly.

Some might be turned off knowing that he has slept with so many women, but it turns me on, I like that he knows what he's doing. It's clear that he's experienced by the way he seems to manipulate my body and by the time he's tugging my jeans off I'm shaking and I'm desperate to take the edge off.

I stand completely naked and normally I'm shy, but he makes me feel beautiful with how he looks at me. He bites his lip in desire.

"Your turn," I tell him as I walk to the draw to collect a condom.

Confidently, he shrugs off his shirt and then kicks his jeans and boxers and then relaxes back on the bed. I'm shameless as I look at him. He's tall and broad, his muscles defined and his pecs and stomach flat and fit. He's probably the most perfect thing I've ever seen in my life.

I jump on the bed excited and I don't hesitate as I bring the packet to my lips and open it. I grab the condom and grip his cock. I can't have been any more right in my life. His cock is long and fat and just perfect and I can't wait to sit on it and have my fill of it. I smooth the latex down and I'm trembling all over in anticipation as I straddle him and balance one hand on his chest, the other hand holding his cock in place.

I glance up and him and he grins, letting me take charge. He holds my hips as I line his cock up and then slowly, I start to sink down on it.

"Oh, oh, fuck, oh God," I moan, the words pouring from me and suddenly I understand everything because this is perfect.

His cock feels huge inside me and at this point, I'm not even sure it will fit but I want it desperately. I want him to wreck my pussy. He stretches me and touches every inch of me, filling me up in a way that I didn't think was possible.

"Fuck, fuck, fuck," I pant, my face lax in pleasure as I lock eyes with him.

"That's it, you can do it, sit on it, babe," he encourages me and shows me how to ease it inside me until I feel like I might cry from the feeling of being so full.

I can't keep still. I start gently, rocking on him but then it's not long until I'm soaking wet and my thighs are burning as I begin to fuck myself on him, my tits exposed and bouncing.

"Fuck," he groans, and he lets out a long sigh.

"Oh, God, fuck me, Daniel," I beg.

He complies and thrusts his hips upwards and meets me halfway. It's perfect and he quickly finds a rhythm that leaves me almost screaming because it's only minutes before I'm coming.

"Fuck, yes, yes, yes," I moan and I reach between my own legs, my fingers slipping through my slick come to play with myself in front of Daniel as he continues to fuck me.

"Ohhh fuck, I can feel you coming on me…"

I nod and bite into my bottom lip, I feel like I can't breathe from the exhaustion and I start to tire, leaning heavily on his chest. I've never had sex like this – hard and out of control and loud and dirty. Daniel takes pity on me and he grabs me by the thighs and then flips us. I squeal and grab at him panicking at the sudden change, but he gives me no time to adjust. He pins my knees to my shoulders and then rolls his hips hard. I scream and scramble for the pillow next to me. I shove it over my face. The whole building must be able to hear me at this point, but I can't stop, I can't keep quiet.

I'm coming again before I know what's happening, sobbing into the pillow and I can't move an inch. I feel like he's in complete control of me, I couldn't move if I tried and I love every second. I'm exhausted, desperate and overstimulated.

"Please, Daniel, please," I beg, my voice muffled in the pillow.

Suddenly, it's ripped away from me and he's looking into my eyes. He steals my breath when he kisses me and then I feel him moan against my lips as he comes. It takes a long time for us to come down from our orgasms. I kind of lay there feeling useless and like every muscle in my body has been thoroughly ravished.

He collapses next to me and then we look at each other.

"So, do I get that date still?" he asks me.

I laugh and throw the pillow at him. "Of course, Sabastian."

Temptation with My Bestfriend's Brother

"Tanya shouldn't have a crush on her best friend's older brother, but she can't help it. They've managed to keep it under control until Tanya is babysitting one night and unexpectedly Jared shows up. What her best friend doesn't know can't hurt her."

"Who's a beautiful boy? You are! Yes, you are!" I coo as I bounce baby Braydon on my knees, delighted as he squeals in joy at something so simple. His tiny hands grip mine as we play together and I feel like my heart is going to burst with my love for him. I haven't seen him since last weekend and I'm excited for us to spend the evening together. I'm sitting on my best friend's bed, watching her get ready for her hot date with her husband, Nick. I promised I would babysit for her so the two of them can have a night out together for their first anniversary together. So here I am on a Friday night, preparing to spend some time with the little man.

"Wow, he's getting so big now, Stella!" I tell her. "I can't believe he's gone one now, it seems like five minutes ago that you were worrying what to do with a baby." It was his birthday just a few months ago. He feels heavier than only a week ago and I'm sure that he's had another growth spurt. He looks adorable in the new sleepsuit that I brought for him, and though the little dinosaur suit is slightly baggy on him, I know it won't be long until he grows out of this one too.

"I know, how do you think I feel?" she asks me as she pulls a face in the mirror, trying to apply liquid eyeliner efficiently to her eyelids as she squints to get a better look. "I still can't believe that this is my life," she says, referring to the fact that she and her husband are now finally settled together and they've been married an entire year. They haven't had a typical romance, that's for sure, but these days, who has? They are happy together and that's what matters.

"Now we just need to find someone for you," Stella says and it distracts me from Braydon for a moment.

I've never been one for relationships, but now my best friend is settled and happy, I must admit, it's hard to watch her and to not want what she has. I would be crazy not to. She and Nick are such a cute couple, and they deserve each other after everything they've been through.

"Oh, you never told me how your date went!" Stella says and then glances at me through her reflection in the mirror and I can feel my face flush.

It's been a week since she set me up on a blind date. I don't know how to tell her that it was awful.

Instead, my mind moves to her brother Jared. The two of us went on a secret date and I've been replaying the night over and over in my mind.

"Oh, that good, eh?" Stella asks me with a knowing smirk, and I feel my stomach drop.

Oops. She thinks I'm thinking about that guy! What am I going to say?!

"Oh, uh, yeah it was okay," I lie, and focus on Braydon so Stella can't see that I'm lying about it from the look on my face.

If she knew that I still had a crush on Jared, then she would be less than pleased. I think every girl has that fantasy where they marry into their best friend's family, and I'm not immune from that. Me and Stella have joked about what would happen if I ended up with one of her brothers. But it's nothing more than that. A joke. I know she thinks that Jared and I are a bad match. She's made passing comments about it in the past. And well, if I'm honest with myself, I have to admit that we wouldn't work too. He doesn't have time for relationships. He's completely obsessed with working – I don't need someone like that. I want someone who is going to put me first, not treat me as an afterthought.

"Well, it looks like it was more than 'okay'... You say that like I don't know you! You're blushing!" she exclaims, and she looks excited. I feel terrible for fooling her.

"I'm not!" I try to deny but I can feel my face burning the more that she looks at me. I try to focus my attention on the gorgeous little boy in my arms as he stands on my knees and smushes his hand against my nose while babbling. "He was a gross loser, wasn't he, Braydon?" I say and Braydon replies by trying to pull my hair which I take as him listening to me.

"Did you sleep with him?" she asks in a hush, turning around in her dressing table chair. She peers at me, her eyes narrowing suspiciously.

I avoid looking at her because as soon as she says those words, my brain goes right to me fantasizing about sleeping with Jared.

"You did!" she hisses in conclusion.

"I didn't!" I squeal in response because there is no way on Earth that I would ever sleep with that man. The very idea of it makes me cringe. "Honestly, it was a bad date."

"Woah. What the hell?! Why didn't you tell me?" she asks clearly surprised. "I assumed you had a good time. You normally tell me everything."

It was true. My first point of call is always Stella.

"It wasn't a big deal," I explain, "it's not like I'm disappointed. I didn't *like* him or anything. It's not like we are dating. It was just a blind date."

"Hmmm, I'm not sure that I believe you, you sound pretty blasé about it," she says skeptically.

I shrug in response. "He was good-looking, but that's about it. If I wanted a one-night stand then I'd hook up with someone on Tinder."

Stella turns around and continues applying her makeup delicately and for the moment I know that I've managed to get escape her curiosity.

"Are you sure you're going to be okay tonight?" she asks me for the thousandth time.

I resist rolling my eyes because I know she's just being a good mom, but I am going to be absolutely fine. I've looked after Braydon so many times. It's strange to think that he's not really family – at least by blood – because I love him so much and I would do anything for him.

"I'm going to be fine," I respond. "I know the routine. I'll call you if I need anything. Medicine's in the cabinet. I have the number of his pediatrician," I reel the information off to reassure her that everything is okay. "But we're going to have a great evening. He's going to have a lovely bottle. Isn't that right?!" I ask him, talking in a baby voice.

"Yeah, yeah, yeah," he replies excitedly, cute as a button with no idea what I'm saying, and Stella and I laugh at how cute he is.

Stella and Nick leave at just gone eight pm and Braydon and I wave them goodbye at the door. "There we go, bye-bye, mommy, bye daddy," I say on his behalf. Braydon sits on my hip, sucking on his hand as I lock the door.

Braydon begins to fuss, his little face scrunching up as he grumbles and I know that it's time for him to go to bed. I go through the routine of warming up a bottle for him knowing that he won't settle without the comfort of a feed. Once it's heated correctly, I take him upstairs and into the nursery. It's such a cute room and it makes me think about what it would be like to have a cute nursery in my apartment. But I know that if that is to ever happen it would probably be a long, long time away.

I sit in his rocking chair, clicking off the main light in his room and turn on his nightlight. I sit and cuddle him, rocking back and forth as he begins to gulp down the bottle. Immediately, his eyes begin to flutter closed. I take the time to enjoy him for a moment and something inside me aches as I hold him close and smell his little head. He smells of baby shampoo and talc. He's asleep within minutes and I gently place him in his crib, careful not to disturb him. I click on the baby monitor before sneaking out of the room and slowly closing the door as not to disturb him.

I make my way to the spare room, ready to get changed and into my own nightwear. I have no idea what time Stella and Nick will be home, but I know they are going to take advantage of the fact they are child-free for the night so I'm happy to make myself at home.

I'm just climbing out of the shower and toweling off when I hear a strange noise. I look towards the baby monitor where it is sitting on the sink and I pause for a moment, listening. I wait for Braydon to make a noise, a little grumble, or the sound of him moving but I hear nothing.

I must have imagined it.

I finish dressing myself when I hear the noise again. I open the bathroom door and walk cautiously down the hallway to peer over the banister, feeling more than a little paranoid.

My heart stops.

The noise isn't coming from Braydon's room. I can hear someone downstairs.

Oh, God, what do I do?

I think about calling the cops and realize that I've left my phone on the kitchen counter downstairs. I look at Braydon's bedroom door which is still firmly shut. I have to get to that phone. Being as light-footed as I can, I immediately run to the hallway closet and grab a baseball bat which I know is hidden in

there. With it gripped tightly in my hand, I make my way downstairs and head for the kitchen to grab my phone.

***

I pull up outside the house in my BMW and park in front of the driveway. It blocks in Nick's car but I don't really think anything of it. They won't be going anywhere at this time of night. So, with a bottle of wine and a six-pack of beer in hand. I knock on the door and wait for a response, but I'm stood there for a few minutes and no-one answers. I knock again, this time a little louder, but it's the same.

Huh, must not be able to hear me. Good job I have a key.

I fish my keys out of my back pocket. I remember to lock it behind me. I don't want the wrath of my little sister. Braydon has started walking now and doors are a point of interest for him. He's forever trying to reach the handles and curiously see what's hiding behind the doors.

"Hello?" I call out as I make my way to the kitchen, letting them know that I've arrived. There's no sign of them but I hear the shower running upstairs so I guess they're up there and showering Braydon. They will come down once they're done and he's settled in bed. "I brought wine and beer!" I call out to them.

I set the drinks down on the kitchen table and set about finding the corkscrew for the wine. It's in the top drawer and I pour myself a drink as I'm waiting for them.

I'm about to turn to put the wine in the fridge when something catches the corner of my eye and I jump in surprise. My glass of wine goes crashing to the floor, smashing on the wooden flooring and instantly shattering into a million pieces. I jump back in alarm as the wine spreads in a puddle across the floor.

"Oh, Jesus Christ, Tanya," I cry out as I notice who has suddenly appeared behind me. "You scared the living daylights out of me!" The last thing that I expected was to be apprehended from behind by Tanya of all people.

"Me?! I thought someone was breaking in the house!" she yells at me, and it's then that I notice she's holding a baseball bat and looking panicked. She looks at me sheepishly before lowering it.

"How is that even possible? I have a key. I let myself in the front door!" I defend myself, trying to make her see sense. I take the bat off her and lay it on the counter. It's only then that I notice she's wearing pajamas and slippers. I raise an eyebrow at her appearance.

"I'm staying here tonight!" she rushes to explain, "It's Stella's anniversary. They're not home."

Ah, that makes sense. "Damn," I say. She had mentioned it, but I thought they were going out tomorrow, not today. "Sorry, I didn't realize."

"No, it's not you. They were going to go out tomorrow, but they changed their plans," she explains, confirming my thoughts.

"Looks like I never got the memo," I joke before looking down at the mess at my feet. I'm glad it's on the wooden floors and not their cream carpets. "I'll clean up this mess and then I'll get out your hair."

"Oh, err..." Tanya blushes and I pause for a moment, wondering what she is trying to say. "Okay, I'll go and get the mop."

"I'll get the vacuum cleaner."

The two of us split up to clean up the mess. I try not to look at Tanya's legs in her cute silky shorts as she mops the red wine but it's hard not to. I've thought about her so many times this week that I didn't even realize that I was doing it until it was too late. She must feel my eyes on her as she catches me as she turns around. I look away.

"I'll get going then," I say, but I don't really mean it. I have nothing else to do for the evening. My plan was to have a drink with my family and to watch bad comedy shows.

"You know… unless you'd prefer that I stay..." I suggest to her, trying to sound nonchalant about it. "I mean I opened the bottle anyway, I might as well drink it. You might be able to have a small one."

I must be crazy. I should keep my mouth shut. I should walk out the door and go home. But for some reason, I can't resist it. The more I see Tanya, the harder it's becoming to deny the attraction between us and it's only growing, getting bigger and harder to resist.

She looks at me with her eyes sparkling and I know she wants it as much as I do. "If you want," she replies. "I guess a small one can't do any harm. I don't think they'll be home for a few hours and Braydon is fast asleep. He usually stays settled."

The smile on my face is instant as I reach back into the cupboard for two glasses. I like her thinking.

I pour the two of us a drink. A large one for myself and Tanya a small one. Then we grab the bottle, taking it with us as we make our way to the family room. We settle on the couch, keeping space between us as we turn on the TV and try to agree on something to watch – not like it matters anyway, the last thing on my mind is watching TV when Tanya is sitting next to me and looking good enough to eat. Even with no makeup on and her curly hair pulled back into a ponytail, she looks pretty and I find myself unable to look away. We settle on a romantic comedy that neither of us has seen before and I'm happy with that if I'm honest. I'm pretty laid back when it comes to media. We sit together and watch the movie quietly, enjoying the moment to relax and enjoy each other's company. I manage to follow the movie a little, it's about two best friends who are both getting married and the lengths they go to have the perfect weddings with their partners, but of course, everything goes wrong.

"I couldn't believe it when they said it was their year anniversary, already," I say, thinking about Stella's wedding. She's the only one of us who is married. "I know how much those two deserve each other. Seems like yesterday I was walking Stella down the aisle."

I glance towards a picture on their mantelpiece of the two of them on their wedding day. Our parents would have been proud of her. She's come a long way. She's grown into a beautiful young lady and I'm glad she's happy.

"Yeah, I think so too," Tanya replies. "Do you… ever think about it?"

I frown for a moment, not understanding what she means. "What? Their wedding?" I ask her.

"Well, yeah, I mean… no. I mean marriage in general. Can you ever see yourself settling down?" she avoids looking at me, her gaze fixed on the movie.

The words shock me. Though I guess they shouldn't. I'm thirty-six after all. I was in love once but… it didn't work out. I'm too much for most women. I work too many hours, I'm too bossy and demanding… I'm better off by myself.

"No," I lie, "I don't have time for that."

"I guess not," she replies. "Me neither," but she says it a little too quickly and I wonder if she's lonely. She glances at me through her thick eyelashes and I feel my mouth go dry.

"So, what are you looking for?" I ask her, pressing for information and I shuffle a little closer, closing the space between us so our thighs are lined together.

She blushes and I know that my words are affecting her. "I don't know."

She shrugs softly. But her body language conflicts with her words. She looks like she does know but she is just too shy to say what she wants.

"You do know, don't you?" I lean in closer and I ask her in a hushed voice. I watch as goosebumps break out on her skin. She squirms in her seat. "Answer me," I demand.

She turns and looks at me. She looks beautiful in the dim light of the TV and I gulp thickly.

"Yes," she says and she glances down at my lips. I feel cocky in the knowledge that even eight years after it happened, I can seduce her all over again.

"You think about us, don't you?" I know she does, so I look right at her, my gaze unwavering. She knows what I'm talking about.

"I-I… of course, I do." She breaks eye contact with me for a moment, glancing down demurely. "Why did you kiss me?" she says quietly and I barely hear the words over the sound of the TV.

"Because I wanted to," I reply, because if I can be honest about anything then it is that. "And I'd kiss you now too."

***

Oh, God. He's so sexy. Did he really just say that he would kiss me?

I'm not sure what to think. But how am I supposed to resist him when he's looking at me like this? He's still dressed immaculately. His sharp-fitted three-piece suit is showing off his toned body and his expensive taste. His face is clean-shaven, and his eyes sharp as they look at me. I feel like he's looking right through me and into my mind.

I should feel self-conscious as I feel his eyes flit down and towards my breasts, but it only makes my heart skip in my chest and my hands grow clammy. He makes me feel like such a silly young girl, lusting over him when he's older than me. But I can't help it. It's as if I'm not in control.

I know I shouldn't play into his hand. I'm giving him exactly what he wants but I can't bring myself to care. I want him to want me.

"W-what if Stella finds out?" I ask, attempting to grasp onto some logic and sanity, but it's hard to resist him when I've been thinking about our date last week non-stop. I feel like the worst friend in the world, sitting in my best friend's house, basically half-naked in front of her older brother but I'm weak. I always am when it comes to Jared.

"She doesn't have to know. We've kept secrets before," he tells me and it sounds so convincing. "I know you can be a good girl."

His words have me clenching my thighs. I look down at his lips again and I wonder if they taste the same. Our last kiss seems like such a distant memory – one that I want to relive.

He smirks at me and I know that he has won. He leans in and I find myself gravitating towards him. Our lips meet in the middle and I relax against him instantly. This is everything I've yearned for. His aftershave smells familiar and comforting and I'm taken back to being eighteen again, making out with him in the back of his car. His lips are soft and plump against my own and I'm filled with satisfaction.

Oh, God. It's so wrong, but I can't stop.

His hand is firm where he cups my face, and I lean into that too. His hand is warm and his embrace makes me feel secure. Something that I haven't felt in a really long time.

I can feel him smile against my lips and it's infectious. Before I know it, we are kissing each other eagerly. I bring my hands to him too and grip at his jacket, my nails digging into the material.

"We should stop," I whisper as a tiny voice in the back of my mind tells that this isn't a good idea. "But I want you," I admit instead, "I want you so bad."

He responds to my words of encouragement by smoothing his hands down my body. He touches my waist and I feel his fingers slip underneath my silk pajamas. I immediately shiver, goosebumps erupting on my skin. I arch into the touch. I want more. I'm hungry for him.

His kisses are hot as they trail down my neck and my eyes flutter closed in pleasure. Arousal blooms in my stomach and I grow warm. It's been a while since I last had sex, not since I've moved back to New York. But it was nothing like this. No-one has ever made me feel the way Jared is making me feel now.

I let out a soft moan and I bite into my lip as I try to quieten myself. Jared kisses me again. This time hot and open, his tongue pushing into my mouth. His touch becomes eager and his grip firm at my waist. He pulls me into his arms and I let out a squeak of surprise. I find myself straddling his thighs and I let out a giggle as I settle there. I realize that I like this feeling. There is something absurd about this situation. I never thought I would find myself like this again, but here I am.

We kiss again and again, and Jared leans forward to shrug out of his jacket. I waste no time in reaching for the buttons of his shirt. I begin to open them, eager to get to his bare skin. I'm not going to

let this chance pass by. I know that this will probably be a one-time thing. I don't want to waste this opportunity. I would be crazy if I did.

"You're eager this evening," he tells me. "I like it."

I grin in response as I finish unbuttoning his clothes and pull his shirt open. I look down at his exposed chest. His toned pecs and stomach catch my interest.

Fuck, he's so hot.

I reach for my blouse and lock eyes with him. Slowly, I start to open it. I'm not wearing a bra but I'm not shy as I show him my tits. It's completely shameless. I drop my blouse to the floor, and it lays there forgotten.

Jared reaches for me, cupping my breasts in his hands as we join again, shifting closer to each other as we start to make out. He caresses my skin, pinching my sensitive nipples and making me shiver with pleasure. I never want him to stop. Everything feels so amazing. I'm willing to take whatever he wants to give me.

He plays my body like an instrument. I feel hot and flushed all over. I can feel my panties growing damp where I'm pressed against him. I would be embarrassed, but I can feel the hard line of his cock in his slacks, and I know that this is actually going to happen.

He's the first to make the next move as he slips one of his hands between my thighs and presses his fingers against where I need him the most. He rubs me through my panties, and I can't stop the moan that rips from me. I bury my face into his shoulder to sniffle the noise.

"I can already feel that you're soaking wet for me," he whispers to me dirtily. The naughty words make my stomach twist pleasantly. I nod because it's true. I probably haven't been this wet in my entire life.

"Ohhh," I moan. "More, please," I beg him.

He doesn't hesitate to comply. He pulls my shorts and panties to the side to dip two fingers into my slick pussy. I cry out softly as he rubs between my labia and moves to my clit. It's like an explosion. My breath becomes shaky, and my heart feels like it's about to beat out of my chest. He rubs gentle circles against my clit, and I rock into the touch. With every gentle movement pleasure curls in my stomach. It travels down into my pussy and seems to explode through me.

I nuzzle my face against his neck, kissing him there desperately for a moment before smashing our mouths together again. It only amplifies what I'm already feeling. It makes everything feel electric.

Oh, God. He's going to make me come.

It surprises me because it's never been this way. It's never happened so quickly or felt so deep. I feel like he's touching me perfectly. It's as if he's looking into my mind. I can't stop it. I don't think anything can. I'm tipping over the edge as an orgasm rips through me, leaving me trembling and clinging to Jared. It takes me a few minutes to come down from the high that it gives me.

He laughs and rubs my back before removing his hand from me and I miss his touch already.

Wow, did that really just happen? I think to myself in disbelieve.

I can still feel that he's hard against me. I want to return the favor. I want to make him feel as amazing as I do. So, I reach down and rub the hard length of him which is trapped between us in his tight pants. He feels hot under my palm and my mouth waters. His cock feels big and long and perfect. I know exactly what I want.

I grin at him. "Let me suck you?" I ask him, smiling at him prettily.

Jared looks at me surprised but he nods eagerly in consent, nonetheless. "What? You expected me to say no?" he asks cockily. I roll my eyes but it's affectionately more than anything else.

I climb off him and then sink to my knees. I rest my hands on his knees before I slowly trail them upwards and towards his cock. The material of his pants is tented and I lick my lips at the sight. I've been curious for so long that I can't help but reach for his belt straight away. I undo the buckle and pull the expensive leather out of the way so I can get to the zipper of his pants. I waste no time as I open the button and immediately the zipper eases downwards. His Armani boxers are exposed to me. I look up at him, into those green eyes and he's smirking down at me. He looks so inviting.

Jared pulls his cock out, giving it a few strokes before he lets it stand proud against his stomach.

Jesus Christ...

I can't help but gasp at the sight of it. It's thick and long, and perfect. I've never seen anything like it in my life. Immediately, I need it. This is my chance to satisfy my curiosity after all these years. I would be a fool to let it pass by.

I reach for him, gripping his cock at the base in a firm grip. I lean forward and I lick the head teasingly for a moment, adjusting to the feel and the taste before I suck it into my mouth. He tastes clean and musky. It's an earthy natural taste that can only be described as intoxicating. I'm hungry for more. I suck him further into my mouth, getting his cock nice and wet as I jerk him off. I can barely fit him in my mouth, and it feels so good to be touching him this way. Above me, he's groaning, and it feels like praise to my ears. I like that he's enjoying this, that me touching him is bringing him pleasure. It's all I can think about.

It tickles as he brushes his fingers over me before he grips the back of my head. I'm encouraged by the gesture as he gently encourages me to suck his cock exactly how he likes it. I can tell when he's getting close as his grip on me becomes a little rough - enough that I know that he's losing control. It's an addictive feeling. One that I know I will treasure.

To my surprise, he warns me mere seconds before he comes, and I pull off obediently as he tugs at my hair. I jerk him maybe three more times before he's coming all over himself, drops of his release splashing onto his abs. He leans down, out of breath, and then he kisses me. It's soft and perfect. As we pull away I can hardly believe what has just happened. The lust begins to clear and I look towards the TV, the movie has finished and I have no idea how long it's been on the end screen. The night is perfect.

Satisfying Our Desire

"Hannah is on a date with a man who she thought was irresistible, that is, until he turns out to be a complete pig. Desperate to escape, she hides in the bathroom and wonders how she will ever get out of this bad date. Luckily, Prince Charming comes running in to save the day – well, stumbling."

I can't help it as I stare across the restaurant table in disbelief.

Is this guy kidding me right now?! I think to myself as I watch him blatantly check out the waitress who has just brought our drinks over to us. *Wow, I'm going to need a lot more alcohol if I'm going to finish this date.*

With that in mind, I pick up my newly arrived Chardonnay and try to focus on not downing it just to get enough Dutch courage to not stand up and storm off. Instead, I focus on the sweet taste and tangy bubbles and the warmth that it gives me. It has been a long time since I've been on a date so I know that I should just try to relax and enjoy myself.

I met Mike at a networking function just a few weeks ago and I felt like there was a connection between us. I was there scoping out the current competition for my job in the New York area as I've recently moved back home from South Carolina. I've been a little out of touch. There is only so much information that Googling can get me. So, therefore, a networking event. Mike seemed like such a nice guy. He was interested in my new App idea and said that he might be able to help with the programming side of things. He looked like my type - tall, dark and handsome, dressed impeccably in an expensive suit… but clearly, I was wrong. I always am when it comes to men. I always have the worst judge of character. This is how I've ended up where I am now – twenty-six and single, and still struggling to find where I want to go with my life.

"So, um… tell me about yourself, Mike," I say to him, trying to prompt the conversation into a direction where I can learn something about this man. "You said you work in IT. Do you enjoy it?" I ask him, attempting to salvage the date before it's completely ruined.

Maybe I'm being too hard on him.

It's not like we are exclusively dating or anything – we've just met - so he can look at other women if he wants to. We are just two acquaintances going for drinks. We can see where things go and to if we can be useful to each other with a business arrangement. At least, that is what I'm telling myself.

"Yes, but you probably wouldn't understand it, so I won't bore you too much," he replies with a chuckle. I'm disappointed. I would have loved to listen about his work. "Why don't you tell me about yourself?" he continues. "You said you were self-employed."

I nod. "Oh. Yes. I made an App a few years ago and it was pretty successful but me and my partner decided to sell it." I try to skim over the details, there's no need to tell him about the drama of my life.

"Oh! Is it still going?" he asks.

"Yes, but... Not... really?" I try to explain. "As I said, my business partner and I sold it to a bigger company. But, to be honest, it kind of crashed and burned after we handed it over. It's a shame, but it was the right thing to do at the time."

It had been. Selling the app and moving was going to be a fresh start after a bit of a health scare I had. I earned enough money to do everything that I wanted. I traveled and relaxed and cleared a lot of things off my bucket list. But now I'm back home and but feeling a bit lonely. My apartment is feeling pretty empty.

"Oh, so did you get a lot of money for it?" he asks nosily and looks more interested in me than he has all night.

I try not to choke on my wine and I hesitate as I try to think of an answer. I don't really want to tell him anything about my finances. What kind of person asks that?

"It... it was a comfortable amount," I reply with a tight smile. I try to hide my uneasiness behind my glass of chardonnay by taking a sip.

"You don't have children do you?" he asks, effectively interrupting my thoughts with a clear look of disgust on his face.

How rude.

This man clearly has no tact at all. Where the hell's he going with this? I struggle to keep the smile on my face. I don't have children. In fact, I can't have children so he's chosen the wrong thing to mention.

"Oh. No, I don't," I say, because how else can I possibly respond to that? I'm feeling more and more awkward with every second that passes. I have to resist looking at my watch to check the time. I've barely been here twenty minutes and I'm already thinking about leaving.

"Oh, good. I don't like children," he tells me.

He reaches for his own drink and takes a big gulp of whatever beer he has ordered. He seems completely oblivious to how he sounds to me.

"The last thing I want to do is to go home with you tonight and for there to be a kid there. Kind of ruins the mood for me," he continues.

Wow, he's really presumptuous... and really digging himself a grave...

I have to physically bite my tongue, so I don't say anything. No matter how attractive this man is, he's starting to look pretty ugly to me. The more that he talks the more it's a struggle for me not to say anything rude. I've never been one of those girls who could sit there quietly and keep my thoughts to myself; I tend to run my mouth sometimes.

Thankfully, I'm rescued by the waitress, Emily, as she arrives with our entrees. I'm glad for the distraction as I feel my stomach rumble. I haven't eaten all day and the chicken wings that arrive make my mouth water. They smell delicious. Emily gives me a kind smile as she places our food down between each of us. I look to Mike, and I'm puzzled to see him looking elsewhere. I follow his line of sight and see that he's definitely not staring at our food. He is staring down Emily's shirt as she leans across and gives us our cutlery.

"Oh, you got the chicken wings. Should you really be eating that?" he asks me nonchalantly.

It's the last straw. Embarrassment floods me and I can see by Emily's face that she has heard his comment. I wait until the waitress leaves before I excuse myself. I don't think I can stay a minute longer with this man. He seems like a completely different person than the one I had met a couple of weeks ago.

"I'll be just a minute," I tell him, although I'm sure to pick up my Gucci bag and my iPhone from where it had been resting face down on the table. I know I'm not coming back.

I should feel bad leaving him with the bill, but I can't bring myself to stay any longer. I know my items are not expensive at all. Plus, I can also transfer him some money later if he needs it. I feel as if Mike's not interested in my app at all. He isn't interested in me. He must be just looking for an insecure, easy target for a one-night stand. That's not something that I'm interested in with someone like him.

I'm horny, not desperate.

I try to stomp down my own disappointment.

Immediately, I make my way towards the bathroom. My Louboutin heels click on the polished marble floor as I try to walk casually away from that disaster of a date.

I can't believe that I got dressed up for this, I think as I look over my reflection in the mirror once I'm inside the bathroom.

It does nothing for my confidence. I've never worried about the way I look, in fact, I think I'm quite pretty. I have big dark eyes and mid-length curly black hair, and curves that leave most men looking – well, apart from Mike, apparently. But for some reason it bothers me that he has made a comment about my weight – even if I was fat, then it's completely out of line. I feel sorry for any woman that crosses his path in the future.

I roll my eyes. I've wasted a full face of makeup for this, I could be at home right now and binge-watching *Bridgerton* on Netflix. I know it's time to leave. Now I simply need to attempt to sneak out of the restaurant without him noticing me. The last thing I want is a confrontation or to be embarrassed any further.

I walk out of the room with my head down, my phone in my hand as I open the Uber app. I'm just about to order a cab. But with no notice and before I can stop myself, I fall and I go crashing to the floor. My phone skids across the floor and I squeak as I fall. My brain tries to frantically catch up with what's happening around me as I tumble to the floor and land on my ass.

Ouch.

"Hannah?!" I hear a familiar voice exclaim and I look up, surprised. I'm sitting on the floor, my dress up to my thighs, and flashing my red panties. Hurriedly, I snap my knees closed and grab the material

to yank it down, my eyes whipping around me to see who else has noticed. Luckily, it's only me and the offender in the small alcove which leads to the ladies' and gents' bathrooms.

"Dr. Ellis?!" I reply in surprise, and sure enough, there stands my doctor, looking sheepish as he's knocked me to the floor. I'm not sure what's redder: my panties, or my face.

"Hannah, I'm so sorry!" He immediately grabs my phone from the floor and then helps me to my feet. My face is flaming.

Oh God, I just flashed him my panties...

I feel like it's written all over my face. Thankfully, he doesn't mention it but instead begins to fuss over me.

"Are you okay? This is completely my fault, I wasn't looking where I was going," he explains. "I've just come from a meeting, I was too distracted - my head lost in the clouds," he explains. "You're not hurt, are you? Your phone seems okay," he says, and he passes it back to me.

I check it over - at least the screen isn't smashed. That would have been the worst.

"I'm fine," I assure him, my pride wounded more than anything else.

"Are you sure? Let me buy you a drink to apologize, this is completely my fault," he offers. I hesitate, thinking about Mike back in the dining room.

"Um..." My face must give me away as I try to figure out how to explain that I was hiding in the bathroom from my date like some kind of teenager.

"Are you here with someone?" he probes, looking at me in a way that makes my stomach pleasantly twist.

"I'm actually having the worse time right now," I admit while pulling a face and nodding.

"Ouch, bad date?" He looks at me sympathetically.

"The worst," I reply, still feeling sorry for myself. Dr Ellis must feel sorry for me too because he looks over my appearance and then gives me a small smile.

"Come on then, let me get you out of here, then," he offers, and he shrugs off his black suit jacket and places it around me, effectively sheltering me. It smells like him, his cologne surrounds me and I blush for an entirely different reason.

"I... one second," I say, feeling relieved because I'm not sure how else I am going to escape Mike. I unlock my phone and open my massager app.

I'm sorry. Thanks for the invitation but I don't think that it's going to work out.

I instantly feel a hundred times better.

Dr. Ellis wraps one arm around me and then walks me directly past the dining room, using his large stature to block me from sight. I am more than thankful as we step out into the night air. I feel a weight lift off me as we begin to walk from the restaurant and into the crisp New York air.

Sorry, Mike, I think, not feeling very sorry at all.

***

I can't stop my eyes from flitting downwards over my patient. I've never seen her dressed up like this. I could hardly believe it when I saw her. I've known her since she was 18, but tonight, it's clear that she's not a cute 18 year old anymore. Tonight, she looks ravishing in her black skintight dress. Her creamy chocolate skin is exposed and her long legs on display; her ample cleavage exposed and showing off exactly what I'm missing out on. I almost want to say something about her date but I know it will be in bad taste. Unquestionably, Hannah is a beautiful woman. I'm happy to help her escape from an asshole. It's his loss, after all.

I scan the street in the darkness and wonder where will be open at this time of night. It isn't exactly late. It's only around eight pm but if we want to go somewhere decent then we may need a reservation.

"Come on, I know somewhere," I tell her. I steer her toward the crosswalk and then down Twenty-Four and Third Avenue.

New York City is alive at night, the city lit up as people go about their business. It has been a long time since I have gone out for a drink simply for fun - without it involving business. I find myself excited at the prospect of spending a little time with Hannah.

I lead her toward the bar, and I'm surprised to see that there is a line outside that circles around the block, but I bypass it in the hope that the owner, Terry, will be in. I ask the doorman who looks like he doesn't believe me when I tell him that I know the owner, but he disappears nonetheless to go and have a look. Tonight, I'm lucky because as soon as he comes to the door.

"Brian! You got my text! How are you?!" he asks, ushering me inside and past his doorman.

"I'm good, thanks. I've been a bit swamped with work at the moment. You know how it is," I explain, knowing that he understands. He's a bit of a workaholic too, so he knows the drill, I've always been obsessed with my job.

Terry's eyes flit towards Hannah and I realize that I haven't introduced her. "This is my good friend, Hannah," I introduce, not wanting to be rude.

"Of course!" Terry replies with a grin, looking excited at the prospect of inviting us inside. He leads us off to the left of the tall, black bar. "Make yourself comfortable," he instructs us as he walks around to the staff side of the bar and then chats with me for a few minutes.

I watch as Hannah looks around the lush surroundings fascinated as she listens to Terry intently. I have to admit, it's tastefully decorated and for a weekend it's not completely overrun which seems like part of its charm. It's nice to be able to have a conversation with someone without having to yell over

tacky overpowering music. Terry leaves us with a pat on my shoulder and a promise for us to talk again soon.

I watch as Hannah shrugs out of my jacket and I find it hard to keep my eyes to myself as she stands in her short, tight dress. I try hard not to think about the fact that I know exactly what underwear she is hiding under there.

"Jesus, I would never be able to just walk into a place like this," she says, effectively distracting me from her attire. "I forget how well-spoken you are sometimes," she says with a small grin as she glances at the drinks menu which stands proudly on the bar.

"I don't know what you mean," I deny, though we both know that is not the truth. I could probably talk my way into anywhere.

She sits down and I join her. I end up buying us a bottle of red to share.

"So, what were you doing at The Royal?" she asks me, looking happy as I pour her a decent-sized glass. The Royal is the restaurant we both snuck out of and it was a popular hangout for a lot of my clients.

"More business," I tell her. It's usually the only thing that I do, whether I'm at work or home, my job always comes first. At this point I know it's an addiction, but it keeps my mind busy.

"Do you ever have a day off?" she asks, and I know that she is teasing me.

"Oh, haha," I reply, but her teasing does bring a smile to my face after a long day. "Without that business, I wouldn't have been there and saved your butt today, so really, you should be thanking me for my dedication," I reply with a smirk. I'm pleased as a smile lights up her face.

"Oh, such a hero," she says playfully and the two of us laugh.

Hannah perks up at the smell of food as a waiter passes us with a large tray and from where I'm sat next to her, I can hear her stomach rumble. She looks at me embarrassed and I let out a chuckle.

"Maybe I can get you a bite to eat too? " I suggest with a grin.

She blushes prettily, her skin reddening around her cheeks and I find it hard to look away. "Sorry, I didn't have any dinner. I was expecting my date to go a lot better than it did." She sighs and looks disappointed, tearing her eyes away from me for a moment to look at her shoes.

"It's okay," I try to assure her. "Maybe it wasn't meant to be. You seemed like you were pretty eager to get away. You don't want to end up with someone like that anyway." She had essentially jumped at the chance to leave with me.

"Yeah, I found him pretty rude." She then proceeds to give me a rundown about his guy, Mike, telling me all about how they'd met and how the offer of a date had come about, and the disaster that followed. I frown as I listen to her story.

"I can't believe he asked you how much you sold your company for. That's like asking someone's salary the first time you meet them," I scoff.

"Thank you!" she exclaims and looks relieved that I can see where she is coming from. "He was so rude. I might just give up on dating altogether. I'd like to say he's the worst guy I've met but I'd be lying."

"Well, as they say, there's plenty more fish in the sea," I say, trying to be optimistic for her. "Anyway, how have you been?" We both know what I am talking about.

Her face lights up at the change of subject. "Really good," she divulges. "I can't thank you enough. You can hardly see the scar anymore."

I had supported her through a complicated surgery about 18 months ago. I hadn't really seen her since then. We'd grown close over that time but I'd taken a step back because of my developing feelings for her. But I'm not her doctor anymore.

"I'm glad," I tell her.

The two of us share a look for a moment and then laugh as Hannah's stomach grumbles again.

"Maybe we should get that food now," I propose. "Burgers?" I ask her, having seen a giant cheeseburger with delicious-looking fries be served across the room.

"Please," she says like I've offered to resolve world peace.

We finish the bottle together and then we both finish our burgers in record time. They're delicious and flavorsome, exactly what we need with our stomachs full of alcohol. I'm surprised at Tiffany being able to polish hers off since it is a very large serving– it's impressive that she's able to hide it.

When I find myself leaning closer into Hannah, I can smell her perfume, and as she looks up at me through her long, pretty eyelashes. I check my phone and it's gone midnight.

Have we really been sitting here this long? Wow, time really does fly when you're having fun. I don't want the night to end.

***

I didn't realize how much I had missed him.

I can't help it, spending time with Dr. Ellis has brought back all the memories from my treatment. All of the kind ways that he went above and beyond to help me and the relationship that bloomed between us at the time. Back then, we couldn't really do anything about our feelings. He could have got fired… but now… I wonder if it's any different.

"So… Dr. Ellis…"

"You know you can call me Brian. I think we're at that point," he tells me, and his voice gives me butterflies.

"O-oh," I stutter. I want to take a chance. I want to see if he wants this too. "Would you… like to come somewhere more private with me this evening." I lay it all out on the table. I don't want any misunderstandings here.

He looks shocked, but he grins. "Hannah, are you sure?"

I roll my eyes. "You know I am. It's not like it's a surprise that I want you. You've known I've always had a crush on you, and you can hardly blame me after…" I trail off, my cheeks red.

He licks his lips as he looks at me and I know that I've won. Instantly, I'm filled with happiness and I can't wait any longer. I never thought that I would be given this opportunity. I can't believe I've just run into him like this.

"Come on," he tells me, and then grabs my hand, leading me to the back of the restaurant. I guess knowing the owner has some perks because Brian seems to know exactly where he is going and takes me through a door named staff and to the back of the building. I find myself in the alleyway. "We can get a cab from here," he suggests, but I already have something else in mind.

I've waited for this for too long. I don't want to wait any longer.

I give him no notice as I kiss him. I simply turn and grab him by his expensive suit. Dragging him down to me and licking into his mouth desperate. Instantly hot and needy to have what I can of this man.

Something breaks between us and he grabs me and shoves me against the wall. I can't believe this is happening. I've thought about it so many times over the years and now it's actually happening. Dr. Ellis… *Brian's* hands are all over me, squeezing my ass as he ravishes my mouth and holds me against the cold brick.

It feels dirty. I can hear the sounds of the street, and if I look to the left, I can see the silhouettes of people walking past, oblivious to the fact I'm about to let this man fuck me in an alleyway.

"God, I want you so badly," he tells me and I feel his words deep inside me. I know he means it, I can feel it in my soul.

"Then take me then," I tell him and I grip at his shirt, pulling it from his belt. I grab the leather and struggle to get it open but it only takes a few seconds in reality. I free his cock from his underwear and I grip it, feeling the heavyweight in my hand and I'm in bliss. I can't believe it. I'm impossibly turned on just by the hot silky feel of him.

He's hiking my dress up and pulling my panties down and I should try to hide, I should tell him no, but I don't. I can't wait. A cab ride is too long. His apartment is too far away. I need him here and now.

My panties drop to the floor and then I feel his hand between my thighs, his fingers dipping inside me.

"Oh, God, you're so wet," he gasps in amazement.

"Yes, I need you," I tell him desperately and I spread my legs as he starts to finger me. It feels so good. I can't imagine what his cock will feel like if I am trembling like this just from his hands.

We kiss again and our bodies press together. His cock is close to my pussy and I bat his hand away from me so I can rub the fat head against the wet slit. My head falls back in bliss as he touches me bare. I'm sure I could come from this alone and I can feel that he needs more. His lips are on my neck and his hand in my hair.

I shouldn't let him fuck me without protection, but the idea of having to stop right now is too much. I can't let that happen. It's a mutual decision as we begin to rock together and it feels natural as I hike my leg up and he grips it, sliding his cock into me in one smooth motion that leaves us both gasping. He fucks me slow and deep as the world carries on around us. It feels filthy but the slide of his cock inside me is addictive and I moan into his kiss.

"Yes, yes," I moan and my hands grip at his expensive suit.

I feel another hand on my thigh and Brian is picking me up, his hands firm under my thighs as he holds me in place and fucks me against the wall. I grip his hips with my thighs. I can feel the brick scratching my ass and my lower back where my dress is hiked up. It hurts but it will only be a reminder of this moment.

"Please, Brian, I need to feel you," I moan and he nods, his hips becoming sharper and his thrusts faster. "Yes, please, right there," I beg him. Every thrust inside me feels perfect and I'm dizzy with pleasure. I need to feel him coming deep inside me. I need to know that I've done this to him, reduced him to such a mess that he's done such a naughty thing like this. A respectable man like him turned to a desperate, out of control mess.

I'm in heaven as I feel him stiffen and I can feel the pulse of him coming, the wetness filling my already soaked pussy. The two of us moan, and gasp and cry out, in the cold New York night and I know something has changed between us forever.

His Secret Mistress

"Beth and Ryder shouldn't be together. Not only are they over ten years apart in age but Ryder is the CEO of a successful literary agency while Beth is a proofreader from the first floor – his employee. If anyone found out, then Ryder would probably get a sexual harassment lawsuit... best not to get caught."

Jackson yawns as he walks through the office door and I take that as a sign that it's been one of those nights with his baby son, Luke. He looks a bit like a zombie. His face is pale and he looks like he's ready to pass out. As if to prove me right he collapses down on the sofa in my office. It makes me glad that I don't have kids.

"Luke kept you up?" I ask him as I buzz my assistant, Kerry. "Is he okay?" I ask, wondering if he's ill or if it's just the usual baby things.

. "Yeah, he's teething, and it sucks," he says. "Nothing seems to work." He throws an arm over his face and groans.

"You should try using Anbesol. Numbs their little gums. Works like a charm," I say, and I freeze as the words leave my mouth.

Shit. Why did I say that?

Jackson turns to me and looks at me puzzled for a moment as I have no reason to know this. I look away and hope that he doesn't notice. Thankfully, Kerry arrives at the door and knocks lightly and completely distracts Jackson from my words.

"You called me?" she asks delicately.

Kerry has been working for us for almost a year now and she's a nice young lady. People tend to misjudge her because of her blonde hair and short skirts, but she has a double major. She's smart and beautiful, but despite that, I only see her as an employee – not like that would stop me if I was interested. Plus, she's not my type. She's tall and blonde which is pretty much the polar opposite of what I find attractive.

"Can you get us some coffee, please?" I ask her politely and give her a little smile.

"Yeah, like with a hundred shots of espresso," Jackson adds with a groan.

She nods and pulls out her phone to jot down what we want. We make our orders and then she disappears with a click of her heels and a perky smile on her face. I know she won't be gone long, there's a Starbucks just around the corner and they take a lot of business from our building and have a system to process our orders quickly and efficiently. It won't be long before I get my coffee fix.

"So, what's on the agenda today?" Jackson asks me. "We're doing the employee audits?" He gives a sigh.

It's the worst part of the job, but it comes with working in upper management. We must keep everything in order and make sure that everyone is doing their job properly. One mistake could cost us our life's work. After all, it's our name that's on the building.

"Yeah, let's wait for coffee first..."

I watch as Jackson slumps back on the sofa, messing around on his phone. He's addicted to those silly cellphone games. I roll my eyes and try to ignore my own phone where it's hiding in my pocket. I sit down at my desk, absentmindedly swinging in my computer chair. I'm tired too and I'm distracted. It's been impossible not to be. It's been almost a week since I made a huge mistake with one of my employees... Well, it would be a mistake if I wasn't planning to do it all over again.

Her name is Beth and she works on the first floor. As soon as I ran into her in the elevator late one evening, it was love at first sight. I never meant for it to happen. It was nothing. A bit of fun. We ended up hooking up right then and there. I thought once I'd had my fill that it would be out of my system. But... it's not. By God, it's not. I can't stop thinking about her. The way she moaned. The way she clung to me. I can't forget the smell of her hair, of her perfume. I want to bathe in it. I want it all over again.

I reach into my pocket for my phone. I think about texting her but I don't know if it's a good idea or not. I'm not sure what I want right now. Before I do anything, I need to figure out exactly what I want. I never do anything without making a plan. It's how I've got where I am now in life, 35 and the CEO of one of the biggest literacy agencies in New York.

I debate what to do about it. There isn't anyone that I can talk to about this. I know I have to think about this logically. I need to weigh the pros and cons of this. I know I want to see her again. I like Beth. Obviously a lot more than I had anticipated otherwise I wouldn't be obsessing about it. She's attractive. Trustworthy. Secretive...

Our encounter was unexpected, and really, I should have handled it better. I shouldn't have left so quickly afterward. It was a mistake. I should have said something... anything... instead of just leaving her hanging like that. It wasn't fair to her. I know that. I'm going to have to apologize. But I know that I can make it up to her.

The only place that I can think that we can meet that is safe from disruptions is my apartment. No-one ever drops by there unannounced and it's not like I can accidentally overhear us like at work. I'm convinced that she wants the same as me. That much is clear. So why shouldn't I do this for myself? When was the last time that I allowed myself to have a good time? I can't even remember. I've been working so hard, surely I deserve this? A little fun. Something to help me relax and to do in my off time which isn't related to my work.

Do I really miss her enough to do this? I think to myself. My mind answers a resounding, yes. *I do.*

I want to see her again, but not in passing. I want to actually spend time with her. I want to carry on what has started between us. I want to see where this goes. I have dreamed about it this week. About what it would feel like being with her, our bodies joining and moving together in ecstasy. It's been keeping me up at night.

But I think my business and I know that I don't have time for anything frivolous. I've worked hard my entire life, sometimes doing things that I am less than proud of. It's just something from the past that I have to learn to live with. Now all my attention goes into my business. I don't have time for relationships. I can't commit to that. I already have too much going on in my life. More than I care to admit...

If Beth wants what I want – something casual, discreet, and fun, then I can do this. I know it would be unfair to promise her anything else because it would be a lie. It's something that I can't commit to. She's a good girl and I don't want to hurt her.

I finally unlock my phone screen and open the messaging app. I know this is my last chance to back out from my plan. I hesitate... I'm not going to know for sure until I speak to Beth. We have to talk face to face to sort this out. Privately. I decide that if she wants what I want then I can do this. But I'll have to give her a choice. Make it clear. Then if she agrees, we can do this. But only if she agrees.

Excited at the prospect, I quickly type out a message and hit send before I'm caught by Jackson.

Champagne at mine. 8 pm.

***

I'm still lying in bed when my phone vibrates. It's my day off today so I think about ignoring it. It's probably another spam notification from someone claiming to be someone who they aren't, or someone trying to sell me something that I don't need. I really need to sort out my email settings... But this time, something tells me that I should just check instead of rolling over and ignoring it. I reach to find my phone from where it's hiding under my pillow. I blearily look at it and I'm instantly awake as I see that it's Ryder Burke that has messaged me. *The* Ryder Burke. As in Burke Publishing. Where I work. I sit up straight in bed, my eyes wide as I unlock my phone. I'm either about to be fired or to open a dick pic. I'm not sure which one would make my heart race more. I read his message.

Champagne at mine. 8 pm.

What? I've got to be dreaming... but I know he's serious because the message after gives his address. I haven't heard anything from Mr Burke since our surprise tryst a week ago and if I'm honest, I didn't really expect to. I knew what I was getting into when that happened. I didn't take it personally. I saw it for what it was, a once-in-a-lifetime experience. A quick tryst with my boss. At least... so I thought...

Oh, God, he wants to see me again.

The thought has me jumping out of my bed and running to the mirror to poke and prod at my face. My eyebrows look a mess and I'm desperate for a trip to the salon. I pull at my hair and wish that I'd not waited so long between trips to my hairdresser. There's no way that I can show up at his apartment looking like this. I need to look my best.

"Crap," I curse to myself.

I knew I shouldn't have put off my appointments this week. I'd been so busy at work that I've just not had time. I need to get my nails done, my hair... I'm going to have to get an appointment today. It's a good job that I have a fantastic beautician.

I grab my phone and immediately call Hermione. I met her at Burke, actually, she trained me before she left on maternity leave and we stayed in touch. Going to the salon together is something that we've started to do together so I have to invite her. It would be odd to go by myself behind her back. It would hurt her feelings not to be invited. It rings three times before she answers.

"Hey, I'm planning to go into the salon this morning. You coming?" I ask her, pulling on the first comfortable clothes that I can reach. It's a soft Versace lounge set.

"This morning? I'll have to bring the baby, he's not in daycare this morning. No wait – I'll call the babysitter, then I'll call you back."

She hangs up the phone and I use the time to text Sasha, our beautician, to let her know me and Hermione will be dropping in and need her urgently. She texts back saying that it's fine and she'll move her clients around a little for us.

My salon is a nice little place on the edge of town, and on my way, I'm planning in my head what I'm going to wear tonight. I want to leave a lasting impression on Mr. Burke. I've been given another chance and I have to take it. Even if it turns out to be just another one-off then that's good enough for me. After our encounter, I can't stop thinking about sleeping with him again. I know that tonight is my chance. I think about what dress to wear and wonder what's going to impress him. I do have a new dress. It's still hung up in the closet with the tags on even though I brought it 6 months ago. Right now, I'm glad for it, I'm hoping I can wear it tonight.

I beat Hermione to the store and wait for her outside. She appears just a few moments later with baby Luke on her hip and carrying a large baby bag on his shoulder. It explains why she was later than usual. She normally beats me here.

"Oh, hello, beautiful," I greet Luke and then take him from her eagerly. I haven't really been going over to Hermione's house as often as I usually do. So it's been a week or so since I last saw him. "No babysitter?" I ask as I hold him close to me.

"No, she's at college this morning," she replies with a yawn. "God, sorry, I'm exhausted. I needed this today, do you think Sasha will mind?"

I roll my eyes. "If anything, she'll thank you, you know that she loves Luke. Everyone loves you don't they, darlin'? You're the cutest. And this means that I get to spend more time with you. even if you are just watching Auntie Beth get her nails done. I'm gonna have to buy you a gift for being such a good boy."

"You know, I think you're becoming that fabulous aunt that doesn't have children but just pops by with expensive gifts and looks perfect all the time."

I scoff. "I definitely don't look perfect right now."

"Oh, shush you," she says, "talk to me again after you've had kids then you'll understand what looking rough actually looks like."

She lets out a laugh before walking into the Salon. We are greeted with the familiar smell of the chemicals from the nail polish and various aromatherapy oils. Sasha sees us straight away and welcomes us over to her therapy room. It's a small room, decorated in pink and black but it's very relaxing. Soft music plays in the background and Sasha's assistant is already there and preparing the nail station.

"Hi," she greets. She's already walking over to the coffee machine to make us a latte in our usual routine. "Oh, I see we've got little man with us today. What a nice surprise! He's getting so big now!"

I place Luke onto the floor, and we watch as he stands unsteadily and peers up at Sasha. "The last time you were in here you couldn't walk!" she says, looking impressed.

"I know how you feel," I agree with her since I think the same thing every time that I see him.

"So, what's the occasion ladies or did you just want a treat?" Sasha asks us.

"Oh, nothing really... just sprucing myself up a little bit," I lie. "Just thought it would be nice for us to have some girl time."

"Yeah, why not treat yourselves."

The two of us set up a little play area on the floor for Luke while Sasha and her assistant Becky make the preparations for what we want this morning. Luke is happily set up with some little blocks and a sippy cup of grape juice on the floor. He's completely preoccupied with some potato chips and the blocks. He's tipping the potato chips on the floor and putting the blocks into the empty chips bag.

"So, ladies, what can I do for you? Nails, brows, lashes, the usual?" Sasha knows me so well.

"Yes, please."

"Oh, good. I was wondering what happened to you two. I haven't seen you guys in a while."

"You know: work, sleep, the usual."

"Yeah, and Luke is teething right now."

I can hardly believe it. I know most children have teeth at this age - he's almost one now. but Lucas has been a late bloomer when it comes to his teeth. He only has his first two cutting through, so to hear he has more is exciting. If I ever have children of my own, I'm going to be unbearable since I get this excited about my nephew – and he's not even related by blood.

"Yeah, I think they're coming in all in the wrong order. It's typical. I blame Jackson." The two of us laugh. Her husband Jackson gets the blame for everything.

"So, are you off today then?" Sasha asks me as we are both settled onto the therapy beds and she settles herself above me, and Becky above Maya.

"Yeah, I'm off for two days now," I explain.

"That's good, you should relax."

I fully plan to. I relax back and close my eyes as Sasha starts prepping my eyebrows with the dye. We all fall silent for a few moments just listening to Luke talk nonsense on the floor.

"I'm glad you called today," Maya tells me, her voice from the right of me, and I open my eyes for a second before settling again when I find her lying next to me.

"It's no problem, it's nice to relax together," I admit.

I have no plans of telling Hermione that I'll be seeing my boss this evening. After all, she still works for the company. What she doesn't know can't hurt her.

***

I'm driving home when my phone vibrates and I realize that it's Beth that has texted me. I can hardly believe my luck. I never expected that she would actually entertain me. But there's the reply. A little winky face and a confirmation.

Eight it is ;)

I never thought that such a short message could make me so happy. All thoughts of my hectic and frustrating morning are completely forgotten.

I push all of that to the back of my mind. Hardly daring to believe. Looking at my phone and not exactly seeing it. Not exactly seeing because my brain has gone on to wonderland and my mind is flying on clouds that I didn't know existed. She'd actually replied and that reply left a lot of things to be said, that reply made everything possible.

I look at the message again, just to be sure, just to be sure I am not seeing wrong or making a mistake with what I am reading. She'd actually sent it though, she wanted to see me. I thought there'd be no way. I thought for sure that she'd never reply.

A horn blares behind me and I drop my phone on my lap, moving forward in a slow crawl like the other cars around me and smiling. I can't wait to get home. The penthouse is kept squeaky clean and I pay good money for the service, but still, I like to make sure everything is perfect and I want this evening to be perfect.

The cars crawl slowly ahead of me and without me even realizing it, the thoughts about what happened that evening creep back to my mind. The two of us kissing hotly, my hands on her silky, dark chocolate skin, gripping at her firmly. Our breath hot between our lips. The sounds of her moans echoing around the small metal room.

I don't feel or know it but my hands have tightened on the steering wheel and now they grip it almost strong enough to break it off while my jaws are clamped shut so tight that my teeth would crack if they could. I get home finally, spending longer on the road than I thought than usual. I am in a bouncy mood. My brain is beginning to feed me thoughts that make it seriously hard to think about anything but Beth.

The woman has tied my brain and my hearts in knots. I only have to think about her and I start imagining things in my mind that I didn't know were even possible. My body reacting to it. It is like I'm a teenager again. I have no control over myself.

My phone beeps, it's Jackson. He's reminding me that he's out of the office today and that I need to sign off our new contracts. I smile. He likes to check and double-check every detail and make sure that it has been covered. Not for the first time, I remind him we have a secretary. I forward it all to Kerry. Work is the last thing on my mind right now.

No. Tonight is going to be about me. About Beth. For the first time ever, I'm going to do something that I want to do. Something for myself. For the two of us.

The penthouse looks perfect but still, that isn't enough, I need to set the mood.

I go to the bar and fetch out a bottle of wine I've saved for a special occasion. I set it in a bucket of ice. I flick on the electric fireplace. I've always thought the realistic logs are a nice touch. I dim the penthouse lights a bit and make sure all the curtains are wide open, giving a breathtaking view of the entire city.

I look around. *This will do nicely.*

***

I take a deep breath before I push the doorbell and then take a step back, waiting for Mr. Burke to answer the door. I've never been to this side of town before, to this apartment building before. I know that his cryptic text message of an invitation must mean something huge. I am hoping I'm not about to make a fool of myself. I'm so lost in thought about what it all might mean that when Mr. Burke finally opens the door that I jump back. I let out a giggle at my nervous behavior.

"Hi," I say to him shyly.

Immediately, I know that I have nothing to be shy about as I feel his eyes wander down my body. He takes in my choice of outfit for the night. My short purple dress, which is mid-thigh, shows off my plump breasts and long legs but leaves just enough to the imagination. His eyes flit back upwards and his jade green lock with my chocolate brown.

"Hello," he greets me. His voice is deep. Suave. I feel like I'm being hypnotized.

He steps aside and opens the door for me welcoming me into his penthouse apartment. I can't keep my eyes to myself as I step inside for the first time. It's impossible to. It feels like I have just stepped into some kind of dream place. Or like something I would see in a magazine or that belongs to a celebrity. Mr. Burke's apartment is immaculate and very tastefully decorated in dark teal and black. It looks striking. Though I guess I shouldn't be surprised for somebody in his line of work. It reminds me that although I am very well off financially and secure working in publishing, I have nothing on Mr. Burke's riches. It is easy to forget that he's one of the most affluent people in New York City.

"Thanks for inviting me, I was more than a little surprised at your text message," I admit. "I honestly wasn't expecting it... I hope I haven't got the wrong idea..." I tell him. I hand him the gift bag containing his a bottle of wine and some chocolates. I didn't want to be rude by arriving without a gift.

"No, not at all," he says, closing the door behind us with a soft click. "In fact, I think you have exactly the right idea."

The tone of his voice has me pausing mid-step and slowly, I turn around to face him. I cannot move from the way he is looking at me. His eyes devour me. I feel like I'm pinned to the spot as he slowly and purposefully strides towards me. I can do nothing but stand there and wait for his next move. He closes the space between us leaving barely an inch separating us.

I feel my heart pick up in my chest. I'm shaking. My palms are sweaty. Even him standing there silently just looking at me is enough to make me desperate for him. I take a small step back to increase the space, but there's nowhere else to go. I'm trapped against the front door and I can't move. I don't want to move. I want to stay exactly as I am now and see what he does next.

He smiles at me and I like how it looks on his face. He's so undeniably attractive and it has such an effect on me. No one has ever made me feel this way by just standing next to me... by entering my aura. I feel like this man has full control over me even though he's barely said a word. I gulp thickly as my mouth goes dry. My eyes remain locked with his beautiful wide green eyes. He stares at me and it makes me feel vulnerable. It makes me feel like I'm naked. I wait for his next move, but it doesn't come. Instead, he winks at me as if he knows exactly what he's doing to me and then he finally steps back and puts some space between us.

"Thank you," he says, finally walking away from me.

I begin to follow him. My Jimmy Choos click loudly on his flooring as I make my way to his kitchen.

"You remembered my favorite wine," he says and this time it's him who is surprised.

"Yes, you served it at our Christmas party this year." I remember looking up at him at the top table, and feeling like my crush on him was something insane. That even looking at him wrong would get me fired, let alone the two of us sleeping together.

He takes his time to collect two wine glasses and make us both a drink. Politely, I take the glass and he holds out his own in a salute. We clink our glasses together in a toast and the noise resounds softly in the silent room.

"To new adventures," he toasts.

I raise an eyebrow at the choice of words but nevertheless, I take a sip of the offered drink. It's delicious and I can tell why he enjoys this specific vineyard so much. Impressed, I grin at him and take another small step.

"So, am I right in thinking that you want to talk to me about something?" I ask directly, because how else can I breach this subject?

I'm not silly. I know why I'm here. I know what he wants from me and I want it too. But this is Ryder Burke we're talking about and I need to be one hundred percent clear. You don't just make

assumptions when it comes to him. Mr. Burke knows exactly what he wants and he's not afraid to take it. If he wants this then I know that I must give him everything that he asks. Nobody says no to someone like Ryder Burke, and I don't want to.

"Well, I was doing some thinking, and something occurred to me. I feel like we have been wasting time skirting around this issue the last week, when it's obvious that we are attracted to each other. We are also very compatible. You please me in a way that a woman hasn't been able to for a very long time."

My eyes go wide at the words. He talks to me so directly, as if what he is telling me is a fact, rather than his personal opinion... He speaks so surely. I don't know what to say, so I just nod at him because he is right.

"Now I'm not saying that I think we should be together formally," he rushes to tell me, "because I feel I can't give you that type of commitment. But what I can give you is a small part of me. You know, just a bit of fun when I'm not preoccupied."

Immediately, I want that. I want whatever Mr. Burke is willing to give me. I nod.

"That... that sounds amazing." Somehow, I manage to keep my voice steady.

"But you need to tell me if that's going to be enough for you," he says. "I don't want there to be any misunderstandings between us. You are my employee."

He gives me a smile which keeps his words soft. I understand his words and I agree with them. I love my job. I'm not stupid enough to divulge our affair to anyone.

"If you agree to this, you must agree to my terms. I'm not going to let my relationship with you compromise my hard work. No matter how pretty you may be."

I can only stare at him for a moment as I try to digest the words. It feels like a lot to process all at once. It's the type of thing that I would hear in my daydreams and late-night fantasies. My rich, billionaire boss wanting to start a sexual relationship. Things like this don't happen to me. Not here in reality. Not my life.

"You're right," I eventually reply. "I'll do whatever you say. I trust you."

Mr. Burke looks pleased with my words and he places his glass on the kitchen counter. He slowly reaches up with his left hand and gently touches my chin, tapping it and encouraging me to look up at him. He's so much taller than me and something is thrilling about how small he makes me feel even in my 4-inch heels.

"Good. I trust you which is why you're the only woman that I could ever do this with," he tells me softly, and I believe him. "But don't make me regret it and no matter how tempting, don't fall in love with me," he says with a laugh. He gives me a smirk.

I can't help but let out a giggle at his presumptuous tone. "As if," I tell him, "you're so full of yourself."

With that our agreement is set, we both understand that we want from this: we want secrecy, we want fun, but most of all we want each other.

We're both grinning as we finish our glass of wine, downing the contents eagerly. My hands tremble slightly in anticipation of what's about to happen.

"You can call my Ryder, by the way," he tells me, and I flush. He's always been so unreachable, yet here he is, inviting me to call him by his first name.

"Ryder," I repeat, seeing how it feels on my lips.

Ryder must like it, because he kisses me, his hands immediately grabbing at my bottom. He hoists me up with little effort, making it easy for me to lock my thighs on his hips. We kiss deeply and I'm impossibly turned on at the feeling of him manhandling me with such ease. Our kisses become deep and frantic and his hands make sure movements across my body, cupping at my hip and at my breast and fondling me through my bra. My arms around his neck and my hands are in his hair and his kiss feels like a drug to me.

Ryder drops me so I'm sitting on the countertop. He stands between my spread thighs. Then his hands are on my bare thighs. Hot and firm, his skin a little rough as it pushes upwards, taking my dress with it. I wiggle my hips allowing him to pull my dress up to my stomach and expose my panties to him.

"Lie down," Ryder growls into my mouth and then pushes me back suddenly.

I find myself staring at the ceiling and I can feel his hands on my underwear, ripping it as if it is offensive to him. He feels out of control. He grabs my legs and opens them and I'm trapped there completely on display for him and ready to let him do whatever he wants to me.

I expect him to fuck me right away, so I'm confused as I feel something far from that. A soft wet sensation slides from my entrance to my clit. I realize that he has his mouth on me.

Oh, God.

It's something that I've never experienced before and my hands scramble to find something to hold onto as I'm tipped into an ocean of pleasure where I feel like I am drowning. His tongue licks at me repeatedly, giving me no respite from the soul-wrenching pleasure. My stomach tenses, my thighs shake, and my toes curl in my shoes before they finally fall from my feet and onto the kitchen floor.

"Oh, fuck," I cry out, moaning and out of control. "Oh, ohhh…"

I've never been one for being loud, but I can't stop the sound exploding from me, and with every moan, Ryder only licks, sucks, and kisses at me more insistently until I can't stop it. Finally, my body can't take it anymore and I come. I sit upon my elbows and look down at Ryder through lidded eyes as I struggle to catch my breath.

"I've wanted to do that for a very long time," he says, placing one last kiss on my pubic mound softly.

I can't do anything but flop back onto the countertop. I feel exhausted.

"Who says I'm done with you yet?" he asks me and my eyes widen. "Tell me, Beth, do you want me to come on you, or do you want me to fuck you?"

My eyes widen at the question. I want him to fuck me. There's no doubt about that.

"Wait, don't tell me. I'll tell you what I want."

I shiver at the words. Something inside me desperate to know what he's going to do to me. I love how he's taking control like this, how he's just taking what he wants from my body.

I'm surprised when I feel him grabbing me and I'm thrown over his shoulder.

"Oh, fuck!" I squeal. I'm instantly impressed by his feat of strength. He lifts me easily, as if I weigh nothing, when I know I'm a healthy strong weight.

He carries me through the apartment and then over to the lounge area. I look at the world upside down for a moment, glancing at the fire and then to the soft rug on the floor before I am turned the right way. I'm placed gently on that rug.

Ryder smirks down at me, attractive in the flickering light. I feel my pussy throb. I'm so wet. I'm still dressed, but he makes quick work of my clothes, stripping me naked and then his eyes devouring me.

"I want you," I tell him, panting slightly. I've never wanted something so much in my life.

But Ryder responds by slowly pulling his tie off, his eyes locked with mine. I don't realize what he is doing until it's covering my eyes, being tied tight across my eyes, and blocking my sight. My hair pulls as he secures it at the back. I can't move it even an inch. My heart palpitates, nervous and excited about what is to come.

I can hear a strange sound, and I'm unsure of what it is, my mind can not come up with an image that matches the sounds. But soon, my hands are grabbed and I feel something rough wrap around them, tugging them together, and then suddenly I can't move them. My wrists are pressed together and there is no room for movement as I try to separate them.

It must be his belt... He's blindfolded me and tied me up.

"What are you doing?" I whisper, my curiosity burning within me.

"I didn't say you could talk," he snaps.

I snap my mouth closed obediently. My mind wanders back to our tryst in the elevator, how commanding and forceful he was. How hard and selfishly he had fucked me. I want it. I want it again. I feel as if he has ruined me for everyone else. His words and actions had made me come so hard.

I can't hear a thing. I'm in complete darkness and the hair on the back of my neck stands up. I can hear him stand, and then the tap of his shoes on the floor, walking away from me.

He doesn't answer, and I feel alone... My heart is beating rapidly. I have never done something so exciting. I am leaving all my faith and trust in Ryder. I'm completely powerless, naked and bound on his floor. I wait for him patiently, listening to the crackle of the fireplace.

I hear him a moment later. It sounds like he walks around me, curling me before he then settles.

"Good girl. You were so patient," he whispers and his voice sends a shiver up my spine.

"I want to be good for you," I admit quietly, not sure if he's going to scold me for talking. But instead, I feel his hands. He spreads my thighs again and I whimper as I feel something cold nudge against my asshole. I tense.

What's he doing? I... I've never...

I feel a vibration against my hole and I jump and cry out in shock.

It's a vibrator... he's putting it inside...

My face burns at his actions and I squirm as I feel the blunt vibrator force my ass to relax. It's pushing inside me slowly and opening me up.

Oh, God, I... I shouldn't like it... It's so wrong... But...

I thrash against the rug, my chest arching towards the ceiling and I spread my legs wider. I want more. I want him to do these things to me. I want him to touch my pussy, to make me come. I don't care where he puts his cock, as long as it's inside of me. I know that it makes me dirty – filthy even – but I can't bring myself to care.

"Ryder... Ryder," I gasp, my hands ball into fists and I clench them tightly, struggling against the confines.

It feels like he's teasing me, slowly pushing the vibrator inside me and then out again in a frustratingly slow rhythm.

"Please..."

I hear him chuckle.

He likes this. He likes doing this to me...

It's so much. Too sensitive. My pussy is aching for me and my legs start to tremble.

"Oh, fuck!" I cry out, as my pussy is suddenly filled, something probing alongside the vibrator which is fucking into me slowly. I'm so full that I don't think I can possibly feel more stretched but I'm wrong as the sensation amplifies.

I struggle against the belt holding my hands in place. I want to grab at something, but I can't do anything but grip at my own hands and shake, thrashing in place.

"Moan my name," he tells me.

I immediately obey. "Ryder, oh, fuck. It feels so good. I love you playing with my pussy and my ass. It's so fucking good."

"More. Louder. Or I'll stop."

"Ryder!" I sob out. "Ryder..."

I feel the soft tender touch of his tongue on my clit and that's it, I'm coming again. The vibrator was so deep inside my ass, and his fingers stuffed inside my pussy and his mouth on me. It's so overwhelming and I realize that I'm crying from relief. My tears soak into the makeshift blindfold.

"Thank you, thank you," I gasp out until finally, I feel the toy and his fingers slip from me. My bones feel like jello and I'm trembling all over.

I have no time for respite, as he grabs me again and lifts me. I land on something soft.

I must be on the sofa. We hardly moved...

I have no time to think about it as suddenly I'm grabbed by my hair and his cock is against my lips. I open my mouth and take his dick inside as he grabs at me and holds onto my shoulders, his fingers sharp against my bare skin.

His hard cock is pushing deep in my mouth, and I can feel how hot and swollen it is. I can feel it pulse, the veins standing out from the surface. I run my tongue around it and he grabs my hair tighter again and pushes it deeper. I gag on it as deeply as I can, trying to shove it down my throat until I can't possibly take any more. I am desperate to make this man feel good. My ass and pussy are still sensitive and throbbing, the ghosts of his expert touch still pleasing me even though it's long gone.

I flick my tongue around the fat head as he pulls out and lets me surface for air. I take deep lungfuls knowing this might be my only chance. I take a few seconds for myself. Everything feels amplified. I am still robbed of my senses, blind and bound.

I kiss the bundle of nerves below the head. He groans and it's like praise to my ears. A reward for my hard work before I try again, taking his long fat length down my throat. I gag and drool, long streams of saliva pouring from me as I start to deepthroat him over and over. Going sloppily at him. Milking him.

He holds onto me as I suck on his hard dick, massaging from the base with my hands for the maximum effect. I keep the head in my mouth and the full length lubricated and wet, jerking what I can't fit in my mouth. I'm pinned against the sofa like this, until he moves away. His cock slips from my lips and my jaw aches from the rough treatment, but I loved every second.

"Gimme your pussy," he demands, and roughly my ass is being dragged to the edge of the couch cushion and my legs forced open.

He teases my pussy lips with his shaft, sliding it against me, moving the hot head up and down while I moan. He pushes in deep. Filling all of me. I moan loud and carefree, my voice echoing around the room unashamed.

I squeak as his hands are suddenly on my neck, choking me, but instead of panicking, I'm begging for more inside my mind. His face close to mine and he holds it there, the two of us breathing the same air as he slides out, before slowly, he digs in deep again.

He gives me no notice. There is no warning. He begins to fuck me brutally. His cock invading every inch of me as I splutter and gasp for air, but his hand is still over my windpipe, blocking me from taking a full breath. I'm dizzy, the world around me spinning as I'm taken to new heights of pleasure. The movement, the feel of him sending alarm bells in my brain. He's digging through me. My pussy is wet with come, with my juices, sloshing as he slides into me with a precision that has me screaming.

My eyes roll into the back of my head, the sensation of his cock fucking me, of his waist clapping against my ass. I moan long and hard. His hands dig into my neck tighter, in a vise grip.

"Just like that," I moan, my words choked. I like this. I like him using me. Treating me like a whore.

He goes harder and faster. His body is pummeling into me wildly. I scream his name, once twice. I'm almost unable to think. His hand is on my tits, grabbing at my nipples one by one, twisting against them, torturing them. I moan at that touch, shying away, but I am unable to escape. I can only lay there and moan, cry and beg for him.

"Ryder," I moan. Held by him completely, savagely.

His huge dick continues fuck me, splitting me apart. His hands leave my breasts after a serious squeeze and separate my ass cheeks and impossibly, he quickens the pace.

Ecstasy fills me completely. I'm caught up in it. Lost. My eyes slid backward and my brain pulses with sensations that run throughout my entire being, shocking me with pleasure, filling me.

"Keep going, Ryder, keep going," I beg him and he groans in response.

He pounds me until the only thing that keeps me glued to this Earth is his hold on me. Finally, after an eternity, his hands let go. He frees me. It's as if I've been electrocuted. Pleasure rushes through me, assaulting me through my entire body and I scream. His cock slides out, pushed out from the force of my pussy as I come. I squirt all over him, screams of my come forced from me and the splatter of wet juices soaking him. I can feel him jerking himself off, his hand tapping against me softly until I feel his hot wet come dripping onto my shaven pussy. Our juices mixing together.

He takes me in his arms, holding me with my legs wrapped around him. We both breathe heavily, drunk on our experience. He gently reaches for his tie and pulls it off my eyes. I blink rapidly in the dim room and we stare at each other, smiling.

CPSIA information can be obtained
at www.ICGtesting.com
Printed in the USA
BVHW021045230623
666309BV00008B/205